Dear Reader,

H·I·S·T·O·R·I·C·A·L
Christmas
S·T·O·R·I·E·S 1·9·9·0

NORA ROBERTS
PATRICIA POTTER
RUTH LANGAN

Harlequin Books

TORONTO • NEW YORK • LONDON
AMSTERDAM • PARIS • SYDNEY • HAMBURG
STOCKHOLM • ATHENS • TOKYO • MILAN

Harlequin Historical first edition November 1990

ISBN 0-373-83218-4

Harlequin Historical Christmas Stories 1990
Copyright © 1990 by Harlequin Enterprises Limited.

The publisher acknowledges the copyright holders of
the individual work as follows:

In from the Cold
Copyright © 1990 by Nora Roberts

Miracle of the Heart
Copyright © 1990 by Patricia Potter

Christmas at Bitter Creek
Copyright © 1990 by Ruth Langan

CONTENTS

IN FROM THE COLD

★

Nora Roberts

A longtime tradition in my family is Christmas breakfast. My parents' home is crowded and noisy, and everyone lends a hand—watching the light on the waffle iron, holding their plates out for more. We are allowed to fry the bacon or flip the pancakes on the griddle. But nobody—*nobody*—makes the pancake batter except my pop. There are two huge bowls of it to feed the horde before we get down to exchanging gifts and ripping colored paper to shreds. Because there are so many of us, we often eat in shifts, crowding around the dining room table and spilling over to the breakfast bar. Wherever I sit, the first bite takes me back to childhood.

POP'S PANCAKES

6 eggs, beaten
1 can evaporated milk
1 stick (¼ cup) butter or margarine, melted
1½ cups regular milk (1 cup for waffles)
3 cups flour
6 tbsp. baking powder

Combine ingredients in the order listed. Mix well. Let stand for 10 minutes to rise.

For pancakes, spoon batter onto hot griddle. Be patient—don't flip until bubbles appear.

Enjoy.

And Merry Christmas.

Chapter One

His name was MacGregor. He clung to that even as he clung to the horse's reins. The pain was alive, capering down his arm like a dozen dancing devils. Hot, branding hot, despite the December wind and blowing snow.

He could no longer direct the horse but rode on, trusting her to find her way through the twisting paths made by Indian or deer or white man. He was alone with the scent of snow and pine, the muffled thud of his mount's hooves and the gloom of early twilight. A world hushed by the sea of wind washing through the trees.

Instinct told him he was far from Boston now, far from the crowds, the warm hearths, the civilized. Safe. Perhaps safe. The snow would cover the trail his horse left and the guiding path of his own blood.

But safe wasn't enough for him. It never had been. He was determined to stay alive, and for one fierce reason. A dead man couldn't fight. By all that was holy he had vowed to fight until he was free.

Shivering despite the heavy buckskins and furs, teeth chattering now from a chill that came from within as well as without, he leaned forward to speak to the horse, soothing in Gaelic. His skin was clammy with the heat of the pain, but his blood was like the ice that formed on the bare branches of the trees surrounding him. He could see the mare's breath blow out in white streams as she trudged on through the deepening snow. He prayed as only a man who could feel his own blood pouring out of him could pray. For life.

There was a battle yet to be fought. He'd be damned if he'd die before he'd raised his sword.

The mare gave a sympathetic whinny as he slumped against her neck, his breathing labored. Trouble was in the air, as well as the scent of blood. With a toss of her head, she walked into the wind, following her own instinct for survival and heading west.

The pain was like a dream now, floating in his mind, swimming through his body. He thought if he could only wake, it would disappear. As dreams do. He had other dreams—violent and vivid. To fight the British for all they had stolen from him. To take back his name and his land—to fight for all the MacGregors had held with pride and sweat and blood. All they had lost.

He had been born in war. It seemed just and right that he would die in war.

But not yet. He struggled to rouse himself. Not yet. The fight had only begun.

He forced an image into his mind. A grand one. Men in feathers and buckskins, their faces blackened with burnt cork and lampblack and grease, boarding the ships *Dartmouth*, *Eleanor* and *Beaver*. Ordinary men, he remembered, merchants and craftsmen and students. Some fueled with grog, some with righteousness. The hoisting and smashing of the chests of the damned and detested tea. The satisfying splash as broken crates of it hit the cold water of Boston Harbor at Griffin's Wharf. He remembered how disgorged chests had been heaped up in the muck of low tide like stacks of hay.

So large a cup of tea for the fishes, he thought now. Aye, they had been merry, but purposeful. Determined. United. They would need to be all of those things to fight and win the war that so many didn't understand had already begun.

How long had it been since that glorious night? One day? Two? It had been his bad luck that he had run into two drunk and edgy redcoats as dawn had been breaking. They knew him. His face, his name, his politics were well-known in Boston. He'd done nothing to endear himself to the British militia.

Perhaps they had only meant to harass and bully him a bit. Perhaps they hadn't meant to make good their threat to arrest him—on charges they hadn't made clear. But when one had drawn a sword, MacGregor's weapon had all but leaped into his own hand. The fight had been brief—and foolish, he could admit now. He was still unsure if he had killed or only wounded the impetuous soldier. But his comrade had had murder in his eye when he had drawn his weapon.

Though MacGregor had been quick to mount and ride, the musket ball had slammed viciously into his shoulder.

He could feel it now, throbbing against muscle. Though the rest of his body was mercifully numb, he could feel that small and agonizing pinpoint of heat. Then his mind was numb, as well, and he felt nothing.

He woke, painfully. He was lying in the blanket of snow, faceup so that he could see dimly the swirl of white flakes against a heavy gray sky. He'd fallen from his horse. He wasn't close enough to death to escape the embarrassment of it. With effort, he pushed himself to his knees. The mare was waiting patiently beside him, eyeing him with a mild sort of surprise.

"I'll trust you to keep this to yourself, lass." It was the weak sound of his own voice that brought him the first trace of fear. Gritting his teeth, he reached for the reins and pulled himself shakily to his feet. "Shelter." He swayed, grayed out and knew he could never find the strength to mount. Holding tight, he clucked to the mare and let her pull his weary body along.

Step after step he fought the urge to collapse and let the cold take him. They said there was little pain in freezing to death. Like sleep it was, a cold, painless sleep.

And how the devil did they know unless they'd lived to tell the tale? He laughed at the thought, but the laugh turned to a cough that weakened him.

Time, distance, direction were utterly lost to him. He tried to think of his family, the warmth of them. His parents and brothers and sisters in Scotland. Beloved Scotland, where they fought to keep hope alive. His aunts and uncles and cousins in Virginia, where they worked for the right to a new life in a new land. And he, he was somewhere between, caught between his love of the old and his fascination with the new.

But in either land, there was one common enemy. It strengthened him to think of it. The British. Damn them. They had proscribed his name and butchered his people. Now they were reaching their greedy hands across the ocean so that the half-mad English king could impose his bloody laws and collect his bloody taxes.

He stumbled, and his hold on the reins nearly broke. For a moment he rested, his head against the mare's neck, his eyes closed. His father's face seemed to float into his mind, his eyes still bright with pride.

"Make a place for yourself," he'd told his son. "Never forget, you're a MacGregor."

No, he wouldn't forget.

Wearily he opened his eyes. He saw, through the swirling snow, the shape of a building. Cautious, he blinked, rubbed his tired eyes with his free hand. Still the shape remained, gray and indistinct, but real.

"Well, lass." He leaned heavily against his horse. "Perhaps this isn't the day to die after all."

Step by step he trudged toward it. It was a barn, a large one, well built of pine logs. His numb fingers fumbled with the latch. His knees threatened to buckle. Then he was inside, with the smell and the blessed heat of animals.

It was dark. He moved by instinct to a mound of hay in the stall of a brindled cow. The bovine lady objected with a nervous moo.

It was the last sound he heard.

Alanna pulled on her woolen cape. The fire in the kitchen hearth burned brightly and smelled faintly, cheerfully, of apple logs. It was a small thing, a normal thing, but it pleased her. She'd woken in a mood of happy anticipation. It was the snow, she imagined, though her father had risen from his bed cursing it. She loved the purity of it, the way it clung to the bare branches of trees her father and brothers had yet to clear.

It was already slowing, and within the hour the barnyard would be tracked with footprints, hers included. There were animals to tend to, eggs to gather, harnesses to repair and wood to chop. But for now, for just a moment, she looked out the small window and enjoyed.

If her father caught her at it, he would shake his head and call her a dreamer. It would be said roughly—not with anger, she thought, but with regret. Her mother had been a dreamer, but she had died before her dream of a home and land and plenty had been fully realized.

Cyrus Murphy wasn't a hard man, Alanna thought now. He never had been. It had been death, too many deaths, that had caused him to become rough and prickly. Two bairns, and later, their beloved mother. Another son, beautiful young Rory, lost in the war against the French.

Her own husband, Alanna mused, sweet Michael Flynn, taken in a less dramatic way but taken nonetheless.

She didn't often think of Michael. After all, she had been three months a wife and three years a widow. But he had been a kind man and a good one, and she regretted bitterly that they had never had the chance to make a family.

But today wasn't a day for old sorrows, she reminded herself. Pulling up the hood of her cape, she stepped outside. Today was a day for promises, for beginnings. Christmas was coming fast. She was determined to make it a joyful one.

Already she'd spent hours at her spinning wheel and loom. There were new mufflers and mittens and caps for her brothers. Blue for Johnny and red for Brian.

For her father she had painted a miniature of her mother. And had paid the local silversmith a lot of pennies for a frame.

She knew her choices would please. Just as the meal she had planned for their Christmas feast would please. It was all that mattered to her—keeping her family together and happy and safe.

The door of the barn was unlatched. With a sound of annoyance, she pulled it to behind her. It was a good thing she had found it so, she thought, rather than her father, or her young brother, Brian, would have earned the raw side of his tongue.

As she stepped inside the barn, she shook her hood back and reached automatically for the wooden buckets that hung beside the door. Because there was little light she took a lamp, lighting it carefully.

By the time she had finished the milking, Brian and Johnny would come to feed the stock and clean the stalls. Then she would gather the eggs and fix her men a hearty breakfast.

She started to hum as she walked down the wide aisle in the center of the barn. Then she stopped dead as she spotted the roan mare standing slack hipped and weary beside the cow stall.

"Sweet Jesus." She put a hand to her heart as it lurched. The mare blew a greeting and shifted.

If there was a horse, there was a rider. At twenty, Alanna wasn't young enough or naive enough to believe all travelers were friendly and meant no harm to a woman alone. She could have turned and run, sent up a shout for her father and brothers. But though she had taken Michael Flynn's name, she was born a Murphy. A Murphy protected his own.

Head up, she started forward. "I'll have your name and your business," she said. Only the horse answered her. When she was close enough she touched the mare on her nose. "What kind of a master have you who leaves you standing wet and saddled?" Incensed for the horse's sake, she set down her buckets and raised her voice. "All right, come out with you. It's Murphy land you're on."

The cows mooed.

With a hand on her hip, she looked around. "No one's begrudging you shelter from the storm," she continued. "Or a decent breakfast, for that matter. But I'll have a word with you for leaving your horse so."

When there was still no answer, her temper rose. Muttering, she began to uncinch the saddle herself. And nearly tripped over a pair of boots.

Fine boots at that, she thought, staring down at them. They poked out of the cow stall, their good brown leather dulled with snow and mud. She stepped quietly closer to see them attached to a pair of long, muscled legs in worn buckskin.

Sure and there was a yard of them, she thought, nibbling on her lip. And gloriously masculine in the loose-fitting breeches. Creeping closer, she saw hips, lean, a narrow waist belted with leather and a torso covered with a long doublet and a fur wrap.

A finer figure of a man she couldn't remember seeing. And since he'd chosen her barn to sleep, she found it only right that she look her fill. He was a big one, she decided, tilting her head and holding the lamp higher. Taller than either of her brothers. She leaned closer, wanting to see the rest of him.

His hair was dark. Not brown, she realized, as she narrowed her eyes, but deep red, like Brian's chestnut gelding. He wore no beard, but there was stubble on his chin and around his full, handsome mouth. Aye, handsome, she decided with feminine appreciation. A strong, bony face, aristocratic somehow, with its high brow and chiseled features.

The kind of face a woman's heart would flutter over, she was sure. But she wasn't interested in fluttering or flirting. She wanted the man up and out of her way so that she could get to her milking.

"Sir." She nudged his boot with the toe of hers. No response. Setting her hands on her hips, she decided he was drunk as a lord. What else was there that caused a man to sleep as though dead? "Wake up, you sod. I can't milk around you." She kicked him, none too gently, in the leg and got only a faint groan for an answer. "All right, boy-o." She bent down to give him a good shake. She was prepared for the stench of liquor but instead caught the coppery odor of blood.

Anger forgotten, she knelt down to carefully push aside the thick fur over his shoulders. She sucked in a breath as she saw the long stain along his shirtfront. Her fingers were wet with his blood as she felt for a pulse.

"Well, you're still alive," she murmured. "With God's will and a bit of luck we might keep you that way."

Before she could rise to call her brothers, his hand clamped over her wrist. His eyes were open now, she saw. They were green, with just a hint of blue. Like the sea. But there was pain in them. Compassion had her leaning closer to offer comfort.

Then her hand plunged deep into the hay as he tugged her off balance so that she was all but lying on him. She had the quick impression of a firm body and raging heat. Her sound of indignation was muffled against his lips. The kiss was brief but surprisingly firm before his head fell back again. He gave her a quick, cocky smile.

"Well, I'm not dead anyway. Lips like yours would have no place in hell."

As compliments went, she'd had better. Before she could tell him so, he fainted.

Chapter Two

He drifted, on a turbulent sea that was pain and relief and pain. Whiskey, the good, clean kick of it, warming his belly and dulling his senses. Yet over it he remembered a searing agony, a hot knife plunged into his flesh. Curses raining on his head. A warm hand clutching his, in comfort. In restraint. Blissfully cool cloths on his fevered brow. Hateful liquid poured down his throat.

He cried out. Had he cried out? Had someone come, all soft hands, soft voice, lavender scent, to soothe him? Had there been music, a woman's voice, low and lovely? Singing in Gaelic? Scotland? Was he is Scotland? But no, when the voice spoke to him, it was without that soft familiar burr, but instead with the dreamy brogue of Ireland.

The ship. Had the ship gone astray and taken him south instead of home? He remembered a ship. But the ship had been in port. Men laughing among themselves, their faces blackened and painted. Axes swinging. The tea. The cursed tea.

Ah, yes, he remembered. There was some comfort in that. They had taken their stand.

He had been shot. Not then, but after. At dawn. A mistake, a foolish one.

Then there had been snow and pain. He had awakened to a woman. A beautiful woman. A man could ask for little more than to wake to a beautiful woman, whether he awakened live or dead. The thought made him smile as he opened his heavy eyes. As dreams went, this one had its virtues.

Then he saw her sitting at a loom beneath a window where the sun was strong. It glistened on her hair, hair as black as the wing of any raven that flew in the forest. She wore a plain wool dress in dark blue with a white apron over it. He could see that she was wand slender, her hands graceful as they worked the loom. With a rhythmic click and clack she set a red pattern among deep green wool.

She sang as she worked, and it was her voice he recognized. The same voice had sung to comfort him when he had toiled through the hot and the cold of his dreams. He could see only her profile. Pale skin of white and rose, a faint curve to a mouth that was wide and generous, with the hint of a dimple beside it, a small nose that seemed to tilt up just a bit at the tip.

Peaceful. Just watching her gave him such a full sense of peace that he was tempted to close his eyes and sleep again. But he wanted to see her, all of her. And he needed her to tell him where he was.

The moment he stirred, Alanna's head came up. She turned toward him. He could see her eyes now—as deep and rich a blue as sapphires. As he watched, struggling for the strength to speak, she rose, smoothed her skirts and walked toward him.

Her hand was cool on his brow, and familiar. Briskly, but with hands that were infinitely gentle, she checked his bandage.

"So, have you joined the living, then?" she asked him as she moved to a nearby table and poured something into a pewter cup.

"You'd know the answer to that better than I," he managed. She chuckled as she held the cup to his lips. The scent was familiar, as well, and unwelcome. "What the devil is this?"

"What's good for you," she told him, and poured it ruthlessly down his throat. When he glared she laughed again. "You've spit it back at me enough times that I've learned to take no chances."

"How long?"

"How long have you been with us?" She touched his forehead again. His fever had broken during the last long night, and her gesture was one of habit. "Two days. It's the twentieth of December."

"My horse?"

"She's well." Alanna nodded, pleased that he had thought of his mount. "You'd do well to sleep some more and I'll be fixing you some broth to strengthen you. Mr...?"

"MacGregor," he answered. "Ian MacGregor."

"Rest then, Mr. MacGregor."

But his hand reached for hers. Such a small hand, he thought irrelevantly, to be so competent. "Your name?"

"Alanna Flynn." His was a good hand, she thought, not as rough as Da's or her brothers', but hard. "You're welcome here until you are fit."

"Thank you." He kept her hand in his, toying with her fingers in a way that she would have thought flirtatious—if he hadn't just come out of a fever. Then she remembered he had kissed her when he'd been bleeding to death in her barn, and carefully removed her hand. He grinned at her. There was no other way to describe that quick curve of lips.

"I'm in your debt, Miss Flynn."

"Aye, that you are." She rose, all dignity. "And it's Mrs. Flynn."

He couldn't remember a swifter or weightier disappointment. Not that he minded flirting with married women, if they were agreeable. But he would never have considered taking it further than a few smiles and murmurs with another man's woman. It was a bloody shame, he thought as he studied Alanna Flynn. A sad and bloody shame.

"I'm grateful to you, Mrs. Flynn, and to your husband."

"Give your gratitude to my father." She softened the order with a smile that made her dimple deepen. He was a rogue, of that she hadn't a doubt. But he was also a weak one and, at the moment, in her care. "This is his house, and he'll be back soon." With her hands on her hips, she looked at him. His color was better, she noted, though the good Lord knew he could use a good clipping on that mane of hair he wore. And a shave wouldn't have hurt him. Despite it, he was an excellent-looking man. And because she was woman enough to have recognized the light in his eyes when he looked at her, she would keep her guard up.

"If you're not going to sleep, you might as well eat. I'll get that broth."

She left him to go into the kitchen, her heels clicking lightly on the plank floor. Alone, Ian lay still and let his gaze wander over the room. Alanna Flynn's father had done well for himself, Ian mused. The windows were glazed, the walls whitewashed. His pallet was set near the fire and its stone hearth was scrubbed clean. Above it was a mantelpiece of the same native stone. On it candles were set and a pair of painted china dishes. There were two fowling pieces above it all and a good flintlock, as well.

The loom was under the window, and in the corner was a spinning wheel. The furniture showed not a speck of dust and was brightened a bit by a few needlepoint cushions. There was a scent—apples baking, he thought, and spiced meats. A comfortable home, he thought, hacked out of the wilderness. A man had to respect another who could make his mark like this. And a man would have to fight to keep what he had made.

There were things worth fighting for. Worth dying for. His land. His name. His woman. His freedom. Ian was more than ready to lift his sword. As he tried to sit up, the cozy room spun.

"Isn't it just like a man?" Alanna came back with a bowl of broth. "Undoing all my work. Sit still, you're weak as a babe and twice as fretful."

"Mrs. Flynn—"

"Eat first, talk later."

Out of self-defense, he swallowed the first spoonful of broth she shoveled into his mouth. "The broth is tasty, mistress, but I can feed myself."

"And spill it all over my clean linens in the bargain. No, thank you. You need your strength." She placated him as she would have her own brothers. "You lost a great deal of blood before you got to us— more when the ball was removed." She spoke as she spooned up broth, and her hand didn't tremble. But her heart did.

There was the scent of herbs and her own lavender fragrance. Ian began to think being fed had its advantages.

"If it hadn't been so cold," she continued, "you would have bled all the quicker and died in the forest."

"So I've nature as well as you to thank."

She gave him a measured look. "It's said the Lord works in mysterious ways. Apparently he saw fit to keep you alive after you'd done your best to die."

"And put me in the hands of a neighbor." He smiled again, charmingly. "I've never been to Ireland, but I'm told it's beautiful."

"So my father says. I was born here."

"But there's Ireland on your tongue."

"And Scotland on yours."

"It's been five years since I've seen Scotland this time." A shadow came and went in his eyes. "I've been spending some time in Boston. I was educated there and have friends."

"Educated." She had already recognized his schooling by his speech and envied him for it.

"Harvard." He smiled a little.

"I see." And she envied him all the more. If her mother had lived... Ah, but her mother had died, and Alanna had never had more than a hornbook to learn to write and read. "You're a ways from Boston now. A day's ride. Would you be having any family or friends who will worry?"

"No. No one to worry." He wanted to touch her. It was wrong, against his own code of honor. But he wanted to see if her cheek could be as beautifully soft as it looked. If her hair would feel as thick and heavy. Her mouth as sweet.

Her lashes lifted, and her eyes, clear and cool, met his. For a moment he could see only her face, drifting over his. And he remembered. He had already tasted those lips once.

Despite his best intentions, his gaze lowered to them. Lingered. When she stiffened, his eyes flickered up. There was not so much apology in them as amusement.

"I must beg your pardon, Mrs. Flynn. I was not myself when you found me in the barn."

"You came to yourself quickly enough," she snapped back, and made him laugh until he winced at the pain.

"Then I'll beg your pardon all the more and hope your husband won't call me out."

"There's little danger of that. He's been dead these three years."

He looked up quickly, but she only shoveled another spoonful of broth in his mouth. Though God might strike him dead, he couldn't say he was sorry to hear Flynn had gone to his Maker. After all, Ian reasoned, it wasn't as if he had known the man. And what better way to spend a day or two than recovering in the lap of a pretty young widow?

Alanna scented desire the way a hound scents deer and was up and out of reach. "You'll rest now."

"I feel that I've rested weeks already." Lord, she was a lovely thing, all curves and colors. He tried his most ingratiating smile. "Could I trouble you to help me to a chair? I'd feel more myself if I could sit, perhaps look out the window."

She hesitated, not because she was afraid she couldn't move him. Alanna considered herself strong as an ox. But she didn't trust the gleam she'd seen come and go in his eyes.

"All right then, but you'll lean on me and take it slow."

"With gladness." He took her hand and raised it to his lips. Before she could snatch it away, he turned it over and brushed his lips, as no man ever had, over the cup of her palm. Her heart bounded into her throat. "You have eyes the color of jewels I once saw around the neck of the queen of France. Sapphires," he murmured. "A seductive word."

She didn't move. Couldn't. Never in her life had a man looked at her this way. She felt the heat rush up, from the knot in her belly along her suddenly taut breasts, up her throat where her pulse hammered and into her face. Then he smiled, that quick, crooked shifting of lips. She snatched her hand away.

"You're a rogue, Mr. MacGregor."

"Aye, Mrs. Flynn. But that doesn't make the words less true. You're beautiful. Just as your name says. Alanna." He lingered over each syllable.

She knew better than to fall for flattery. But the center of her palm still burned. "It's my name, and you'll wait till you're asked to use it." It was with relief that she heard the sounds outside the house. Her brow lifted a bit when she saw that Ian had heard them as well and braced. "That'll be my father and brothers. If you'd still be having a mind to sit by the window, they'll help you." So saying, she moved to the door.

They would be cold and hungry, she thought, and would gobble down the meat pies and the apple tarts she had made without a thought for the time and care she had given them. Her father would fret more over what hadn't been done than what had. Johnny would think about how soon he could ride into the village to court young Mary Wyeth. Brian would put his nose into one of the books he loved and read by the fire until his head drooped.

They came in bringing cold and melting snow and loud masculine voices.

Ian relaxed as he noted it was indeed her family. Perhaps it was foolish to think the British would have tracked him all this way in the snow, but he wasn't a man to let down his guard. He saw three men—or two men and a boy nearly grown. The elder man was barely taller than Alanna and toughly built. His face was reddened and toughened by years of wind and weather, his eyes a paler version of his daughter's. He took off his work cap and beneath it his hair was thin and sandy.

The older son had the look of him but with more height and less bulk. There was an ease and patience in his face that his father lacked.

The younger matched his brother inch for inch, but there was the dew of youth still on his cheeks. He had the same coloring as his sister.

"Our guest is awake," Alanna announced, and three pairs of eyes turned to him. "Ian MacGregor, this is my father, Cyrus Murphy, and my brothers, John and Brian."

"MacGregor," Cyrus said in a voice that rumbled. "An awkward name."

Despite the pain, Ian stiffened and pushed himself as straight as possible. "One I'm proud of."

"A man should be proud of his name," Cyrus said as he took Ian's measure. "It's all he's born with. I'm glad you decided to live, for the ground's frozen and we couldn't have buried you till spring."

"It's a bit of a relief to me, as well."

Satisfied with the answer, Cyrus nodded. "We'll wash for supper."

"Johnny." Alanna detained her brother with a hand on his arm. "Will you help Mr. MacGregor into the chair by the window before you eat?"

With a quick grin, Johnny looked at Ian. "You're built like an oak, MacGregor. We had the very devil of a time getting you into the house. Give me a hand here, Brian."

"Thanks." Ian bit back a groan as he lifted his arms over the two pairs of shoulders. Cursing his watery legs, he vowed to be up and walking on his own by the next day. But he was sweating by the time they settled him into the chair.

"You're doing well enough for a man who cheated death," Johnny told him, understanding well the frustrations of any sick man.

"I feel like I drank a case of grog then took to the high seas in a storm."

"Aye." Johnny slapped his good shoulder in a friendly manner. "Alanna will fix you up." He left to wash for supper, already scenting the spiced meat.

"Mr. MacGregor?" Brian stood in front of him. There was both a shyness and intensity in his eyes. "You'd be too young to have fought in the Forty-five?" When Ian's brow lifted, the boy continued hurriedly. "I've read all about it, the Stuart Rebellion and the bonny prince and all the battles. But you'd be too young to have fought."

"I was born in '46," Ian told him. "During the Battle of Culloden. My father fought in the rebellion. My grandfather died in it."

The intense blue eyes widened. "Then you could tell me more than I can find in books."

"Aye." Ian smiled a little. "I could tell you more."

"Brian." Alanna's voice was sharp. "Mr. Mac-Gregor needs to rest, and you need to eat."

Brian edged back, but he watched Ian. "We could talk after supper if you're not weary."

Ian ignored Alanna's stormy looks and smiled at the boy. "I'd like that."

Alanna waited until Brian was out of earshot. When she spoke, the barely controlled fury in her voice surprised Ian. "I won't have you filling his head with the glory of war and battles and causes."

"He looked old enough to decide what he wants to talk about."

"He's a boy yet, and his head is easily filled with nonsense." With tense fingers, she pleated the skirt of her apron, but her eyes remained level and uncompromising. "I may not be able to stop him from running off to the village green to drill, but I'll have no talk of war in my house."

"There will be more than talk, and soon," Ian said mildly. "It's foolish for a man—and a woman—not to prepare for it."

She paled but kept her chin firm. "There will be no war in this house," she repeated, and fled to the kitchen.

Chapter Three

Ian awoke early the next morning to watery winter sunlight and the good yeasty smell of baking bread. For a moment he lay quiet, enjoying the sounds and scents of morning. Behind him the fire burned low and bright, shooting out comforting heat. From the direction of the kitchen came Alanna's voice. This time she sang in English. For a few minutes he was too enchanted with the sound itself to pay attention to the lyrics. Once they penetrated, his eyes widened first in surprise, then in amusement.

It was a bawdy little ditty more suitable to sailors or drunks than a proper young widow.

So, he thought, the lovely Alanna had a ribald sense of humor. He liked her all the better for it, though he doubted her tongue would have tripped so lightly over the words if she had known she had an audience. Trying to move quietly, he eased his legs from the pallet. The business of standing took some doing and left him dizzy and weak and infuriated. He had to wait, wheezing like an old man, one big hand pressed for support against the wall. When he had his breath back he took one tentative step forward. The room tilted and he clenched his teeth until it righted again. His arm throbbed mightily. Concentrating on the pain, he was able to take another step, and another, grateful that no one was there to see his tedious and shambling progress.

It was a lowering thought that one small steel ball could fell a MacGregor.

The fact that the ball had been English pushed him to place one foot in front of the other. His legs felt as though they'd been filled with water, and a cold sweat lay on his brow and the back of his neck. But in his heart was a fierce pride. If he had been spared to fight again, he would damn well fight. And he couldn't fight until he could walk.

When he reached the kitchen doorway, exhausted and drenched with the effort, Alanna was singing a Christmas hymn. She seemed to find no inconsistency in crooning about amply endowed women one moment and heralding angels the next.

It hardly mattered to Ian what she sang. As he stood, watching, listening, he knew as sure as he knew a MacGregor would always live in the Highlands that her voice would follow him to his grave. He would never forget it, the clear, rich notes, the faint huskiness that made him imagine her with her hair unbound and spread over a pillow.

His pillow, he realized with a quick jolt. It was there he wanted her without a doubt, and so strongly that he could all but feel the smooth, silky tresses shift through his fingers.

Most of those thick raven locks were tucked under a white cap now. It should have given her a prim and proper look. Yet some strands escaped, to trail—seductively, he thought—along the back of her neck. He could easily imagine what it would be like to trail his fingers just so. To feel her skin heat and her body move. Against his.

Would she be as agile in bed as she was at the stove?

Perhaps he wasn't so weak after all, Ian mused, if every time he saw this woman his blood began to stir and his mind shot unerringly down one particular path. If he hadn't been afraid he would fall on his face and mortify himself, he would have crossed the room and spun her around, against him, into him, so that he could steal a kiss. Instead he waited, hopefully, for his legs to strengthen.

She kneaded one batch of dough while another baked. He could see her small, capable hands push and prod and mold. Patiently. Tirelessly. As he watched her, his rebellious mind filled with such gloriously lusty thoughts that he groaned.

Alanna whirled quickly, her hands still wrapped around the ball of dough. Her first thoughts shamed her, for when she saw him filling the doorway, dressed in rough trousers and a full open shirt, she wondered how she might lure him to kiss her hand again. Disgusted with herself, she slapped the dough down and hurried toward him. His face was dead white and he was beginning to teeter. From previous experience, she knew that if he hit the ground she'd have the very devil of a time getting him back into bed.

"There now, Mr. MacGregor, lean on me." Since the kitchen chair was closer, and he was of a considerable weight, she led him to that before she rounded on him. "Idiot," she said with relish more than real heat. "But most men are, I've found. You'd best not have opened your wound again, for I've just scrubbed this floor and wouldn't care to have blood on it."

"Aye, mistress." It was a weak rejoinder, but the best he could do when her scent was clouding his mind and her face was bent so close to his. He could have counted each one of her silky black eyelashes.

"You had only to call, you know," she said, mollified a bit when she noted his bandage was dry. As she might have for one of her brothers, Alanna began to fasten his shirt. Ian was forced to suppress another groan.

"I had to try my legs." His blood wasn't just stirring now but was racing hot. As a result, his voice had a roughened edge. "I can hardly get on my feet again by lying on my back."

"You'll get up when I say and not before." With this she moved away and began to mix something in a pewter cup. Ian caught the scent and winced.

"I'll not have any more of that slop."

"You'll drink it and be grateful—" she slapped the cup on the tabletop "—if you want anything else in your belly."

He glared at her in a way he knew had made grown men back away or run for cover. She simply placed her fisted hands on her hips and glared back. His eyes narrowed. So did hers.

"You're angry because I talked with young Brian last night."

Her chin lifted, just an inch, but it was enough to give her anger an elegant haughtiness. "And if you'd been resting instead of jabbering about the glory of war, you'd not be so weak and irritable this morning."

"I'm not irritable or weak."

When she snorted, he wished fervently that he had the strength to stand. Aye, then he'd have kissed her to swooning and shown her what a MacGregor was made of.

"If I'm irritable," he said between clenched teeth, "it's because I'm near to starving."

She smiled at him, pleased to hold the upper hand. "You'll get your breakfast after you've drained that cup, and not a moment before." With a twitch of her skirts she returned to her bread making.

While her back was turned, Ian looked around for a handy place to dump the foul-tasting liquid. Finding none, he folded his arms and scowled at her. Alanna's lips curved. She hadn't been raised in a house filled with men for naught. She knew exactly what was going through Ian's mind. He was stubborn, she thought as she pushed the heels of her hands into the dough. But so was she.

She began to hum.

He no longer thought about kissing her but gave grave consideration to throttling her. Here he sat, hungry as a bear, with the enticing smell of bread baking. And all she would give him was a cup of slop.

Still humming, Alanna put the bread into a bowl for rising and covered it with a clean cloth. Easily ignoring Ian, she checked the oven and judged her loaves were done to a turn. When she set them on a rack to cool, their scent flooded the kitchen.

He had his pride, Ian thought. But what good was pride if a man expired of hunger? She'd pay for it, he promised himself as he lifted the cup and drained it.

Alanna made certain her back was to him when she grinned. Without a word, she heated a skillet. In short order she set a plate before him heaped with eggs and a thick slab of the fresh bread. To this she added a small crock of butter and a cup of steaming coffee.

While he ate, she busied herself, scrubbing out the skillet, washing the counters so that not a scrap of dough or flour remained. She was a woman who prized her mornings alone, who enjoyed her kitchen domain and the hundreds of chores it entailed. Yet she didn't resent his presence there, though she knew he watched her with his steady, sea-colored eyes. Oddly, it seemed natural, even familiar somehow, that he sit at her table and sample her cooking.

No, she didn't resent his presence, but neither could she relax in it. The silence that stretched between them no longer seemed colored by temper on either side. But it was tinted with something else, something that made her nerves stretch and her heart thud uncomfortably against her ribs.

Needing to break it, she turned to him. He was indeed watching her, she noted. Not with temper but with . . . interest. It was a weak word for what she saw in his eyes, but a safe one. Alanna had a sudden need to feel safe.

"A gentleman would thank me for the meal."

His lips curved in such a way that let her know he was only a gentleman if and when he chose to be. "I do thank you, Mrs. Flynn, most sincerely. I wonder if I might beg another cup of coffee."

His words were proper enough, but she didn't quite trust the look in his eyes. She kept out of reach as she picked up his cup. "Tea would be better for you," she said almost to herself. "But we don't drink it in this house."

"In protest?"

"Aye. We won't have the cursed stuff until the king sees reason. Others make more foolish and dangerous protests."

He watched her lift the pot from the stove. "Such as?"

She moved her shoulders. "Johnny heard word that the Sons of Liberty arranged to destroy crates of tea that were sitting in three ships in Boston Harbor. They disguised themselves as Indians and boarded the ships all but under the guns of three men-of-war. Before the night was done, they had tossed all of the East Indian Company's property into the water."

"And you think this foolish?"

"Daring, certainly," she said with another restless movement. "Even heroic, especially in Brian's eyes. But foolish because it will only cause the king to impose even harsher measures." She set the cup before him.

"So you believe it best to do nothing when injustice is handed out with a generous hand? Simply to sit like a trained dog and accept the boot?"

Murphy blood rose to her cheeks. "No king lives forever."

"Ah, so we wait until mad George cocks up his toes rather than stand now for what is right."

"We've seen enough war and heartache in this house."

"There will only be more, Alanna, until it's settled."

"Settled," she shot back as he calmly sipped his coffee. "Settled by sticking feathers in our hair and smashing crates of tea? Settled as it was for the wives and mothers of those who fell at Lexington? And for what? For graves and tears?"

"For liberty," he said. "For justice."

"Words." She shook her head. "Words don't die. Men do."

"Men must, of old age or at sword's point. Can you believe it better to bow under the English chains, over and over until our backs break? Or should we stand tall and fight for what is ours by right?"

She felt a frisson of fear as she watched his eyes glow. "You speak like a rebel, MacGregor."

"Like an American," he corrected. "Like a Son of Liberty."

"I should have guessed as much," she murmured. She snatched up his plate, set it aside, then, unable to stop herself, marched back to him. "Was the sinking of the tea worth your life?"

Absently he touched a hand to his shoulder. "A miscalculation," he said, "and nothing that really pertains to our little tea party."

"Tea party." She looked up at the ceiling. "How like a man to make light of insurrection."

"And how like a woman to wring her hands at the thought of a fight."

Her gaze flew back down and locked with his. "I don't wring my hands," she said precisely. "And certainly wouldn't shed a tear over the likes of you."

His tone changed so swiftly she blinked. "Ah, but you'll miss me when I've gone."

"The devil," she muttered, and fought back a grin. "Now go back to bed."

"I doubt I'm strong enough to make it on my own."

She heaved a sigh but walked to him to offer him a shoulder. He took the shoulder, and the rest of her. In one quick move she was in his lap. She cursed him with an expertise he was forced to admire.

"Hold now," he told her. "Differences in politics aside, you're a pretty package, Alanna, and I've discovered it's been too long since I've held a warm woman in my arms.''

''Son of a toad,'' she managed, and struck out.

He winced as the pain shimmered down his wounded arm. ''My father would take exception to that, sweetheart.''

''I'm not your sweetheart, you posturing spawn of a weasel.''

''Keep this up and you'll open my wound and have my blood all over your clean floor.''

''Nothing would give me more pleasure.''

Charmed, he grinned and caught her chin in his hand. ''For one who talks so righteously about the evils of war, you're a bloodthirsty wench.''

She cursed him until she ran out of breath. Her brother John had said nothing but the truth when he'd claimed that Ian was built like an oak. No matter how she squirmed—absolutely delighting him—she remained held fast.

''A pox on you,'' she managed. ''And on your whole clan.''

He'd intended to pay her back for making him drink the filthy medicine she'd mixed. He'd only pulled her into his lap to cause her discomfort. Then, as she'd wiggled, he'd thought it only right that he tease her a little and indulge himself. With just one kiss. One quick stolen kiss. After all, she was already fuming.

In fact, he was laughing as he covered her mouth with his. It was meant in fun, as much a joke on himself as on her. And he wanted to hear the new batch of curses she would heap on his head when he was done.

But his laughter died quickly. Her struggling body went stone still.

One quick, friendly kiss, he tried to remind himself, but his head was reeling. He found himself as dizzy and as weak as he'd been when he'd first set his watery legs on the floor.

This had nothing to do with a wound several days old. Yet there was a pain, a sweet ache that spread and shifted through the whole of him. He wondered, dazedly, if he had been spared not only to fight again but to be given the gift of this one perfect kiss.

She didn't fight him. In her woman's heart she knew she should. Yet in that same heart she understood that she could not. Her body, rigid with the first shock, softened, yielded, accepted.

Gentle and rough all at once, she thought. His lips were cool and smooth against hers while the stubble of his beard scraped against her skin. She heard her own sigh as her lips parted, then tasted his on her tongue. She laid a hand on his cheek, adding sweetness. He dragged his through her hair, adding passion.

For one dazzling moment he deepened the kiss, taking her beyond what she knew and into what she had only dreamed. She tasted the richness of his mouth, felt the iron-hard breath of his chest. Then heard his sharp, quick curse as he dragged himself away.

He could only stare at her. It unnerved him that he could do little else. He had dislodged her cap so that her hair streamed like black rain over her shoulders. Her eyes were so dark, so big, so blue against the creamy flush of her skin that he was afraid he might drown in them.

This was a woman who could make him forget— about duty, about honor, about justice. This was a woman, he realized, who could make him crawl on his knees for one kind word.

He was a MacGregor. He could never forget. He could never crawl.

"I beg your pardon, mistress." His voice was stiffly polite and so cold she felt all the warmth leach out of her body. "That was inexcusable."

Carefully she got to her feet. With blurred vision she searched the floor for her cap. Finding it, she stood, straight as a spear, and looked over his shoulder.

"I would ask you again, MacGregor, to go back to your bed."

She didn't move a muscle until he was gone. Then she dashed away an annoying tear and went back to work. She would not think of it, she promised herself. She would *not* think of him.

She took out her frustrations on the newly risen dough.

Chapter Four

Christmas had always given Alanna great joy. Preparing for it was a pleasure to her—the cooking, the baking, the sewing and cleaning. She had always made it a policy to forgive slights, both small and large, in the spirit of giving. She looked forward to putting on her best dress and riding into the village for Mass.

But as this Christmas approached, she was by turns depressed and irritated. Too often she caught herself being snappish with her brothers, impatient with her father. She became teary over a burnt cake, then stormed out of the house when Johnny tried to joke her out of it.

Sitting on a rock by the icy stream, she dropped her chin onto her hands and took herself to task.

It wasn't fair for her to take out her temper on her family. They'd done nothing to deserve it. She had chosen the easy way out by snapping at them, when the one she truly wanted to roast was Ian MacGregor. She kicked at the crusty snow.

Oh, he'd kept his distance in the past two days. The coward. He'd managed to gain his feet and slink out to the barn like the weasel he was. Her father was grateful for the help with the tack and animals, but

Alanna knew the real reason MacGregor had taken himself off to clean stalls and repair harnesses.

He was afraid of her. Her lips pursed in a smug smile. Aye, he was afraid she would call down the wrath of hell on his head. As well she should. What kind of man was it who kissed a woman until she was blind and deaf to all but him—then politely excused himself as if he had inadvertently trod on her foot?

He'd had no right to kiss her—and less to ignore what had happened when he had.

Why, she had saved his life, she thought with a toss of her head. That was the truth of it. She had saved him, and he had repaid her by making her want him as no virtuous woman should want a man not her husband.

But want him she did, and in ways so different from the calm, comforting manner she had wanted Michael Flynn that she couldn't describe them.

It was madness, of course. He was a rebel, once and forever. Such men made history, and widows out of wives. All she wanted was a quiet life, with children of her own and a house to tend to. She wanted a man who would come and sleep beside her night after night through all the years. A man who would be content to sit by the fire at night and talk over with her the day that had passed.

Such a man was not Ian MacGregor. No, she had recognized in him the same burning she had seen in Rory's eyes. There were those who were born to be warriors, and nothing and no one could sway them. There were those who were destined, before birth, to fight for causes and to die on the battlefield. So had been Rory, her eldest brother, and the one she had loved the best. And so was Ian MacGregor, a man she had known for days only and could never afford to love.

As she sat, brooding, a shadow fell over her. She tensed, turned, then managed to smile when she saw it was her young brother, Brian.

"It's safe enough," she told him when he hung back a bit. "I'm no longer in the mood to toss anyone in the stream."

"The cake wasn't bad once you cut away the burnt edges."

She narrowed her eyes to make him laugh. "Could be I'll take it in my mind to send you swimming after all."

But Brian knew better. Once Alanna's hot temper was cooled, she rarely fired up again. "You'd only feel badly when I took to bed with a chill and you had to douse me with medicine and poultices. Look, I've brought you a present." He held out the holly wreath he'd hidden behind his back. "I thought you might put ribbons on it and hang it on the door for Christmas."

She took it and held it gently. It was awkwardly made, and that much more dear. Brian was better with his mind than with his hands. "Have I been such a shrew?"

"Aye." He plopped down into the snow at her feet. "But I know you can't stay in a black mood with Christmas almost here."

"No." She smiled at the wreath. "I suppose not."

"Alanna, do you think Ian will be staying with us for Christmas dinner?"

Her smile became a frown quickly. "I couldn't say. He seems to be mending quickly enough."

"Da says he's handy to have around, even if he isn't a farmer." Absently, Brian began to ball snow. "And he knows so much. Imagine, going to Harvard and reading all those books."

"Aye." Her agreement was wistful, for herself and for Brian. "If we've a good harvest the next few years, Brian, you'll go away to school. I swear it."

He said nothing. It was something he yearned for more than breath, and something he'd already accepted he would live without. "Having Ian here is almost as good. He knows things."

Alanna's mouth pursed. "Aye, I'm sure he does."

"He gave me the loan of a book he had in his saddlebag. It's Shakespeare's *Henry V*. It tells all about the young King Harry and wonderful battles."

Battles, she thought again. It seemed men thought of little else from the moment they were weaned. Undaunted by her silence, Brian chattered on.

"It's even better to listen to him," Brian continued enthusiastically. "He told me about how his family fought in Scotland. His aunt married an Englishman, a Jacobite, and they fled to America after the rebellion was crushed. They have a plantation in Virginia and grow tobacco. He has another aunt and uncle who came to America too, though his father and mother still live in Scotland. In the Highlands. It seems a wondrous place, Alanna, with steep cliffs and deep lakes. And he was born in a house in the forest on the very day his father was fighting the English at Culloden."

She thought of a woman struggling through the pangs of labor and decided both male and female fought their own battles. The female for life, the male for death.

"After the battle," Brian went on, "the English butchered the survivors." He was looking out over the narrow, ice-packed stream and didn't notice how his sister's gaze flew to him. "The wounded, the surrendering, even people who were working in fields nearby. They hounded and chased the rebels, cutting them down where they found them. Some they closed up in a barn and burned alive."

"Sweet Jesus." She had never paid attention to talk of war, but this kept her riveted, and horrified.

"Ian's family lived in a cave while the English searched the hills for rebels. Ian's aunt—the one on the plantation—killed a redcoat herself. Shot him when he tried to murder her wounded husband."

Alanna swallowed deeply. "I believe Mr. Mac-Gregor exaggerates."

Brian turned his deep, intense eyes on her. "No," he said simply. "Do you think it will come to that here, Alanna, when the rebellion begins?"

She squeezed the wreath hard enough for a sprig of holly to pierce through her mittens. "There will be no rebellion. In time the government will become more reasonable. And if Ian MacGregor says any different—"

"It isn't only Ian. Even Johnny says so, and the men in the village. Ian says that the destruction of tea in Boston is only the beginning of a revolution that was inevitable the moment George III took the throne. Ian says it's time to throw off the British shackles and count ourselves for what we are. Free men."

"Ian says." She rose, skirts swaying. "I think Ian says entirely too much. Take the wreath in the house for me, Brian. I'll hang it as soon as I'm done."

Brian watched his sister storm off. It seemed that there would be at least one more outburst before her black mood passed.

Ian enjoyed working in the barn. More, he enjoyed being able to work at all. His arm and shoulder were still stiff, but the pain had passed. And thanks to all the saints, Alanna hadn't forced any of her foul concoctions on him that day.

Alanna.

He didn't want to think about her. To ease his mind, he set aside the tack he was soaping and picked up a brush. He would groom his horse in preparation for the journey he had been putting off for two days.

He should be gone, Ian reminded himself. He was surely well mended enough to travel short distances. Though it might be unwise to show his face in Boston for a time, he could travel by stages to Virginia and spend a few weeks with his aunt, uncle and cousins.

The letter he had given Brian to take to the village should be on its way by ship to Scotland and his family. They would know he was alive and well—and that he wouldn't be with them for Christmas.

He knew his mother would weep a little. Though she had other children, and grandchildren, she would be saddened that her firstborn was away when the family gathered for the Christmas feast.

He could see it in his mind—the blazing fires, the glowing candles. He could smell the rich smells of cooking, hear the laughter and singing. And with a pang that was so sudden it left him breathless, he hurt from the loss.

Yet, though he loved his family, he knew his place was here. A world away.

Aye, there was work to do here, he reminded himself as he stroked the mare's coat. There were men he had to contact once he knew it was safe. Samuel Adams, John Avery, Paul Revere. And he must have news of the climate in Boston and other cities now that the deed was done.

Yet he lingered when he should have been away. Daydreamed when he should have been plotting. He had, sensibly, he thought, kept his distance from Alanna. But in his mind she was never more than a thought away.

"There you are!"

And she was there, her breath puffing out in quick white streams, her hands on her hips. Her hood had fallen from her head and her hair swung loose, inky black against the plain gray fabric of her dress.

"Aye." Because his knuckles had whitened on the brush, he made an effort to relax his hand. "It's here I am."

"What business are you about, filling a young boy's head with nonsense? Would you have him heave a musket over his shoulder and challenge the first redcoat he comes to?"

"I gather you are speaking of Brian," he said when she stopped to take a breath. "But when I go a step further than that, I lose my way."

"Would you had lost it before you ever came here." Agitated, she began to pace. Her eyes were so hot a blue he wondered they didn't fire the straw underfoot. "Trouble, and only trouble from the first minute I came across you, sprawled half-dead in the hay. If I'd only known then what I've come to know now, I might have ignored my Christian duty and let you bleed to death."

He smiled—he couldn't help it—and started to speak, but she plunged on.

"First you nearly pull me down in the hay with you, kissing me even though you'd a ball in you. Then, almost on the moment when you open your eyes, you're kissing my hand and telling me I'm beautiful."

"I ought to be flogged," he said with a grin. "Imagine, telling you that you're beautiful."

"Flogging's too kind for the likes of you," she snapped with a toss of her head. "Then two days ago, after I'd fixed you breakfast—which is more than a man like you deserves—"

"Indeed it is," he agreed.

"Keep quiet until I'm done. After I'd fixed you breakfast, you drag me down on your lap as though I were a—a common..."

"Do words fail you?"

"Doxy," she spit out and dared him to laugh. "And like the great oaf you are, you held me there against my will and kissed me."

"And was kissed right back, sweetheart." He patted his horse's neck. "And very well, too."

She huffed and stammered. "How dare you?"

"That's difficult to answer unless you're more specific. If you're asking how I dared kiss you, I'll have to confess it was more a matter of not being able to stop myself. You've a mouth that's made for it, Alanna."

She felt herself go hot and began to pace again on unsteady legs. "Well, you got over it quickly enough."

His brow lifted. So she wasn't in a temper over the kiss but over the fact that he'd stopped. Looking at her now, in the dim light of the barn, he wondered how he'd managed to do so. And knew he wouldn't again.

"If it's my restraint that troubles you, sweet-heart—"

"Don't call me that. Not now, not ever."

Gamely, he swallowed a chuckle. "As you wish, Mrs. Flynn. As I was saying—"

"I told you to be still until I've finished." She stopped to catch her breath. "Where was I?"

"We were talking about kissing." Eyes glowing, he took a step toward her. "Why don't I refresh your memory?"

"Don't come near me," she warned, and snatched up a pitchfork. "I was simply using that as a reference to the trouble you've caused. Now, on top of everything else, you've got Brian's eyes shining over the thought of a revolution. I won't have it, Mac-Gregor. He's just a boy."

"If the lad asks questions, I'll give him true answers."

"And make them sound romantic and heroic in the bargain. I won't see him caught up in wars others make and lose him as I did my brother Rory."

"It won't be a war others make, Alanna." He circled her carefully, keeping away from the business end of the pitchfork. "When the time comes we'll all make it, and we'll win it."

"You can save your words."

"Good." Quick as a flash he grabbed the staff of the pitchfork, dodged the tines and hauled her against him. "I'm tired of talking."

When he kissed her this time, he was prepared for the jolt. It was no less devastating, no less exciting. Her face was cold and he used his lips to warm it, running them over her skin until he felt them both begin to shudder. He dragged a hand through her hair until he cupped the back of her neck. His other arm banded her hard against him.

"For God's sake, kiss me back, Alanna." He murmured it against her mouth. His eyes were open and hot on hers. "I'll go mad if you don't, mad if you do."

"Damn you then." She threw her arms around him. "I will."

She all but took him to his knees. There was no hesitation, no demur. Her lips were as hungry as his, her tongue as adventurous. She let her body press to his and thrilled at the sensation of his heart hammering against her.

She would never forget the scent of hay and animals, the drifting motes of dust in the thin beams of sunlight that broke through the chinks in the logs. Nor would she forget the strong, solid feel of him against her, the heat of his mouth, the sound of his pleasure. She would remember this one moment of abandonment because she knew it could never last.

"Let me go," she whispered.

He nestled into the sweet, fragrant curve of her neck. "I doubt I can."

"You must. I didn't come here for this."

He trailed his mouth to her ear and smiled when she shivered. "Would you really have stabbed me, Alanna?"

"Aye."

Because he believed her, he smiled again. "Here's a likely wench," he murmured, and nipped at her ear.

"Stop it." But she let her head fall back in surrender. Lord help her, she wanted it to go on. And on, and on. "This isn't right."

He looked at her then, his smile gone. "I think it is. I don't know why or how, but I think it's very right."

Because she wanted so badly to lean against him, she stiffened. "It can't be. You have your war and I have my family. I won't give my heart to a warrior. And there's the end of it."

"Damn it, Alanna—"

"I would ask you for something." She eased quickly out of his arms. Another moment in them and she might have forgotten everything—family and all her secret hopes for her own future. "You could consider it your Christmas gift to me."

He wondered if she knew that at that moment he would have pledged her all that was his, even his life. "What is it you want?"

"That you'll stay until Christmas is passed. It's important to Brian. And," she added before he could speak, "that you will not speak of war or revolts until the holy day is over."

"It's very little to ask."

"Not to me. To me it is a very great deal."

"Then you have it." She took a step back, but with a lift of his brow he took her hand firmly in his, raised it to his lips and kissed it.

"Thank you." She regained her hand quickly and hid it behind her back. "I have work to do." His voice stopped her as she hurried toward the door.

"Alanna...it is right."

She pulled the hood over her head and hurried out.

Chapter Five

The snow that fell on Christmas Eve delighted Alanna. In her heart she held the hope that the storm would rage for days and prevent Ian from traveling, as she knew he planned to do in two days' time. She knew the hope was both selfish and foolish, but she hugged it to her as she bundled into scarf and cloak to walk to the barn for the morning milking.

If he stayed, she would be miserable. If he left, she would be brokenhearted. She allowed herself the luxury of a sigh as she watched the flakes whirl white around her. It was best if she thought not of him at all, but of her responsibilities.

Her footsteps were the only sound in the barnyard as her boots broke through the new dusting to the thin crust beneath. Then, in the thick hush, the door creaked as she lifted the latch and pulled it open.

Inside, she reached for the buckets and had taken her first step when a hand fell on her shoulder. With a yelp, she jumped, sending the buckets clattering to the floor.

"Your pardon, Mrs. Flynn." Ian grinned as Alanna held both hands to her heart. "It seems I've startled you."

She would have cursed him if there had been any breath remaining in her lungs. Not for a moment could she have held her head up if he'd known she'd just been sighing over him. Instead, she shook her head and drew air in deeply. "What are you doing, sneaking about?"

"I came out of the house moments behind you," he explained. He had decided, after a long night of thought, to be patient with her. "The snow must have masked my approach."

Her own daydreaming had prevented her from hearing him, she thought, irritated, and bent down to snatch the buckets just as he did the same. When their heads bumped, she did swear.

"Just what the devil would you be wanting, MacGregor? Other than to scare the life from me?"

He would be patient, he promised himself as he rubbed his own head. If it killed him. "To help you with the milking."

Her narrowed eyes widened in bafflement. "Why?"

Ian blew out a long breath. Patience was going to be difficult if every word she spoke to him was a question or an accusation. "Because, as I have observed over the past days, you've too many chores for one woman."

Pride was stiff in her voice. "I can care for my family."

"No doubt." His voice was equally cool. Again, they reached down for the buckets together. Ian scowled. Alanna straightened to stand like a poker as he retrieved them.

"I appreciate your offer, but—"

"I'm only going to milk a damn cow, Alanna." So much for patience. "Can't you take the help in good grace?"

"Of course." Spinning on her heel, she stalked to the first stall.

She didn't need his help, she thought as she tugged off her mittens and slapped them into her lap. She was perfectly capable of doing her duty. The very idea of his saying she had too much to do. Why, in the spring there was twice as much, with planting and tending the kitchen garden, harvesting herbs. She was a strong, capable woman, not some weak, whimpering girl.

He was probably used to *ladies*, she thought with a sneer. Polished sugar faces that simpered and fluttered behind fans. Well, she was no lady with silk dresses and kid slippers, and she wasn't a bit ashamed of it. She sent a glare in Ian's direction. And if he thought she pined for drawing rooms, he was very much mistaken.

She tossed her head back as she began the tug and squeeze that squirted the brindled cow's milk into the bucket.

Ungrateful wench, Ian mused as he, with less ease and finesse, milked the second cow. He'd only wanted to help. Any fool could see that her duties ran from sunup to sundown. If she wasn't milking she was baking. If she wasn't baking she was spinning. If she wasn't spinning, she was scrubbing.

The women in his family had never been ladies of leisure, but they had always had daughters or sisters or cousins to help. All Alanna had were three men who obviously didn't realize the burdens that fell on her.

Well, he was going to help her if he had to throttle her into accepting.

She finished her bucket long before Ian and stood impatiently tapping her foot. When he was done, Alanna reached for the bucket, but he held it away from her.

"What are you doing?"

"I'm carrying the milk in for you." He took up the other bucket.

"Now why would you be doing that?"

"Because it's heavy," he all but bellowed, then muttering about stubborn, empty-headed women, he marched to the door.

"Keep swinging those buckets like that, Mac-Gregor, and you'll have more milk on the ground than in your belly." She couldn't quite catch what he muttered at her, but it wasn't complimentary. Suspicious, she brushed snow from her face. "Since you insist on carrying the milk, I'll just go gather the eggs."

They stalked off in different directions.

When Alanna returned to her kitchen, Ian was still there, feeding the fire.

"If you're waiting for breakfast, you'll wait a while longer."

"I'll help you," he said between gritted teeth.

"Help me what?"

"With breakfast."

That did it. With little regard for how many eggs cracked, she slammed down the bucket. "You find fault with my cooking, MacGregor?"

His hands itched to grab her shoulders and give her a brisk shake. "No."

"Hmm." She moved to the stove to make coffee. Turning, she all but plowed into him. "If you're going to be standing in my kitchen, MacGregor, then move aside. You're not so big I can't push you out of my way."

"Are you always so pleasant in the morning, Mrs. Flynn?"

Rather than dignify the question with an answer, she took the slab of ham she'd gotten from the smokehouse and began to slice. Ignoring him as best she could, she began to mix the batter for the pancakes she considered her specialty. She'd show Ian MacGregor a thing or two about cooking before she was done.

He said nothing but clattered the pewter dishes he set on the table to make his point. By the time her family joined them, the kitchen was filled with appetizing smells and a tension thick enough to hack with an ax.

"Pancakes," Johnny said with relish. "Sure and it's a fine way to start Christmas Eve."

"You look a bit flushed, girl." Cyrus studied his daughter as he took his seat. "You're not coming down sick, are you?"

"It's the heat from the stove," she snapped, then bit her tongue as her father narrowed his eyes. "I've applesauce made just yesterday for the pancakes." She set the bowl she was carrying on the table, then went back for the coffee. Flustered because Ian had yet to take his eyes from her, she reached for the pot without remembering to wrap a cloth around the handle. As she singed the tips of two fingers, she let out a cry and followed it with an oath.

"No use bringing the Lord into it when you've been careless," Cyrus said mildly, but he rose to smear cooling butter on the burns. "You've been jumpy as a frog with the hiccups these past days, Alanna."

"It's nothing." She waved him back to the table with her good hand. "Sit, the lot of you, and eat. I want you out of my kitchen so I can finish my baking."

"I hope there's a fresh raisin cake on the list." Johnny grinned as he heaped applesauce on his plate. "No one makes a better one than you, Alanna. Even when you burn it."

She managed to laugh, and nearly mean it, but she had little appetite for the meal as she joined the table.

It was just as well, she decided some time later. Though the men in her life had chattered like magpies through breakfast, they hadn't left a scrap for the rest of the birds. With relief she watched them bundle up for the rest of the day's work. She'd have the kitchen, and the rest of the house, to herself in short order. Alone, she should be able to think about what and how she felt about Ian MacGregor.

But he had been gone only minutes when he returned with a pail of water.

"What are you up to now?" she demanded, and tried in vain to tuck some of her loosened tresses into her cap.

"Water for the dishes." Before she could do so herself, he poured the water into a pot on the stove to heat.

"I could have fetched it myself," she said, then felt nasty. "But thank you."

"You're welcome." He shrugged out of his outer clothes and hung them on a hook by the door.

"Aren't you going to go with the others, then?"

"There are three of them and one of you."

She tilted her head. "That's true enough. And so?"

"So today I'm helping you."

Because she knew her patience was thin, she waited a moment before speaking. "I'm perfectly capable—"

"More than, from what I've seen." He began to stack the dishes she'd yet to clear. "You work like a pack mule."

"That is a ridiculous and a very uncomplimentary description, boy-o." Her chin jutted forward. "Now get out of my kitchen."

"I will if you will."

"I've work to do."

"Fine. Then let's be at it."

"You'll be in my way."

"You'll work around me." When she drew her next breath he cupped her face in his hands and kissed her, hard and long. "I'm staying with you, Alanna," he said when she managed to focus on him again. "And that's that."

"Is it?" To her mortification, her voice was only a squeak.

"Aye."

"Well, then." She cleared her throat, stepped back and smoothed her skirts. "You can fetch me apples from the storage cellar. I've got pies to bake."

She used the time it took him to return to try to compose herself. What was becoming of her when she lost her brains and every other faculty over a kiss? But it wasn't an ordinary kiss, not when they were Ian's lips doing the work. Something strange was happening when one moment she was pinning her heart on the hope that he would stay a while longer—the next she was resenting him so that she wished him a thousand miles away. And a moment later, she was letting him kiss her, and hoping he'd do so again at the first opportunity.

She'd been born in the Colonies, a child of a new world. But her blood was Irish—Irish enough that words like fate and destiny loomed large.

As she began to scrub dishes, she thought that if her destiny was in the shape of one Ian MacGregor, she was in trouble deep.

"It's simple enough to peel an apple," she insisted later, fuming over Ian's clumsy, hacking attempts. "You put the knife under the skin."

"I did."

"And took most of the meat with it. A little time and care works wonders."

He smiled at her, all too strangely for her comfort. "So I'm thinking, Mrs. Flynn. So I'm thinking."

"Try again," she told him as she went back to her piecrusts and rolling pin. "And you'll be cleaning up all those peelings you're scattering on my floor."

"Aye, Mrs. Flynn."

Holding the rolling pin aloft, she glared at him. "Are you trying to rouse my temper, MacGregor?"

He eyed the kitchen weaponry. "Not while you're holding that, sweetheart."

"I've told you not to call me that."

"So you have."

He watched her go back to her pies. She was a pleasure to watch, he thought. Quick hands, limber fingers. Even when she moved from counter to stove and back again, there was a nimbleness in her movements that sent his heart thudding.

Who would have thought he'd have had to be shot, all but bleed to death and end up unconscious in a cow stall to fall in love?

Despite her criticism, and her tendency to jump whenever he got too close, he was having the best day of his life. Perhaps he didn't want to make a habit out of peeling apples, but it was a simple way to be near her, to absorb that soft lavender scent that seemed to cling to her skin. It melded seductively with the aromas of cinnamon, ginger and cloves.

And in truth, though he was more at home in political meetings or with a sword in his hand than in the kitchen, he had wanted to ease what he saw as an unfair burden of responsibility.

She didn't appear to deem it so, he mused. Indeed, she seemed content to toil away, hour by hour. He wanted—needed, he admitted—to show her there was more. He imagined riding with her through the fields of his aunt's plantation. In the summer, he thought, when the rich green might remind her of an Ireland she'd never seen. He wanted to take her to Scotland, to the glory of the Highlands. To lie with her in the purple heather by a loch and listen to the wind in the pine.

He wanted to give her a silk dress, and jewels to match her eyes. They were sentimental, romantic notions, he knew. Surely he would have choked on the words if he had tried to express them.

But he wanted to give, that much he knew. If he could find a way to make her take.

Alanna felt his stare on her back as though it were tickling fingers. She'd have preferred the fingers, she thought. Those she could have batted away. Struggling to ignore him, she covered the first pie, fluted and trimmed the crust and set it aside.

"You'll slice a finger off if you keep staring at me instead of watching what you're about."

"Your hair's falling out of your cap again, Mrs. Flynn."

She took a hand and shoved at it, only succeeding in loosening more curls. "And I don't think I care for the tone you use when you call me Mrs. Flynn."

Merely grinning, Ian set aside a pared apple. "What should I call you then? You object to sweetheart, though it suits so nicely. Your nose goes in the air when I call you Alanna—without your permission. Now you're ready to spout into temper when I, very respectfully, call you Mrs. Flynn."

"Respectfully, hah! You'll go to hell for lying, Ian MacGregor." She waved the rolling pin at him as she turned. "There's not a dab of respect in your tone when you use it—not with that smug smile on your mouth and that gleam in your eye. If you don't think I know just what that gleam means, you're mistaken. Other men have tried it and gotten a good coshing for their pains."

"It gratifies me to hear it . . . Mrs. Flynn."

She made a sound he could only describe as hot steam puffing out of a kettle. "You'll call me nothing at all. Why I took Brian's part and asked you to stay for Christmas will always be a mystery to me. The good Lord knows I don't want you here, cluttering up my kitchen, giving me another mouth to cook for, grabbing me and forcing your unwelcome attentions on me at every turn."

He leaned against the counter. "You'll go to hell for lying, sweetheart."

It was the reflex of the moment that had the rolling pin flying out of her hand and toward his head. She regretted it immediately. But she regretted it even more when he snagged the flying round of wood the instant before it cracked into his forehead.

If she had hit him, she would have apologized profusely and tended his bruise. The fact that she'd been foiled changed the matter altogether.

"You cursed Scotsman," she began, lathering up. "You spawn of the devil. A plague on you and every MacGregor from now till the Last Reckoning." Since she'd missed with the rolling pin, she grabbed the closest thing at hand. Fortunately, the heavy metal pie plate was empty. Ian managed to bat it away from his head with the rolling pin.

"Alanna—"

"Don't call me that." She hefted a pewter mug and tried her aim with that. This time Ian wasn't so quick and it bounced off his chest.

"Sweetheart—"

The sound she made at that would have caused even a battle-tried Scotsman to shudder. The plate she hurtled struck Ian's shin. He was hopping on one leg and laughing when she reached for the next weapon.

"Enough!" Roaring with laughter, he grabbed her and swung her around twice, even when she bashed him over the head with the plate.

"Damned hardheaded Scot."

"Aye, and thank God for it or you'll have me in my grave yet." He tossed her up and caught her nimbly at the waist. "Marry me, Mrs. Flynn, for your name was meant to be MacGregor."

Chapter Six

It was a close thing as to whom was the most shocked. Ian hadn't realized he'd meant to ask her. He'd known he was in love, was both amused and dazzled by it. But until that moment his heart hadn't communicated to his brain that marriage was desired. Marriage to Alanna, he thought, and let loose another laugh. It was a fine joke, he decided, on the pair of them.

His words were still echoing in Alanna's head, bouncing from one end of her brain to the other like balls in a wheel. *Marry me.* Surely she hadn't mistaken what he'd asked her. It was impossible, of course. It was madness. They had known each other only days. Even that was long enough for her to be certain Ian MacGregor would never be the life companion of her dreams. With him, there would never be peaceful nights by the fire but another fight, another cause, another movement.

And yet... Yet she loved him in a way she had never thought to love. Wildly, recklessly, dangerously. Life with him would be...would be... She couldn't imagine it. She put a hand to her head to still her whirling brain. She needed a moment to think and compose herself. After all, when a man asked a woman to marry him, the very least she could do was . . .

Then it occurred to her that he was still holding her a foot off the floor and laughing like a loon.

Laughing. Her eyes narrowed to sharp blue slits. So it was a great joke he was having at her expense, tossing her in the air like a sack of potatoes and chortling. Marry him. Marry him indeed. The jackass.

She braced a hand on his broad shoulder for balance, rolled the other into a fist and struck him full on the nose.

He yelped and set her down so abruptly she had to shift to keep upright. But she recovered quickly and, feet planted, stuck her hands on her hips and glared at him.

Tentatively, he touched his fingers to his nose. Aye, it was bleeding, he noted. The woman had a wicked right. Watching her warily for any sudden moves, he reached for his handkerchief.

"Is that a yes?"

"Out!" So deep was her rage her voice shook even as it boomed. "Out of my house, you pox-ridden son of Satan." The tears that sprang to her eyes were tears of righteous fury, she assured herself. "If I were a man I'd murder you where you stand and dance a jig on your bleeding body."

"Ah." After an understanding nod, he replaced his handkerchief. "You need a bit of time to think it over. Perfectly understandable."

Speechless, she could only make incoherent growls and hisses.

"I'll speak with your father," he offered politely. She shrieked like a banshee and grabbed for the paring knife.

"I will kill you. On my mother's grave, I swear it."

"My dear Mrs. Flynn," he began as he cautiously clamped a hand on her wrist. "I realize a woman is sometimes overcome with the proposal or marriage, but this . . ." He trailed off when he saw that tears had welled from her eyes and run down her cheeks. "What is this?" Uncomfortable, he brushed a thumb over her damp cheek. "Alanna, my love, don't. I'd rather have you stab me than cry." But when he gallantly released her hand, she tossed the knife aside.

"Oh, leave me be, won't you? Go away. How dare you insult me this way? I curse the day I saved your miserable life."

He took heart that she was cursing him again and pressed a kiss to her brow. "Insult you? How?"

"How?" Behind the veil of tears her eyes burned like blue suns. "Laughing at me. Speaking of marriage as if it were a great joke. I suppose you think because I don't have fine clothes or fancy hats that I have no feelings."

"What do hats have to do with it?"

"I suppose all the elegant ladies in Boston just smile indulgently and rap your hand with their fans when you play the flirt, but I take talk of marriage more seriously and won't stand by while you speak of it and laugh in my face at the same time."

"Oh, sweet God." Who would have thought that he, a man reputed to be smooth and clever with the ladies, could muck things up so badly when it mattered? "I was a fool, Alanna. Please listen."

"Was and are a fool. Now take your paws off me."

He gathered her closer. "I only want to explain."

Before he could, Cyrus Murphy pushed open the door. He took one look at the wreckage of the kitchen, at his daughter struggling against Ian, and reached calmly for the hunting knife in his belt.

"Let go of my girl, MacGregor, and prepare to die."

"Da." Eyes widened at the sight of her father, pale as ice with a knife in his hands, Alanna threw herself in front of Ian. "Don't."

"Move aside, lass. Murphys protect their own."

"It isn't the way it looks," she began.

"Leave us, Alanna," Ian said quietly. "I'll have a word with your father."

"The hell you will." She planted her feet. Perhaps she would have shed his blood herself—and had, if one counted his nose—but she wouldn't have her father kill him after she'd worked for two days and nights to keep him alive. "We had an argument, Da. I can handle it myself. He was—"

"He was proposing marriage to your daughter," Ian finished, only to have Alanna round on him again.

"You lying polecat. You didn't mean a word of it. Laughing like a loon while you said it, you were. I won't be insulted. I won't be belittled—"

"But you will be quiet," he roared at her, and had Cyrus raising a brow in approval when she did indeed subside. "I meant every word," he continued, his voice still pitched to raise the roof. "If I was laughing it was at myself, for being so big a fool as to fall in love with a stubborn, sharp-tongued shrew who'd as soon stab me as smile at me."

"Shrew?" Her voice ended on a squeak. "Shrew?"

"Aye, a shrew," Ian said with a vicious nod. "That's what I said, and that's what you are. And a—"

"Enough." Cyrus shook the snow from his hair. "Sweet Jesus, what a pair." With some reluctance, he replaced his knife. "Get on your coat, MacGregor, and come with me. Alanna, finish your baking."

"But, Da, I—"

"Do as I say, lass." He gestured Ian out the door. "With all the shouting and the wailing it's hard for a body to remember it's Christmas Eve." He stopped just outside and planted his hands on his hips in a gesture his daughter had inherited. "I've a job to do, MacGregor. You'll come with me and explain yourself."

"Aye." He cast a last furious look at the window where Alanna had her nose pressed. "I'll come with you."

Ian trudged across the snow and through the billowy curtain that was still falling. He hadn't bothered to fasten his coat and stuck his ungloved hands in its pockets.

"Wait here," Cyrus said. He went inside a small shed and came out with an ax. Noting Ian's cautious stare, he hefted it onto his shoulder. "I won't be using it on you. Yet." He moved off toward the forest with Ian beside him. "Alanna's partial to Christmas. As was her mother." There was a pang, as there always was when he thought of his wife. "She'll be wanting a tree—and time for her temper to cool."

"Does it ever?"

As a matter of habit, Cyrus studied the forest floor for signs of game. They'd want fresh venison soon. "You're the one who's thinking of shackling his leg to hers. Why is that?"

"If I could think of one good reason, I'd give it to you." He hissed his breath out between his teeth. "I ask the woman to marry me, and she hits me in the nose." He touched the still sore appendage, then grinned. "By God, Murphy, I'm half-mad and in love with the woman—which amounts to the same thing. I'll have her to wife."

Cyrus stopped in front of a pine, studied it, rejected it, then moved on. "That remains to be seen."

"I'm not a poor man," Ian began. "The bloody British didn't get everything in the Forty-five, and I've done well enough with investments. I'll provide well for her."

"Mayhap you will, mayhap you won't. She took Michael Flynn and he had no more than a few acres of rocky land and two cows."

"She won't have to work from dawn to dust."

"Alanna doesn't mind work. She takes pride in it." Cyrus stopped in front of another tree, nodded, then handed the ax to Ian. "This'll do. When a man's frustrated, there's nothing like swinging an ax to sweat it out of him."

Ian spread his legs, planted his feet and put his back into it. Wood chips flew. "She cares for me. I know it."

"Might," Cyrus agreed, then decided to treat himself to a pipe. "'Tis her habit to shout and slap at those she cares for most."

"Then she must love me to distraction." The ax bit into the meat of the pine's trunk. Ian's expression was grim. "I'll have her, Murphy, with or without your blessing."

"That goes without saying." Cyrus patiently filled his pipe. "She's a woman grown and can make up her own mind. Tell me, MacGregor, will you fight the British with as much passion as you'll woo my daughter?"

Ian swung the ax again. The blade whistled through the air. The sound of metal on wood thudded through the forest. "Aye."

"Then I'll tell you now, it may be hard for you to win both." Satisfied the pipe was well packed, he struck a match against a boulder. "Alanna refuses to believe there will be war."

Ian paused. "And you?"

"I've no love for the British or their king." Cyrus puffed on his pipe and sent smoke drifting through the snow. "And even if I did, my vision's sharp enough yet to see what will come. It may take a year, or two, or more, but the fight will come. And it will be long, and it will be bloody. When it comes I'll have two more sons to risk. Two more sons to lose." He sighed, long and heavy. "I don't want your war, Ian Mac-Gregor, but there will come a point when a man will have to stand for what is his."

"It's already begun, Murphy, and neither wanting it nor fearing it will change history."

Cyrus studied Ian as the tree fell to the cushioning snow. A strong man, he thought, one of those damned Scot giants, with a face and form a woman would find pleasing enough. A good mind and a good name. But it was Ian's restless and rebellious spirit that concerned him.

"I'll ask you this, will you be content to sit and wait for what comes to come, or will you go out in search of it?"

"MacGregors don't wait to stand for what they believe in. Nor do they wait to fight for it."

With a nod, Cyrus helped Ian heft the fallen tree. "I won't stand in your way where Alanna is concerned. You may do that for yourself."

* * *

Alanna rushed into the front of the cabin the moment she heard Ian's voice. "Da, I want to... Oh." She stopped short at the sight of her father and Ian with a pine tree held between them. "You've cut a Christmas tree."

"Did you think I'd be forgetting?" Cyrus took off his cap and stuffed it in his pocket. "How could I with you nagging me day and night?"

"Thank you." It was with both pleasure and relief that she crossed the room to kiss him. "It's beautiful."

"And I suppose you'll want to be hanging ribbons and God knows what else on it." But he gave her a quick squeeze as he spoke.

"I have Mama's box of ornaments in my room." Because she understood him so well, she kissed him again. "I'll fetch it after supper."

"I've other chores to see to. You can devil MacGregor about where you want the thing." He gave her hand a quick pat before he went out again.

Alanna cleared her throat. "By the front window, if you please."

Ian dragged it over, balancing it on the flat wooden boards Cyrus had hammered to the trunk. The only sound was the rustling of needles and the crackle of the fire.

"Thank you," she said primly. "You can go about your business now."

Before she could escape to the kitchen again, he took her hand. "Your father has given me permission to wed you, Alanna."

She tugged once on her hand, then wisely gave up. "I'm my own woman, MacGregor."

"You'll be mine, Mrs. Flynn."

Though he stood a foot over her head, she managed to convey the impression of looking down her nose at him. "I'd sooner mate a rabid skunk."

Determined to do it right this time, he brought her rigid hand to his lips. "I love you, Alanna."

"Don't." She pressed her free hand to her nervous heart. "Don't say that."

"I say it with every breath I take. And will until I breathe no more."

Undone, she stared at him, into those blue-green eyes that had already haunted her nights. His arrogance she could resist. His outrageousness she could fight. But this, this simple, almost humble declaration of devotion left her defenseless.

"Ian, please..."

He took heart because she had, at long last, called him by his given name. And the look in her eyes as the word left her lips could not be mistaken. "You will not tell me you're indifferent to me."

Unable to resist, she touched a hand to his face. "No, I won't tell you that. You must see how I feel every time I look at you."

"We were meant to be together." With his eyes on hers, he pressed the palm of her hand to his lips. "From the moment I saw you bending over me in the barn I felt it."

"It's all so soon," she said, fighting both panic and longing. "All so quick."

"And right. I'll make you happy, Alanna. You can choose whatever house you want in Boston."

"Boston?"

"For a time, at least, we would live there. I have work to do. Later we could go to Scotland, and you could visit your homeland."

But she was shaking her head. "Work. What work is this?"

A shield seemed to come down over his eyes. "I gave you my word I would not speak of it until after Christmas."

"Aye." She felt her bounding heart still and freeze in her breast. "You did." After a deep breath, she looked down at their joined hands. "I have pies in the oven. They need to come out."

"Is that all you can say?"

She looked at the tree behind him, still bare, but with so much promise. "I must ask you for time. Tomorrow, on Christmas, I'll give you my answer."

"There is only one I'll take."

That helped her to smile. "There's only one I'll give."

Chapter Seven

There was a scent of pine and wood smoke, the lingering aroma of the thick supper stew. On the sturdy table near the fire Alanna had placed her mother's prized possession, a glass punch bowl. As had been his habit for as long as Alanna could remember, her father mixed the Yuletide punch, with a hand generous with Irish whiskey. She watched the amber liquid catch the light from the fire and the glow from the candles already lighted on the tree.

She had promised herself that this night, and the Christmas day to follow, would be only for joy.

As well it should be, she told herself. Whatever had transpired between her father and Ian that morning, they were thick as thieves now. She noted that Cyrus pressed a cup of punch on Ian before he ladled one for himself and drank deeply. Before she could object, young Brian was given a sample.

Well, they would all sleep that night, she decided, and was about to take a cup herself when she heard the sound of a wagon.

"There's Johnny." She let out a huff of breath. "And for his sake he'd best have a good excuse for missing supper."

"Courting Mary," Brian said into his cup.

"That may be, but—" She broke off as Johnny came in, with Mary Wyeth on his arm. Automatically, Alanna glanced around the room, relieved everything was as it should be for company. "Mary, how good to see you." Alanna went quickly to kiss the girl's cheek. Mary was shorter and plumper than she, with bright gold hair and rosy cheeks. They seemed rosier than usual, Alanna noted—either with cold from the journey from the village, or with heat from Johnny's courting.

"Merry Christmas." Always shy, Mary flushed even more as she clasped her hands together. "Oh, what a lovely tree."

"Come by the fire, you'll be cold. Let me take your cape and shawl." She shot her brother an exasperated look as he just stood by and grinned foolishly. "Johnny, fetch Mary a cup of punch and some of the cookies I baked this morning."

"Aye." He sprang into action, punch lapping over his fingers in his rush. "We'll have a toast," he announced, then spent considerable time clearing his throat. "To my future wife." He clasped Mary's nervous hand in his. "Mary accepted me this evening."

"Oh." Alanna held out her hands, and since Mary didn't have one to spare, grabbed the girl by the shoulder. "Oh, welcome. Though how you'll stand this one is beyond me."

Cyrus, always uncomfortable with emotion, gave Mary a quick peck on the cheek and his son a hearty slap on the back. "Then we'll drink to my new daughter," he said. "'Tis a fine Christmas present you give us, John."

"We need music." Alanna turned to Brian, who nodded and rushed off to fetch his flute. "A spritely song, Brian," she instructed. "The engaged couple should have the first dance."

Brian perched himself with one foot on the seat of a chair and began to play. When Ian's hand came to rest on her shoulder, Alanna touched her fingers briefly, gently, to his wrist.

"Does the idea of a wedding please you, Mrs. Flynn?"

"Aye." With a watery smile, she watched her brother turn and sway with Mary. "She'll make him happy. They'll make a good home together, a good family. That's all I want for him."

He grinned as Cyrus tossed back another cup of punch and began to clap his hands to the music. "And for yourself?"

She turned, and her eyes met his. "It's all I've ever wanted."

He leaned closer. "If you gave me my answer now, we could have a double celebration this Christmas Eve."

She shook her head as her heart broke a little. "This is Johnny's night." Then she laughed as Johnny grabbed her hands and pulled her into the dance.

A new snow fell, softly, outside the cabin. But inside, the rooms were filled with light and laughter and music. Alanna thought of her mother and how pleased she would have been to have seen her family together and joyful on this most holy of nights. And she thought of Rory, bright and beautiful Rory, who would have outdanced the lot of them and raised his clear tenor voice in song.

"Be happy." Impulsively she threw her arms around Johnny's neck. "Be safe."

"Here now, what's all this?" Touched, and embarrassed, he hugged her quickly then pulled her away.

"I love you, you idiot."

"I know that." He noted that his father was trying to teach Mary to do a jig. It made him almost split his face with a grin. "Here, Ian, take this wench off my hands. A man's got to rest now and then."

"No one can outdance an Irishman," Ian told her as he took her hand. "Unless it's a Scotsman."

"Oh, is that the way of it?" With a smile and a toss of her head, she set out to prove him wrong.

Though the candles had burned low before the house and its occupants slept, the celebrations began again at dawn. By the light of the tree and the fire, they exchanged gifts. Alanna gained a quiet pleasure from the delight on Ian's face as he held up the scarf she had woven him. Though it had taken her every spare minute to work the blue and the green threads together on her loom, the result was worth it. When he left, he would take a part of her.

Her heart softened further when she saw that he had gifts for her family. A new pipe for her father, a fine new bridle for Johnny's favorite horse and a book of poetry for Brian.

Later, he stood beside her in the village church, and though she listened to the story of the Savior's birth with the same wonder she had had as a child, she would have been blind not to see other women cast glances her way. Glances of envy and curiosity. She didn't object when his hand closed over hers.

"You look lovely today, Alanna." Outside the church, where people had stopped to chat and exchange Christmas greetings, he kissed her hands. Though she knew the gossips would be fueled for weeks, she gave him a saucy smile. She was woman enough to know she looked her best in the deep blue wool dress with its touch of lace at collar and cuffs.

"You're looking fine yourself, MacGregor." She resisted the urge to touch the high starched stock at his throat. It was the first time she'd seen him in Sunday best, with snowy lace falling over his wrists, buttons gleaming on his doublet and a tricornered hat on his mane of red hair. It would be another memory of him to treasure.

"Sure and it's a beautiful day."

He glanced at the sky. "It will snow before nightfall."

"And what better day for a snowfall than Christmas?" Then she caught at the blue bonnet Johnny had given her. "But the wind is high." She smiled as she saw Johnny and Mary surrounded by well-wishers. "We'd best get back. I've a turkey to check."

He offered his arm. "Allow me to escort you to your carriage, Mrs. Flynn."

"Why that's kind of you, Mr. MacGregor."

He couldn't remembered a more perfect day. Though there were still chores to be done, Ian managed to spend every free moment with Alanna. Perhaps there was a part of him that wished her family a thousand miles away so that he could be alone with her at last and have her answer. But he determined to be patient, having no doubt what the answer would be. She couldn't smile at him, look at him, kiss him that way unless she was as wildly in love as he. He might have wished he could simply snatch her up, toss her on his horse and ride off, but for once, he wanted to do everything properly.

If it was her wish they could be married in the church where they had observed Christmas. Then he would hire—or better, buy—a carriage, blue picked out in silver. That would suit her. In it they would travel to Virginia, where he would present her to his aunt and uncle and cousins.

Somehow he would manage a trip to Scotland, where she would meet his mother and father, his brothers and sisters. They would be married again there, in the land of his birth.

He could see it all. They would settle in Boston, where he would buy her a fine house. Together they would start a family while he fought, with voice or sword, for the independence of his adopted country.

By day they would argue and fight. By night they would lie together in a big feather bed, her long slender limbs twined around him.

It seemed since he had met her he could see no further than life with her.

The snow did fall, but gently. By the time the turkey and potatoes, the sauerkraut and biscuits were devoured, Ian was half-mad with impatience.

Rather than join the men by the fire, he grabbed Alanna's cloak and tossed it over her. "I need a moment with you."

"But I haven't finished—"

"The rest can wait." As far as he could see, her kitchen was already as neat as a pin. "I will speak with you, in private."

She didn't object, couldn't, because her heart was already in her throat when he pulled her out into the snow. He'd barely taken time to jam on his hat. When she pointed out that he hadn't buttoned his coat against the wind, he swept her up in his arms and with long strides carried her to the barn.

"There's no need for all of this," she pointed out. "I can walk as well as you."

"You'll dampen your dress." He turned his head and kissed her snow-brushed lips. "And I like it very well."

After he set her down inside, he latched the door and lighted a lamp. She folded her hands at her waist. It was now, Alanna told herself firmly, that the Christmas celebration had to end.

"Ian—"

"No, wait." He came to her, put his hands gently on her shoulders. The sudden tenderness robbed her of speech. "Did you not wonder why I gave you no gift this morning?"

"You gave me your gift. We agreed—"

"Did you think I had nothing more for you?" He took her hands, chilled because he had given her no time for mittens, and warmed them with his. "On this, our first Christmas together, the gift must be special."

"No, Ian, there is no need."

"There is every need." He reached into the pocket of his doublet and withdrew a small box. "I sent a village lad into Boston for this. It was in my quarters there." He placed the box in her hand. "Open it."

Her head warned her to refuse, but her heart—her heart could not. Inside she saw a ring. After a quick gasp, she pressed her lips together. It was fashioned of gold in the shape of a lion's head and crown.

"This is the symbol of my clan. The grandfather whose name I carry had it made for his wife. Before she died, she gave this to my father to hold in trust for me. When I left Scotland, he told me it was his hope I would find a woman as strong, as wise and as loyal to wear it."

Her throat was so tight the words hurt as she forced them out. "Oh, Ian, no. I could not. I don't—"

"There is no other woman who will wear it." He took it from the box and placed it on her finger. It might have been made for her, so perfect was the fit. At that moment, he felt as though the world were his. "There is no other woman I will love." He brought her ring hand to his lips, watching her over it. "With this I pledge you my heart."

"I love you," she murmured as she felt her world rip in two. "I will always love you." There would be time, she knew, as his mouth came to hers, for regrets, for pain, for tears. But tonight, for the hours they had, she would give him one more gift.

Gently, she pushed his coat from his shoulders. With her mouth moving avidly beneath his, she began to unbutton his doublet.

With unsteady hands, he stilled hers. "Alanna—"

She shook her head and touched a finger to his lips. "I am not an untried girl. I come to you already a woman, and I ask that you take me as one. I need you to love me, Ian. Tonight, this Christmas night, I need that." This time it was she who captured his hands and brought them to her lips. It was reckless, she knew. But it was right. "And I need to love you."

Never before had he felt so clumsy. His hands seemed too big, too rough, his need too deep and intense. He swore that if he accomplished nothing else in his life he would love her gently and show her what was written in his heart.

With care, he lowered her onto the hay. It was not the feather bed he wished for her, but her arms came willingly around him, and she smiled as she brought his mouth to hers. With a sound of wonder, he sank into her.

It was more than she'd ever dreamed, the touch of her love's hands in her hair, on her face. With such patience, with such sweetness, he kissed her until the sorrows she held in her heart melted away. When he had unbuttoned her frock, he slipped it from her shoulder to kiss the skin there, to marvel at the milky whiteness and to murmur such foolish things that made her want to smile and weep at once.

He felt her strong, capable fingers push aside his doublet, unfasten his shirt, then stroke along his chest.

With care he undressed her, pausing, lingering, to give pleasure and to take it. With each touch, each taste, her response grew. He heard her quick, unsteady breath at his ear, then felt the nip of her teeth as he gave himself over to the delights of her body.

Soft, lavender scent twining with the fragrance of hay. Smooth, pale skin glowing in the shadowed lamplight. Quiet, drifting sighs, merging with his own murmurs. The rich shine of her hair as he gathered fistfuls in his hands.

She was shuddering. But with heat. Such heat. She tried to say his name but managed only to dig her nails into his broad shoulders. From where had come this churning, this wild river that flowed inside her? And where would it end? Dazzled, desperate, she arched against him while his hands traveled like lightning over points of pleasure she hadn't known she possessed.

Her mouth was on his, avid, thirsty, as he pushed her to the first brink, then beyond. Her stunned cry was muffled against his lips and his own groan of satisfaction.

Then he was inside her, deep. At the glory of it, her eyes flew open. She saw his face above her, the fire of his hair glinting in the lamplight.

"Now we are one." His voice was low and harsh with passion. "Now you are mine."

And he lowered his mouth to hers as they gave each other the gift of self.

Chapter Eight

They dozed, turned to each other, her cloak carelessly tossed over their tangled forms, their bodies warmed and replete from loving.

He murmured her name.

She woke.

Midnight had come and gone, she thought. And her time was over. Still, she stole a bit more, studying his face as he slept, learning each plane, each angle. Though she knew his face was already etched in her head, and on her heart.

One last kiss, she told herself as she brushed her lips to his. One last moment.

When she shifted, he mumbled and reached out.

"You don't escape that easily, Mrs. Flynn."

Her heart suffered a new blow at the wicked way he said her name. "'Tis almost dawn. We can't stay any longer."

"Very well then." He sat up as she began to dress. "I suppose even under the circumstances, your father might pull his knife again if he found me naked in the hay with his daughter." With some regret he tugged on his breeches. He wished he had the words to tell her what the night had meant to him. What her love meant to him. With his shirt unbuttoned, he rose to kiss the back of her neck. "You've hay in your hair, sweetheart."

She sidestepped him and began to pluck it out. "I've lost my pins."

"I like it down." He swallowed and took a step forward to clutch handfuls of it. "By God, I like it down."

She nearly swayed toward him before she caught herself. "I need my cap."

"If you must." Obliging, he began to search for it. "In truth, I don't remember a better Christmas. I thought I'd reached the peak when I was eight and was given a bay gelding. Fourteen hands he was, with a temper like a mule." He found her cap under scattered hay. With a grin, he offered it. "But, though it's close in the running, you win over the gelding."

She managed to smile. "It's flattered I am, to be sure, MacGregor. Now I've breakfast to fix."

"Fine. We can tell your family over the meal that we're to be married."

She took a deep breath. "No."

"There's no reason to wait, Alanna."

"No," she repeated. "I'm not going to marry you."

For a moment he stared, then he laughed. "What nonsense is this?"

"It isn't nonsense at all. I'm not going to marry you."

"The bloody hell you aren't!" he exploded, and grabbed both her shoulders. "I won't have games when it comes to this."

"It's not a game, Ian." Though her teeth had snapped together, she spoke calmly. "I don't want to marry you."

If she had still had the knife in her hand and had plunged it into him, she would have caused him less pain. "You lie. You look me in the face and lie. You could not have loved me as you did through the night and not want to belong to me."

Her eyes remained dry, so dry they burned. "I love you, but I will not marry you." She shook her head before he could protest. "My feelings have not changed. Nor have yours—nor can yours. Understand me, Ian, I am a simple woman with simple hopes. You'll make your war and won't be content until it comes to pass. You'll fight in your war, if it takes a year or ten. I cannot lose another I love, when I have already lost so many. I will not take your name and give you my heart only to see you die."

"So you bargain with me?" Incensed, he paced away from her. "You won't share my life unless I'm content to live it ignoring all I believe in? To have you, I must turn my back on my country, my honor and my conscience?"

"No." She gripped her hands together tightly and fought not to twist them. "I offer you no bargain. I give you your freedom with an open heart and with no regrets for what passed between us. I cannot live in the world you want, Ian. And you cannot live in mine. All I ask is for you to give me the same freedom I give you."

"Damn you, I won't." He grabbed her again, fingers that had been so gentle the night before, bruising. "How can you think that a difference in politics could possibly keep me from taking you with me? You belong with me, Alanna. There is nothing beyond that."

"It is not just a difference in politics." Because she knew she would weep in a moment, she made her voice flat and cold. "It is a difference in hopes and in dreams. All of mine, and all of yours. I do not ask you to sacrifice yours, Ian. I will not sacrifice mine." She pulled away to stand rigid as a spear. "I do not want you. I do not want to live my life with you. And as a woman free to take or reject as she pleases, I will not. There is nothing you can say or do to change that. If in truth you do care for me, you won't try."

She snatched up her cape and held it balled in her hands. "Your wounds are healed, MacGregor. It's time you took your leave. I will not see you again."

With this, she turned and fled.

An hour later, from the safety of her room, she heard him ride off. It was then, and only then, that she allowed herself to lie on the bed and weep. Only when her tears wet the gold on her finger did she realize she had not given him back his ring. Nor had he asked for it.

It took him three weeks to reach Virginia, and another week before he would speak more than a few clipped sentences to anyone. In his uncle's library he would unbend enough to discuss the happenings in Boston and other parts of the Colonies and Parliament's reactions. Though Brigham Langston, the fourth earl of Ashburn, had lived in America for almost thirty years, he still had high connections in England. And as he had fought for his beliefs in the Stuart Rebellion, so would he fight his native country again for freedom and justice in his home.

"All right, that's enough plotting and secrets for tonight." Never one to pay attention to sanctified male ground, Serena MacGregor Langston swept into the library. Her hair was still fiery red as it had been in her youth. The few strands of gray didn't concern a woman who felt she had earned them.

Though Ian rose to bow to his aunt, the woman's husband continued to lean against the mantel. He was, Serena thought, as handsome as ever. More perhaps. Though his hair was silver, the southern sun had tanned his face so that it reminded her of oak. And his body was as lean and muscular as she remembered it from nearly thirty years before. She smiled as her eldest son, Daniel, poured her brandy and kissed her.

"You know we always welcome your delightful company, Mama."

"You've a tongue like your father's." She smiled, well pleased that he had inherited Brigham's looks, as well. "You know very well you wish me to the devil. I'll have to remind you again that I've already fought in one rebellion. Isn't that so, *Sassenach*?"

Brigham grinned at her. She had called him by the uncomplimentary Scottish term for the English since the first moment they had met. "Have I ever tried to change you?"

"You're not a man who tries when he knows he must fail." And she kissed him full on the mouth. "Ian, you're losing weight." Serena had already decided she'd given the lad enough time to stew over whatever was troubling him. As long as his mother was an ocean away, she would tend to him herself. "Do you have a complaint for cook?"

"Your table, as always, is superb, Aunt Serena."

"Ah." She sipped her brandy. "Your cousin Fiona tells me you've yet to go out riding with her." She spoke of her youngest daughter. "I hope she hasn't done anything to annoy you."

"No." He caught himself before he shifted from foot to foot. "No, I've just been a bit, ah, distracted. I'll be sure to go out with her in the next day or so."

"Good." She smiled, deciding to wait until they were alone to move in for the kill. "Brig, Amanda would like you to help her pick out a proper pony for young Colin. I thought I raised my eldest daughter well, but she apparently thinks you've a better eye for horseflesh than her mama. Oh, and, Daniel, your brother is out at the stables. He asked me to send for you."

"The lad thinks of little but horses," Brigham commented. "He takes after Malcolm."

"I'd remind you my younger brother has done well enough for himself with his horses."

Brigham tipped his glass toward his wife. "No need to remind me."

"I'll go." Daniel set down his snifter. "If I know Kit, he's probably working up some wild scheme about breeding again."

"Oh, and, Brig. Parkins is in a lather over something. The state of your riding jacket, I believe. I left him up in your dressing room."

"He's always in a lather," Brigham muttered, referring to his longtime valet. Then he caught his wife's eye, and her meaning. "I'll just go along and see if I can calm him down."

"You won't desert me, will you, Ian?" Spreading her hooped skirts, she sat, satisfied that she'd cleared the room. "We haven't had much time to talk since you came to visit. Have some more brandy and keep me company for a while." She smiled, disarmingly. It was another way she had learned—other than shouting and swearing—to get what she wanted. "And tell me about your adventures in Boston."

Because her feet were bare, as she had always preferred them, she tucked her legs up, managing in the wide plum-colored skirts to look both ladylike and ridiculously young. Despite the foul mood that haunted him, Ian found himself smiling at her.

"Aunt Serena, you are beautiful."

"And you are trying to distract me." She tossed her head so that her hair, never quite tamed, flowed over her shoulders. "I know all about your little tea party, my lad." She toasted him with her snifter. "As one MacGregor to another, I salute you. And," she continued, "I know that the English are already grumbling. Would that they would choke on their own cursed tea." She held up a hand. "But don't get me started on that. It's true enough that I want to hear what you have to say about the feelings of those in New England and other parts of America, but for now I want to know about you."

"About me?" He shrugged and swirled his drink. "It's hardly worth the trouble to pretend you don't know all about my activities, my allegiance to Sam Adams and the Sons of Liberty. Our plans move slowly, but they move."

She was nearly distracted enough to inquire further along these lines, but Brigham, and her own sources, could feed her all the information she needed. "On a more personal level, Ian." More serious, she leaned forward to touch his hand. "You are my brother's first child and my own godchild. I helped bring you into this world. And I know as truly as I sit here that you're troubled by something that has nothing to do with politics or revolutions."

"And everything to do with it," he muttered, and drank.

"Tell me about her."

He gave his aunt a sharp look. "I have mentioned no 'her.'"

"You have mentioned her a thousand times by your silence." She smiled and kept his hand in hers. "'Tis no use trying to keep things from me, my lad. We're blood. What is her name?"

"Alanna," he heard himself saying. "Damn her to hell and back."

With a lusty laugh, Serena sat back. "I like the sound of that. Tell me."

And he did. Though he had had no intention of doing so. Within thirty minutes he had told Serena everything from his first moment of regaining hazy consciousness in the barn to his furious and frustrated leave-taking.

"She loves you very much," Serena murmured.

As he told his tale, Ian had risen to pace to the fire and back, to the window and back and to the fire again. Though he was dressed like a gentleman, he moved like a warrior. He stood before the fire now, the flames snapping at his back. She was reminded so completely of her brother Coll that her heart broke a little.

"What kind of love is it that pushes a man away and leaves him with half a heart?"

"A deep one, a frightened one." She rose then to hold out her hands to him. "This I understand, Ian, more than I can tell you." Pained for him, she brought his hands to her cheeks.

"I cannot change what I am."

"No, you cannot." With a sigh, she drew him down to sit beside her. "Neither could I. We are children of Scotland, my love. Spirits of the Highlands." Even as she spoke, the pain for her lost homeland was ripe. "We are rebels born and bred, warriors since time began. And yet, when we fight, we fight only for what is ours by right. Our land, our homes, our people."

"She doesn't understand."

"Oh, I believe she understands only too well. Perhaps she cannot accept. By why would you, a MacGregor, leave her when she told you to? Would you not fight for her?"

"She's a hardheaded shrew who wouldn't listen to reason."

"Ah." Hiding a smile, she nodded. She had been called hardheaded time and again during her life—and by one man in particular. It was pride that had set her nephew on his horse and had him licking his wounds in Virginia. Pride was something she also understood very well. "And you love her?"

"I would forget her if I could." He ground his teeth. "Perhaps I will go back and murder her."

"I doubt it will come to that." Rising, she patted his hand. "Take some time with us here, Ian. And trust me, all will be well eventually. I must go up now and rescue your uncle from Parkins."

She left him scowling at the fire. But instead of going to Brigham, she went into her own sitting room and composed a letter.

"I cannot go." Cheeks flushed, eyes bright and blazing, Alanna stood in front of her father, the letter still clutched in her hand.

"You can and will," Cyrus insisted. "The Lady Langston has invited you to her home to thank you in person for saving the life of her nephew." He clamped his pipe between his teeth and prayed he wasn't making a mistake. "Your mother would want this for you."

"The journey is too long," she began quickly. "And in another month or two it will be time for making soap and planting and wool carding. I've too much to do to take such a trip. And...and I have nothing proper to wear."

"You will go, representing this house." He drew himself up to his full height. "It will never be said that a Murphy cowered at the thought of meeting gentry."

"I'm not cowering."

"You're shaking in your boots, girl, and it makes me pale with shame. Lady Langston wishes to make your acquaintance. Why, I have cousins who fought beside her clan in the Forty-five. A Murphy's as good as a MacGregor any day—better than one if it comes to that. I couldn't give you the schooling your good mother wanted for you—"

"Oh, Da."

He shook his head fiercely. "She will turn her back on me when I join her in the hereafter if I don't push you to do this. 'Tis my wish that you see more of the world than these rocks and this forest before my life is done. So you'll do it for me and your mother if not for yourself."

She weakened, as he'd known she would. "But... If Ian is there..."

"She doesn't say he is, does she?"

"Well, no, but—"

"Then it's likely he's not. He's off rabble-rousing somewhere more like."

"Aye." Glumly, she looked down at the letter in her hand. "Aye, more like." She began to wonder what it would be like to travel so far and to see Virginia, where the land was supposed to be so green. "But who will cook? Who will do the wash and the milking. I can't—"

"We're not helpless around here, girl." But he was already missing her. "Mary can help, now that she's married to Johnny. And the Widow Jenkins is always willing to lend a hand."

"Aye, but can we afford—"

"We're not penniless, either," he snapped. "Go and write a letter back and tell Lady Langston you kindly accept her invitation to visit. Unless you're afraid to meet her."

"Of course I'm not." That served to get her dander up. "I will go," she muttered, stomping up the stairs to find a quill and writing paper.

"Aye," Cyrus murmured as he heard her door slam. "But will you be back?"

Chapter Nine

Alanna was certain her heart would beat so fast and hard that it would burst through her breast. Never before had she ridden in such a well-sprung carriage with such a fine pair of matched bays pulling it. And a driver all in livery. Imagine the Langstons sending a carriage all that way, with a driver, postilions and a maid to travel all the miles with her.

Though she had traveled by ship from Boston to Richmond, again with a companion the Langstons had provided, she would journey by road the remainder of the way to their plantation.

They called it Glenroe, after a forest in the Highlands.

Oh, what a thrill it had been to watch the wind fill the sails of the ship, to have her own cabin and the dainty maid to see to her needs. Until the maid had taken sick from the rocking of the boat, of course. Then Alanna had seen to *her* needs. But she hadn't minded a bit. While the grateful lass had slept off her illness, Alanna had been free to walk the decks of the great ship and watch the ocean, glimpsing occasional stretches of coastland.

And she wondered at the vastness and beauty of the country she had never truly seen.

It was beautiful. Though she had loved the farm, the forest and the rocks of her native Massachusetts, she found the land even more glorious in its variety. Why, when she had left home, there had still been snow on the ground. The warming days had left icicles gleaming on the eaves of the house and the bare branches of the trees.

But now, in the south, she saw the trees greening and had left her cloak unfastened to enjoy the air through the carriage window. In the fields there were young calves and foals, trying out their legs or nursing. In others she saw dozens and dozens of black field hands busy with spring planting. And it was only March.

Only March, she thought again. Only three months since she had sent Ian away. In a nervous habit, she reached up to touch the outline of the ring she wore on a cord under her traveling dress. She would have to give it back, of course. To his aunt, for surely Ian wouldn't be on the plantation. Couldn't be, she thought with a combination of relief and longing. She would return the ring to his aunt with some sort of explanation as to her possession of it. Not the full truth, she reflected, for that would be too humiliating and painful.

She wouldn't worry about it now, she told herself, and folded her hands in her lap as she studied the rolling hills already turning green in Virginia's early spring. She would think of this journey, and this visit, as an adventure. One she would not likely have again.

And she must remember everything to tell Brian, the curious one. She would remember everything, she thought with a sigh, for herself. For this was Ian's family, people who had known him as a babe, as a growing lad.

For the few weeks she remained on the plantation with Ian's family, she would feel close to him again. For the last time, she promised herself. Then she would return to the farm, to her family and her duties, and be content.

There was no other way. But as the carriage swayed, she continued to hold her fingers to the ring and wish she could find one.

The carriage turned through two towering stone pillars with a high iron sign that read Glenroe. The maid, more taxed by the journey than Alanna, shifted in the seat across from her. "You'll be able to see the house soon, miss." Grateful that the weeks of traveling were almost at an end, the maid barely restrained herself from poking her head out the carriage window. "It's the most beautiful house in Virginia."

Heart thudding, Alanna began to fiddle with the black braid that trimmed the dove-gray dress she had labored over for three nights. Her busy fingers then toyed with the ribbons of her bonnet, smoothed the skirts of the dress, before returning to pluck at the braid again.

The long wide drive was lined with oaks, their tiny unfurling leaves a tender green. As far as she could see, the expansive lawns were tended. Here and there she saw trimmed bushes already in bud. Then, rising over a gentle crest, was the house.

Alanna was struck speechless. It was a majestic structure of pristine white with a dozen columns gracing the front like slender ladies. Balconies that looked like black lace trimmed the tall windows on the second and third stories. A wide, sweeping porch skirted both front and sides. There were flowers, a deep blood red, in tall urns standing on either side of stone steps that led to double doors glittering with glass.

Alanna gripped her fingers together until the knuckles turned as white as the house. It took all her pride and will not to shout to the driver to turn the carriage around and whip the horses into a run.

What was she doing here, in such a place? What would she have to say to anyone who could live in such richness? The gap between herself and Ian seemed to widen with each step of the prancing bays.

Before the carriage had drawn to a halt at the curve of the circular drive, a woman came through the doors and started down the porch. Her billowing dress was a pale, watery green trimmed with ivory lace. Her hair, a lovely shade of red gold, was dressed simply in a coil at her neck and shone in the sunlight. Alanna had hardly alighted with the assistance of a liveried footman when the woman stepped forward, hands extended.

"Mrs. Flynn. You're as beautiful as I expected." There was a soft burr to the woman's speech that reminded Alanna painfully of Ian. "But I will call you Alanna, because I feel we're already friends." Before Alanna could decide how to respond, the woman was smiling and gathering her into an embrace. "I'm Ian's aunt, Serena. Welcome to Glenroe."

"Lady Langston," Alanna began, feeling dusty and crumpled and intimidated. But Serena was laughing and drawing her toward the steps.

"Oh, we don't use titles here. Unless they can be of some use to us. Your journey went well, I hope."

"Aye." She felt she was being borne away by a small, red-haired whirlwind. "I must thank you for your generosity in asking me to come, in opening your home to me."

"'Tis I who am grateful." Serena paused on the threshold. "Ian is as precious to me as my own children. Come, I'll take you to your room. I'm sure you'll want to refresh yourself before you meet the rest of the family at tea. Of course we don't serve the bloody stuff," Serena continued blandly as Alanna gaped at the entrance hall with its lofty ceilings and double curving stairs.

"No, no of course not," Alanna said weakly as Serena took her arm to lead her up the right-hand sweep of the stairs. There was a shout, a yell and an oath from somewhere deep in the house.

"My two youngest children." Unconcerned, Serena continued up. "They squabble like puppies."

Alanna cleared her throat. "How many children do you have, Lady Langston?"

"Six." Serena took her down a hall with pastel wall covering and thick carpeting. "Payne and Ross are the ones you hear making a din. They're twins. One minute they're bashing each other, the next swearing to defend each other to the death."

Alanna distinctly heard something crash, but Serena didn't blink an eye as she opened the door to a suite of rooms.

"I hope you'll be comfortable here," she said. "If you need anything, you have only to ask."

What could she possibly need? Alanna thought dumbly. The bedroom was at least three times the size of the room she had slept in at home. Someone had put fresh, fragrant flowers into vases. Cut flowers in March.

The bed, large enough for three, was covered in pale blue silk and plumped with pillows. There was a wardrobe of carved wood, an elegant bureau with a silver-trimmed mirror, a dainty vanity table with a brocade chair. The tall windows were open so that the warm, fragrant breeze ruffled the sheer white curtains. Before she could speak, a maid scurried in with a steaming pitcher of water.

"Your sitting room is through there." Serena moved past a beautifully carved fireplace. "This is Hattie." Serena smiled at the small, wiry black maid. "She'll tend to your needs while you're with us. Hattie, you'll take good care of Mrs. Flynn, won't you?"

"Oh, yes, ma'am." Hattie beamed.

"Well, then." Serena patted Alanna's hand, found it chilled and unsteady and felt a pang of sympathy. "Is there anything else I can do for you?"

"Oh, no. You've done more than enough."

I've not even begun, Serena thought but only smiled. "I'll leave you to rest. Hattie will show you down whenever you're ready."

When the door closed behind the indomitable Lady Langston, Alanna sat wearily on the edge of the bed and wondered how she would keep up.

Because she was too nervous to keep to her rooms, Alanna allowed Hattie to help her out of the traveling dress and into her best frock. The little maid proved adept at dressing hair, and with nimble fingers and a chattering singsong voice, she coaxed and brushed and curled until Alanna's raven locks were draped in flirty curls over her left shoulder.

Alanna was just fastening her mother's garnet eardrops and drumming up her courage to go downstairs when there were shouts and thumping outside her door. Intrigued, she opened her door a crack, then widened it at the sight of two young male bodies rolling over the hall carpet.

She cleared her throat. "Good day to you, gentlemen."

The boys, mirror images of each other with ruffled black hair and odd topaz eyes, stopped pummeling each other to study her. As if by some silent signal, they untangled themselves, rose and bowed in unison.

"And who might you be?" the one with the split lip asked.

"I'm Alanna Flynn." Amused, she smiled. "And you must be Payne and Ross."

"Aye." This came from the one with the black eye. "I'm Payne, and the eldest, so I'll welcome you to Glenroe."

"I'll welcome her, as well." Ross gave his brother a sharp jab in the ribs with his elbow before he stepped forward and stuck out a hand.

"And I'll thank both of you," she said, hoping to keep the peace. "I was about to go down and join your mother. Perhaps you could escort me."

"She'll be in the parlor. It's time for tea." Ross offered his arm.

"Of course we don't drink the bloody stuff." Payne offered his, as well. Alanna took both. "The English could force it down our throats and we'd spit it back at them."

Alanna swallowed a smile. "Naturally."

As the trio entered the parlor, Serena rose. "Ah, Alanna, I see you've met my young beasts." With a considering look, she noted the black eye and bloody lip. "If it's cake the pair of you are after, then you'll wash first." As they raced off, she turned to introduce Alanna to the others in the room. There was a boy of perhaps eighteen she called Kit, who had his mother's coloring and a quick smile. A young girl she measured as Brian's age, with hair more blond than red, dimpled prettily.

"Kit and Fiona will drag you off to the stables at every opportunity," Serena warned. "My daughter Amanda hopes to join us for dinner tonight with her family. They live at a neighboring plantation." She poured the first cup of coffee and offered it to Alanna. "We won't wait for Brigham and the others. They're off overseeing the planting and the good Lord knows when they might come in."

"Mama says you live on a farm in Massachusetts," Fiona began.

"Aye." Alanna smiled and relaxed a little. "There was snow on the ground when I left. Our planting season is much shorter than yours."

The conversation was flowing easily when the twins came back, apparently united again as their arms were slung around each other's shoulders. With identical grins they walked to their mother and kissed each cheek.

"It's too late," Serena told them. "I already know about the vase." She poured two cups of chocolate. "It's a good thing it happened to be an ugly one. Now sit, and try not to slop this over the carpet."

Alanna was at ease and enjoying her second cup of coffee when a burst of male laughter rolled down the hall.

"Papa!" The twins cried and leaped up to race to the door. Serena only glanced at the splotch of chocolate on the rug and sighed.

Brigham entered, ruffling the hair of the boys on either side of him. "So, what damage have you done today?" Alanna observed that his gaze went first to his wife. There was amusement in it, and something much deeper, much truer, that lighted a small spark of envy in her breast. Then he looked at Alanna. Nudging the boys aside, he crossed the room.

"Alanna," Serena began, "this is my husband, Brigham."

"I'm delighted to meet you at last." Brigham took her hand between both of his. "We owe you much."

Alanna flushed a little. Though he was old enough to be her father, there was a magnetism about him that set a woman's heart aflutter. "I must thank you for your hospitality, Lord Langston."

"No, you must only enjoy it." He shot his wife a strange and, what seemed to Alanna, exasperated look. "I only hope you will remain happy and comfortable during your stay."

"How could I not? You have a magnificent home and a wonderful family."

He started to speak again, but his wife interrupted. "Coffee, Brig?" She had already poured and was holding out the cup with a warning look. Their discussions over her matchmaking attempt had yet to be resolved. "You must be thirsty after your work. And the others?"

"Were right behind me. They stopped off briefly in the library."

Even as he spoke, two men strode into the room. Alanna only vaguely saw the tall, dark-haired man who was a younger version of Brigham. Her stunned eyes were fixed on Ian. She wasn't even aware that she had sprung to her feet or that the room had fallen into silence.

She saw only him, dressed in rough trousers and jacket for riding, his hair windblown. He, too, had frozen into place. A dozen expressions crossed his face, as indeed they crossed hers. Then he smiled, but there was an edge to it, a hardness that cut her to the quick.

"Ah, Mrs. Flynn. What an...unusual surprise."

"I—I—" She stumbled to a halt and looked around wildly for a place to retreat, but Serena had already risen to take her hand. She gave Alanna's fingers a short, firm squeeze.

"Alanna was good enough to accept my invitation. We wanted to thank her in person for tending you and keeping you alive to annoy us."

"I see." When he could tear his gaze from Alanna, he sent his aunt a furious look. "Clever, aren't you, Aunt Serena?"

"Oh, aye," she said complacently. "That I am."

At his side, Ian's hands curled into fists. They were twins of the one in his stomach. "Well, Mrs. Flynn, since you're here, I'll have to welcome you to Glenroe."

"I..." She knew she would weep and disgrace herself. "Excuse me, please." Giving Ian a wide berth, she raced from the room.

"How gracious of you, Ian." With a toss of her head, Serena went after her guest.

She found Alanna at the wardrobe, pulling out her clothes.

"Now, what's all this?"

"I must go. I didn't know—Lady Langston, I thank you for your hospitality, but I must go home immediately."

"What a pack of nonsense." Serena took her firmly by the shoulders and led her toward the bed. "Now sit down and catch your breath. I know seeing Ian was a surprise, but—" She broke off as Alanna covered her face with her hands and burst into tears.

"Oh, there, there, sweetheart." In the way of all mothers, she put her arms around Alanna and rocked. "Was he such a bully, then? Men are, you know. It only means we must be bigger ones."

"No, no, it was all my fault. All my doing." Though humiliated, she couldn't stem the tears and laid her head on Serena's shoulder.

"Whether it was or not, that's not something a woman should ever admit. Since men have the advantage of brawn, we must use our better brains." Smiling, she stroked Alanna's hair. "I wanted to see for myself if you loved him as much as I could see he loved you. Now I know."

"He hates me now. And who could blame him? But it's for the best," she wept. "It's for the best."

"He frightens you?"

"Aye."

"And your feelings for him frighten you?"

"Oh, aye. I don't want them, my lady, I can't have them. He won't change. He'll not be happy until he gets himself killed or hanged for treason."

"MacGregors don't kill easily. Here now, have you a handkerchief? I can never find one myself when it's most needed."

Sniffling, Alanna nodded and drew hers out. "I beg your pardon, my lady, for causing a scene."

"Oh, I enjoy a scene, and cause them whenever possible." She waited to be sure Alanna was more composed. "I will tell you a story of a young girl who loved very unwisely. She loved a man who it seemed was so wrong for her. She loved in times when there was war and rebellion, and death everywhere. She refused him, time and time again. She thought it was best."

Drying her eyes, Alanna sighed. "What happened to them?"

"Oh, he was as pigheaded as she, so they married and had six children. Two grandchildren." Her smile blossomed. "I've never regretted a single moment."

"But this is different."

"Love is always the same. And it is never the same." She brushed the hair from Alanna's cheek. "I was afraid."

"You?"

"Oh, aye. The more I loved Brigham, the more frightened I was. And the harder I punished us both by denying my feelings. Will you tell me of yours? Often it helps to speak with another woman."

Perhaps it would, Alanna thought. Surely it could hurt no more than it already did. "I lost my brother in the war with the French. I was only a child, but I remember him. He was so bright, so beautiful. And like Ian, he could think of nothing but to defend and fight for his land, for his beliefs. So he died for them. Within a year, my mother slipped away. Her heart was broken, and it never mended. I've watched my father grieve for them, year after year."

"There is no loss greater than that of ones you love. My father died in battle twenty-eight years ago and I still see his face, so clear. I left my mother in Scotland soon after. She died before Amanda was born, but still lives in my heart." She took both of Alanna's hands, and her eyes were damp and intense. "When the rebellion was crushed, my brother Coll brought Brigham to me. He had been shot and was near death. In my womb I carried our first child. We were hiding from the English in a cave. He lingered between life and death."

So Ian's stories to Brian were true, she thought as she stared at the small, slender woman beside her. "How could you bear it?"

"How could I not?" She smiled. "He often says I willed him back to life so that I could badger him. Perhaps it's true. But I know the fear, Alanna. When this revolution comes, my sons will fight, and there is ice in my blood at the thought that I could lose them. But if I were a man, I would pick up a sword and join them."

"You're braver than I."

"I think not. If your family were threatened, would you hide in a corner, or would you take up arms and protect them?"

"I would die to protect them. But—"

"Aye." Serena's smile bloomed again, but it was softer, more serious than before. "The time will come, and soon, when the men of the Colonies will realize we are all one. As a clan. And we will fight to protect each other. Ian knows that now. Is that not why you love him?"

"Aye." She looked down at their joined hands.

"If you deny that love, will you be happier than if you embraced it and took what time God grants you together?"

"No." She closed her eyes and thought of the past three months of misery. "I'll never be happy without him—I know that now. And yet, all of my life I dreamed of marrying a strong, quiet man, who would be content to work with me and raise a family. With Ian, there would be confusion and demands and risks. I would never know a moment's peace."

"No," Serena agreed. "You would not. Alanna, look into your heart now and ask yourself but one question. If the power were yours, would you change him?"

She opened her mouth prepared to shout a resounding "Aye!" But her heart, more honest than her head, held another answer. "No. Sweet Jesus, have I been so much a fool not to realize I love him for what he is, not for what I wish he might be?"

Satisfied, Serena nodded. "Life is all risk, Alanna. There are those who take them, wholeheartedly, and move forward. And there are those who hide from them and stay in one place. Which are you?"

For a long time Alanna sat in silence. "I wonder, my lady—"

"Serena."

"I wonder, Serena," she said, and managed a smile, "if I had had you to talk with, would I have sent him away?"

Serena laughed. "Well, that's something to think about. You rest now, and give the lad time to stew."

"He won't want to talk to me," she muttered, then set her chin. "But I'll make him."

"You'll do," Serena said with a laugh. "Aye, you'll do well."

Chapter Ten

Ian didn't come to dinner, nor did he appear at breakfast the next morning. While this might have discouraged most women, for Alanna it presented exactly the sort of challenge she needed to overcome her own anxieties.

Added to that were the Langstons themselves. It was simply not possible to be in the midst of such a family and not see what could be done with love, determination and trust. No matter what odds they had faced, Serena and Brigham had made a life together. They had both lost their homes, their countries and people they loved, but had rebuilt from their own grit.

Could she deny herself any less of a chance with Ian? He would fight, certainly. But she began to convince herself that he was too stubborn to die. And if indeed she were to lose him, was it not worth the joy of a year, a month or a day in his arms?

She would tell him so. If she ever ran the fool to ground. She would apologize. She would even, though it grated, beg his forgiveness and a second chance.

But as the morning whiled away, she found herself more irritated than penitent. She would apologize, all right, Alanna thought. Right after she'd given him a good, swift kick.

It was the twins who gave her the first clue as to where to find him.

"You were the one who spoiled it," Payne declared as they came poking and jabbing at each other into the garden.

"Hah! It was you who set him off. If you'd kept your mouth shut we could have gone off with him. But you've such a bloody big—"

"All right, lads." Serena stopped clipping flowers to turn to them. "Fight if you must, but not here. I won't have my garden trampled by wrestling bodies."

"It's his fault," they said in unison, and made Alanna smile.

"I only wanted to go fishing," Ross complained. "And Ian would have taken me along if *he* hadn't started jabbering."

"Fishing." Alanna crushed a blossom in her hand before she controlled herself. "Is that where Ian is?"

"He always goes to the river when he's moody." Payne kicked at a pebble. "I'd have convinced him to take us, too, if Ross hadn't started in so Ian was snarling and riding off without us."

"I don't want to fish anyway." Ross stuck up his chin. "I want to play shuttlecock."

"*I* want to play shuttlecock," Payne shouted, and raced off to get there first.

"I've a fine mare in the stables. A pretty chestnut that was a gift from my brother Malcolm. He knows his horseflesh." Serena went on clipping flowers. "Do you like to ride, Alanna?"

"Aye. I don't have much time for it at home."

"Then you should take advantage of your time here." She gave her young guest a sunny smile. "Tell Jem at the stables I said to saddle Prancer for you. You might enjoy riding south. There's a path through the woods just beyond the stables. The river's very pretty this time of year."

"Thank you." She started to dash off, then stopped. "I—I don't have a riding habit."

"Hattie will see to it. There's one of Amanda's in my trunk. It should suit you."

"Thank you." She stopped, turned and embraced Serena. "Thank you."

Within thirty minutes, Alanna was mounted.

Ian did indeed have a line in the water, but it was only an excuse to sit and brood. He'd given brief consideration to strangling his aunt for her interference, but before he'd gotten the chance she had burst into his room and raked him so completely over the coals that he'd had nothing to do but defend himself.

Aye, he'd been rude to her guest. He'd meant to be.

If it didn't smack so much of running away, he'd have been on his horse and headed back to Boston. He'd be damned if he'd ride away a second time. This time, she could go, and the devil take her.

Why had she had to look so beautiful, standing there in her blue dress with the sun coming through the window at her back?

Why did it matter to him how she looked? he thought viciously. He didn't want her any longer. He didn't need a sharp-tongued shrew of a woman in his life. There was too much work to be done.

By God, he'd all but begged her to have him. How it grated on his pride! And she, the hussy, had lain with him in the hay, given herself to him, made him think it mattered to her. He'd been so gentle, so careful with her. Never before had he opened his heart so to a woman. Only to have it handed back to him.

Well, he hoped she found some weak-kneed spineless lout she could boss around. And if he discovered she had, he would cheerfully kill the man with his own two hands.

He heard the sound of a horse approach and swore. If those two little pests had come to disrupt his solitude, he would send them packing soon enough. Taking up his line, he stood, feet planted, and prepared to roar his nephews back to the house.

But it was Alanna who came riding out of the woods. She was coming fast, a bit too fast for Ian's peace of mind. Beneath the jaunty bonnet she wore her hair had come loose so that it streamed behind her, a midnight flag. A few feet away, she reined the horse. Even at the distance, Ian could see her eyes were a brilliant and glowing blue. The mare, well used to reckless women riders, behaved prettily.

When he got his breath back, Ian shot her a killing look. "Well, you've managed to scare away all the fish for ten miles. Don't you have better sense than to ride through unfamiliar ground at that speed?"

It wasn't the greeting she'd hope for. "The horse knew the way well enough." She sat, waiting for him to help her dismount. When he merely stood, glaring, she swore and struggled down herself. "You've changed little, MacGregor. Your manners are as foul as ever."

"You came all the way to Virginia to tell me so?"

She fixed the mare's reins to a nearby branch before she whirled on him. "I came at your aunt's kind invitation. If I had known you were anywhere in the territory, I wouldn't have come. Seeing you is the only thing that has spoiled my trip, for in truth, I'll never understand how a man such as yourself could possibly be related to such a fine family. It would be my fondest wish if you would—" She caught herself, blew out a breath and struggled to remember the resolve she had worked on all through the night. "I didn't come here to fight with you."

"God help me if that had been your intention, then." He turned back to pick up his line. "You got yourself off the horse, Mrs. Flynn. I imagine you can get yourself back on and ride."

"I will speak with you," she insisted.

"Already you've said more than I wish to hear." And if he stood looking at her another moment, he would crawl. "Now mount and ride before you push me too far."

"Ian, I only want to—"

"Damn you to hell and back again." He threw down the line. "What right have you to come here? To stand here and make me suffer? If I had murdered you before I left I'd be a happy man today. You let me think you cared for me, that what happened between us meant something to you, when all you wanted was a toss in the hay."

Every ounce of color fled from her cheeks, then rushed back again in flaming fury. "How dare you? How dare you speak so to me?" She was on him like a wildcat, all nails and teeth. "I'll kill you for that, MacGregor, as God is my witness."

He grabbed wherever he could to protect himself, lost his balance and tumbled backward with her into the river.

The dunking didn't stop her. She swung, spit and scratched even as he slid on the slippery bottom and took her under with him.

"Hold, woman, for pity's sake. You'll drown us both." Because he was choking, coughing up water and trying to keep her from sinking under again, he didn't see the blow coming until his ears were already ringing. "By God, if you were a man!"

"Don't let that stop you, you bloody badger." She swung again, missed and fell facedown in the river.

Cursing all the way, he dragged her onto the bank, where they both lay drenched and breathless.

"As soon as I've the strength to stand, I'll kill her," he said to the sky.

"I hate you," she told him after she'd coughed up river water. "I curse the day you were born. And I curse the day I let you put your filthy hands on me." She managed to sit up and drag the ruined bonnet out of her eyes.

Damn her for being beautiful even wet and raging. His voice was frigid when he spoke. A dangerous sign. "You asked me to put them on you, as I recall, madam."

"Aye, that I did, to my disgust." She threw the bonnet at him. "'Tis a pity the roll in the hay wasn't more memorable."

"Oh?" She was too busy wringing out her hair to note the reckless light in his eyes. "Wasn't it now?"

"No, it wasn't. In fact, I'd forgotten all about it until you mentioned it." With what dignity she still had in her possession, she started to rise. He had her flat on her back in an instant.

"Well, then, let me refresh your memory."

His mouth came down hard on hers. She responded by sinking her teeth into his lip. He cursed her, gathered her dripping hair in his hand and kissed her again.

She fought herself, all the glorious feelings that poured through her. She fought him, the long firm body that so intimately covered hers. Like scrapping children, they rolled over the grassy bank, blindly seeking to punish for hurts old and new.

Then she whimpered, a sound of submission and of joy. Her arms were around him, her mouth opening hungrily to his. All the force of her love burst out in that one meeting of lips and fueled a fire already blazing.

Frantic fingers tore at buttons. Desperate hands pulled at wet, heavy clothing. Then the sun was steaming down on their damp bodies.

He wasn't gentle now. She didn't wish it. All the frustration and the need they had trapped within themselves tore free in a rage of passion as they took from each other under the cloudless spring sky.

With her hands in his hair, she pulled his mouth to hers again and again, murmuring wild promises, wild pleas. As they lay on the carpet of new grass, he absorbed the scent that had haunted him for weeks. He stroked his hands along the smooth white skin he had dreamed of night after night.

When she arched against him, ruthlessly stoking his fires, he plunged into her. Her name was on his lips as he buried his face in her hair. His was on hers as she wrapped her long limbs around him. Together they raced toward the end they both craved, until at last they lay still, each hounded by their own thoughts.

He drew himself up on his elbow and with one hand cupped her face. As she watched, loving him, she saw the temper return slowly to his eyes.

"I give you no choice this time, Alanna. Willing or weeping we marry."

"Ian, I came here today to tell you—"

"I don't give a bloody damn what you came to tell me." His fingers tightened on her chin. He had emptied himself in her, body and soul. She had left him with nothing, not even pride. "You can hate me and curse me from now until the world ends, but you'll be mine. You are mine. And by God, you'll take me as I am."

She gritted her teeth. "If you'd let me say a word—"

But a desperate man didn't listen. "I'll not let you go again. I should not have before, but you've a way of scraping a man raw. Whatever I can do to make you happy, I'll do. Except abandon my own conscience. That I cannot do, and won't. Not even for you."

"I don't ask you to, and never would. I only want to tell you—"

"Damn it, what is it that's digging a hole in my chest?" Still swearing he reached between them. And held up the MacGregor ring that dangled from a cord around her neck. It glinted in the sunlight as he stared at it. Slowly, he closed his fingers around it and looked down at her. "Why..." He took another moment to be sure he could trust his voice. "Why do you wear this?"

"I was trying to tell you, if you would only let me speak."

"I'm letting you speak now, so speak."

"I was going to give it back to you." She moved restlessly beneath him. "But I couldn't. It felt dishonest to wear it on my finger, so I tied it to a cord and wore it by my heart, where I kept you, as well. No, damn you, let me finish," she said when he opened his mouth. "I think I knew even as I heard you ride away that morning that I had been wrong and you had been right."

The beginnings of a smile teased his mouth. "I have river water in my ears, Mrs. Flynn. Would you say that again?"

"I said it once, I'll not repeat it." If she'd been standing, she would have tossed her head and lifted her chin. "I didn't want to love you, because when you love so much, it makes you afraid. I lost Rory in the war, my mother from grief and poor Michael Flynn from a fever. And as much as they meant to me, I knew that you meant more."

He kissed her, gently. "Don't let me interrupt."

"I thought I wanted a quiet home and a family, a husband who would be content to work beside me and sit by the fire night after night." She smiled now and touched his hair. "But it seems what I wanted all along was a man who would never be content, one who would grow restless by the fire after the first night or two. One who would fight all the wrongs or die trying. That's a man I would be proud to stand beside."

"Now you humble me," he murmured, and rested his brow on hers. "Only tell me you love me."

"I do love you, Ian MacGregor. Now and always."

"I swear to give you that home, that family, and to sit by the fire with you whenever I can."

"And I promise to fight beside you when the need comes."

Shifting, he snapped the cord and freed the ring. His eyes were on hers as he slipped it onto her finger. "Never take it off again."

"No." She took his hand in hers. "From this moment, I'm a MacGregor."

Epilogue

Boston. Christmas Eve, 1774

No amount of arguments could keep Ian out of the bedroom where his wife struggled through her first birthing. Though the sight of her laboring froze his man's heart, he stood firm. His aunt Gwen in her quiet, persuasive way had done her best, but even she had failed.

"It's my child, as well," he said. "And I'll not leave Alanna until it's born." He took his aunt's hand and prayed he'd have the nerve to live by his words. "It's not that I don't trust your skills, Aunt Gwen. After all, I wouldn't be here without them."

"It's no use, Gwen." Serena chuckled. "He's as stubborn as any MacGregor."

"Hold her hand then, when the pain is bad. It won't be much longer now."

Alanna managed a smile when Ian came to her side. She hadn't known it would take so long to bring such a small thing as a child into the world. She was grateful that he was with her and for the comforting presence of Gwen, who had brought so many dozens of babies into the world. Gwen's husband, who was a doctor, would have attended the birth as well, had he not been called away on an emergency.

"You neglect our guests," Alanna said to Ian as she rested between contractions.

"They'll entertain themselves well enough," Serena assured her.

"I don't doubt it." She closed her eyes as Gwen wiped her brow with a cool cloth. It pleased her that her family was here for Christmas. Both the Murphys and the Langstons. She should have been doing her duties as hostess on this first Christmas in the house she and Ian had bought near the river, but the babe, not due for another three weeks, was putting in an early appearance.

When the next pang hit, she squeezed Ian's hand and tensed.

"Relax, relax, mind your breathing," Gwen crooned. "There's a lass."

The pains were closer now, and stronger. A Christmas baby, she thought, struggling to rise over the wave. Their child, their first child, would be a priceless gift to each other on this the most holy night of the year.

As the pain passed, she kept her eyes closed, listening to the soothing sound of Ian's voice.

He was a good man, a solid husband. She felt his fingers twine around hers. True, her life was not a peaceful one, but it was eventful. He had managed to draw her into his ambitions. Or perhaps the seeds of rebellion had always been inside her, waiting to be nurtured. She had come to listen avidly to his reports of the meetings he attended and to feel pride when others sought his advice. She could not but agree with him that the Port Bill was cruel and unjust. Like Ian, she scorned the idea of paying for the tea that had been destroyed in order to escape the penalty.

No, they had not been wrong. She had learned there was often right in recklessness. She had to smile. It was recklessness, and right, that had brought her here to a birthing bed. And she thanked God for it.

And hadn't other towns and provinces rallied to support Boston, just as her family and Ian's had rallied to support them in this, the birth of their first child?

She thought of their honeymoon in Scotland, where she had met his family and walked in the forests of his childhood. One day they would go back and take this child, show him, or her, the place of roots. And to Ireland, she thought as the pain returned, dizzying. The child would not forget the people who had come before. And while the child remembered, he would choose his own life, his own homeland. By their struggles, they would have given him that right.

"The babe's coming." Gwen shot Ian a quick, reassuring smile. "You'll be a papa very soon."

"The birth of our child," Alanna panted, fighting to focus on Ian. "And soon, the birth of our nation."

Though he could taste his own fear, for her, he laughed. "You're becoming more of a radical than I, Mrs. MacGregor."

"I do nothing by half measures. Oh, sweet Jesus, he fights for life." She groped for her husband's hand. "There can be little doubt he will be his father's son."

"Or her mother's daughter," Ian murmured, looking desperately at Gwen. "How much longer?" he demanded. "She suffers."

"Soon." She let out a little sound of impatience as there was a knock on the door.

"Don't worry." Serena pushed at her already rolled-up sleeves. "I'll send them packing." It surprised her to find her husband at the threshold. "Brig, the babe's all but here. I don't have time for you now."

"You'll have time." He stepped inside, tossing one arm around his wife. "I've just gotten a message I've waited for, a confirmation from London I wanted before I spoke to you."

"Damn messages from London," Serena muttered as she heard Alanna groan.

"Uncle, news can wait."

"Ian, you need to hear this as well, tonight of all nights."

"Then say it and be gone," his wife snapped at him.

"Last month a petition was debated by Parliament." Brigham took Serena by the shoulders and looked into her eyes. "The Act of Proscription has been repealed." He cupped her face in his hands as her eyes filled. "The MacGregor name is free."

With her tears fell a weight she had carried all of her life. "Gwen. Gwen, did you hear?"

"Aye, I heard, and I thank God for it, but I've my hands full at the moment."

Dragging her husband with her, Serena hurried to the bed. "Since you're here," she told Brigham, "you'll help."

Within minutes there was the sound of church bells heralding midnight and the birth of a new Christmas. And the sound of a baby's lusty cry, heralding life.

"A son." Gwen held the squirming child in her arms.

"He's all right?" Exhausted, Alanna lay back against Brigham's bracing hands. "Is he all right?"

"He's perfect," Serena assured her, mopping her own tears. "You'll hold him in a moment.

"I love you." Ian pressed Alanna's hand to his lips. "And I thank you for the greatest gift that man can have."

"Here now." Gwen shifted the newly swaddled infant to his father's arms. "Take your son."

"Sweet God." Stunned, he looked from the baby to Alanna. It was an image she would treasure all of her life. "He's so small."

"He'll grow." Serena smiled up at her husband. "They always do." She put an arm around her sister as Ian transferred the baby to Alanna's waiting arms.

"Oh, he's so beautiful." Reaching for Ian, she drew him down beside her. "Last Christmas we were given each other. This Christmas we're given a son." Gently, she stroked the downy dark hair on the baby's head. "I can't wait to see what the years will bring."

"We'll give you time alone—" Brigham took his wife and his sister-in-law by the hand "—and go down and tell the others."

"Aye, tell them." Ian stood, and because she understood, Alanna gave him the child to hold once again. "Tell them that Murphy MacGregor is born this Christmas day." After kissing his son, he held him up for the others to see, and the baby let out a lusty wail. "A MacGregor who will say his name proudly to all that can hear. Who will walk in a free land. Tell them that.''

''Aye, tell them that,'' Alanna agreed as Ian's hand closed around hers. ''From both of us.''

* * * * *

A Note from Nora Roberts

I can't help it. Christmas is my favorite time of year. I like the music, the cards, the big bright bows, the anticipation. Decorating the tree is one of my favorite family events. It's the only time of year you'll find me—almost happily—in the kitchen every day. And it's the only time of year my husband and children will find freshly baked cookies in the cookie jar.

Has it become commercial? Sure. I don't care. I get a tremendous charge out of buying gifts, out of wrapping them, arranging them under the tree. And, yes, shaking anything that has my name on it. When we drive around and see the lights strung over houses, trees glimmering in windows, I feel a kinship with the people who live in those houses, behind those windows. The pleasure that gives me has nothing to do with marketing and everything to do with magic.

Christmas is family, and I have a huge one. I have four brothers; my husband has four sisters. Most of them have taken the advice to "go forth and multiply" seriously. We spend the entire day with family, starting in our own home before dawn, just the four of us. Though my two sons are nearly grown, Christmas mornings are still exciting, chaotic and magic.

After the sun's up and the house is in shambles, we head down to my parents' house to have a late breakfast with them, my brothers, sisters-in-law, nieces, nephews, my grandmother, and anyone else who happens along. Then it's back up the road again to visit my husband's parents, sisters, brothers-in-law, nieces, nephews. By the time we finally get home, we're exhausted, and have an entire videotape to remind us of the day. I wouldn't trade one hectic moment of it.

I suppose that's why I went back to the MacGregors when I started to write a Christmas story. Over the years, they have become my family, too. I hope you enjoy Ian's story, "In from the Cold." It isn't wrapped in pretty paper, but it's my Christmas gift to you, from the heart.

Happy Holidays,

Nora Roberts

MIRACLE OF THE HEART

★

Patricia Potter

To my mother and father,
and all the Miracles of the Heart
they've given to me over the years.

One of the highlights of each Christmas when I was growing up was the making of the fudge and, of course, the age-old ritual of licking the pan and spoon, a chore most eagerly sought by my brother and me.

It was always my father who made the fudge, and no one, no matter how hard they tried, could ever quite make this wonderful delicacy just the way he did.

Here's how he says he does it. I personally believe there's an added touch of magic someplace.

GRANDPA'S FUDGE

2 squares Baker's unsweetened chocolate
¾ cup half-and-half or whole milk
2 cups granulated sugar
1 tsp salt
1 tbsp corn syrup
2 tbsp butter
1 tsp vanilla
½ cup black walnuts or pecans

Butter sides of a heavy, two-quart saucepan. In the pan, melt chocolate in half-and-half or whole milk over low heat. Add sugar and salt. Cook over medium heat, stirring constantly until sugar is dissolved and mixture boils. Add corn syrup and continue cooking until mixture reaches 238° F. (soft-ball stage).

Immediately take from heat. Add butter and vanilla. Beat vigorously until mixture stiffens and dulls. Quickly stir in nuts. Spread mixture on a buttered plate.

Let cool. Cut as desired.

Chapter One

Shenandoah Valley, 1864

Blythe Somers buried her face in the fragrant boughs of pine she and the children had gathered earlier in the afternoon. She wanted to cry, but the tears wouldn't come. They had all been used up.

Christmas Eve, 1864. A time of joy and thankfulness.

A time of death.

A time of loneliness that reached outside the heart and even into the bones, until every movement became an act of supreme will.

She took a deep breath, but it came out more a sob as she thought of Christmas four years past. Memories, both joyful and agonizingly painful, came rushing back with the impact of a runaway locomotive.

Her father had been alive then, and the house was filled with the delightful smells of cooking. Laughter had crowded out all other sounds, echoing through each room, permeating every cranny of the comfortable farmhouse.

But the most wonderful moment of all that Christmas had been when Rafe Hampton, his face slightly chagrined, had awkwardly bent to one knee and asked for her hand in marriage. A Hampton on his knee was a most unusual sight indeed, and despite the seriousness of the event, Blythe had not been able to help laughing.

Rafe had frowned for a moment at her reaction to his most earnest of efforts before breaking into a full grin. "Is that a yes?"

"Oh, yes," she had said, still giggling slightly, partly from the sight of him on the floor, partly from plain undiluted joy.

Together, they had told his brother Seth, who had stilled for a moment, conflicting emotions blazing across his face before he shook Rafe's hand and lightly kissed her cheek. The two brothers had competed with each other for years for her favor. Yet the three had been very close, and neither Rafe nor Seth had allowed their common desire to break the strong bond they shared.

"Oh, Rafe...where are you?" Blythe's words were no more than a whisper in the semidarkness. The room was lit by only two candles, for they, like everything else, were in short supply. Oil to feed the lamps was long gone.

She and Rafe had planned to be married in the May of 1861. Seth was, of course, to be the best man. Instead, the two men had become enemies. Rafe, the attorney, had joined the North. Seth, the doctor, had joined the South.

Blythe would never forget the day Rafe had ridden away. Knowing how badly the South would need doctors, Seth had already joined the Army of Virginia. His brother had been battling his conscience for months, torn between his loyalty to his family and state, and his strong belief in the Union.

Rafe had stopped by the Somers's farm to tell Blythe of his decision. His usually smiling mouth was grim, his green-blue eyes without the mischievous gleam she often found there.

He was going west, he said, to join the Tennessee volunteers. He would not fight in Virginia against family and lifelong friends. Yet in good conscience he could not sit out the war, or join Virginia. He would not ask Blythe to wait for him.

"I'll wait forever," she had replied, feeling as if her world was falling apart.

He had taken her chin in his hand and stared at her as if afraid he would never see her again, as if he were memorizing every inch of her. "I know you will," he said in the deep drawling voice that she loved, yet there was a tension in it she had never heard before. "But I'll not hold you to it."

"The war won't last long...."

She had seen the despair settle on his beloved features. "I fear it will be much longer than anyone believes." His arms had gone around her with a crushing strength, and his mouth caught hers hungrily, as if he could never get enough of her.

And then he was gone.

Four years he had been gone. His prediction had been much more accurate than all the optimistic platitudes voiced by his fellow Southerners.

The war was almost over now. The South lay in waste, so many of its young men dead or wounded. Blythe's father was dead. Along with one of Rafe's brothers. Thank God, Seth had survived thus far, but in these last furious months of fighting she had lived in fear for him. And for Rafe.

"Where are you, my love?" she whispered again. She had heard from Rafe during the first two years of the war although communication had been difficult at best. Rafe had always found a way.

But there had been no word for two years. Blythe didn't even know whether he was dead or alive, although she believed, deep in her heart, that she would have felt something if he had died. They had been too close for it to be otherwise. She looked down at the ring she never removed from her finger. It was the only thing of value left her, but she would sooner sell her heart than sell the one thing she had left of Rafe.

Don't think of it, she told herself. *Think of tomorrow and of trying to give the children some kind of Christmas.*

Blythe straightened her back and returned to the task at hand. She had found some red ribbon in one of the trunks upstairs, and now she draped it around the greenery. It would add some festivity to a house grown gray and shabby.

It was nearly midnight when she finished. She went up to her room and gathered up the presents she had so painstakingly made and hidden. They weren't much, she thought sadly. Scarves cut down from her father's old cloak. Two rag dolls she had made, one for small Benji and the other for Suzie. She bit her lip, once more wanting to cry. They had so little . . . these children of hers. So very little.

They had come to her from such tragedy . . . first one, then a second, and a third, until she now had ten orphans with no other place to go. But how could she continue to care for them, to feed them?

If it had not been for Seth, they probably would have all starved months ago....

She placed the gifts around the fireplace, so the children would see them first thing in the morning. *Now for the pies.* She had saved the last apples for these pies. Seth had brought her some precious sugar two days earlier. He was assigned to Mosby's raiders and was sometimes given spoils from their raids on Yankee supply trains. She knew he never used any for himself but always passed them on to her.

This whole area was alive with Yankees now, but somehow Mosby's raiders filtered through Yankee lines like water leaking through a sieve. Seth would suddenly appear with saddlebags full of supplies. He would play with the children, tease smiles from too-solemn faces, then disappear as silently and quietly as he had come.

Blythe put on an old coat and, taking a candle lamp, went outside. A water trough was situated on a small incline under a huge spreading oak tree. She set the lamp down beside the trough, and using both hands and all the strength her tired body still possessed, she pushed until it slid sideways, revealing an opening in the ground beneath it. Blythe quickly picked up the candle and descended into the cold black fruit cellar that now served as a hideaway for their small supply of food.

After one disastrous visit by Confederate troops who confiscated much of their foodstuffs, giving them nearly worthless Confederate bills in exchange, Seth had built the trough. When the wooden tub was in place, it neatly disguised the narrow entrance to the cellar built into the well-shaded hill. Despite subsequent visits by both Confederate and Union forces,

Blythe had been able to conceal the remainder of what little food they had.

The cellar, however, was now almost empty. Biting her lips as she shone the light around the shelves, she wondered how much longer they would have even the barest of meals. *Don't think about it tonight.*

Blythe gathered up the last of the apples, took several cups of flour from the nearly empty barrel and returned to the house. There was a blazing fire in the warm kitchen. At least they had enough wood. Blythe started a fire in the iron stove, a luxury her father had bought before the war, and went to work mixing the dough for her precious pies. They too would be a surprise for the children, the pies and the two chickens she had been keeping safe in a cave not far away. At least they would have a decent Christmas dinner.

The thought heartened her, and she started to hum a Christmas song. She would make this a good Christmas for the children who had lost so much. She would.

Her mind ran over her young charges now. Benji, at five, was the youngest. He had come with his sister, Margaret, who was eight, after their father had been killed and their mother had died of fever. More from heartbreak, Blythe thought sadly. The two had no relatives, and Blythe and her father had agreed to take them in. That had been two years ago. Then came Jaime, an embittered twelve-year-old who had shown up asking to work in exchange for a meal and had stayed. He was now thirteen. Blythe didn't know his story; although he was a hard worker he said little and had distrusted everyone at first. In many ways, he had become the man of the house, doing much of the work in the one field Blythe had tried to keep under cultivation.

Nine-year-old Suzie had been found on the road one day, her huge eyes reflecting a terror that no child should know. After weeks of nightmares, Blythe had discovered that deserters had killed her father and raped and murdered her mother.

Soon after, Abraham and Micah had appeared on the porch. The nine- and eight-year-old brothers had been abandoned by their father and had set off together for Petersburg looking for jobs. Instead, they had found Blythe.

Sarah had come early this year. She had been a house slave, until Yankees had burned the plantation where she lived and the owners had fled. Left to fend for themselves, the few remaining slaves had decided to go north. During the journey, Sarah had gone looking for berries and gotten lost.

There were two others like Sarah, sisters who had been purchased away from their families as babies. Katy and July had also become separated from the group they had attached themselves to. Ragged, hungry and terrified, they had somehow found their way to Blythe's door.

The last, and saddest of all, was Maria. A fair-skinned mulatto, she was large with child—the result of a brutal rape by blue-coated soldiers. She was fourteen, and the babe was due any day. Strangely enough, Maria looked forward to the birth, to having a child of her own. There was a gentleness, a sweetness in the girl, despite all that had happened, that always made Blythe's heart constrict.

This was her family now. All of them. Innocent victims of a war they had had no part in creating.

They had soothed some of her grief when her father had died a year ago of wounds received at the Second Battle of Manassas. They had eased the agony of not knowing where Rafe was, or whether he was alive. She had little time for loneliness, except for moments like this when Rafe was so strong in her mind and heart. There had been, in the beginning, some resentment from her neighbors when she took in the slave children, but many in this area had not owned slaves, nor did they like the institution. And everyone had problems of their own just staying alive and trying to hold on to their land.

As did Blythe. The Somers's farm had been small but prosperous, relying much on the fine horseflesh Ben Somers bred. Ben had never believed in slavery and had only two freemen, both of whom left to join the Northern army when the Somers's horses were taken. Ben and Blythe had tended one small wheat field and a vegetable garden themselves until her father's health, never robust after a Yankee bullet took one of his lungs, steadily declined until he died last year.

How she wished she could turn back the clock for all of them.

But you can't, she scolded herself. *You can only make the best of what you have. And you have a great deal. You still have the farm, and the children, and Seth. And some day, Rafe will return. It's more than most Southerners have today.*

The dough was taking shape. She mixed the pie filling... the sugar and apples and precious cinnamon. The smell of spices joined with that of evergreen coming from the parlor, and Blythe felt a surge of hope, of excitement that, despite the pain during the past years, had always been with her at Christmas. It was just coming a bit late this year. *It will be a good Christmas!*

She was pouring the mixture into the pie crusts when she heard the light knock on the door.

With the caution bred of years spent in the center of a war, Blythe picked up her father's pistol before she opened the door. She had had far too many unwanted visitors in months past.

She opened the door with the same wariness. She could not refuse someone food or shelter, not tonight of all nights, but she would be very careful in doing so.

Seth!

Seth was standing there, one arm clutching a medical bag, the other around a man in gray, holding him tightly underneath the arms. Blood covered the stranger's gray coat.

"There are Yankees behind us," Seth said, his breath coming in gasps from the effort of holding the man up. "No place else to go. The fruit cellar?"

Blythe didn't waste time asking for explanations. Seth wouldn't have come here if it hadn't been urgent. He had taken great care in the past not to endanger them.

Picking up the candle lamp, she hurried out to the trough. As Seth continued to hold the other officer up, she pushed open the secret door and led the way down, holding the light so Seth could see the steps. At the bottom, he lowered the officer to the floor.

"General Massey," he said to Blythe as his hands stripped off the man's coat. "The Yanks want him bad. He's been in on the war-planning in Richmond. He came to see Mosby, and we were returning to Richmond with him when we were caught in a trap east of here. The others stayed behind to give us enough time to get back to our lines. But he can't make it any farther. He's bleeding too badly.''

She stared at him. "You were going to Richmond?''

"I've been reassigned, Blythe. The need is desperate there. I was going to send you a note. It was the best I could do.''

Her legs nearly gave way under her. Seth gone. Like Rafe. She depended on him so much. Dear God, how would she manage alone? She only saw him once every couple of weeks, but knowing he was never far away had given her courage. She watched his strong fingers move surely, but incredibly gently, over the wound as he examined it. Looking up, he smiled reassuringly. "You'll be all right, Blythe. No man, Southern or Northern, is your match when you get that determined look on your face.''

"I'll miss you.''

"I'll miss you, too . . . and the children. But my orderly has instructions to look out for you. He'll bring what food he can.''

His gaze was demanding strength from her, and she gave it to him. It was the least she could do. She nodded and turned away, not wanting him to see the tears forming in her eyes.

"You should be safe here," she said, changing the subject, desperately trying not to think about what lay ahead. "The children know how important it is to keep the cellar secret." Even if they didn't, she knew they wouldn't say anything. They usually hid when any stranger came. Strangers represented danger.

"I didn't want to come here...but I had no place else to go." This time, his drawl, so like Rafe's, was as strained as she knew her own voice had been.

Blythe studied Seth's face. It was so very thin and weary. He was only twenty-eight, but he looked so much older at the moment. His tawny blond hair, usually shining with gold from the sun, looked unkempt and faded. The shimmering blue-green eyes, the one feature he shared with Rafe, were dulled with fatigue. But the compassion was still there. The compassion, she knew, would always be there.

"What can I do? Your horses? Should I hide them?"

"I already did...in the cave with the chickens. But, if you have them, blankets...rugs...anything to keep him warm. And some water. Hot water." He turned back to his patient.

Leaving the candle with Seth, she hurried out, closing the trough entrance behind her. She hated to waste the time and energy, but she couldn't afford not to take the precaution. And neither could Seth.

It was clear and cold. Blythe could see the sparkling stars above in a midnight-blue sky. She shivered, for she had not taken time to put on a coat. But the trembling came from something more. Fear for Seth. Heart-deep fear. She had heard of the Yankee prisons, the treatment afforded Mosby's guerrillas. It wouldn't matter that he was a doctor, a healer. They were treated no differently, although their role was life, not death.

The fear and concern hastened her footsteps. Seth had said the Yankees were not far behind. She put some water on the stove to heat while she went to find some covering for the injured man. The blankets were nearly gone, parceled out between the children, but she had a thick quilt that could be doubled. There was also a treadbare rug in her bedroom; it would at least protect the officer from the damp cold earth of the fruit cellar. She bundled them up, and then poured the water into a bucket. Loaded down, she returned to the cellar, struggled with the opening and took her booty down the narrow steps.

Seth had taken off his coat. The general's shirt was open, and Blythe saw the jagged open wound, and she sucked in her breath.

Seth gave her a wry smile as she set down the bucket of steaming hot water along with several pieces of clean cloth, the quilt and rug. "Thank you."

"What can I do to help?"

"Slide the rug under him as I lift him," he said gratefully.

Blythe didn't miss the pain on the man's face as Seth lifted him, but it seemed to revive the officer. His glazed eyes caught Blythe, and hesitated there.

"My thanks, madam." The words croaked out, and Blythe was flooded with sympathy. She knelt beside him with the quilt, covering as best she could the area that was not being attended by Seth.

Seth took his eyes away from the wound long enough to glance at the open door. "You'd better get back, Blythe, and close the door."

She nodded, knowing she was risking them all by hesitating. But she wanted to help. So much.

Seth shook his head, understanding her only too well. "I can handle it now. No more risks. Don't come back here tonight."

Blythe nodded reluctantly and started for the stairs.

"Blythe?"

She turned back.

"Thank you," he said softly. "And Merry Christmas."

Tears threatened to blind her on the way back into the house. She hated to think of the two men in the cellar, and especially tonight of all nights. But Seth was right. He was safer that way. Safer? Would any of them ever really be safe again?

The pies were in the oven when Blythe heard hoofbeats. Dozens of them. Her hands stilled as she heard a hard command through the window, and then a certain silence.

Her heart quivering, she looked out the window. The lawn in front was filled with horses and men in blue uniform. She couldn't see faces; their hats were all pulled low against the cold. It wasn't the first time Yankees had been here, and each time they had taken what they wanted from her home. Now there was much more at risk. She looked at the pistol and decided against flaunting it. It wouldn't do any good against the scores of men, except possibly to make them more inquisitive, more suspicious. She tucked it under some aprons in the pantry and went to the door, opening it with unsteady hands.

A blast of cold air hit her, but it was nothing compared to the impact of the sight of the tall lean major standing in front of her.

A hat covered the hair she knew was as black as a raven's wing, and a tense expression tightened the lips that once laughed and teased. His brilliant green-blue eyes, so like those of his brother in the fruit cellar, swept her warily. . . .

Rafe. Dear God. It was Rafe!

Chapter Two

The face carved so strongly in her memory was miraculously there in front of her. For a moment, Blythe felt faint, and she steadied herself against the door. She wanted to rush into his arms, but something harsh and unfamiliar about him stopped her.

"Rafe," she whispered.

He hesitated, his eyes defensive. "Am I welcome, Blythe?"

The coolness in his voice, the tautness in his posture, kept her from doing what she so badly wanted to do... touch him and assure herself he was real, not a Christmas apparition, but flesh-and-blood real.

There was something wrong... terribly, terribly wrong. And then horror struck her. Was he looking for Seth? She suddenly stiffened.

"It depends on why you're here," she said, wondering how such impersonal words came off her tongue when her heart was beating loud enough for all the Yankees outside to hear. There was something in the stiff way he held himself, in his own cool words, in his hooded eyes that searched her face so warily, even hostilely. As if she were the enemy.

He moved inside despite the fact she hadn't answered his question, and he closed the door. He didn't want his men to hear. "Why?" The question was cold and objective. "Do you have something...or someone...to hide?"

Blythe froze, her blood turning as cold as the icy water that ran in the stream down from her farm. "Why are you here, Rafe...to rob what little we have left? You're too late. Your soldiers have taken nearly everything...."

"As the Rebs have burned Hampton Farms," Rafe responded. "I thought Seth might have had some little influence."

"Both sides have found reasons to destroy everything," Blythe retorted, her heart crumbling. "The South because it's in need, and the North to stop the South. One side takes; the other burns."

Rafe hesitated a moment before asking the question that he had to ask, the question that had been draining his spirit and soul for months. "How's Seth?"

"He's alive...the last time I heard," Blythe replied, her voice shaking slightly.

He wanted to ask more, to know whether she and his brother had married yet, whether Seth lived here now. But he couldn't. He tried to control his voice, to keep it calm. "And Mother?"

"She's in South Carolina with your sister."

He leaned against the door, the back of his hand rubbing eyes that looked as tired as Seth's. "There was nothing there at Hampton Farms...no one, no life at all," he said.

"It was too dangerous. The Yankees attacked because Seth was with Mosby. The Rebs attacked because you had gone to the North. After three of your workers were killed, Seth sent your mother, and all your people who wanted to go, South.''

There was an agonized sound from his throat, like an animal in pain.

"Francis?" The taut question referred to his older brother, who had inherited Hampton Farms.

"He was killed a year ago. By deserters.''

His fist knotted, and his face was a study in agony. Blythe desperately wanted to take him in her arms, to wipe away his pain, her own grief and loneliness, and the years of terror being caught in the middle of a war. Yet...there was something about him, something that warned her to keep away. She played with the ring that hadn't left her finger in four years.

She saw his eyes lower to her hands, watched them fasten on the ring.

"You're still wearing the ring?" There was an uncertainty in his voice that didn't match the cool arrogance that had been with him when he'd arrived.

"I said I would wait forever.''

"And I said I would not hold you to it.''

"It was not your decision to make for me.''

"And...Seth?''

"What about Seth?''

"I'd heard...''

Her eyes widened in question. "Heard what?''

"That...you were to marry Seth. I thought...''

The confusion on her face told him he had been lied to. A Southern prisoner, an old neighbor, had goaded him with the news that Blythe was going to marry a true Southerner—his brother. For eighteen months he had believed it true, and bitterness and grief had eaten him inside like a worm destroying an apple. A muscle worked in his cheek as he took a step toward her, suddenly hoping against hope. "It's not true?"

"Dear God, Rafe . . . I've always loved *you*, always you." She took a step toward him as she started to comprehend his strange behavior.

"But Seth . . . ?" His mouth closed, tightened into a grim line as he struggled to understand.

"Seth has been the best friend anyone could have, and I love him dearly, but not the way I love you. Rafe, how could you even . . . ?" She stopped. That was why the letters had ended, why she had heard no more. He hadn't even given her the courtesy of a question, just condemned and forgotten her while she had waited . . . and waited. . . .

"Damn you," she said, her hand flying up and making contact with his cheek, the impact loud in the quiet house.

He raised his hand to his stinging cheek. Suddenly his mouth twisted crookedly in a half smile. "You always did have a powerful right." He reached for her flushed cheek and touched it wonderingly. How smooth it was. How smooth and warm and lovely. How fiery those golden eyes when she was angry. He had almost forgotten how lovely. He had worked at making himself forget.

Rafe felt her tremble at his touch, saw the mist of tears form in her eyes, and wondered how he could have been such a fool. War did that. War made you believe the worst, made you believe that nothing could ever be right again. His fingers shook as they traced a pattern from her mouth to her eyes, relishing the soft feel of her skin, the way her body tensed in response.

He thought briefly of his men. He had asked them to wait, explaining curtly that he knew these people.

But they seemed a long way away now. There was, at the moment, no one in the world except Blythe Somers, whose face reflected so much hurt, yet something else. Love?

Rafe couldn't help himself. He bent down and touched his lips to hers, at first feeling their resistance, and then their yielding. Her mouth was suddenly as searching as his, as wanting. Four years were gone, and she was his girl who could charm and laugh and . . . love. Most of all, love. His mission, his duty, were both lost in the recapture of something he had thought dead and gone.

"Oh, Blythe," he whispered. "It's been so long, so damnably long . . . you'll never know . . ."

But his next words never came. They both started at the creak of a door. As they turned, the long barrel of an antique musket appeared. Rafe whirled around, his hand going for his holstered pistol.

"No!" Blythe screamed.

Rafe hesitated, his gun in his hand, as the door widened and a towheaded youngster glared at him with pale blue eyes. The ancient musket was leveled right at his stomach.

Rafe slowly lowered his pistol, looking questioningly at Blythe.

"Jaime is man of the house now," she said, keeping her hand on Rafe's arm, not wanting to let him go. "You can put that gun down, Jaime. This is Major Hampton, an old neighbor of mine."

Jaime's eyes widened but lost none of their distrust. "But he's a Yank."

Blythe tried a faint smile, but she knew it was stiff. "Are any of the others awake?"

"No ma'am. I checked before coming down. Didn't want 'em gittin' in the way."

Blythe smiled despite herself. Jaime took care of the others as though they were his own. He disclaimed any sentimentality over it and admitted to no such weakness as love. But it was there, even when he scolded them.

"Do you think you can lower that musket?" Rafe asked cautiously.

"Not 'lessen I know you won't hurt Miss Blythe. There's a passel of them thieves out there," Jaime insisted, his hands still securely on the musket. "I guess we got us their leader," he said with some satisfaction.

"Jaime, put the gun down." There was a strength and resolution in Blythe's voice that startled Rafe, and he looked at her again. All these years, he had equated laughter and gaiety with Blythe Somers. Her eyes had been full of sparkle and life; her feet light and fast, whether in play or at a dance; her lips teasing and smiling. But now there was a maturity about her that was even more appealing than the girlish beauty had been. Damn, but he wanted her in his arms. He had dreamed of it for years until that day eighteen months ago when Jason Cole, with taunting viciousness, had told him she was going to marry Seth. Damn his own soul for believing it.

The lie had deadened his heart and stolen what little faith he had had after years of brutal killing. Perhaps that was why he had so readily accepted it. He had become so immersed in misery and death that hope had seemed to die in him. Perhaps it had been easier to survive that way.

Coming here tonight had been one of the hardest things he had ever done. But he had had no choice. He had arrived in the Shenandoah Valley less than a week ago from Sherman's army in Savannah. Sherman would now march up the coast and meet Grant to close the circle around General Lee's remaining troops. Much against his will, Rafe had been sent to Virginia to help Sheridan's staff since he knew the area. While he was in camp, a group of Sheridan's cavalry encountered a small Confederate detail, and a Union officer had recognized one of the escaping Rebs as a general on Lee's planning staff. The Union officer didn't know what the enemy general was doing here, perhaps trying to coordinate the various Reb cavalry units, many of which, like Mosby's, operated almost entirely on their own. In any event, the Confederate general was seen slumping over his saddle before another Confederate officer grabbed the reins from the wounded man's hands and raced away. An outnumbered but stubbornly determined group of Rebs had kept Sheridan's men from following until it was too late to go after them.

Knowing that Rafe was from the area, Sheridan had assigned him to track the general down before the officer could reach safety.

Blythe's farm was the first on the road the Rebs had taken.

Rafe had approached the house with a leaden heart, believing the only woman he had ever loved was either affianced or married to his brother.

But she still wore *his* ring, no other, and he realized he had lived in his own hell for eighteen months for no reason other than a bitter enemy's lies.

He took a step toward her, the boy with the gun forgotten for the moment.

Jaime stepped between them, his chin up. "You leave Miss Blythe alone."

"You have a gallant protector, Miss Blythe," Rafe said softly, partly amused, partly annoyed.

"Jaime," she said, wondering whether she wanted him to leave or not. "Jaime," she said again. "Please put the gun down."

"Ya sure?"

She smiled and Rafe's heart constricted. It was the first time since his arrival that she had smiled, and he thought the expression was incredibly beautiful. Tender. Wistful. So damned fresh and clean and pure. He had to fight himself to keep from grabbing her. Almost from a distance, he heard her voice continue....

"There are two pies in the stove," she was saying to the boy. "Will you get them for me?"

"Aw...that's women's work."

"Then you would rather not have pie later today?"

Indecision twisted Jaime's face as his greed fought with his idea of a man's responsibilities.

"Find a place the Yanks won't discover them," she added slyly.

"What about 'im?" Jaime asked suspiciously, casting a dark look at Rafe.

"I won't tell," Rafe promised solemnly, seeking a way to mollify the young intruder and once more be alone with Blythe, "but you'd best hide them well for my men have orders to search."

Jaime looked at the oven and quickly made up his mind. They hadn't had sweets in a very long time, and here they were just begging the Yanks to steal them. He had to protect them for the young 'uns. He put a towel around his hands and lifted the pies from the stove, sending a spicy aroma throughout the kitchen. He disappeared through the door, the musket tucked in his arm.

"He doesn't trust me," Rafe said ruefully.

"He doesn't trust anyone. For good reason."

"Blythe..." Rafe started, but then there was a knock at the door. Frustrated, Rafe opened it to find two of his men standing there awkwardly.

One, whom Blythe recognized as a sergeant, looked apologetically at her, then saluted smartly to Rafe. "Fresh tracks, sir, not far from here. We also found blood. They must be in this vicinity."

Rafe's face changed, hardened. Reluctantly he turned back to Blythe. "Are there Rebs here?"

"No."

"Blythe, I meant it when I told the boy we have orders to search. We're looking for a Reb general. His capture could shorten the war."

"No one is here," Blythe said, a knot of fear growing inside her. Several of Mosby's men had been hung or shot as guerrillas. Seth's commission as a physician would mean little to Union troops ravaged by Mosby's men. And she had no guarantee Rafe could, or even would, try to protect him. He had changed greatly in four years.

Rafe's expression was grim as he turned to the sergeant. "Search the house and barn. But you are to take nothing. Absolutely nothing. Any man who does will be court-martialed."

"There are children here," Blythe said in one last attempt to stop the search.

Rafe had seen the one, now he remembered Blythe asking if any of the "others" were awake. He had assumed she meant her workers. Jason Cole, who had lied about Seth and Blythe, had also told him that Ben Somers had died. It was one of the reasons he had believed the lie. Blythe would need someone to help, and Seth was there while he . . .

"Children?"

"Orphans . . . made so by one side or the other. What difference does it make? It's Christmas. Give them at least this one day of peace."

He turned his bleak eyes to her. "He's too important to us, Blythe."

Blythe bit her lip. She could well imagine the younger children's reactions to uniformed men coming into their rooms at night. "You don't understand. Some of these children lost their parents to men in uniform . . . one was raped . . . they're terrified of them."

Rafe's green-blue eyes pierced her, seeking the truth. "Do you swear there are no Rebs in the house?"

"I don't need to swear anything to you," she said in dismayed fury. She had waited for him four years, four pain-filled years, two of them without a word. And now this . . . this cold, inhuman invasion. "Don't ask me to help you now."

"Show me where the children are," he replied quietly. Perhaps she had still loved him . . . until tonight. He wondered if she still would after today.

Resentment and anger made her eyes flash.

"I'll be very quiet," he said, motioning for two men to accompany him.

She gave him one more angry stare, knowing if she didn't take him, he would search without her. She took the one remaining candle and moved gracefully to the stairs, her head high and defiant.

Rafe looked quietly through the doorways she opened, seeing two small bodies on one bed, and a third on a cot. He moved to another and, with the two men behind him, looked in. It had one bed and two cots. On the bed, a girl saw him and cried out in fear, cowering under the covers, and Rafe felt as if a knife had pierced his body. He was not accustomed to instilling fear in children, and the realization that he had hurt unbearably. He watched as Blythe went over to the figure, bent down and made soothing, crooning sounds. He backed out, not missing the fact that two other children were crouched on one bed in what looked like protective fetal positions. They were still, too still, and Rafe sensed that they knew he was there. What, in Christ's name, had happened to them? He waited for Blythe for several moments, and she finally emerged from the room, anxiety written all over her face.

But he had to finish. He could not leave without doing so. Duty, instilled in him so long and so hard, was impossible to shake. Even now. Even with Blythe standing there, proud and hurt and confused. There were two more rooms, and once again he sensed that the two children in the first were awake, but afraid to move, to reveal themselves. Their terror was palpable. Once again, Blythe moved gracefully to their sides, comforting and soothing until their bodies relaxed. The last room had been a small nursery, and it was occupied now by a glowering Jaime with his arm around a small boy.

"You don't want to look under the beds?" Blythe said with a biting challenge in her voice.

"Dear God, Blythe, do you think I enjoy this?" There was so much regret in his voice that Blythe couldn't help but feel a certain unwanted sympathy for him. She wanted to hate him at the moment. She had to, for Seth's sake, for the sake of the wounded man. Not a Confederate officer, or a Union one. But simply a man who needed help.

They returned to the first floor, and Rafe hesitated. "I'm sorry, Blythe. It was necessary. I *do* have orders to search all properties."

"Do you want to see my bedroom? There might be a general under my bed," she said sarcastically.

Rafe looked at the two men following them with sheepish, embarrassed looks on their faces. "Every room," he said shortly.

With pieces of her heart dying a little more each moment, she led the way and stood aside as he entered her bedroom, glancing at the low set bed and the one blanket there.

He turned and looked at her frozen face. "Blythe . . ." he tried again.

"There's the parlor and Papa's study. They might be hiding there."

Her voice was cold, and her lips were no longer soft and yielding as they had been so few minutes ago. Damn this war, he thought.

He dutifully followed her, knowing now the search was in vain. Otherwise she would not have been so docile in allowing it.

They ended back in the kitchen.

"Smells mighty fine, ma'am," the sergeant said hopefully. "Just like Christmas at my home."

"And where's your home, sergeant?" Blythe asked, unable to resist the plea in the man's eyes.

"Indiana. And I sure hope I git back soon. You have a Merry Christmas, ma'am. Sorry for the intrusion."

Rafe was unaccountably annoyed by the sergeant. "Have the men check the barn and outbuildings. Remember what I told you . . . nothing is to be taken."

"Yes sir."

The sergeant and the other man disappeared out the door, leaving Blythe and Rafe alone in awkward silence.

Blythe didn't know what she was feeling at the moment. Emotions warred inside her like the discordant notes of a broken harpsichord. She wanted to touch him, to hold him, to whisper love words to him, yet part of her held back.

"Don't you think you should be conducting the search personally, Major?" Blythe asked. "You wouldn't want to miss anything." There were so many things causing her to hurt inside: his assumption that she had abandoned him, his coldness when he had arrived, his heartless search of her house.

The longing to feel his lips against hers.

She could have them again; she could have the strength of his body again. It was there in his eyes. Waiting. Wanting. Pleading.

But she knew it would be a mistake. He might stay or come back. He might, dear God, find Seth.

And she couldn't let that happen. Not for any of them.

She looked down at the ring on her finger. There was only one way she knew to send him away, to keep him away. Feeling as if a heavy hand had reached down and was squeezing her soul, she slowly took the ring off and held it out to him.

"Don't," he said achingly. "Please don't, Blythe."

"I didn't think we could ever be enemies, Rafe, but you just proved we are."

His face closed, a curtain falling over the vivid glittering eyes. Only a muscle flexing in his cheek revealed his emotion.

"Keep it," he said, his fist clenching in a knot to keep from touching her, from taking her in his arms. "I told you once I would not hold you to our engagement...."

"I held to it," Blythe said, hoping he would leave before her tears revealed themselves. "You didn't."

"I love you," he said stubbornly.

"Do you? You have a strange way of showing it."

His hand, almost under its own volition, reached out and folded her hand around the ring, pressing it there tightly. "I have to go, but I'll be back."

"Not like this, Rafe," she said softly. "Not as a Union officer invading my home."

He stood there, staring at her, not quite believing he had found her again, only to lose her. Then he whirled away from the penetrating golden eyes.

At the door, he turned around. "I've been assigned to Sheridan. If you need anything...?"

"I won't," she said, turning away, because now the tears were falling.

Rafe went out in the cold air, bracing himself against the chill both inside and outside. He watched his men search methodically through the buildings, knowing again it was wasted effort. Yet he sensed Blythe had been hiding something. He hoped not. For her sake, he hoped not.

He looked up at the sky. Christmas. It was Christmas morning now, although dawn was still several hours away. The empty place inside, the familiar black hole where he had hidden emotions for so long, yawned wide and deep.

Christmas. A time of celebration and joy. How wonderful it used to be as a boy! His was a large family—six children—and, at Christmas, Hampton Farms overflowed with laughter and love. The day was always climaxed by a play, presented by the combined efforts of the children as their Christmas gift to their parents.

Those times were a war away now. His father dead, one brother dead, another—Seth—an enemy. His oldest brother, Tristan, was in Santa Fe and had fought only briefly when Confederate forces marched into New Mexico. One sister had died giving birth, and the other was in South Carolina with his mother.

And Blythe. Beautiful, caring, compassionate Blythe. Mother now to how many orphans? She was more beautiful than ever; the grief and trouble had bestowed on her a loveliness born of character...not just surface attractiveness.

Dear God, he couldn't lose her now. But now, he knew, was not the time to press his case...not after he had so clumsily invaded her home, had told her he had not believed her commitment. They both needed time to allow their emotions to settle. But he knew he would not let her go.

And where was Seth this Christmas Eve? He had not seen a member of his family in nearly four years.

Dear Lord, but he was lonely. He had not known how much so until tonight. Or maybe he had. He just hadn't admitted it to himself.

The men were finishing, going to the trough now to water their horses before continuing on. Rafe took a last look around the farm he remembered so well. Everything was much the same...except the fences had once been filled with fine horses, and chickens had scratched happily outside a well-kept henhouse. And then he noticed the other things. The paint on the barn and the house, even in the pale moonlight, was faded and dingy. Part of the porch railing was sagging.

He thought of Blythe struggling to keep everything going. Whether she liked it or not, he would find a way to help. God help him, but he would find a way.

Distractedly he led his horse over to the trough.

The trough? There was something different about the trough. He remembered it as being inside the barn fence. He looked around and saw something on the ground and leaned down, touching it.

Blood.

And then Rafe remembered something else. The fruit cellar. It used to be around here; the three of them—his brother, Blythe and himself—had raided it enough times.

One thought led to another, each leading to a damning conclusion. His quarry was right below him.

He scuffed the blood stain with his boot, covering it with dirt as his mind ran over the ramifications of his discovery. If he were to alert his men and a Confederate general were found here, the Somers's farm was sure to be destroyed in retaliation. That was, he had discovered soon enough, the way of things in the Shenandoah Valley.

Rafe suddenly realized he had not really expected the general to be here, despite the tracks. Blythe had never been a fervent rebel, and her family had fought just as bitterly against secession as his own family had. Although her father and Seth had joined the South, they had done so reluctantly, out of loyalty to Virginia, not to the cause of slavery.

And Rafe also knew he had simply used the Confederate general as an excuse to see Blythe Somers.

Now he was caught in his own trap, for he could not let the man go, not when Sheridan thought the Confederate's capture could mean days, if not weeks, off the war.

He took one last look at the trough and hurried back to the front of the house where Blythe, now in a threadbare coat, had come out to watch. The sergeant met him there, shaking his head. "Nothing here, Sir."

Blythe spoke up. "I told your sergeant that Jaime and I went riding for greenery to decorate the house."

"Where are the horses?"

"Hidden from army thieves," Blythe said bitterly.

Rafe studied her face, and his heart constricted. She had learned to lie well in the past four years. She had probably needed to.

He turned to the sergeant. "Saddle the detail and follow the road. Search every residence. I'll do some looking on my own and meet you back at camp."

The sergeant looked at him curiously. He had seen the tension between the young lady and his new major. But he had not served under the officer long enough to interpret his moods. "Yes sir," he said cautiously.

Blythe turned around and went back into the kitchen without a word.

Rafe stood on the porch, his hand on the railing as he watched the troop ride away. As the last of the hoofbeats faded into the distance he returned to the kitchen.

Blythe was leaning against a wall, her face pale. Her father's pistol was in her hand, hidden in the folds of her skirt. The moment she had seen Rafe's eyes on the trough and his back stiffen, she knew he had found the hiding place. She had been surprised that he had sent his men away. But any illusions she had were quickly shattered.

"I want him," Rafe said softly. "I know he's in the fruit cellar."

"Then why didn't you tell your men?"

"I didn't want you hurt. I'll explain I found him somewhere else. I doubt he'll contradict me."

"Let them go," she pleaded.

"Them?"

Blythe bit her lip, knowing she had revealed more than she'd intended. "Please."

"I can't, Blythe. I think you know that."

"No, I don't know it," she cried stubbornly.

"How many are there?"

Blythe was silent.

Rafe drew his pistol and went to the door, striding out to the water trough. Blythe followed him out and watched as he lay down the gun and played with the wooden tub, trying to discover how it opened. As it started to move, he reached for the gun.

"Don't touch it, Rafe." Her voice was trembling slightly, but he didn't mistake the determination in it.

He turned around and stared into a pistol pointed directly at him.

Chapter Three

In the pale moonlight, Rafe's eyes raked over Blythe's stiff posture, the glint of tears in her eyes and the gun held quite firmly in her hands.

"You won't shoot," he said softly, his back now turned to the trough. His attention was so riveted on her he didn't hear the quiet sound of leather boots against the dirt of the cellar stairs.

"Perhaps she won't, brother, but I will. Your gun arm will do quite nicely. I know how to patch it up again." The voice was deadly serious.

Rafe stood straight as he heard the words from behind him. But he kept his eyes fastened on Blythe. "Seth?"

"None other. Now lay down the gun and stay very still. Blythe, give me your gun and get some rope. I don't want him tempted into doing something rash."

Rafe stooped gracefully and set down the gun, then turned around slowly, regarding his brother with a rueful smile. "I should have known it was you down there."

"It would have been much better if you had left it alone. Now I have to decide what to do with you."

Rafe ignored the implication of his words. It was Seth. Alive. Thin. Much too thin. But alive. Once more that night, a swell of joy, of deep though complicated pleasure, grew deep inside him. Despite Seth's warning and the gun held unwavering in his hand, Rafe couldn't quite stop the smile that twisted his lips.

"It's been a long time, Seth...good Lord, too long. Damn, but I'm glad to see you."

"Even under the circumstances?"

"Even under the circumstances," Rafe admitted slowly. His left eyebrow crooked upward in a disarming manner only too familiar to Seth. It usually foretold mischief. "Would you really shoot me?"

"I wouldn't like it, Rafe, but yes, I would."

"I wish I didn't believe you."

"Believe me, and save us both a great deal of pain."

Rafe was silent a moment, weighing the words. He didn't doubt them for a moment. Seth never bluffed. Rafe himself often did, but Seth, never. He was much too earnest for that, and had been since they were children.

"The war could be over sooner if I take him," Rafe finally ventured. "Lives saved on both sides..." It was, he knew, the only appeal that would work with Seth.

"And how would he fare in a Union hospital and prison?" Seth asked, not even bothering to debate the presence of the man below.

"Our interest is that he stay alive," Rafe answered frankly. "He'll have the best of care. I can promise that."

"He already has that," Seth retorted immodestly. "I think I'll trust my care above that of the Yankee surgeons. He won't tell you anything, anyway. And then what will you do with him? Put him in some damn Yankee pesthole of a prison?''

"If I don't get back to camp, my men will come looking for me."

"I doubt if they will ever find us in the fruit cellar, brother," Seth replied lazily. "You are the only one who knew it was here. It was damnable luck that you happened along."

Seth's tone was deceptive, Rafe knew. His brother's eyes were wary, missing nothing, and his body poised to act, his finger firm on the trigger. "You won't have any better luck from now on. The noose is tightening, Seth. The South can't last much longer."

"I know," Seth said softly. "All I can do is save as many lives as possible."

"I want Massey," Rafe insisted.

Seth shook his head slowly.

"You'll never get back with him alive."

"Perhaps. But right now I'm holding the gun. That doesn't make your position much better."

Rafe considered jumping Seth, but he didn't doubt for a moment that his brother would pull the trigger to protect the man under his care. And damned if he fancied sitting out the rest of the war in a hospital. Just as he was considering the odds, Blythe returned, a length of rope in her hand and a look of profound misery on her face.

"Clasp your hands together in front of you, Rafe," Seth said softly.

Rafe hesitated.

"Don't test me, Rafe. I don't want to spend Christmas sewing you up."

Rafe reluctantly did as he was told, and Seth nodded to Blythe to tie his brother's wrists. Blythe hesitated as she looked from one man to the other. The steely determination in the eyes of both told her something terrible might happen if she didn't. She slowly looped the rope around Rafe's wrists and drew it tight. But then she stopped. She had tied knots a hundred times in the barn when working with the horses, but now her hands fumbled with the rope, her fingers disobeying her mind's commands. She made the mistake of looking up at him, up into the eyes she had loved . . . still loved . . . so much.

They were fathomless, impenetrable. There was tension between the two brothers, but little real animosity, and for that, at least, she was supremely grateful. Yet neither of them, she knew, would back down; it was a supreme test of wills with Seth, who had the gun, having the advantage. Like Rafe, she believed he would do exactly what he said he would do. Nothing was more important to Seth than someone under his immediate care . . . not her, not his family. She had experienced his singlemindedness before.

Momentarily paralyzed, her hands remained unmoving on Rafe's wrists which were partially bound.

Seth handed her the two pistols he held and took the ends of the rope, which already were secure enough that Rafe couldn't quite jerk away. Tightening them, he tied surgeon knots that Rafe could not unravel.

As Rafe watched, Seth leaned down and picked up the gun his brother had placed on the ground beside the trough. Tucking the weapon into his worn frock coat, he took Rafe's arm, propelling him down the steep steps to where a candle lit the dim interior.

From beneath the thick quilt covering his body, the Confederate general stared at the newcomer in a blue military cloak.

Seth took the pistols from Blythe and dropped them into a worn leather bag and then moved quickly to the side of his patient. "It's all right. It was only one man, and we have him here."

The wounded man turned to Blythe, his pain-etched features strained. "I hope I haven't brought you trouble." He was only too aware of the reprisals often conducted by Union forces to families protecting Confederates.

Seth thought to reassure him. "I don't think so...I doubt this particular Yank will report it." He looked up at Rafe, who was standing against the wall of the cellar. "Sit down, Rafe."

The general looked confused at the familiar, even friendly tone as the Yank obediently slid to the ground and casually propped his tied wrists on one bent knee.

"My brother," Seth explained in a dry tone.

"Your brother?" The exclamation was weak but nonetheless concerned as the general scanned the stranger's campaign hat with the major's insignia on it. His eyes moved slowly across Rafe's face, resting on his alert and intelligent eyes.

"Every family has a rogue," Seth explained cheerfully as he grinned wearily and turned back to Rafe.

"And a fool," Rafe retorted. His eyes went from Blythe to Seth, recalling how well the two had worked together minutes earlier, his mind absorbing the knowledge that Seth had chosen to come here when in danger. The ache in him grew deeper as he realized how much the woman he loved had come to depend on his brother during the past four years. It was an excruciating thought, exacerbated by the poisonous jealousy he had felt during the past eighteen months. There was a bond between Seth and Blythe from which he had been excluded. And it hurt, God, how it hurt. Even though he could hold it against neither of them. He was the one who had left.

The general grimaced suddenly with pain, and Seth's hands soothed him before reaching for his medical bag. He took out a vial and mixed part of its contents in a cup with some water from the pail Blythe had fetched earlier. Seth lifted Massey's head and held the cup while the general sipped slowly, his hand moving convulsively with pain. In minutes, Massey's eyes closed and his breathing came easier.

Seth thanked God for the morphine Mosby's men had stolen from a Yank supply train. He leaned against the wall of the cellar. In the flickering light of the candle, he looked at Rafe, his brother, and Blythe, his friend. Rafe's eyes were wary and filled with smoldering anger... or perhaps some other emotion Seth couldn't identify. Blythe was still standing as if unsure of what to do. But her eyes reflected how much her heart was hurting.

"Hell of a Christmas," Seth said softly. "But I'm damned glad to see you alive."

Rafe's mouth was grim. "Hell of a Christmas is right. Would you have really shot me?"

"Yes," Seth replied frankly. "Though I would have been damned unhappy about it."

"That's comforting at least," Rafe said dryly.

"It's only that I don't have that much morphine left," Seth said with a slight grin. "And you always were a terrible patient. I remember when we had measles as kids...."

"You gave them to me," Rafe complained. "Anyway, it gives me some satisfaction to know I didn't misjudge you...I would have hated to give up my gun on a bluff.''

"Hell, you just hate to lose, period.''

A strained silence filled the air. The teasing, so common between them as boys and young men, only served to cover deeper emotions, emotions that were fettered. Emotions that had to remain that way. There was too much at stake for it to be otherwise. Yet memories pounded at the three of them...silent, accusing memories. Seth's throat choked with the thought of the closeness he and his brother, as the two youngest of a large boisterous family, had once shared.

Seth stood and walked over to Rafe, his hand going out to touch his brother's shoulder, to touch if not embrace. It lingered there, not wanting to lose contact after four years during which neither knew whether the other lived. He saw the same aching hurt in Rafe's eyes.

"I'm sorry," Seth whispered.

Rafe swallowed the lump that had risen in his chest. He nodded, and both knew it was his way of saying the same thing.

Seth looked at Blythe, and wondered how this small room could hold so much anguish. Misery was stark on Blythe's face, and Rafe's was closed in a way he remembered, in a manner that only happened when agony was too great to reveal. He had seen it that way once before...when their father had died.

They needed time alone, these two. His brother and Blythe. Perhaps he could help them reach each other again, heal the raw wounds that were so evident between them. This *was* Christmas.

Seth leaned over and checked the bonds around Rafe's wrists once more, his eyes mentally sizing the length of rope dropping from where the knot was tied. He then cut the remnant with a knife from his medical bag and used it to tie his brother's ankles together. Grimacing slightly with distaste for the necessity of doing so, he kept his eyes from Rafe's once-again bleak expression. He then looked around the cellar. There was nothing Rafe could use to free himself except the contents of his medical bag. He took that in hand.

"I think I'll have a little look around," he said.

"I'll go with you," Blythe said, suddenly afraid of being left alone with Rafe and all her tumultuous feelings.

"Someone has to stay with the general," Seth said gently. "And I think you and Rafe have some talking to do."

"There's . . . there's nothing to talk about," Blythe said wretchedly. "Not anymore."

"I think there is, or you wouldn't look so infernally unhappy." He turned to Rafe. "Sometimes you can be a damned idiot."

On that brotherly note, he left, leaving the trough almost but not completely in place so that he could descend rapidly if need be. Pulling his gray coat around him against the cold, he went to the old oak tree paces away and swung up on a strong lower branch, settling himself against the trunk. From his perch he could hear hoofbeats during the silent night, probably long before riders appeared. Feeling infinitely lonely, he looked up, searching for the North Star.

Nearly two thousand years before, a birth had heralded peace on earth.

Would it ever come?

And would any peace come to the two people he loved best in the world?

A silence settled between Rafe and Blythe. Their eyes locked together, searching, wary, guarded. Her eyes involuntarily went down to his bound hands, and his own eyes followed her gaze.

Rafe waited for her to speak.

He stretched his legs uncomfortably, now that they were bound together. But despite the restraint, he looked to Blythe like a graceful, lazy cat. Lazy and deceptively dangerous.

"You wouldn't consider untying me?" he said finally.

She shook her head slowly, wishing at the moment she was anyplace else. Or did she?

"Do you see much of Seth?" It wasn't the question he wanted to ask, but it came, anyway. God, he hated the jealousy that still nagged at him.

"In the beginning," Blythe answered slowly, seeing the glitter in his eyes and not entirely understanding its cause. "Now it's terribly dangerous for him." She paused, then continued as much to break the uncomfortable silence as to impart any information. "He designed the trough," she said. "Without it, we might have starved. The Confederates raided us, then the Yanks, then the Confederates again."

Rafe looked around, at the closing above. "It's very clever, but then Seth has always been very clever."

"He's been a very good friend. I don't know what we would have done without him," she said hesitantly, partially happy that the subject had moved away from themselves. Yet there was something in Rafe's expression, something raw and wounded.

"It's been very hard for you, hasn't it?" His voice gentled, and there was some of the old tenderness in it.

"No worse than for many others. Perhaps even better. I still have a roof, some food, a farm. Not many have that anymore." It was said matter-of-factly, with no pity or accusation. Rafe had followed his conscience, as had Seth. That their consciences led them down different paths did nothing to make either of them lesser men.

But she saw the shadows cross Rafe's face in the flickering candlelight and wondered about the horrors he had seen, had participated in. Her hand reached out to touch the sleeve of his uniform.

"Where have you been?"

"Every place there was hell," he said. "Shiloh, Vicksburg, Chickamauga, Atlanta, the march through Georgia. That, I think, was the worst. We had orders to burn everything—homes, barns, whole towns." His hands clenched together, and Blythe could only imagine the nightmare he was reliving. She touched his hands, trying to ease some of the tension so evident in them.

He looked down and smiled wryly. "I tried to stay away from Virginia, Blythe, from something like this. God, how I tried, even as I was aching for you, to be with you, to help you. Even..."

"Even when you thought I had married your brother?" Now there was pain in her voice, in her face.

"Even then...perhaps especially then. It hurt, God it hurt, but I love both you and Seth . . . nothing could have changed that."

"You were so cold when you came tonight."

"I thought by being cold, distant, perhaps I wouldn't grab you as I wanted, to hold you close as I have dreamed so many nights." Rafe was silent for a moment, holding her hand as if it were a lifeline. "Then I saw the ring and knew I had been wrong, and damn, everything else happened." He laughed bitterly. "My timing was not the best."

"Would you have come . . . even without orders?"

"Ah, Blythe. You can't imagine how I felt when I was ordered this way . . . wanting to see you, afraid to see you." His hands trembled with emotion held tightly inward. "I tried my damnedest not to come here from Savannah, but when the orders were finalized, I think I was elated. Elated and scared." His wrists strained against the rope as he tried to take more of her hand in his. "Tonight when I knew I had to come by here, I felt like a small boy about to take the whipping of his life. Wanting to put it off, wanting to get it over with." He shook his head. "God, I wanted to see you . . . but . . ." He stopped, hesitating. Then slowly, he continued, "I didn't expect to find anything . . . certainly not a Confederate general, knowing how you felt about the war."

Both of their eyes turned to the sleeping officer. "He's wounded, Rafe."

"And then there was Seth?"

"Yes," she said, seeing the pain return once more to his face. But it disappeared quickly under a wry grin.

"You always did bring home every injured critter you could find," he said. "Remember that baby fox? I thought your father would have apoplexy."

Her hand clutched his tighter with the memory. "You rode two days to release him far enough away that he couldn't return and raid our chickens... so Papa wouldn't shoot him." She looked at the back of his hand, which still carried a bite scar from that fox, and felt waves of love for him. Like Seth, he had a deep compassionate streak, but Rafe had always hid it well under an easy smile and mischievous, teasing eyes. Now there was a bitter facade around the heart that had always been so giving, so warm, but she suspected those qualities still there. Walled, perhaps, because that was the only way he could survive the war. But still there. She had seen them earlier in the kitchen with Jaime, and when he so carefully and quietly searched the house so as not to disturb the children.

But she had not wanted to recognize it as that. She had been too afraid for Seth and the wounded man. So she had protected herself with anger, just as he had protected himself with coldness when they first met. The anger that had frothed in her earlier had slowly seeped away. He was Rafe. Beloved Rafe, who had come back to her.

And dear God, she was trembling with need for him, need to have his arms around her.

It was as if he read her mind. With a questioning look, he lifted his hands high above her, and wordlessly invited her to snuggle up to him. She needed no second invitation.

Blythe fit her curves into his, and felt his arms go around her, his bound wrists tight against her waist.

She felt his lips on her hair, and then alongside her cheeks. Tender, soft, wistful, yearning.

"My God, I love you. I've missed you," he finally whispered.

It was enough, at the moment, to relax against him, to let her hands touch and caress his long strong fingers, the back of his hands burned brown with sun. She drew them up to her mouth and showered them with kisses, letting her tongue lick the cool skin, and feeling his body tense under her ministrations.

All the old feelings were flowing between them...the tenderness they had shared, the strong emotional love, the barely restrained passion that had so tormented them. There were still questions, still hesitancy, still wariness, but those were submerged in the joy of their touching, of sharing the warmth of their bodies.

Rafe silently cursed the ropes that bound him, for he could not touch her the way he wished, but he would not ruin this moment by asking for something that could reestablish the barriers they had just so carefully, so tentatively, breached. His arms tightened around her, feeling the thinness of her body under the coat. Once more, he felt rivers of guilt running through him. He had not been here when her father died...when she had needed someone. As she still did. He looked around the nearly empty fruit cellar, totaling the few pitiful supplies. What food she could scrounge probably went to her young orphans.

"Tell me about the children," he said. "How many are there?" He had seen bundles wrapped in blankets but had not stopped to count them. He had not wanted to disturb them more than he had.

"Ten now," Blythe said in a voice that was like music to him. "Soon to be another. One of the girls is pregnant, raped by a Union soldier. She's ready to give birth any time now.''

She felt him tense at her words, at her mention of rape by a Union soldier.

"It could just as well have been a Southern one," Blythe continued in a world-weary voice that pierced him to the core. "The gallantry left this war a long time ago."

"How old is she?"

"Fourteen. She was the one who cried out when you came into the room. She's terrified of all uniforms."

"I'm sorry, Blythe. So damned sorry I had to search the house."

She rested her head against his heart, listening to its steady beat. Her own heart stopped a moment as she heard the raw anguish in his voice. Now secure in his arms, she understood. He had done what he had to do, just as Seth had done what he had to do by threatening the brother he loved and tying him up. Both Hamptons had an overabundant sense of honor and duty. Perhaps, she thought, that was why she loved them both so much. Yet while she realized it, she also felt a deadening sense of fear that this was not over, that the play was not finished.

Dear God, what was going to happen? How were any of them going to get out of this tragedy between two brothers? Between the three of them? She shifted slightly in his arms and looked up at his face, and saw the same deep worry there.

His lips came down and caught hers, and she was swept away on a voyage of infinite tenderness, a gentleness spurred in both of them by fear—not physical fear but the fear of doing irreparable damage to those they loved best in the world. The touch was so fragile, so yearning, that Blythe wanted to die with the bittersweet longing of it.

He had taken off his cocky cavalry hat, and now she fondled a tuft of hair that fell over his forehead, then moved her hand to the back of his head and lost it in the thick dark richness of his hair.

His lips hardened on her mouth, and she could feel the barely leashed emotions in his every movement. The rope bit into her side, where it strained against his bound wrists, and she knew it must be agonizing for him. Yet there was something more painful that hung between the two of them...the hunger of years wasted, and dreams unfulfilled, of lonely days and nights, of wounded hearts and longing souls. The passion that had been building between them roared into bright painful flames.

Blythe felt her bones quiver as the kiss deepened. It reached down into the most lonely part of her...and filled her with a quiet joy. Christmas. And he was giving her the greatest gift in the world. Love. The urgent pressure of his lips searched and promised and gave, and she responded in kind, wanting him to share the glorious oblivion of these few moments that were theirs alone. His lips parted, and his tongue sought entrance to her mouth, nuzzling and teasing until her lips opened and he made his loving invasion.

They had stolen kisses before, quiet passionate kisses, but there had always been a reserve between them. They had known they would be married, and they had decided to wait. It had been the way she had been raised, and he had respected that. Neither of them had realized, until too late, that it would be months, perhaps years, before their vows could be said. Certainly neither had expected four years to pass.

Now their passion was deep and wild, having been denied so long.

And uncontrollable.

Rafe's tongue seduced. It probed and teased and loved. An exquisite tingling started in her, in a place deep and secret, and reached to her toes, to the tips of her fingers. It made her tremble with a need overwhelming in its urgency.

He suddenly, almost violently, withdrew his lips. "God in heaven," he groaned. "I need you. I need you so much."

Her lips still red and swollen, Blythe leaned back against his arms and watched the violent emotions cross his face.

"I love you," she whispered. "I'll always love you."

"Even an invader?" The question was part bitter, part wistful.

"*This* invader," she replied, nestling securely back into him, stretching her head to deliver a feather-light yet promising kiss.

"Oh, Blythe, I don't know how I stood the last two years... when I thought I had lost you. There were times..."

Her hand went to his face. "Don't say it. I know. If it hadn't been for the children and Seth...at least I had them. And when I didn't hear from you, when there was no word, no letters, I was so afraid. Yet I knew. I knew in my heart you weren't dead, because then I would have died, too. I would have known. Somehow I would have known." A tear snaked down her cheek.

"I'm sorry, love. God, I'm sorry," he said with a huskiness she had never heard in his voice before. "I thought... it would be better for you... and Seth." There was so much pain in the words that she raised her hand and touched his mouth, telling him silently that it didn't matter. Not now.

"My pretty Blythe. My lovely Blythe," he said, closing his eyes and his mind against the future, against tomorrow. He moved slightly, and his wrists stung like hell as the rope bit farther into him, reminding him only too well of the situation. He opened his eyes again, and he looked at the Confederate general.

Could his capture really shorten the war? Lessen the number of casualties these last weeks were sure to bring? He wondered. But Sheridan seemed so damnably sure. If there was the slightest chance...

But his brother would never let his patient go without a fight. Seth had indicated he would stop him with a bullet if necessary, but Rafe knew he couldn't do the same. He was too damned accurate with a pistol, and he had none of Seth's surgical skill. Still, he might bluff.

What in the hell could he do with his hands bound like this? Which was, he knew, exactly why Seth had done it. And trusted Blythe not to interfere. His brother had known Rafe would never ask it of her, never ask her to make a choice between loyalties of a lifetime.

Seth had changed. And hardened.

As if his very thoughts had summoned his brother, the door above opened, and Seth descended, a slight smile of satisfaction obvious on his face as he saw Blythe tucked in Rafe's arms.

"That must be deucedly uncomfortable," he observed as he saw the deep red marks in Rafe's wrists. "I'll cut you loose, if you swear you haven't seen anything."

Rafe slowly shook his head. "I can't do that, Seth. Besides, you know you can't get far. Our troops will be swarming the area, looking for him, looking for me."

Seth grinned rakishly despite his tired look. "I should have some assistance myself when I don't reach Richmond."

Rafe's eyes met Seth's. Blythe turned around and stared at both of them.

"Dear Mother in heaven," she said. "The children."

It was then that all three realized the Somers's farm could be caught directly in the middle of two armies. Just as they were all silently struggling for an answer, there was a scrabbling on the door and they all heard Jaime's panic-stricken voice.

"Miss Blythe, Miss Blythe. Maria's baby is on the way, and she's hurting something awful."

Chapter Four

Blythe ducked from under Rafe's bound arms.

Seth took a quick look at his general, saw that the man still slept peacefully and quickly calculated that his patient should continue that way for several more hours.

He grabbed the bag he had just dropped, took out a knife and quickly cut the rope around Rafe's ankles. "Rafe, you'll have to come with us. I need Blythe, and I won't leave you alone with General Massey."

Rafe shrugged and lazily got to his feet, sliding up the wall of the fruit cellar.

"You first," Seth said to him, and Rafe led the way, meeting the young boy at the top of the stairs. Jaime's quick wary eyes rested on Rafe's wrists, then went to Seth in puzzlement.

"Cap'n Seth?" he said. He had not known the man who had so often brought them food and other supplies was at the farm. He had frantically searched for Blythe, ending at the fruit cellar in one last desperate attempt to find her. He had thought all the Yankees had gone, having heard the hoofbeats retreat and seen them leave through the window. He had stayed and comforted the younger ones and, hearing no alarm from Blythe, had fallen asleep himself until he heard Maria's cries. Now he wondered what had gone on: the Yankee officer tied; Cap'n Seth, whom he knew to be a doctor, seeming to be in charge. His eyes went to the entrance of the fruit cellar, wondering if more mysteries were below, but Seth quickly closed the door before he could see anything.

His momentary puzzlement fled, however, when all three of them heard a scream, and Seth hurried toward the house, his complete concentration focused on the girl within. Even muffled by the windows, the scream sounded frantic.

His footsteps turned into a half run, and Blythe followed quickly, Rafe by her side, Jaime behind them. Blythe and Seth went through the front door and up the staircase, taking the steps two at a time as another scream came.

Rafe, forgotten for the moment except by Jaime, remained at the bottom of the steps. He gave the boy a rueful smile. "I don't think we're needed at the moment," he said.

The boy stared at the Yank's wrists suspiciously, not certain what he should do.

"They might need some hot water," Rafe offered helpfully.

Jaime glared at him. His experience with soldiers, with the exception of Cap'n Seth, had been uniformly unfavorable. "I ain't leaving you alone."

Rafe wanted to smile, but decided it wouldn't be wise at this moment. He wondered whether his ego could survive this night. Captured by a doctor, guarded by a woman, and now a boy. His men would have a big belly laugh if they learned of it. But by then, he intended to be free, and firmly in control of the Confederate general. His heart lurched as he thought how such an action might once more build a wall between him and Blythe.

But he had no choice. None at all.

"I'll go with you," he offered helpfully to the boy.

Jaime hesitated, looking at the man carefully. Now that he thought about it, this Yank looked a lot like Cap'n Seth. "You and Cap'n Seth related?" he asked.

"Brothers," Rafe replied cheerfully.

"Then why did he tie ya?"

Rafe shrugged. "I 'spect he didn't want me to get in any trouble." So the boy didn't know about the Confederate in the cellar.

Jaime knit his brows together as he tried to understand. It didn't make sense to him.

Rafe noted the confusion. "The water," he reminded the boy gently.

Jaime nodded. Miss Blythe said the tall lean Yankee had been a neighbor, and she certainly had seemed unafraid of him. And he was Cap'n Seth's brother. He couldn't be too bad. Some of Jaime's hard-earned caution seeped away. "Go first," he said.

Rafe led the way into the kitchen he knew so well. It still smelled of apple pie and spices. He looked out the window. It was dark, but it must be close to dawn now. Christmas day. Renewal. Hope. Joy. He had been given all in the past few hours, the most precious gifts of all.

Yet, duty nagged at him, digging its claws in a heart that wanted nothing more than to spend this Christmas with the woman and brother he loved.

Duty's call.

Heart's call.

They were warring each other inside him.

He sat in the window seat and stared out at the last blinking stars of the night. The moon's brightness was already fading and soon there would be a glow to the east.

There was another scream, and he flinched at the sound of it. The boy, Jaime, had finished lighting the fire in the woodstove and was putting a pail of water on it. When he finished, Jaime started stacking wood in the huge fireplace that dominated the kitchen.

Rafe looked around the kitchen until his eyes found what he was searching for. He quietly moved several steps until his hands reached a kitchen knife. His right fist grasped it and started sawing through the rope just as Jaime turned around. The boy's eyes widened as the pieces of rope fell to the ground.

Jaime started for the door to warn Cap'n Seth and Miss Blythe, but strong hands grabbed him and one went over his mouth. He twisted and squirmed, but realizing his helplessness he finally quieted.

"I'll not hurt anyone," Rafe said in a low voice. "Not if you keep still. Do you understand?"

Jaime tensed, every muscle and bone in his thin body rebelling. Yet he didn't know what to do. The Yank was much too strong for him. Slowly, he nodded.

Rafe let him go, yet his hands were ready when Jaime bolted for the door, and once more the boy was caught tightly. "I don't want to tie you, Jaime."

The boy squirmed around, his wrist in the steellike grasp of the Yankee. "What are ya going to do?"

That, Rafe thought, was an excellent question. He wished he knew the answer. "I don't want to hurt anyone," he repeated, avoiding the question.

"You ain't like Cap'n Seth." The accusing observation burned a raw, hurtful hole in Rafe. He had always been good with children. But then that was years ago, before war had altered him. The hole gaped wider as Rafe recalled the admiring looks the boy had given Seth, while his own presence was surveyed with deep suspicion and dislike.

"No," he said slowly. "I suppose I'm not. But I love your Miss Blythe. Does that count for something?"

"'Pends on what you do with it," the boy responded skeptically but with a wisdom, Rafe thought, far beyond his years.

Heart's call. Duty's call.

Rafe could not find a reply to Jaime's observation. Instead, he went over to the stove and picked up the now-boiling water. "Let's take the water up. You lead the way."

The boy hesitated, then finally moved toward the stairs.

"The baby's turned around," Seth told Blythe. Maria bit her teeth on a piece of cloth to hold back another scream. Her dark eyes were filled with pain and fear.

"It will be all right, Maria," Seth said softly, "and you'll have a fine Christmas baby. Just hold on. Do you know what you'll call him?"

Maria's tear-glazed eyes lit. "Yes, sir, I know."

"But you're not telling?" Seth teased, knowing the next few moments were going to be extraordinarily painful while he tried to turn the baby around.

"No, sir," Maria said. "It's . . . bad luck." She gritted the last out as another terrible pain ripped through her.

"Just a few more moments, Maria," Seth said. "Damn, I need some hot water to wash, Blythe. And you'd better check on Rafe. . . ."

"Too late." The drawl came from the doorway, and Seth spun around. Rafe's rangy form leaned against the doorjamb. One of his hands held a steaming bucket of water; the other, a gun Seth recognized as his own, the one he had left on the table outside the room. "Damn," Seth whispered.

Rafe ignored the comment. "Where do you want the water?"

Seth nodded to a table beside the bed.

Rafe set down the water. His eyes went to the bureau where two guns lay, probably taken from the medical bag in haste when Seth reached the pregnant girl's side. Rafe scooped them up quickly before Seth could react. His brother eyed him ruefully, but then he leaned back over Maria as her body convulsed, and an animallike noise came from deep in her throat. Seth ignored Rafe and washed his hands. Unlike most physicians, he had come to believe that cleanliness was the best weapon against infection.

He darted a look at Rafe. "Hell of a Christmas," he said, repeating his words of several hours earlier.

Rafe said nothing as he holstered his own gun and pocketed Blythe's, tucking Seth's into his belt. Damn, but he felt like an arsenal. He looked at Blythe's tired face and wondered how long it had been since she had slept. She looked as if she would drop any moment. Yet her hands were steady as they held the girl's.

"I'll wait outside," he finally said, and, turning, he faced a group of children, all of them looking at him as if he were the devil incarnate.

"Is Maria gonna die?" one small girl managed fearfully.

Seth turned from where he was washing. "No, sweetheart. She's going to be just fine." He raised his eyes to Rafe. "Take care of them, will you?" he said, totally ignoring the gun. "I need Blythe." Seth turned back to his patient, sure Rafe would do exactly as told.

Rafe stood there, towering above a number of small, strange faces, all obviously terrified.

A tiny hand clutched at his blue trouser leg. "I'm 'fraid," a small trembling voice said.

Rafe felt something he hadn't felt in a long time. But then he was feeling many things he hadn't felt in a long time. He hadn't let himself. But now the walls were coming down, and his heart quaked, his stomach tightened with need. Need to reassure, need to help, need to comfort.

Need to belong.

He knelt down until his eyes met the boy's. "What is your name?"

"B...B...Benji," came the stuttered reply.

"Well, Benji, everything is going to be fine. Maria...is it Maria?" At a nod, he continued. "Maria is going to have a fine baby. My brother, Cap'n Seth, is the best doctor there is."

"You're a soldier," accused a voice. "Are you gonna rob us?" The words were said in a resigned tone and with the general assumption that robbing was what all soldiers did.

"No," Rafe said softly, his heart hurting at what these children must have endured. He looked at the thin, pale faces, the frightened eyes, the stiff bodies, and thought about his own childhood. God, it had been happy. Happy and safe and full of love. There had been six of them, four brothers and two sisters, and a mother and father who had provided all the security, the safety, the love one could ever desire. Christmas had been a marvelous time of gaiety and magic. Not fear.

But that was all he saw in these children.

There was a muffled cry from inside the room, and tears started down Benji's cheeks.

Rafe picked him up. "Let's all go down to the parlor," he said, "and I'll tell you a story."

The gaggle of children looked at him dubiously, Jaime most of all, but finally, hesitantly, one of the girls nodded, and then another.

Rafe, holding Benji, led the way. He knew the house nearly as well as his own. When he reached the parlor, he saw the children's eyes widen as they saw the boughs of holly wrapped in the red ribbon, and then their eyes went to the scarves and dolls lying out.

"Father Christmas," said a minute-size imp with black hair and an expression of awe.

They all looked to Rafe for confirmation. "Must have been," he agreed.

Rafe carefully placed Benji down and leaned over, looking at one of the dolls. It had a paper with a name written on it. "Benji. This says Benji," and he was rewarded with a huge smile. The second doll had "Suzie" written on it.

"Suzie?"

The smallest of the girls hung back, looking longingly at the gift but fearfully at Rafe. Once more, an aching pain filtered through him as the child flinched when he reached over to hand the doll to her. But she took it, and he regarded that as a victory.

"You're not Father Christmas!" accused one of the girls with narrowed eyes.

"No, little darlin'," he said. "I'm afraid not." All of a sudden, he wished he had something in his saddlebags . . . some sweet, some food, something. All he had was a story.

There was another cry from upstairs, and nine pairs of eyes looked up toward the staircase. "Maria's gonna die," said one girl. "That's what happened to my ma. She was having another baby." It was said so matter-of-factly that Rafe's heart turned.

Good Lord, what was happening to him? He should be thinking about the Confederate general outside. But his mind, instead, was filled with the luminous green-gold eyes of Blythe upstairs, and the frightened ones of the children down here.

The general. Damn it, the confounded general. Massey's capture could shorten the war. The general knew Lee's plans. Not that he would talk, not willingly, but with right questioning Massey could let something slip. Something important. And nothing was more vital than that. Not himself, not Seth. Nothing was more important than trying to shorten this damnable war. Rafe tried desperately to convince himself of that.

"Story," Benji demanded, his fingers tugging on Rafe's leg.

Damn, the general wasn't going anyplace. A few more minutes wouldn't make any difference.

Rafe went to a desk and placed Blythe's gun in one drawer, and Seth's in another, leaving his own in its holster. He didn't want the children jostling one of the weapons and possibly discharging it. He then sat down in the soft leather chair that used to be Blythe's father's favorite resting place. Benji crawled up on his knee, and the others sat around him, peering skeptically at him. Jaime stood suspiciously in the doorway.

"Once upon a time," Rafe started a bit awkwardly. Damn, but it had been a long time. Could he even remember the words from those Christmases when he and his brothers and sisters had sat at their father's feet and listened avidly to the Christmas story? No matter how many times his father had told it, he had always made it fresh and exciting, adding some new little twist of his own. He would invent a burro named Sam, or an angel named after one of his daughters, or a stubborn shepherd named Rafe . . . or Seth. Rafe smiled at the memory.

But it had been years now, and Rafe had ignored the season the last three Christmases. It was too painful. He on one side of this bloody war, his brothers on another. It wasn't so bad for Seth. He saved lives. And that avocation had little to do with the color of uniforms. But he, Rafe, had taken them. Many of them. Too damned many of them. And each and every one would always haunt him. He had built a shell around his heart, his emotions. It had been the only way to survive.

"Once upon a time," prompted a girlish voice, and Rafe looked over to her.

"What's your name, darlin'?"

"Suzie," the girl replied shyly, ducking her head as she did.

"And you?" he asked the next child.

"Abraham," the boy said, "and this is my brother, Micah," he volunteered about the boy next to him.

Then there was Margaret, Sarah, Katy and July. He smiled slightly at the last name, wondering briefly if he would ever get them straight, and he particularly wondered how in tarnation Blythe had been able to care for them all.

"Story," Benji prodded. His head, now on Rafe's chest, felt just like it should, warm and sweet.

"Once upon a time," he started again, "in a faraway land...a very faraway land, there was a girl, just like Maria, who was about to have a child." It was strange how all the words came back after so many years, and how quickly the little faces became awestruck with the story.

"...So into Bethlehem they came...looking for an inn, for a place for Mary to stay. It was cold, very cold, and Mary was very tired." His deep baritone voice, rich and warm, had settled into a rhythm, and the children moved closer to him, like pieces of metal drawn to a magnet.

"Just like me and Margaret," said Benji, snuggling farther into his arms.

"And me," said Suzie.

"And me," chimed another.

"And we found Miss Blythe," said a fourth.

His throat tightened, and his chest pounded. Blythe had mentioned the children so easily, yet in the confusion and heightened emotions of the evening he had not truly understood the extent of their need...nor Blythe's commitment. While he had been causing this destruction, she had been gathering its tiny victims.

Blythe. His giving, beautiful Blythe.

"But for Mary," he said gently, "there was no place in the inn...."

A few of them knew the story, but others did not, and their eyes opened wider as they squirmed with curiosity.

"But a kind innkeeper said they could rest in the stable, and there, with all the animals watching, Mary's baby was born." There was a joint sigh of relief among the listeners. Rafe looked up at the doorway where Jaime still stood sentry. The young boy's face had softened with the alluring magic of Rafe's deep, drawling voice and the retelling of a story Jaime had heard as the boy he no longer considered himself.

"And shepherds faraway were visited by angels and told of the small baby, and they traveled many miles to see the child...."

"Like you?" asked one of the small pixies.

He grinned. He had forgotten how children loved questions that were unanswerable.

"Like me," he conceded wryly. Some shepherd! Armed with anger and guns.

"What's an angel like?"

He thought for a moment. A spiritual being draped in white? Would they understand that? No, something they could see and comprehend.

"Like Miss Blythe," he answered finally, his throat once more constricting.

Suzie nodded with satisfaction. "I *love* Miss Blythe."

"I do, too," Rafe admitted a bit awkwardly.

"What happened to the baby?" said one impatient voice.

"He grew up and was called the Prince of Peace."

"Where is he?"

"He died a long time ago," Rafe said.

"Is that why there's war?"

Again a question without answers. Why was there war? Principle? Wealth? Land? Honor? Were any of them worth the pain it caused? *Dear Lord, I wish you could answer that for me.*

"I don't know, darlin'," he said, and they all fell silent, each aware of the war's rage outside the warmth and security of this house.

Honor!

That damned general. He had to get the man out of the cellar and back to camp. He had to!

He lifted Benji up and started to suggest that the children go back to bed.

But the girl he knew as Margaret tugged on his hand. "Sir," she said in a small shy tone.

He looked down, his mouth gentling once more, and waited for her to speak.

"We...we want to give Miss Blythe a present, but we don't have anything."

There was a muffled sound from upstairs, and all the heads once more turned anxiously to the staircase. Rafe had an inspiration. "When I was a boy, I had lots of brothers and sisters...like you. Each Christmas we gave a play for our mother and father that told the story of Christmas. I think Miss Blythe would like that very much."

He was very pleased with himself when eight faces beamed up at him. Only Jaime's dour look remained unchanged.

The general. He would be able to take the general back now.

"Willya help us?" Benji said, his small, narrow face earnestly pleading.

"Yes sir, please," added a quiet little girl who had been still until now. It was July, he thought. A girl named July.

The general could wait.

Rafe thought about the production for several seconds, then paused conspiratorially. "First we need..."

While the children scurried off in search of the items Rafe mentioned, he went up to the bedroom and knocked lightly. The door was opened by Blythe, her face tired but her mouth smiling.

"It's a girl," she whispered, nodding over to Seth who was washing a tiny little bit of humanity. Rafe caught a glimpse of little arms and legs, and that was all.

"I'll tell the others," Rafe said, noticing that his brother was still well-occupied and hopefully would be for a while. He had all the guns now, he thought, except Jaime's old musket, and he wasn't overly worried about that now. He had his own, Blythe's and the one Seth had. He rather suspected that weapon had come from General Massey, since Seth wore no holster.

Blythe looked surprised when she heard one of the children in the hall behind him. "They're still up?"

"I don't think they could have gone back to sleep until they knew about their Maria," Rafe said ruefully.

Seth turned around, a small smile on his face. "Keeping you busy?"

Rafe shrugged and turned around, feeling like the Pied Piper as Benji, Margaret, Suzie and the others began to gather behind him.

"Maria's fine," Rafe explained gently. "She has a baby girl."

"Just like Jesus," said Benji.

"Jesus was a boy," Suzie scolded scornfully.

"But it's a miracle all the same," Rafe said. "So Benji's right."

"What about the play?" Margaret whispered.

Rafe, glad to be diverted, quickly took the children back downstairs and staged a rehearsal, helping Benji tuck a sheet around himself as a costume of sorts. He did the same with the others, appointing Margaret as Mary and Suzie and the other girls as angels. He came to Jaime.

"Do you want to be Joseph?" he asked.

Jaime regarded him carefully as if it were some trap and shook his head.

"Then Benji can be Joseph. What would you . . ." he started to ask Jaime.

"Nothing," Jaime said rudely. "I'll watch out for the damn Yankees for Cap'n Seth."

Rafe flinched at the obvious rejection, then shrugged. He finished assigning parts and going over everyone's lines, finishing as quickly as he could. He then lifted Benji, Joseph's sheet and all, and carried him to his bedroom upstairs while Jaime and Margaret saw to the others. He started to tuck the small body in when two arms reached up around his neck and hugged him tightly, giving him a wet kiss.

"Willya watch me be Joseph?" he asked with six-year-old anxiety.

Rafe looked out the window. It was dawn. A thin layer of silver was stretching over the horizon.

He needed to return to camp. With General Massey. And he needed to do it while Seth was still occupied.

"Please...."

Perhaps the damned general could wait a few hours longer. He would keep an eye on Seth.

He finally nodded and received a beatific smile in response.

Weary, thoroughly exasperated with himself for succumbing so easily to what he now believed was Seth's insidious plan to keep him busy with the children, he started to rise, only to find Blythe framed in the door, her mouth curved wonderingly. *How long had she been there?*

"You're very good with him," she said as she came toward him and put her hand in his.

He grinned wryly. "It would be difficult not to be...he's so...affectionate." Needy was more the word for it, he thought. A deep need for security and safety.

She gave him a puzzled look. "Not usually," she said. "Not with strangers."

"Probably because I look like Seth...they all seem fond of him." There was a lonely vulnerability in his voice that reached out to Blythe.

She tightened her hold on his hand. "Do you want to see the baby?"

Rafe looked down at her face. In the dim light of the dawning day, her face appeared infinitely soft and beautiful, her eyes wide and luminous. He could no more say no to her than shoot her.

He nodded, and she led the way back to the room. The baby had been washed and was now settled sleepily in her mother's arms. Maria looked impossibly young, but she had a contented glow as she held the tiny bundle next to her. Her eyes changed only slightly as they regarded the blue uniform with apprehension.

"He's a friend," Blythe said, and the girl relaxed. In seconds there was soft breathing, and the three of them—Rafe, Blythe and Seth—exchanged glances as they realized Maria was finally asleep.

"She'll be all right?" Rafe asked.

Blythe nodded. "Thanks to Seth." Then with a breathtaking smile, she added, "Maria's named the baby Blythe."

Seth smiled, looking uncommonly pleased with himself until his eyes fastened on Rafe and traveled down to the gun still tucked in his brother's uniform trousers. "What now, Rafe?"

"I have to take him back. You know that," Rafe replied softly.

"If the general goes, I go," Seth said. "He's badly wounded... I don't trust your prison doctors."

"Then you'll join him as a prisoner. You probably couldn't stay with him, anyway. Don't be a fool."

Seth shrugged. "Part of the job." He turned toward the door. "And speaking of General Massey, I need to check on him."

"Seth!" Rafe's voice held a sharp warning.

Seth turned back. "You'll have to kill me to stop me." Then he turned around and walked slowly, almost tauntingly, down the stairs.

Chapter Five

Rafe cursed to himself. Seth had always had a way of making him feel wrong. Even when Rafe knew he was right.

And damn it, he was right this time.

He stood there hesitantly, seeing Blythe's eyes on him, reading her thoughts.

How much soldier stood there? How much brother? How much lover? He could see each question reflected in her eyes.

And he didn't know. God help him, he didn't know.

He had known when he had arrived here hours ago. He had been all soldier then. But the past hours had made him uncertain.

Uncertain about right and wrong, about love and duty, about honor.

Where did honor lie in this case?

He had been so sure earlier. Now he wondered. The war was nearly over. The south was battered; only its pride was keeping it going. What good would one general make now? He had seen General Massey's face; it had been determined even in pain. He would never talk, never reveal any plans. In any event, the man's wounds would probably keep him out for the remainder of the war. And Seth was right. The general, with his wounds, might easily die in a Union prison. They were all bad, worse than bad. More like hell. And Seth . . . what would prison do to Seth if he persisted in accompanying the general? Which he would. Rafe didn't doubt that for a second.

Pain struck deep and raw and bleeding within him. Dear God, there had been enough death in his family. In so many families.

But even as he sought justification to disregard orders, dismiss duty, he knew it wasn't that simple. Near defeat as it was, the Confederacy was still delivering lethal blows to Union forces. The coming fight for Petersburg and Richmond would be devastating in terms of dead and wounded. If there was any chance, any chance at all, to unravel Lee's plans or do injury by depriving him of one of his principal aides, Rafe had to take it. Regardless of the personal cost to him or his.

Damn. Goddamn it.

He looked at Blythe. Her shoulders were slumped with exhaustion; her eyes, though still glowing about the birth, were nonetheless not nearly as wide and alert as usual. He had seen the same signs in Seth, and God knew he himself was tired.

"Go to bed," he said gently, dismissing for the moment his heavier thoughts. He put his fingers to her cheek, caressing it. "The children are all in bed and should sleep awhile."

"You and Seth?" she asked anxiously.

"I think we can arrange a truce for a few hours."

"I'll go with you," she replied with a trace of suspicion.

"No." Rafe's tone was firm. "I need some time alone with him."

"You won't..."

He leaned down and kissed her cheek. "No, love, I won't do anything. Not right now. We all need time."

"I don't want you to go...I can't bear..."

He could hold back no longer. He took her in his arms, cherishing the feel of her body next to his...the softness, the giving response. He hugged her tightly to him, his hands wandering through her thick chestnut hair. He leaned his cheek against it, feeling the silkiness, smelling its flowery scent.

For the first time in four years, he felt clean. Whole.

He closed his eyes, reveling in the feelings flooding him. Feelings of love and hope and belonging. But for how long? His arms tightened around her in quiet desperation.

Blythe could sense his every emotion. She had been able to do that for as long as she could remember. Except for those first few moments in the kitchen hours ago. Then he had seemed a stranger. But no more. Now he was Rafe. Her Rafe. With all the tenderness and strength she remembered.

Her Christmas gift. The one she had wanted more than any other.

She lifted her head and met his eyes. Their green-blue depths were swirling with turmoil. She stood on her tiptoes and raised her lips to his, seeking a more intimate touch, a stronger commitment, a greater promise.

And she received it. Rafe's firm mouth first teased, then claimed her own with a need and passion that made her legs unsteady. She raised her arms and intertwined them around his neck.

It had been so long, so very long since she had felt his strength, the warmth of his body. Waves of pleasure swept her, and her blood pulsed like warm, thick syrup in every part of her. An ache, like none she had known before, started throbbing in the depth of her, and her heart sang with sadly sweet carols. He was here. He was hers.

But deep in her soul, she knew nothing had been really settled. Seth was still in danger. The wounded man was still at risk. How could she think only of herself?

Yet she did. At the moment, she concentrated on that. On her own need, on her own joy of being with him. She surrendered to it completely, needing these minutes so desperately, needing to keep the soldier at bay and the young man she had known, with her.

There was a small cry from the bed, and the sound jerked them both back to reality. Rafe reluctantly released Blythe, and she hurried over to Maria, putting a comforting hand on the girl who then relaxed in her sleep.

When she returned to Rafe, he gave her the wry smile she was now beginning to remember only too well. "If you don't get to bed, I'll carry you there."

Blythe smiled with a challenge in her golden eyes, her invitation only too clear.

His smile widened into a grin, and his hands caught her easily and swung her up in his arms. "Where?"

"The next room," she said, relishing the confident strength of his arms, the sureness of his long strides as, within seconds, he deposited her on her own bed, leaning over to leave one tender kiss on her lips before he turned to leave.

"Will you come back to me when you finish talking to Seth?"

He hesitated. She was disastrous to his will. To his duty. Hell, this whole situation was disastrous. Seth. The children. Blythe. He shrugged in surrender. And nodded.

What had Seth said? "It's a hell of a Christmas." It was both. A heaven of a Christmas. A hell of a Christmas.

As he walked outside, the golden glow had turned pink as the sun peaked the hills. He had put his heavy coat and cloak back on, but he had left his cavalry gloves in the kitchen and his fingers tingled with cold.

The trough was back in place, and he marveled again at the ingenuity of his brother as he sprung the catch and pushed the cover open. As he walked down the steep stairs, memories came crowding back.

His family and Blythe's had been close friends, and they had visited often. Blythe was much younger than either he or Seth, but there had always been an enchantment about her, an enthusiasm and kindness that had amused and entranced both brothers, and they were often drawn into her adventures, particularly her frequent rescues of animals and people in distress. During the hot summer days, she would laughingly lure them down into the cellar to munch on apples.

But neither one had thought of her as a woman until they had returned to the farm after university as young men and found their lanky disciple had grown into a beautiful young lady....

"Close the door," Seth commanded from below, and Rafe turned back and did as asked. He didn't want to fight with his brother, not now.

It had been four years since they had parted with a warm embrace, knowing they were taking opposite directions, each committed to his own path. He and Seth had been as close as twins when they were growing up. Separated by only a year, they were the youngest in the family and had always looked out for each other. Despite the fact that Rafe was the eldest, neither had emerged as a leader or sacrificed his independence for the other; there had always been an equality between them, a mutual respect for the other's strengths and differences.

As their eyes adjusted to the darkness, Rafe held out his arms to where Seth was standing and the two men did what they had hesitated to do until now: embraced each other with affection and a deep silent gratitude that the other was still alive after four terrible years.

But still there was a certain reserve, the strain of tension. There remained much that divided them.

Seth slowly backed away, his tired but always lively eyes bright in the darkness. They were full of questions.

"A truce, Seth?"

"For how long?"

"The children want to give Blythe a present...a play. Until then, at least."

"You said your men would be returning...."

"It will be a while...they had a number of places to search, and they'll return to camp...they will be tired."

"Where is it...your camp?"

"Ah, Seth, you know better than that."

Seth chuckled. "It seemed worthy of a try."

"How is your patient?"

"In a lot of pain. I just gave him more morphine. I still can't move him. At least not for a few hours."

A silence hung heavy between them. Then Rafe spoke. "You said you might have some Rebs joining you."

"That's right," Seth said quietly. "Some of the men with us would have gotten back and reported. When I don't reach units south of here, there will be search parties . . . and they know I come here often."

"We'll just try to give Blythe . . . and her children . . . Christmas first. Agreed?"

"And then?"

"Damned if I know . . ."

Seth laughed again, but there was little amusement in it. "Make it up as you go along . . . a typical lawyer."

"A truce, Seth? You didn't answer."

"God almighty, Rafe, you have the guns."

"I don't want to keep them trained on you and your patient all day, or tie you up," Rafe said broodingly. "I want your word you won't try anything until, say, two o'clock. Then we'll take up where we left off."

Seth stared at him, and slowly nodded. He owed at least that to Blythe. "We're both trapped," he said slowly. "There's no easy way out for either of us. But yes, a truce . . . until this afternoon, and we'll both pray that neither of our armies come looking for us in the meantime."

Rafe noticed his brother was shivering slightly in the worn coat he wore. He took off his own cloak and handed it to Seth, making no reference to his threadbare clothes. They both knew the condition of the Confederacy. Seth was lucky to have a coat at all.

"Tell me about Francis?" Rafe asked after a pause.

Seth took the cloak and wrapped it around himself, and then slid tiredly to the floor.

"It was plain hell this spring in the valley, but Francis and mother wouldn't give up. They kept planting, and the Yanks kept burning."

"The Yanks?"

Seth shrugged in the dim light. "I was able to keep Mosby's men away. But then some Reb deserters attacked the farm, and Francis went against them with a gun. He was shot. Mother killed the man who shot him, and the others ran. I finally convinced mother to go stay with Samantha in South Carolina. It helped that Samantha was ready to have a baby and really needed her. Once they left, the place was burned. Damn if I know by whom."

Rafe was silent. "I went by there. There was so damned little left."

"We'll rebuild," Seth said.

"Together," Rafe said.

"Together," Seth acknowledged.

But first they had to get through today, and they both knew it.

"Go to Blythe," Seth said.

"What about you? It's damn cold down here. Why don't you take him into the house?"

"Is that humanitarian or professional concern?"

"Damn you, Seth. What difference does it make?"

"Curiosity."

Rafe couldn't stop a small chuckle. Seth had always been impertinent and provocative. To some, it appeared to be cynicism, but Rafe knew better. No one was more idealistic than his brother. Even now, after four years of war, Seth still wanted to see the best in everything.

"Professionalism, then. A dead Confederate general will do me little good."

"Nor will this one live," Seth retorted. "You don't know him. I do."

Rafe shrugged. "That's not my concern. Getting him to headquarters is. And there's no advantage now to staying down here. I know you're here."

Seth smiled faintly. "I'm taking the chance you won't tell your troops if they come back."

Rafe considered the words. "You're wrong."

Seth merely continued smiling.

Rafe could only shake his head. "You're a damned fool optimist."

"That's probably why I'm on the side I'm on, and you're on the one you are," Seth admitted wryly.

Rafe shook his head and took off his coat. "Give it to the general," he said with something like a smile. He offered his hand. "Merry Christmas, Seth."

"Merry Christmas, Rafe."

Rafe let his gaze linger on Seth for a moment. He felt a wetness in his eyes, and blinked it back. He turned abruptly and left, carefully replacing the trough as it had been.

When he reached the house again, Jaime was waiting for him.

"I thought you were in bed," Rafe said, hoping the boy didn't see what he knew must be an unnatural brightness in his eyes.

"I have to look out for Miss Blythe. I'm the man of the house now," Jaime said jealously.

"She couldn't have a better one," Rafe said sincerely, remembering the musket.

Jaime looked at him with his usual suspicion.

"Will you do something for me...for Miss Blythe?" Rafe asked.

"'Pends on what it is."

"Let us know if any riders approach."

"I'll tell Miss Blythe...and Cap'n Seth."

Rafe nodded, not satisfied but at least comforted slightly that he would know through Blythe.

As he left the kitchen, he turned around and watched Jaime, the musket in hand, stride manfully out the door.

Rafe ascended the stairs slowly, knowing that rejoining Blythe was probably the last thing he should do. Rocked by so many conflicting emotions, he felt more battered tonight than at any time during the war. Battered and tired and apprehensive.

Yet something fine and optimistic was running through him. It had been so damned good to see Seth alive, and to touch Blythe, and to hold young Benji. To hold life once more.

He bargained with himself. If Blythe were asleep, he would leave and find a bed of his own for an hour or so. He couldn't even remember the last time he had closed his eyes. It seemed a lifetime.

He wondered how long he could continue to function this way. His thinking was already fuzzy. Otherwise, why would he be doing everything he was?

Perhaps Christmas was wrapping its magic around him?

He had ignored Christmas for so long, unable to bear the memories, the losses. Unable to recall that Christmas of 1860 when a dew-eyed Blythe had agreed with laughter to be his wife. His wife. Dear God, how much time they had lost.

Rafe could remember everything about that Christmas. The huge yule log in the fireplace, the Christmas carols sung by young people around the piano, Blythe's father contentedly watching from his chair. There had been many smells that Christmas: the rich aroma of pine, roasting meats, sugared confections, hot mulled wine. So much food. So much laughter. So much joy. His heart had sung that day as they planned their future: a home in Fredericksburg, where he would practice law. But they would return often, to this valley, to his home and to hers.

She had been wearing a red velvet dress that day, its sleeves long and flowing, the bodice modest but still showing the gentle swell of her breasts, the skirt immense over hoops. Her eyes had sparked like gemstones, and her hair had been dressed with red bows. He thought he had never seen anything lovelier.

Until today. In a plain, worn dress and with her hair dressed in a practical bun, she was more beautiful than ever. The life was still there. The gentleness. The sweetness. And also the courage . . . that much was evident when she had threatened him with a gun. It was the combination that he loved. Sugar and spice. It had taken rare strength and ingenuity to keep this farm together, to support the growing number of children. It had taken real grit and determination, and that made her incredibly precious.

He put the two pictures of Blythe together in his mind: the carefree girl in the red dress, and the woman, blood-splattered and weary, who looked at Maria and the newborn baby with such delight, never considering the fact that the child meant another mouth to feed.

His arms ached to hold her, to take some of the burden from her, and, he knew, to make his own world right once more.

He had been so lonely. He had never let himself think of it before. Thinking of such things only got you killed. So he had locked his heart in a shell he allowed no one to enter, not even himself. But it had cost. It had cost so much. In terms of being a human being, of being a man.

Rafe leaned against the wall at the top of the stairs. He knew his eyes were still wet with tears. Tears of regret, of gratitude at coming to life again. Of seeing Seth, of holding a child, of loving Blythe. His throat constricted, and his heart thumped against his ribs with the unaccustomed feelings of incredible sadness, incredible joy. How could they exist together without crushing him?

His hand brushed aside the wetness, and he opened the door to Blythe's room.

She wasn't asleep, although she had changed to a flowing dressing gown. Her hair had been released from its simple knot and brushed until it appeared alive with golden streaks. She was standing at the window, but she had turned when she heard the door open.

She held out her hand to him, and he moved quickly to her, taking it in his damp one. She brought his palm to her mouth, and kissed it, before leaning back in his arms. "It's beautiful this morning," she said softly.

And it was. The sun was gliding up in the sky, leaving trails of gold across the still-green earth of the valley. He swallowed with the apparent peace of it. It seemed impossible that two armies were not far away, poised to poison the earth with their carnage. His arms tightened around her, longing to prolong this moment forever.

He rested his chin on her head. "You are so very lovely, Blythe."

She tipped her head toward him. "I had so many plans for when you returned. I would greet you in my best dress and my hair laced with flowers and . . ."

"Instead of flour on your nose. . . ."

"And my very worst dress . . ."

"I thought I had never seen anyone so beautiful in my life," he interrupted gently.

"You seemed so cold and angry."

"I was so damned scared, love. So damned scared you had married Seth, or that you hated me now after all that has happened here . . ."

"I could never hate you. . . ."

"I wouldn't blame you if you did. So much has changed. I've changed."

She looked into his eyes, at the fear that still lingered there. At the hope and love. She shook her head slowly. "No. I thought you had until I saw you with Benji. And then I knew. I knew that all I loved in you was just waiting. . . ."

He couldn't stand it any longer. He crushed her to him, feeling her arms going up around his neck, and her own desperate clinging to bring them as close as possible, to forget the years and once more fuse their souls.

"Will you marry me?" he asked, knowing it was not the time yet unable to resist the words.

"You repeat yourself, sir," she said with the old enchanting mischief. "Am I to understand you did not mean it before?"

He leaned down and nibbled her ear before answering. "I mean right away...."

She stiffened slightly in his arms, and her eyes studied him intently. "You realize you will be getting much more than you intended four years ago?"

"The children?"

She nodded. "I could never abandon them."

He drew her tightly against him. "I would never ask you to. I always wanted a big family."

"That big?" she giggled.

"Maybe," he said with a bit of a leer in his voice, "even a bit bigger."

"I love you," she said.

"Then you will...?"

There was one question remaining before she could answer. "What about Seth?"

His strong hand caught her chin and tipped it toward him. "I don't know, love," and there was such resigned hopelessness in his voice that she wanted to cry.

"Let them go," she said. "The war is almost over. It won't make any difference."

"If it were only Seth..."

"You know Seth won't leave him."

"I know," he said, his fingers tracing patterns on her cheek.

She leaned against him again, her mind turning to the two brothers. Stubborn. They were both so blasted stubborn...

She closed her eyes. She didn't want to think. Only to feel. Only this moment existed.

She felt his lips nuzzle her eyes, then her cheek, before drawing back and leading her to the bed.

"I think we both need some rest," he said, sensing the hesitancy, confusion in her. He could not press the issue of marriage now, not when Seth stood between them.

"Don't leave me," she pleaded.

"No," he whispered. "I won't. Never again."

He sat on the bed and took off his boots, and his uniform jacket, leaving on his blue uniform shirt. He stretched out and held his arms out to her. She lay down, and he turned her so that her back was to his chest, and he drew his arms around her.

She closed her eyes, feeling safe and loved. This was enough at the moment, this quiet, gentle touching. The past two days caught up with her, and she sank quietly into a peaceful sleep.

But Rafe, despite his great need for sleep, could not do the same.

Gentle Christ. What was he going to do?

Chapter Six

A restless movement beside him woke Seth. Despite the fact he had gone nearly sixty hours without sleep before he lay down just a few hours earlier, he was immediately awake. Training, he thought with unusual resentment, was both a blessing and a curse.

It took several minutes for his eyes to accustom themselves sufficiently to the dimness to find a match and the remnants of the candle. He struck the match against a stone and watched as the wick caught and blazed.

"General Massey?"

The fruit cellar was small enough that he needed only to move several feet to reach his patient. He felt Massey's forehead and was relieved to find it cool. At least there was no infection. Not yet.

"Captain Hampton...?"

Seth looked at his patient inquiringly.

"The Yank...?"

"We declared a temporary truce. But he has the guns now, I'm afraid."

"He's...really...your brother?"

"Yes, but that won't help. Not in this situation. He's determined to take you, and I'm just as determined he won't."

"I'm damned...sorry."

"So am I, General. It was just confounded bad luck he returned now...no one else would have known about this cellar."

"Where is he...now?"

"Sleeping, I think."

"There are no more...Yankees?"

"No."

Massey tried to move but fell back, agony etched in his face. "We...have to leave."

"You can't ride, sir. Not yet. It'll kill you for sure. You've lost too much blood, and we can't chance opening that wound again."

"Better...that way."

"No," Seth said. "It'll be suicide, and I'm not in that business."

"A Yank prison would do the same."

"Not if I go with you."

Massey shook his head. "Damn you, Hampton. I'll make it an order."

"I'm sorry, sir. I can't do it." Seth mentally added a court-martial to everything else facing him. But his hands were gentle as they removed the bandage and he studied the wound carefully. The bullet, thank God, had gone straight through, but the opening and exit wounds were large. He had sewn them up, but they were still leaking blood. A few more hours. He needed at least a few more hours.

"I think Mosby's men will come looking for us, General. They knew where I was heading...."

"And the Yanks?"

"They'll probably come looking for my brother. We just have to hope our troops get here first. With some protection, we won't have to move so fast."

Massey closed his eyes, and Seth wasn't sure if it was from pain or prayer. Then they opened. "What time is it, Captain?"

"I'd say about nine in the morning, Christmas Day."

"Christmas," Massey murmured. A trace of a bitter smile touched his lips. "Not the way I would choose to spend it . . . buried like a mole waiting for a passel of Yanks."

Seth nodded, sharing the feeling completely. "Can I get you something?"

"Some water."

"Morphine?"

"No...don't waste it on me...we have too damned little as it is. And I want to know what's going on. Just water."

Seth studied him. Pain was engraved deep in Massey's face, and every time he moved, it became more pronounced. But he had courage. Damn, if he didn't have courage. Seth resolved then and there that he would, somehow, get Massey away. He poured the general a cup of water and held the man's head with one hand while pressing the cup to his lips in the other. Another flash of pain ripped across his patient's face as he moved only fractionally. *Dear God, how can I get him on a horse?*

"Don't worry, Captain, I'll make it," Massey said, reading Seth's thoughts. He dug into his trousers with his left hand and brought out a gold watch. "Six hours. It's nine now. We'll leave at three o'clock."

Doubt filled Seth's face.

"Three o'clock, Captain. Even if you have to take a corpse."

Seth nodded. Rafe had established the truce until two o'clock, and Seth had sworn to do nothing until then. It would give him one hour. One hour to get one of the guns and then . . .

Then what? Could he really shoot Rafe? Rafe had believed him earlier. Would he now?

Massey saw the agony in the captain's face and understood it only too well. He reached over to Seth. "I'm sorry, Captain," he said once again.

"Merry Christmas, General," Seth replied, and for the first time in the past twelve hours his tone was bitter.

Blythe didn't know at first what had wakened her. For a moment she felt captive, and then she remembered where she was and smiled. Her bonds were his arms, his beloved arms. She felt his breath against her neck, knew the glorious sensation of his lean powerful body next to hers.

She knew from the soft rhythmic sound of his breathing that he was asleep. And she didn't want to wake him. Not yet. He had been so tired.

Blythe wondered what time it was. Morning light was flooding the room which faced the east, so it was about midmorning. She was surprised she heard no sounds from the children, although they were usually fairly quiet. They had not yet learned to be noisy, to laugh, to play. They had not learned to be unafraid again. And wouldn't, she thought. Not as long as the war continued, and men in gray and blue uniforms visited the Somers's farm.

Maria, assisted by Margaret, had looked after the other children when Blythe and Jaime were in the fields. Blythe imagined sleepily that, this morning, Jaime and Margaret had probably already fixed bread and butter and the honey Seth had brought several days ago. But still, she should rise and check on Maria.

But she simply couldn't bear to leave the loving shelter of Rafe's arms. And she knew if she moved, he would wake. And once more there would be the problem of Seth and his Confederate patient. A few more minutes of happiness. Just a few. She snuggled, as quietly as she could, farther into Rafe's body, wanting desperately to turn and look at his sleeping face. She had never seen him asleep. She wondered how he would look with the thick black lashes covering his eyes, and his mouth relaxed. She had to be satisfied with looking at the strong, competent hands, one of which had settled on the portion of the dressing gown covering her right breast.

Something stirred deep inside her, just as it had earlier. A yearning ache for something she really didn't understand. There had always been electricity between them, a smoldering fire, but in the past hours it had become an inferno, jumping from one location to another.

Rafe. She couldn't say it aloud. Not now. But she felt the sound on her tongue. *I love you. I love you so much.* But she also knew a great fear. If he couldn't compromise with himself, and anything happened to Seth, he would never forgive himself. She wondered whether he could live with it.

So strong. So tender. So giving. So stubborn.

She could scarcely believe he would take on her children, all of them. And more, he had said. She knew by the inflection in his voice earlier that he meant theirs.

He moved then, and she felt him stretching against her.

"Hmm," she heard him murmur as his hand tightened on the dressing gown at her breast. She felt a tickling in her ear and anything she had felt in the past few hours was minor compared to the sensations she now suffered.

She turned around and looked at his lazy, sleepy eyes. "I was afraid I was dreaming," he said. "I didn't want to wake up."

His cheeks were slightly dark with fresh beard, and a lock of his dark hair fell over his forehead. He looked like a rascal, more a handsome rogue than an officer hell-bent on accomplishing a difficult duty.

She felt like a cat herself, as her tongue instinctively started licking the slightly rough skin of his bronzed face. It tasted wonderful, salty and compelling, and as she moved toward his throat she could hear the chuckle starting deep inside him.

"Keep this up," he whispered, "and we'll be here all Christmas."

The thought gave her new impetus, even while she wondered at her daring. Nice women, she was afraid, didn't do this. Yet she couldn't think of a reason why not. It was really quite...marvelous. She felt his body respond to her ministrations, felt the growing, throbbing excitement of her own.

Why, dear God, had they waited? She wasn't willing to wait any longer. She didn't know what would happen today. But she wasn't going to lose him. She couldn't.

"Blythe." His voice was a groan.

It echoed her own personal torment, as craving, wild and abandoned, replaced the sensibility of past years. A fear of impending loss was just as strong as the happiness of rediscovery. Everything was so fleeting, so full of risks. Life had become a gamble. Love even more so. And she wasn't going to give it up without ever experiencing its fullness.

She lifted her lips to him, and he took them with an urgency that shook both of them to the core. His hands played with her hair, becoming servants of the silky strands.

The kiss deepened, and his tongue invaded every sensitive corner and curve of her mouth until she trembled all over with need for something greater. It moved with unrestrained passion, then tenderness, playing on her nerves like a master musician. One of his hands went from her hair to her breast, still hidden under the cotton of her nightdress, yet she could feel it swell and harden under his touch, just as she felt him grow and stiffen within his restraining trousers. Her hand went down to a place she had never touched before, and she felt every part of him tense.

"Blythe . . . you don't know what you're doing . . ."

"Our Christmas gift . . . to each other."

"Not this way, love. If anything happens . . ."

"I won't let it," she said so fiercely he had to believe her. Yet he couldn't let this happen. Not today. Not this way. Not with Seth below and so much unfinished business. He wanted her, God, he wanted her, but even more than the physical binding, he wanted her happiness, he wanted the light in her to continue to burn bright.

And he was afraid, so damned afraid that something today would quench it.

"Miss Blythe..."

A child's voice came anxiously through the door.

Whatever might have happened no longer would.

He kissed her, then spun up and to the window, looking below with the caution he usually maintained...until last night. There was nothing there...no sign of Seth, the children, riders—either Reb or his own.

Rafe heard Blythe's soft reply to the question. "What is it, Margaret?"

"Jaime was worried about you."

"I'm fine, love," Blythe said as she and Rafe exchanged wryly amused looks. "I'll be down soon."

They heard retreating footsteps, and Rafe was beside her again. "Merry Christmas," he said gravely.

Blythe couldn't take her eyes from him. The neck of his shirt was unbuttoned, and she saw a wool undershirt stretched tight against his broad chest. His dark blue uniform trousers hugged his lean hips and muscular legs. There was so much masculine strength, so much power in him, and yet there was also an animal grace. Each movement was measured and restrained. The dark stubble on his cheeks was even more pronounced in the light streaming into the room. His mouth was quirked in question, and his green-blue eyes were frothing with emotion. She leaned against him, but was afraid another messenger would soon be at her door. Jaime could be very determined when he set his mind on it.

Yet she couldn't move, particularly when he smiled, a sweet, tender smile full of longing. They stood there, as if frozen in time, their eyes fixed on one another as if frightened the other would disappear in a wisp of smoke.

She was so incredibly lovely, Rafe thought. Her hair tumbled halfway to her waist in thick waves. Her golden eyes shone with passion and understanding and gentleness. Her kiss-swollen mouth was soft and inviting. The white nightdress, high-necked and virginal, nonetheless showed every sleek curve to perfection. Although she seemed too thin to him, her breasts stood out proudly, and gently rounded hips added beauty to the plain garment she wore. She would be beautiful in sackcloth. She had the kind of beauty, the radiance of a beacon on a black night.

Rafe touched her with reverence.

The sound of steps on the staircase outside stirred him. "I think, Miss Blythe, your brood awaits you," Rafe said slowly, regretfully. Despite the tumultuous feelings battling inside him, his tone was light, made so by supreme self-control.

He turned and went back to the window, trying to give her privacy to dress. He thought about leaving but decided to wait until he could slip out, no one the wiser as to where he had spent the early morning hours.

Trying to ignore the sounds behind him, and the temptation to watch, Rafe stared out the window toward the trough. He wondered how Seth was faring…it was blasted cold last night. He could only hope his cloak had given his brother some comfort.

And Massey? Would he be well enough to travel today? How in the devil was he going to pry the man loose from Seth? Rafe squared his shoulders, trying to

summon the well-honed determination, the old sin-
gle-mindedness that had kept him alive these many
months.

He felt a hand on his arm, and he turned slowly, a
smile replacing the frown on his face.

"I need your help," she said with a twinkle in her
eyes before she turned around, showing her back to
him.

She was wearing the red velvet gown she had worn
four years ago...the day she had agreed to be his wife.
There were numerous buttons in the back, and his
hands went to them, but they didn't function as they
should. They faltered slightly, then continued on,
taking much more time than they should. When he
was finished, she turned, and he knew he was gaping.
He remembered the way the red velvet brought out the
ivory of her skin and the blush of her cheeks, the way
it hugged her breasts and tapered to the slender waist.
How long had he held the picture of her this way in his
mind? It had gotten him through fields of death,
nights of terrible dreams. It had seen him through
more battles than he wished to remember. It had made
him go on when everything seemed hopeless. Until
eighteen months ago, when he had thought he had lost
her....

Now, by wearing the dress, she seemed to be reaf-
firming that promise of four years ago.

His hands settled on her bare shoulders. "Does this
mean...?"

"I love you, Rafe. I'll never let anything come between us."

"Not even Massey?" he questioned stiffly, a lump
lodged firmly in his throat. "Or Seth?" He couldn't
prevent the last question. A part of him was terribly

afraid that this might be a bribe of some type. He didn't think he could bear that.

She leaned against him. "You have always done what you had to do. I suppose that's one reason I love you so much." She looked up at him, and he couldn't doubt her feelings as she continued slowly. "I love you whatever you decide . . . I'll never stop loving you, no matter what." He could see her swallow as she continued painfully. "But I worry about you and Seth. What this could do to you, to both of you."

There was infinite sadness in his voice as he replied. "I do, too, love." He felt sick in the pit of his stomach as he said the words, and his heart pounded painfully. This should be the most beautiful day of his life. It might be the worst.

For her sake, he banished the sorrow he knew must show in his eyes, and he moved her slightly from him, as once more he memorized her every feature, just as he had four years earlier.

"I love that dress," he said caressingly.

"I haven't worn it since the day you left," she said, a hint of wetness in her eyes. "I was never going to wear it until you came home to me."

"You are so beautiful," he said. "The most beautiful woman I have ever seen."

Suddenly self-conscious, she looked down at her work-roughened hands and then to a snarled curl falling over her shoulder.

"I'll brush it for you," he said, relishing the thought of holding the long silken mane in his hands.

She looked up quickly under teasing lashes. "The Yankee major acting as lady's maid. Your men would be shocked."

"I think they would be shocked by many things that I've done in the past hours," he said ruefully, thinking of his story telling, of passing his coat to a Reb, even if he was his brother. Rafe knew he had a hard reputation. But strict discipline had been the best way to keep his men alive.

Rafe found the brush on a cherrywood bureau, and led her to the bed where he sat next to her. One of his hands ran the brush through the thick chestnut hair while the other touched the strands, enjoying their silky richness.

Blythe wondered how anything could feel so wonderful as the brush stroked lightly, even lovingly. She could feel his hand work out the snarls before the brush reached them. Once again, she felt the restrained power in his movements, the innate gentleness warring with his natural impatience, and she wondered that he could rein such a strong part of himself for her.

She loved him. She loved him so much. Her hand settled on his leg and moved up and down it, wanting to express her overwhelming emotions in some direct way.

And then all too quickly, it was done. As much as he wanted to linger, his mind was now moving quickly. He had promised Benji his play. And after that . . .

Had Seth bluffed when he said he could expect some of Mosby's troops? And when would his own come?

Not for a while yet. But possibly by late afternoon. And he had to have Massey by then, had to have him as prisoner and away from the farm so no blame would rest here.

His hands tightened compulsively. Why? Why today of all days, of all times, was he faced with this? He wanted to erase it all, to dismiss Seth and Massey from his mind, from his life. But he couldn't. Honor and duty were at stake, and Rafe knew that he was compulsive about both. Compulsive to a point where he feared they were no longer strengths but weaknesses. Yet there was something in him that wouldn't let go. It just wouldn't let go, God help him.

He put down the brush and touched her face with a hand that shook slightly. "You must go down," he said. "I'll be there in a few minutes."

She turned and regarded him gravely, once more as if she could read every one of his thoughts. "It will be all right," she whispered. "I know it will. Somehow it will."

Rafe wished he felt the same, that the nagging fear of calamity wasn't with him. He nodded, and walked her to the door, reluctant to leave her.

Then she was gone, and he was left with his own thoughts. He went back to the window, and his eyes fell on the trough, the damned trough. Why had he noticed it last night? Damn it, why?

Seth, why didn't you go anyplace else? Anyplace at all?

The kitchen was full of children, and they all turned and stared at Blythe as she entered. They had never seen her in a fine dress before.

"Oh, Miss Blythe, you are beautiful," Margaret said in awe.

"Ya look like an angel," Benji said, clutching the doll she had made for him in his arms. "Jest like that Yank said."

Blythe looked at the boy with a questioning expression.

"He told us a story last night . . . about a baby, and shepherds and angels. . . ." Benji's eyes were wide with appreciation, and Blythe grinned at the thought of her brusque major telling the Christmas story.

"Has anyone taken food up to Maria?" she asked. It was only about five or six hours since the birth, and Maria was probably still asleep.

Margaret smiled shyly. "We peeked at the baby. It's beautiful, too. Maria was still sleeping."

"All of you?" Blythe asked the question with a smile. She could see them all creeping in on tiptoes to regard the newest arrival.

Margaret nodded.

"Where's Jaime?"

"He went out to make sure no one is coming."

God bless Jaime, Blythe thought. "Have you all had breakfast?"

Margaret's slow shy smile shone again with pride. "We knew you were tired because of Maria. I fixed some bread and butter and honey."

"Good for you, sweetheart." She thought of Seth and the general outside. She needed to take some food out to them, but though Jaime suspected someone was there, none of the others did. She had not wanted them to, but now she doubted whether she could keep it a secret.

She looked at each of their faces. There was a suppressed excitement about them, like they knew a secret, an exciting happy secret. A sudden uncertainty seized her. Was she putting them all at risk with Seth's presence? Yet she could not force him to leave. She knew him well enough to realize he must be suffering with the knowledge that he had unwittingly put them all in danger, danger that would never have been there had his brother not returned. He would leave as soon as humanly possible.

And Rafe would try to stop him.

Several possible solutions flew through her mind. But none of them, she knew almost instantly, were possible. She could try to knock Rafe out and tie him again, but she suspected he would be very much on guard against that particular maneuver. She could try to lure him someplace and lock the door. But he was strong enough to break open any door in the house, not to mention any available windows that would allow escape. The house had not been designed as a prison.

A host of faces looked up at her expectantly. "Merry Christmas," she said, her hand touching each one.

"Father Christmas came last night," Suzie said, beaming. "He brought me and Benji a doll."

Blythe leaned down and looked at Benji's doll. Suzie's was sitting in a chair. "That's wonderful. Have you named it?"

Suzie shook her head. "I'm thinkin' on it."

"That's good," Blythe agreed solemnly. "It's a very important decision," and Suzie nodded sagely.

"I'm gonna call mine Rafe," Benji said, "'cause he came last night jest like the doll."

Blythe grinned. "I think he will like that." A new baby named Blythe. A new doll named Rafe. A secret delight bobbed up in her. Surely nothing bad could happen today.

She turned to Margaret. "Why don't you go see if Maria is awake?"

Margaret nodded, and Blythe suggested other chores for the youngsters. When the kitchen was finally empty, she cut several thick slices of bread and spread it thick with Seth's honey. She looked in the pitcher that contained the last of the milk obtained yesterday from their cow concealed in the woods. She tucked the pitcher and bread under her arm, looked around and, seeing no small, curious faces, hurried out to the trough. She started to put everything down when Rafe approached, opening it for her.

He had shaved, and he looked incredibly handsome to her...except for the haunted look in his eyes.

"Are you going down with me?" she said slowly, praying this was not the confrontation she had been dreading.

"Just for a moment," he said. "I want to know how Massey is."

"You won't..."

"Not now," he said gently. "Seth and I have a temporary truce."

"How temporary?"

He shifted uncomfortably before answering slowly. "This afternoon."

Blythe swallowed but could not think of anything to say. Everything had already been said.

Seth had been sitting next to Massey, but rose quickly as the door opened. His eyes adjusted to the sudden light, and then a trace of a smile touched his lips as he saw Rafe and Blythe together...and the offerings in her arms.

"Rafe," he acknowledged carefully.

Rafe looked over at the patient, noted that the general's eyes were open and regarding him warily.

"General Massey," he said respectfully. "You look much improved over last night."

"Thanks to your brother," Massey said shortly. "What do you plan to do?"

Rafe had to smile at the direct question. He had heard that Massey was tough.

"Nothing...at the moment," he replied, glancing at Blythe's tense face and Seth's carefully blank one.

"When will he be able to ride?" he asked Seth.

Seth shrugged. "Not for a while 'less you want to kill him."

Rafe's eyes went from the doctor to the general, and back again. "And you, Seth. Did you get any sleep?"

"A little. Your coat was a godsend, Rafe...even if it is the wrong color."

Rafe's expression gentled. Seth's face was drawn and blond with new stubble. His eyes looked immeasurably tired. Rafe's chest constricted. How in hell could he send his brother to prison? He swallowed deep, and his left hand knotted as he observed, "You look terrible."

"It's been a long war."

Rafe nodded, then turned to go up the stairs to the still-open door. He wanted to say more to his brother, so much more, but he couldn't. Not now.

When he was gone, Seth looked at Blythe. "I see a sparkle back in those eyes. It looks good there. I've missed it."

Blythe tried to smile. "What are you going to do, Seth?"

"That's up to Rafe."

"What can I do?" Her question was soft and heartfelt.

His hand went to her shoulder. "Lovely Blythe. Caught in the middle. I wish to God I had never come here last night."

"There was no place else...otherwise I know you wouldn't have..."

"Whatever happens, Blythe, don't let it come between you and Rafe. You belong together. You always have." There was a certain resigned sadness in his voice that cut her to the quick.

"It's Christmas, Seth. A time of miracles. It will work out. It will."

He nodded, but there was little hope in his eyes. "Thank you for the food."

Blythe turned to the Confederate general. "I'm glad you're better."

"One of your miracles, young lady," he said with a bit of a smile.

"There will be others. I know it," she replied. She turned to Seth. "Merry Christmas, Seth."

She fled up the stairs.

Chapter Seven

Despite the more than usual cheerful sound of the children, tension radiated between Blythe and Rafe. It was in the words unsaid, the questions unasked, decisions not fully made.

Blythe started dinner, preparing the chickens she had cleaned the evening before. Rafe disappeared toward the barn where his horse and one elderly mare, which had been disdained by both armies, were stabled. Minutes later, she saw him riding out.

Where is he going?

"Miss Blythe, who's in the fruit cellar?"

Blythe stared at Margaret.

"You took some food down there."

Blythe shook her head in self-disgust. She should have known she couldn't keep a secret from ten pairs of young eyes.

"Captain Seth," she said. "But no one must know."

Margaret's eyes grew large. "Uncle Rafe knows?"

"Uncle Rafe?"

"He told us to call him that."

Blythe released a long breath. "Uncle Rafe." She wouldn't have believed it last night when she had first seen Rafe's cold face. Now, in a few short hours, it was as if he had been here forever.

Where did he go?

She nodded. "Yes, sweet, he knows." She put the chickens on a spit in the fireplace, tucking a pan under them for drippings. She would make some biscuits for gravy. And then there would be the pies. There were no vegetables, no potatoes. All and all, she feared, it would be a skimpy meal, especially with the added mouths to feed. Panic struck her for a moment. Their food supply was getting scarce, and without Seth to supplement it, she wondered how she would manage....

She had depended on him for so long. And now, even if he did get back to his own lines, he was being recalled to Richmond.

Of course, there was Rafe now. But his presence was still too new, too unreal to emotionally accept. A chill creeped down her spine despite the heat from the fireplace, and she tried to shake it off. It's Christmas, she told herself. It's Christmas, and fine things happen on Christmas.

If only she could believe it.

Once the chickens were started, she took a glass of milk upstairs to Maria's room. The girl was awake, the baby in her arms sucking noisily on a breast. Maria looked up, her face soft and wondering. "It's a miracle, isn't it. That something so small and sweet could..." She stopped.

"I know," Blythe said, not wanting Maria to continue, to recall how the child was conceived. "And she's a lovely baby. How do you feel?"

Maria smiled, and one of her hands played with a tiny finger. "I'm fine. Jaime was here. And the others." Her eyes held a secret, and Blythe wondered momentarily what it might be.

Blythe nodded. "I'll send dinner up to you."

"Miss Blythe?"

"Yes."

"Thank you. You and little Blythe are the best things that ever happened to me."

Blythe felt tears crowd her eyes. Dear Mother in heaven, but she had cried more in the past few hours than she had in her entire life. But then, she considered, these were tears of another kind, of shared happiness with someone else.

"And you, sweetheart, are one of the nicest things that has ever happened to me."

She hurried back downstairs, this time humming a carol with complete sincerity. There had been one miracle today. Perhaps it would not be too much to ask for several more.

Blythe found a kitchen full of children and urged them to join her in the song. Margaret was first, and then Suzie in a small voice, and then one by one, the others joined in. Blythe had been teaching them carols during the past week, and all of them soon caught the spirit in Blythe's voice and the smile on her lips.

The tall clock in the parlor struck twelve. Noon.

The last carol died away, and several of the children left on various errands while Blythe started thinking about portions. She had thought the meal would be meager for eleven, and now, in addition to her and the children there were two healthy strong men and one ill one. She wished for another miracle, like the multiplying of fish.

She needed so many miracles today.

Blythe looked down at the apron that covered her dress. The skirt dragged a bit since she had used narrow hoops instead of the great wide ones so fashionable, and impractical, before the war.

Her heart clenched and unclenched as she waited for Rafe's return. She could only imagine he was scouting the area, or perhaps he only needed to exorcise some of his devils in private. He had always gone off by himself to think, to weigh everything before coming to a decision. Yet she knew, in the deepest part of her heart, that his decision had already been made.

She sensed his presence before actually seeing him. Her back was toward the door, her hands busy turning the chickens when she felt a trickle of excitement zigzag down her back. The air was filled with pulsating ripples of force . . . like an underwater storm.

"No trouble?" she asked, not turning to him.

"No," he said softly, but there was an underlining uneasiness in it.

"The children know Seth's still here. I think they feel that something is going on."

Blythe turned finally, and saw him leaning against the door, his hat and gloves in his hands. He looked frozen, and he might well have been for he had neither his cloak nor his coat.

"Come by the fire," she said. "Now that the children know, we might as well bring Seth and the general inside."

"I tried last night. Seth seems to believe as long as he stays there he can protect Massey. Like the children's tale, *The Emperor's New Clothes*. He still doesn't realize he's naked." There was such quiet desperation in Rafe's voice that Blythe turned to him.

"I found their horses," Rafe said, knowing well every inch of the farm, especially the hidden places, "and watered and fed them."

"Jaime?"

"Firmly lodged in a tree, that damned musket with him. It's more likely to kill him than anyone else."

"You'd be surprised. He's already killed several rabbits with it."

"Maybe I should have taken that gun, too?"

Blythe didn't ask what he had done with Seth's gun, nor the general's he had taken earlier. His own was in its holster at his side. She looked up and saw his steady gaze on her. She looked around, and as if by magic, all the children had disappeared.

Rafe went to her and put his hand on her shoulder. He couldn't get enough of her, of touching her. "I wish I had something to give you," he said hesitantly.

"You've already given me the best present I could have. Just to know you're alive and . . ."

"And all I do is bring you trouble and grief." His voice was broken, and she saw a glimmer of wetness in his eyes. "God knows what else."

He fought himself. Just as he had fought himself on the ride he had taken. He knew he should leave now, and take Massey with him. Along with Seth . . . if that was the only option his brother gave him. But he had promised Benji to stay for the play, and he wanted every minute he could have today . . . with Blythe. Every second, every minute, every hour. Benji's promise was a convenient excuse, and he knew it.

He didn't even have the right to wish her a Merry Christmas, not when he most likely would ruin it. That hurt him infinitely more than any physical wound could. So he touched her instead, telling her as best he could that he loved her.

"I know," she whispered. "Is Jaime coming to dinner?"

"He said to save him some...he'll be along soon," Rafe said. "And he said the pies are in the old toy box in the nursery."

"Is he looking for your men or Seth's?"

"I don't think he knows," Rafe said. "He's trying very hard not to like me because he likes Seth. But I'm your friend, so he figures I can't be too bad. He just wants to protect you from everyone."

"Divided loyalties," she said sadly. "So many divided loyalties."

"It won't be much longer, love. Seth and I were talking about rebuilding the farm. We can go back to raising horses."

If you both live...

The thought hung in the air between them, unsaid.

"We will, love."

But then the kitchen became crowded again with children and eager appetites. Again, Blythe caught the unusual whiff of excitement among them, of secrets, and she couldn't help but wonder what they might be. It took her mind from other things.

Blythe had made a small dish of chicken soup, and put a bowl, biscuits and gravy on a tray. She handed it to Rafe. "For General Massey. Ask Seth to come up for dinner. I want both Hamptons at my table today," she said softly. "Tell him Jaime's keeping watch."

Side by side with Rafe, Seth came into the kitchen minutes later, his thin body nearly swallowed by Rafe's coat, but wearing a tentative smile on his face. The children greeted him affectionately, making him examine the new dolls and scarves. They were, Rafe noted, extremely comfortable with Seth, and he realized again how much Blythe had probably come to depend on his brother. He wished the image didn't hurt so much. It was no longer jealousy that he felt, but guilt. Guilt that he hadn't been around when he was needed. He wondered if those feelings would always burn through him like a white-hot poker.

Neither Seth nor Rafe ate much, although both Rafe and Blythe tried to tempt Seth into eating more. Instead, the three adults received their own pleasure in watching small mouths consume their food with undisguised greed, especially the apple pies. A particularly large slice was saved for Jaime.

When they had finished, Margaret stood up and went to Blythe.

"Miss Blythe. We have a present for you."

Blythe looked dumbfounded, and Seth watched as she glanced over at Rafe.

Rafe stood up and offered her his arm. "May I?"

Margaret giggled, and she and the other children ran off, rare laughter trailing after them.

"I have orders to take you outside in approximately five minutes," Rafe said. "I think Seth has other duties."

Blythe looked at them both suspiciously. Rafe leaned over and kissed her. "You have to close your eyes, and no fair opening them."

Blythe closed them tight, relishing the sensation of depending on Rafe, the feel of his supporting arm on hers. What were they up to? What possible present could they have? She heard feet running up and down the steps, and muffled whispers, and the door opening and closing. She knew they were alone when Rafe's lips touched her neck with teasing kisses.

Then she felt herself being guided forward. "Keep your eyes shut," he insisted, and she obediently squinched them tighter, feeling an anticipatory joy. Her arms were fitted into coat sleeves, and then he was lifting her, holding her body tight to his. She heard the opening of the door and shivered at the blast of cold air.

And then she was being lowered again. "You may open them," he said in a voice warm enough to heat her to her core.

Blythe opened her eyes to the beautiful brightness of a clear day. She looked around, adjusting her eyes to the light, when her lips widened in spontaneous delight. In some enchanted way, her front lawn had been transformed. All the comings and goings this morning had apparently had a reason.

A rough shelter, apparently intended as a stable, had been constructed out of several fence posts and a sheet. A cradle sat just inside. A chair, with a bundled-up Maria and her baby, was not far away. Their one cow had been brought out of hiding and munched contentedly next to the makeshift stable. Blythe turned and saw the door to the fruit cellar open, and Seth emerging, half holding, half carrying General Massey.

Seth helped the wounded general sit down against the big spreading oak near the cellar and shrugged hopelessly. "When I told him what was going on, he insisted on coming up."

Blythe looked over at the soldier. His face was pale and strained, but his eyes were bright. He smiled crookedly, painfully, and looked over to Rafe. "He knows I'm here. And . . . it is Christmas."

She turned to Rafe and saw some fleeting emotion cross his face. Respect. Chagrin. Even a trace of suspicion as he looked from the general to Seth. She could read his mind, and her hand went to his and clutched it tightly.

Rafe returned the pressure, his mind racing ahead. Damn Seth. It was just like his brother to disarm him, throw him off balance. How in the hell could he take the man prisoner in front of the children, after sharing Christmas day? He should have known Seth would use every trick at his disposal.

Seth's mouth bent in amusement as he read his brother's expression, and he spread out his hands innocently.

But then the clip-clopping of a horse captured their attention. Dressed in a white sheet, Margaret approached on the back of their old mare, while Benji carefully, and with great dignity, held the reins.

Abraham met them at the stable.

"We need a place ta stay," Joseph, alias Benji, said.

"No room," Abraham said abruptly.

"But it's cold and Maria's, I mean Mary's, gonna have a baby."

Abraham pursed his mouth as he considered the problem. "Ya can stay in the stable."

Benji suddenly looked blank and glanced frantically toward Rafe for help.

Rafe nodded his head, indicating for Benji to do the same. Out of the corner of his mouth he explained to Blythe, "We didn't have much practice."

Looking relieved, Benji turned back to Abraham and nodded his consent, his head moving with exactly the same proud tilt Rafe's had.

Margaret looked exasperated and slid down from the horse, taking Joseph's arm with more than a little force and leading him to the cradle. She picked up a small bundle.

From another direction came the shepherds, dressed in blankets tied with cord around their waists.

"We come from far away," Micah, Abraham's brother, said solemnly. "Far, far away," he added, caught up in his part. "Very far away."

The other shepherd shoved an elbow into Micah's side, and Blythe, trying to keep her laughter inside her throat, heard Sarah's high excited voice, "We wuz minding sheeps, and angels came and said..." She hesitated.

Margaret hissed something to her, and Blythe heard Rafe's choked chuckle.

"...lo an' behold, a child is born..." Again, she hesitated. "Lo an' behold," she started once more, and Margaret looked disgusted as she whispered again.

"And his name is Jesus," Sarah said triumphantly.

Three angels appeared from the side of the house, singing "Hark, The Herald Angels Sing" in sweet, high voices.

Blythe's hand pressed deeper into Rafe's, her heart swelling as she realized Rafe had helped plan this— that her children, all of them, had thrown off the bonds of reserve and shyness to offer her something of themselves today. Next to Rafe's love, it was the best Christmas present in the world.

She looked up at him, her heart in her eyes, her smile tremulous with emotions too deep, too wonderful to put into words. He bent over and kissed her lightly, and the world was wonderful...bright and hopeful.

"Yanks coming...down the road." It was Jaime's voice, high and piercing in the cold winter air, shattering the peace of a centuries-old time and place. "Yanks," the boy hollered again as he came running down the drive. Seth spun around toward General Massey, and Rafe tensed, his hand automatically going to his pistol, while confused children looked around in sudden terror.

"And over there," yelled Abraham, and Blythe swung around. From the direction opposite the road, dozens of silent figures were emerging from the woods bordering the river. Like the gray ghosts Mosby's men were often called, the Southerners were almost invisible as they filtered from the trees until they knelt, weapons at the ready, aiming at the mass of blue pounding down the hard dirt drive.

And in the middle, between the gray and the blue, were nine terrified children in costume; a newborn babe; one hostile 12-year-old with an ancient musket; two warring brothers; Blythe; and one wounded Confederate general.

Chapter Eight

For moments, those in the middle were absolutely still, as if they were all painted figures on canvas.

The scene seemed to tip and spin as Blythe's legs trembled beneath her. She felt herself caught by one of Rafe's strong arms, and she watched helplessly as the men in blue threw themselves from their horses and the men in gray leveled their pistols and rifles. The world suddenly hushed. Nothing broke the silence as the two armies stared at each other over a tableau that defied imagination.

Rafe's arm tightened around Blythe protectively, keeping her shaking legs from falling under her. His eyes quickly surveyed the scene, a quick glance noting that Seth had moved to his general and stood between him and the Yanks, protecting his patient with his own body.

A loud demanding cry broke the silence, loud but undeniably new.

Jaime lifted his musket, but he didn't know where to aim it. Cautiously he moved next to Maria, who held her crying infant in her arms. He was, quite obviously, ready to protect her and the baby with his life. The other children stood like statues, fear on their faces as the strains of their song drifted agonizingly away.

"My God," said one officer in gray, moving warily, but steadily, toward Seth, a pistol in his hand.

"Sweet Jesus," blurted an officer in blue not far away. The rifle in his hands shook slightly.

The two troops stared at each other, the children, the two men they had come to find, and back at each other, uncertain as to what to do, each waiting for the other to make a move.

But Blythe could only see the stark terror on Maria's face, and she shook loose of Rafe's hold and moved swiftly to the girl's side, putting her arms around her as the baby cried hungrily in a warbling voice.

As Blythe had moved, so did Benji, once more making for Rafe, throwing his arms around his leg and hiding his face in the blue trousers.

The officer in blue, a colonel whom Rafe knew only slightly as a martinet, walked over to him. "Major, we came looking for you...." He noted that Rafe had a gun, and the Confederate officer, standing next to Massey, did not. He inclined his head toward General Massey. "I take it he's your prisoner."

The Confederate officer who had just appeared out of the woods, heard the exchange and tore his eyes away from the bundle being held by Maria, and went to Seth. "We were told to assist you...and the general." The eyes of each of the blue and gray clad troops went to the figure of the blanket-covered man now trying to rise.

Seth moved even closer to his patient. Automatically Rafe moved protectively to shield Seth as one of the Union men cocked his rifle.

Once more, there was a stillness as both the gray and blue troops were caught by the similarity in the two faces and the dangerously shimmering green-blue eyes, in the determined jaws and the proud tilt of their heads. Although one had gold hair, and the other dark, they were undeniably brothers.

A murmur ran among both groups of soldiers and, as if by common unspoken consent, guns lowered, although each figure was poised warily to bring his up again...if need be.

The Confederates were obviously Mosby's men, known to be among the most ruthless and elusive fighters in Virginia. Sheridan's men were no less skilled, or merciful, after bitter years of fighting. Distrust radiated between them.

Benji, still attached to Rafe's leg, sniffled loudly. "Tell 'em to go 'way, Uncle Rafe."

It was said in a loud plaintive voice, and several men smiled at its innocence before their mouths turned grim again as they waited for their leaders' decisions.

"A standoff, I would say," the officer in gray said in a deep, drawling voice.

The Union officer hesitated. He very deliberately, carefully, holstered his pistol, and walked to where Rafe and Seth stood in front of Massey, who, despite his best efforts, had fallen back to the ground. The Union officer's eyes measured the quarry, gauged the extent of his injury, studied the fearlessness and pain in Massey's eyes. The blue-coated officer then sighed and smiled wryly as he looked at the rows of Southern guerrillas. He didn't doubt for a moment that they would do anything to keep their general. The man, injured as he was, just damned well wasn't worth the blood that would be spilled. Not today. He shook his head defeatedly. "He doesn't look like he can do us much harm."

One junior officer spoke up. "But he has information...."

"I imagine all his documents are destroyed by now," the Union officer said, waiting for Massey's nod. "And I doubt he'll tell us anything." He looked around wearily. "I'm not going to start a battle with these children in the middle. Damn it, it's Christmas."

He looked at the officer in gray, whose pistol was pointed directly at his chest, and said slowly, "My name's Buckley. A truce?"

"The general?"

"He can go with you." There was tired resignation in Buckley's voice.

The confederate officer slowly holstered his own gun and held out his hand. "Captain Forester. Truce, it is."

"Until midnight?"

"Until midnight," the Confederate agreed, "and far away from here." He leaned down and offered his arms to Benji, who surprisingly accepted them and allowed himself to be lifted.

"Them young 'uns look mighty thin," said a voice someplace in the back of the Union troops.

"Them Rebs don't look no better," chimed in another.

A drawling Southern voice broke in. "I'd kinda like to see them kids go on with what they were doing."

The Union colonel looked around at the eager faces of troops on both sides too long without families, without warmth. There was a longing in each face, a yearning that was universal. And there was hope.

Hope that somehow this Christmas wouldn't be like the other angry, lonely ones.

He turned to Captain Forester. "Would you and your men, and the children, care to share Christmas dinner with us...it's not much, just what we could carry. But there is bacon and potatoes and coffee...?"

Forester bowed. "We'd be..." He stopped. He couldn't quite say the word "honored." There had been so much vicious fighting between them. "What in the hell would we be?" he said in perplexity to Seth.

"Grateful," Seth supplied. "Very, very grateful."

"Very well," Forester agreed. "We would be that," he said, slightly bemused.

The Yanks were already prowling through their saddlebags for sweets which they now handed to the slightly less statuelike children. The youngsters looked to Blythe for reassurance before reaching out eagerly and taking them.

"Ma'am?" A Southerner came up to Blythe, whose arms were still around Maria.

Blythe looked up through eyes that again were becoming suspiciously wet. "Yes?"

The man shuffled awkwardly, his mouth moving in a shy smile. "Do you think I could take a peek at that thar baby...it's been so long...and...well...you see my wife had one not so long ago and I ain't never seen it."

Blythe looked down at Maria, whose arms were still trembling, although much of the tense, hovering violence was filtering away. "Maria?" she said softly.

The girl looked up at the anxiety and desperate longing on the man's face, and slowly, cautiously, she held the baby out for inspection.

"Ain't he the purtiest little thing," the soldier exclaimed with awe.

"She," Maria said, in a surprisingly strong voice. "She."

"She's the purtiest little thing," he corrected himself, and suddenly there were other men crowding around, each taking their turn to look at the baby despite the color of their uniform.

"She's mighty bitsy," one man said in a soft voice that didn't go at all with the hard eyes and jagged scar across his face.

"She was born just this morning," Maria said quietly, and her shoulders straightened pridefully for the first time since she had come to Blythe seven months earlier.

"You shouldn't be up then, ma'am," one man said. He looked at Blythe. "Can I help her into the house?"

Blythe saw the fear return to Maria's eyes. "I'll go with you," she said, and Maria then nodded, her expression relaxing as she saw the kindness in the man's expression. Blythe took the child from Maria and followed as the soldier gently supported her up the porch stairs.

Blythe tucked the young girl into bed, the baby in her arms, its small mouth eager to suckle again.

"I don't understand what happened," the girl said hesitantly. "They were all so angry, then..."

"It's Christmas, sweetheart. Wonderful things happen at Christmas. Like your baby."

Maria nodded, satisfied. "I wish Christmas was every day."

Blythe nodded, her throat choking with those tears she hadn't shed.

She turned around and went downstairs, back out onto the lawn. Rafe and Seth were standing together, pleased grins on their faces as they introduced each other to their acquaintances. All the men had heard of sets of brothers divided by war, but they had never met one. It was somehow reassuring, comforting, that these two still had powerful protective feelings for each other. Perhaps it meant that when the war was over, peace wouldn't be so difficult.

Rafe saw Blythe and put his arm around her, pulling her close to him. As close as possible, because Benji was back, his security apparently Rafe's leg.

The embrace was shattered by Benji's voice. "Are you gonna be our papa?"

Approximately fifty pairs of Confederate faces and an equal number of Union ones, turned to the couple with growing smiles. "Am I?" Rafe questioned. He waited anxiously, even fearfully, for her answer. Although she had declared her love for him, she had avoided answering his proposal. He had believed it was because of Seth, but perhaps . . . there was something else. Perhaps he had changed too much. . . . Perhaps . . .

But all his fears fled as he looked down at her. Her eyes were as bright as candles as she whispered, "Oh, yes."

The Confederate captain, Forester, cocked his head at the words, his hard, bleak face breaking into a grin. "We have a preacher with us if you're of a mind to make it a Christmas occasion."

Blythe looked up at Rafe, hope singing in her heart, eagerness and adoration in her eyes, and Rafe needed no more urging.

He nodded. "Thank you," he said slowly, and then turned to Seth. "You'll be the best man?"

"Who else?" Seth replied with a wink. "I'm pleased you've finally recognized it."

There were chuckles among the throng, traveling from man to man as they repeated the words to those who hadn't heard.

"I can play a passing good harmonica," one soldier commented.

"I have a guitar," offered another in a different uniform.

Blythe looked out at the waiting soldiers. For the moment, the uniforms didn't matter, not to any of them. This was Christmas, and for most of them, it was the first time in many months, even years, that life abounded. Birth. Marriage. Love. Laughter. Giving instead of taking. Bound by a commonality of hope that was universal, they each reached inside themselves for their own memories. Memories of their own loves, of their own children, of Christmases past and visions of Christmases future.

Blythe's heart swelled with a joy and faith so great she thought her heart would burst as she searched the faces around her. Tomorrow, they would be enemies again, but today... today... well, today showed what could be. Would be.

She held one hand out to Rafe and the other to Seth, who took it with tenderness.

Seth leaned close to her. "You told me there would be a miracle." He looked around. "I never believed there would be so many. You have a very special way of making them happen."

Blythe glowed as her hand tightened on his, and she stretched on tiptoe to kiss his cheek. "Thank you, Seth. Thank you for everything."

It was not the ceremony Blythe had envisioned, a church wedding celebrated with lifelong friends.

It was much, much better.

Standing under the golden sunlight of a bright Christmas Day, she and Rafe held hands, his reassuringly tight, as their eyes loved and promised. Promised so very much.

The preacher was a soldier, who used a gun when he wasn't using a Bible, but his tone was soft and reverent as he said the familiar words. Familiar, but not familiar, Blythe thought, because now their meaning was so much more precious.

"We are gathered here together..." Blythe's eyes left Rafe's for a moment and went from man to man, many of them with tears in their eyes. The soft sound of a guitar was barely audible in the background. A love song.

Together. Men who had put aside their differences to rejoice with them. There was something extraordinarily beautiful about it. And about the children whose faces were rapt with the mystery of what they were seeing.

"To join in holy wedlock . . ." But they were joined long ago, Blythe thought. Joined in so many ways. In heart and soul, and now, finally, in the sight of God, "and these witnesses."

"To have and to hold..." Blythe trembled as Rafe's hand spontaneously tightened on hers. So long. It had been so long . . . but never again. Never again.

"From this day forward..." Until eternity, Blythe knew. Her eyes, her smile, promised Rafe at least that long.

"I now pronounce you man and wife."

Rafe didn't wait any longer. His lips touched hers with a frantic need to confirm the ceremony, to make real the words that he had only dreamed of for so long. Only then did Blythe, in some part of her mind, realize the preacher had not included the usual words, "Until death do you part..."

Her own touch, the gentle shining avowal of love, reassured him as his had done earlier during the ceremony. The kiss deepened until her very bones seemed to melt and her heart seemed unable to contain the exquisite joy that swelled there.

There was a chuckle, first one, and then another, before they broke loose and accepted congratulations and bashful smiles from the war-weary men.

The harmonica broke out into "Lorena," and Rafe bowed low as the guitar added its soft sound to the music. He took Blythe in his arms, and the two of them danced, their eyes locked on each other, their touches gentle yet possessive. Minutes later, the Union officer danced with her, and then the Confederate leader. Carols were sung and food shared. The children looked with wonder at men who gave instead of took. As the shadows started to fall, Union Colonel Buckley and Confederate Captain Forester announced regretfully that it was time to leave.

Blythe looked for Seth, but he was gone...as was General Massey. Rafe saw her searching look, and a sudden bleak shadow crossed his face. But it was gone almost as quickly as it had come, and he smiled with wry understanding. "I don't think he's taking any chances with his general."

It was a bittersweet reminder of the war, yet there lingered around them a kind of peace. The magical, illusory mood lasted as the soldiers emptied their saddlebags and piled what food they had on the porch. It continued as each approached Rafe and Blythe and wished them well, even the hard, lean Confederates who knew they might soon be facing Rafe in battle.

Blythe and Rafe watched the last ones leave. The children were, for once, completely full with food, and their eyes full of wonder as they watched the gray figures disappear once more through the woods, and the mounted blue ones trot off in formation in the other direction.

Benji and the others were still dressed in their blankets and sheets. All of them had crumbs around their mouths and happy smiles in their eyes . . . like ordinary children. Even Jaime looked content for once.

The sun set, spreading a golden glow over the woods as if blessing them.

Blythe's mind wandered over the events since Seth had knocked on her door last night. Could everything have happened in less than twenty-four hours . . . in one day? In one enchanted day? She felt Rafe's arm tighten around her.

Just one day. And so many miracles. So many.

And now she knew there would be more. Against the dying blaze of the sun, she could see Rafe and Seth working together, building again. She could see the children playing, laughing, unafraid, and envision the horses in the fields beyond. The earth would spring back to life, and heal itself.

She knew it now. Today had shown that it could.

Blythe looked up at Rafe, and they rose together. They knew exactly how to begin.

But at the top step, Blythe looked back at the now-deserted lawn, at the trees standing silent sentinel, at the first stars blinking above. Her gaze hesitated there. "Thank you," she whispered. "Thank you."

* * * * *

A Note from Patricia Potter

Christmas has always been a special holiday for me, and there have been many memorable ones. But none more so than the year I spent Christmas Eve with strangers.

It was my first Christmas after completing college, and I was working with the *Atlanta Journal*. Since newspapers don't close down for the holidays and I was the new kid on the block, I had to work on Christmas Eve in Atlanta, Georgia. But I was determined to get home to Huntsville, Alabama, some 180 miles away, for Christmas.

I was planning to drive, but a sudden ice storm changed my mind, and at the last moment, I booked a flight and begged off work several hours early. I drove to the airport and happily boarded a plane for Huntsville around 2:00 p.m., Christmas Eve. The plane took off an hour late, and just as we were about to land in Huntsville, the runway iced over. We continued on to Memphis and, there, too, the runway iced over minutes before our arrival. They sent us back to Atlanta! After more than seven hours on board, we were right where we started.

Undaunted, I asked whether anyone wanted to risk the drive to Huntsville. Although we'd heard the roads were closed, three other frustrated passengers volunteered. There was a widow who had five children waiting for her, a Sunday school teacher with polio who wanted to get home to her family, and a businessman who had caught pneumonia in Ohio and had been released from the hospital on the condition that he would fly straight home.

Sleet was falling, ice was forming on the roads and Huntsville was a range of mountains away—a route of steep hills and lonely roads. Being Southerners, none of us knew how to drive in icy weather. But by then we were four musketeers, united and resolute in our purpose. We climbed into my car, the gentleman driving, and started off. Within an hour, the headlights died. Our driver, still recovering from pneumonia, stepped out into the rain and sleet and snow, lifted the hood, jiggled some wires and off we went again. Over the next several hours, this little excercise became a common occurrence.

We were one of the few cars on the road, and nothing was open: no stores, no gas stations, no place to phone about the weather. The conditions were treacherous, even without the fact that the headlights went off at the most awkward and dangerous of times. The trip was often one of extreme terror. (A solid preparation for a career in writing about adventure.) But we exchanged stories and sang, even though our driver suffered fits of coughing.

Strangers became family. Christmas became the warmth of sharing. The moments seemed touched with a special kind of magic.

We finally arrived in Huntsville during the bleak gray hours of Christmas morning, and we parted, never to see one another again. But that Christmas Eve, frightening at times, funny at others, seemed to me what Christmas was all about: the coming together of strangers and family in comfort and friendship.

For that reason, it was my most memorable Christmas and will always hold a special place in my heart.

Patricia Potter

CHRISTMAS AT BITTER CREEK

★

Ruth Langan

To my Mom and Dad,
Who always made Christmas so special
for my sisters and me;

And to my children
Who keep Christmas in my heart;

And, of course, to Tom
Who adds the magic.

WALNUT PUMPKIN CHIFFON PIE

1½ cups walnuts, finely chopped
3 tbsp granulated sugar
2 tbsp soft butter
1 envelope unflavored gelatin
¼ cup cold water
3 eggs, separated
½ cup milk
¾ cup brown sugar, packed
½ tsp salt
1½ tsp pumpkin-pie spice
1 cup canned pumpkin
¼ tsp cream of tartar
⅓ cup granulated sugar
whipped cream
walnut halves

Preheat oven to 350° F.

Crush chopped walnuts with rolling pin. Mix together crushed walnuts, 3 tbsp sugar and 2 tbsp butter. Cover sides and bottom of a 9″ pie plate to form crust. Bake for 10 to 12 minutes or until lightly browned. Cool and chill.

Soften gelatin in water.

In a large sauce pan, beat together egg yolks and milk. Beat in brown sugar, salt and pumpkin-pie spice. Add gelatin and pumpkin. Blend well. Cook over moderate heat, stirring until gelatin dissolves and mixture thickens. Remove from heat and let cool.

When pumpkin mixture begins to gel, in a separate bowl, beat together egg whites and cream of tartar until soft peaks form. Gradually beat in ⅓ cup sugar to make meringue.

Fold meringue into pumpkin mixture. Turn into chilled crust. Chill for 4 hours or until firm.

Garnish with whipped cream and walnut halves.

Chapter One

He was good at waiting. Hadn't he spent a lifetime perfecting the art?

He sat astride the big roan, watching as the first snowflakes drifted through the canopy of evergreen boughs. At this altitude the air was thin. He breathed it in, filling his lungs. Then he spotted the hoofprint. It wasn't much more than a small depression in the hard-packed soil. But it was what he'd been looking for. He slid from the saddle and studied the print for long seconds. Leading his mount, he walked a few paces, then crouched over a second set of similar prints. He followed them until they disappeared along the rocky path.

He studied the trail ahead. There were a hundred places where a man could hide himself. Until he wanted to be seen.

Drawing his hat low on his forehead, he pulled himself into the saddle and checked his rifle. Very soon now, he'd be called upon once more to use his skill with a gun. It was, he thought with a grimace, the only thing he did well.

"With Christmas approaching, I thought you might all enjoy writing about that first Christmas, and what it means to us today." Laura Conners glanced around at the dozen children who filled the small schoolhouse.

They seemed puzzled. Though she had often spoken about the meaning of Christmas, the children of this tough land had little time to contemplate the significance of anything except the constantly changing weather and how it would affect crops and livestock.

At the thought of the weather, Laura cast a speculative glance through the schoolhouse window and came to a decision. "It appears to be snowing harder. Put away your slates, children. Your parents will be concerned. I'll dismiss you earlier than usual."

Though no one actually cheered, she saw the looks that passed from one student to another. How well she remembered the joy of being given an unexpected break from the dull routine, of being allowed to romp in the snow instead of fretting over the sums on her slate.

As if on cue, coming up the path toward the schoolhouse was Anna Thompson, whose five lively sons seemed to throw her into a constant state of confusion. Anna had confirmed just this morning that there would be another baby on the way next spring. As she had five times before, she had begun knitting a lovely pink blanket.

"Beth, will you help me with the little ones?" Laura asked, leading the way to the cloakroom.

"Yes, Miss Conners."

Working alongside her, a shy dark-haired girl of fourteen buttoned coats and tied scarves. When the younger children were bundled into their warm clothes, her teacher gave her a grateful smile.

"Thank you, Beth."

"You're welcome. I'll help you clean up, Miss Comers."

"Another time. That snow is coming down much too fast. I want you to go straight home before the trails get covered."

"Yes, Miss Conners."

Her teacher heard the note of regret in the girl's voice. Beth Mills was never happier than when she was allowed to stay after school and help with chores. The bright little girl desperately wanted to learn all she could, so that one day she could be a teacher, too. But now that her father had died and her mother had taken a job in the Red Garter, Beth's chances of continuing her education seemed over. Wanda Mills needed her daughter's help. At fourteen, Beth's childhood was almost over.

Laura understood the girl's need to linger at the school. There was little reason for Beth to hurry home to the small cramped room she shared with her mother at Mrs. Cormeyer's rooming house.

Anna Thompson breezed into the school and held out her arms to embrace the sons who bustled about her.

Laura couldn't help chuckling at the sight of the plump overworked woman surrounded by her always busy active boys.

As Beth began to follow the others from the school, Laura hesitated, then called her back. "I baked some apple spice cake last night. Early Christmas presents." She lifted a loaf wrapped in a linen towel. "I thought you and your mother might enjoy this."

The girl's mouth rounded in surprise. "Oh, thank you, Miss Conners." She lowered her head, breathing in the fragrance of cinnamon and apples, avoiding her teacher's eyes. "Mama used to bake when my pa was alive. But she doesn't much care what she eats anymore. Or even if she eats."

"Maybe this will help."

Laura glanced at the sweet child beside her. There was a time when Beth had been part of a happy, loving family. When Bill had died suddenly of a ruptured appendix, Wanda and her young daughter had been devastated. Wanda had simply turned her back on the ranch she and her husband had built in the wilderness, and taking far less for the herd than it was worth, had moved into town. From that moment on, she had spent every waking moment trying to keep herself and her daughter together.

Everyone knew that it was a struggle. There were no secrets here. The town of Bitter Creek was so small, everyone knew everyone else's business almost before it happened.

"I'll see you Monday, Beth."

Laura watched as the girl ran to catch up with the other children. Most of them lived in town, and walked the scant mile to the schoolhouse. A few, whose ranches scattered for miles in either direction, rode horseback or drove small pony carts.

When the schoolhouse was empty, Laura straightened the desks, swept the floor and banked the fire in the small stone fireplace before carefully bracing the door against the north wind.

As she stepped into the cold, she watched the figure of Ned Harrison, mayor of Bitter Creek, trudging toward her.

"Going home early, are you, Laura?"

"Didn't want the parents to worry after their children."

He brushed snow from his whiskers and cleared his throat. "I had hoped to give you a few dollars extra in your pay for Christmas, Laura. But the town just doesn't have enough money right now. And since you don't have any family..." He shrugged his shoulders in an embarrassed gesture as his voice trailed off.

Laura swallowed. She'd been counting on that money to keep the ranch going. But she understood what he meant. Times were hard for everyone. And those with children suffered the most at this time of year.

She forced a cheerful note to her voice that she didn't feel. "It's all right, Ned. I'll be fine."

He smiled and seemed relieved to be finished with this unpleasant duty. "I knew you'd understand, Laura." He touched his hand to his hat and turned away. "You'd better get going. Snow's coming down hard."

Climbing into her wagon, Laura drew a heavy blanket around her shoulders and flicked the reins. She would not think about the flour that money would have bought. Or the good wool fabric in Ned's mercantile. She would get by. Hadn't she always? Besides, it was almost Christmas. And from her earliest days, she had always believed that Christmas was a special time, a magical time.

By the time she reached home, her dark hair and eyebrows were frosted with snow.

In the barn she turned the horse into a stall and forked hay and water into troughs before milking the cow and gathering the eggs that should have been gathered that morning. But there had been a pump to prime, and wood to chop for the fireplace before she left for the tiny schoolhouse. Her days always began before sunup, and never seemed to end until the logs in the fireplace had long since burned to embers.

With a bucket in one hand and a basket in the other, she ran the hundred yards to the darkened ranch house. The door hung at a lopsided angle on rusted hinges and gave a squeal of protest as she swung it wide.

"I swear, Papa, I'll fix that door tomorrow," she muttered under her breath.

Inside she lit a lantern and set it on the kitchen table. Within minutes she had a fire started in the fireplace. Blowing on her cold hands, she draped a shawl around her shoulders and set about fixing herself a supper of cold meat, bread and preserves.

"I know you wouldn't approve, Papa," she said, glancing at the empty chair across the table. "You always said supper wasn't supper without hot biscuits and gravy." A little smile touched her lips. "But maybe I'll kill the old rooster for Sunday supper. And I'll make bread pudding for dessert."

She knew, even before the words were out of her mouth, that she wouldn't follow through on the threat. There were never enough hours in the day to do all she planned. But it was pleasant just thinking about the way Sunday suppers used to be when she was a girl and Mama and Papa were alive.

When the table was cleared she pulled her chair close to the fire. Dear Lord, it was cold tonight. She thought about staying here a few minutes longer. It was heaven to be warm, full, contented. But with idleness came unbidden thoughts. Thoughts of where her life was going. Thoughts of what might have been.

What had Papa always said? "An idle mind is the devil's workshop." She picked up a broom and swept the porch clean of the snow that had already begun piling up against the door. That finished, she retreated indoors and gathered her mending into her lap as she settled once more into the chair. Squinting in the fading light of the fire, she plied needle and thread. Mama's old gowns had been made over so many times, the fabric was threadbare. Still, she thought, examining the seams of a pale blue calico dress, she might get one more year out of this. There was no money left over for fancy clothes. What little money she made teaching had to go back into the ranch. She glanced around at the snug house. It was all she had. But with Papa's passing away, it took everything she had to keep it going. She had turned it into a somewhat comfortable if shabby retreat. There were several needlepoint pillows on the rockers. There was a colorful rag rug in the center of the floor. And the delicate lace curtains at the windows had once been Mama's wedding dress. Since the gown had begun to rot and fall apart, it seemed a sin not to make use of what was left. Besides, Laura thought with a sudden pain around her heart, she'd never have a chance to wear Mama's wedding gown.

Oh, not that there weren't men around who'd marry her. If she'd have them. Nate Burns was a widower with two small children. Lord knows, those little ones needed a mother. And Nate had let it be known among the townspeople that he considered it his duty to offer his home to the spinster teacher. But Laura knew she'd have to be hog-tied and gagged before she'd consent to marry a man as mean-mouthed as Nate.

There was the banker, Jed McMasters. Some in town figured he'd be the richest man in the territory one day. But the only time she'd ever seen Jed smile was when he was counting money. The rest of the time he looked like he'd just swallowed something vile.

There'd been a man. Once. She pricked her finger with the needle and felt tears fill her eyes. There she was again; thinking thoughts that had no place in her life now.

She sewed until the fire burned low and her eyelids grew heavy. Then, setting aside her mending, she carefully folded her lap robe and picked up the lantern.

With a sigh of exhaustion she crossed to her bedroom. The woman in the looking glass startled her for a moment. Her hair was pulled back in a severe bun and secured with several pins. Despite the pains she took to look like a proper teacher, a few corkscrew curls had pried themselves loose to drift about her cheeks and neck. She touched a finger to the fine lines that had begun to be etched around her eyes. Some days her hazel eyes seemed more green than amber. This night, by the light of the lantern, they were a dull copper. By her own design, the shapeless dress hid all traces of the slender form beneath. Pa had often warned her that the good people of Bitter Creek expected the town's teacher to be neither man nor woman, but rather an authority figure akin to a doctor or preacher.

She had held to her papa's strict upbringing. She had earned the town's respect. She was careful to do or say nothing that could be construed as improper. She lived her life, as Papa had instructed, according to a very rigid code.

"Miss Conners," she said with a trace of sarcasm, studying her reflection. The very name conjured up visions of a crochety old woman wielding a slate, a Bible and a hickory stick.

She slipped out of her prim gown and petticoats and pulled on a warm homespun nightgown. Brushing her long hair until it crackled, she stared at the woman in the mirror. She'd heard the whispers of the children outside the schoolhouse. Old Miss Conners. Perhaps the children were right. Though she was not yet thirty, she probably looked to them like a withered old crab apple. She was becoming more and more like her papa. Tough. Strict. Unyielding. But without her constant reminders, she knew that many of the town's children would grow up wild, with little regard for moral principles.

It was this rugged land, she thought, gazing at the snow that curtained her window. The men and women who came here were so busy trying to survive in this wilderness, they had little time left over for the basic rules of civilization. Hadn't she seen it time and again?

Hadn't it even happened to people she'd known and...loved?

"You're turning into an old prune, Laura Conners."

With a clatter she dropped her mother's ivory-handled brush and turned away, refusing to look at herself again. It hurt too much.

She blew out the lantern and climbed wearily into bed.

The horse crested the hill, then paused, feeling its rider shift in the saddle.

The moon was a pale thin sliver, almost obliterated by the falling snow.

Slumped low over the horse's neck, Matt Braden gripped his rifle tightly in his right hand. His left arm dangled uselessly at his side. While the horse stamped and snorted, the snow at his feet was stained crimson.

He was growing weaker by the minute. Matt knew that if he hadn't tied himself to the saddle, he would already be lying face down somewhere back there on the trail. But he had to find shelter quickly, before he froze to death.

He saw the light below. Too small for a camp fire. A candle or lantern most likely. Squinting against the falling snowflakes, he saw the light flicker and die.

Had it been his imagination? Or was there a cabin somewhere below?

He gave only the slightest nudge with his knees. But it was enough to signal his horse into a slow walk. Picking through the drifts, the horse moved ahead, sensing the need to carry its burden gingerly. Each movement brought a stab of pain to the rider, who clung to consciousness by a mere thread. When Matt thought he could bear it no longer, the horse came to an abrupt halt. Matt lifted his head. Looming directly in front of him was a wall.

He knew he should check out the cabin before entering. They could be here ahead of him, waiting to finish the job. But there was no way he could slide from the saddle and crawl to a window. He closed his eyes, then blinked them open. For a minute he thought he was home. He knew this cabin. Knew every stick of furniture he would find inside.

There would be the table his father had made out of the bottom and sides of the wagon. And six chairs carved from saplings. In the loft above was a feather mattress, where his father and mother slept. Below, the bunks were lined up against the south wall of the sod shack. Four small bunks, for Matt and his three brothers.

He smiled. What hellions they'd become. Especially after Ma died. They'd grown up wild, free, with no restrictions issued by their grieving father.

Were they inside now, waiting for him?

He shook his head as if to clear it. His mind was playing tricks on him. This wasn't home. There was no home anymore. His father had followed his mother to the grave. And his brothers? They were dead. All three of them. Jase had been shot in a bank robbery. Cal had been gunned down in a saloon in Texas. Dan had met a crazy tenderfoot who wanted to prove to the world that he could draw faster than one of the legends of Arizona Territory. All dead. And all before they had barely tasted life.

Was his lot in life any better? He felt a wave of anger and despair. Did it matter which side of the law a man chose? When he was dead, he was just as dead. And soon, very soon now, he would join his brothers. But at least he would be free of this pain.

The reins slipped from his fingers. He leaned down until his cheek was resting on the horse's quivering neck. He was so cold he could no longer feel his hands or feet.

He couldn't seem to focus on what to do. And then the fury inside him brought it back to him. Seek shelter. Bind his wounds. Stay alive.

Through a haze of pain he forced his useless hand to seek the knife at his waist. Sweat beaded his forehead as he strained to cut the rope holding him secure. As the knife sliced through the rope, he felt himself falling helplessly. Tumbling into a pit of blackness.

At the sound of something crashing onto her porch, Laura sat straight up in bed. In her years in this wilderness she had faced the fury of nature as well as the fury of man. And though she was never prepared for such battles, she had never backed down.

In the darkness she fumbled for the rusted rifle she always kept on the table beside her bed. The gleaming coals from the fire cast a pale glow over the big front room, lighting it enough to show her the way to the door. Though her hands were trembling, she threw open the door, prepared to face any danger.

The first thing she saw was the riderless horse. Then she saw the man lying at her feet. He was as still as death.

"Dear Lord in heaven!"

She dropped the rifle and touched a hand to the man's throat. A heartbeat. Erratic but strong.

"Here," she said, bending close to his ear. "You'll have to help me if I'm ever going to get you inside."

The man moaned, then struggled to move. Laura draped his arm over her shoulder, then staggered under his weight. With a tremendous pull, she managed to drag him inside and across the floor to her father's room. With great effort she got him settled in the big bed. Then she hurried back to the porch, where she retrieved her rifle. She quickly slammed the door against the biting cold.

Touching a match to the wick in the lantern, she carried it close and bent over the man. He wore a cowhide jacket and a wide-brimmed hat pulled low over his face. Several days' growth of beard darkened his chin.

From the amount of blood oozing through his faded shirt and staining his jacket, she knew that he was gravely wounded. She poured a generous amount of water into a pan, then set the pan atop the hot coals of the fire. While waiting for the water to boil, she took up her father's sharp hunting knife and began the difficult task of cutting away the man's clothes. When that was done, she leaned back and studied him closely by the light of the lantern.

Despite the beard and the shaggy growth of dark hair that curled over the collar of his shirt and spilled across his forehead, she felt the jolt of recognition.

"Matthew. Matthew Braden!" His name was expelled in a rush of air.

His lips moved as if he were speaking. But though she leaned close, she could not make out what he was saying. His eyes remained closed.

"Hush now, Matthew, you're safe here," she whispered, blinking away the tears that had mysteriously filled her eyes.

But though she spoke the words with fervor, she couldn't dispel the doubt in her heart. He had lost a lot of blood, judging from the looks of his jacket. And he was cold. So cold.

With trembling hands she cut away the last of his jacket and shirt. The sight of his wound caused her to sit back on her heels a moment, feeling light-headed.

It was a bullet wound. Somehow, she had known it would be. Matthew had always lived on the edge of danger.

The skin was jagged and torn; the flesh swollen with infection. Though Laura knew what she had to do, she wasn't certain she had the strength or the nerves for such a task.

She placed the hunting knife in the pan of boiling water, then went off in search of clean linens. Moving the lantern closer, she bent to her task.

With the tip of the knife, she probed the wound until she located the bullet. Though Matt moaned, he made no movement. That fact frightened her. He must indeed be weak to lie so quietly while she inflicted such searing pain. Once the bullet was removed, she cleansed the wound, then dressed it with strips of linen.

With that task done, she removed his heavy boots before drawing the blankets tightly about him.

From the wood piled neatly in the corner of the cabin she selected a log and some kindling. Within minutes she had a fire crackling in the big stone fireplace of her father's old room.

The sound of a horse outside caused her to jump. Her nerves, she realized, were stretched to the breaking point.

After peering out the window to be certain no one else was around, she drew on her shawl and led Matthew's horse to the barn. There she unsaddled the stallion and settled him into a stall with food and water. Shivering, she raced back to the house and stood in front of the fire until the trembling stopped.

At a moan from the bed, she looked up sharply. Though the sound of his pain brought her fresh anguish, there was comfort in it, as well. At least Matthew was still alive.

She took the quilt from her bed and walked to the bedroom where he lay as still as death. Pulling a chair close to the bed, she draped the quilt around her and watched as his blankets rose and fell with each measured breath.

She would stay as close as possible and see him through the night.

Fighting exhaustion, Laura's lids fluttered.

Matthew Braden had come back to Bitter Creek. But had he come back to live? Or to die?

Chapter Two

Laura slept fitfully. Each time she awoke, she leaned close to touch a hand to Matt's forehead. His skin was on fire. Lord, he was so hot.

Without realizing it, she curled her lips into a smile of remembrance. Papa had always called Matt a hothead.

"Damned troublemaker." It took a lot for Will Conners to swear. But Matthew Braden always seemed to bring out the worst in her father. From the time Matt and his brothers first showed up in Bitter Creek, Papa was as nervous as a herd of mustangs stalked by a wildcat.

"A man who lives by the gun will perish by the gun," Papa used to intone regularly. "And believe me, that boy and his brothers are headed for nothing but destruction."

"That isn't fair, Papa. Matthew isn't bad—he's just wild."

Had it been that wild streak that had attracted her to him? She didn't know. She knew only that from the first moment she'd seen Matthew Braden, she'd lost her heart. And her common sense. The more others put him down, the more she seemed driven to defend him.

Papa had recognized it even before she did. He saw the soft look that came into her eyes whenever Matt passed her in town. Matt had a roguish way of touching a hand to his hat and winking. She had a curious way of blushing and studying the toe of her boot. Matt's tone, though gruff, was always respectful in her presence. Papa heard the way her voice caught in her throat whenever the wild youth had spoken to her. And when her father pointed it out to her, he'd made her feel ashamed of the way her heart had betrayed her.

"You watch yourself, girl. You're better than that. I know his kind. Without the proper guidance, they go from bad to worse. One of these days his mischief will get out of hand. Those brothers of his will persuade him to help them steal some cattle or rob a bank. And once the law is after them, their only recourse is a gun. They'll shoot their way out of one scrape after another, until someone comes along with a faster gun."

As much as she hated to admit it, Papa had been right. She'd heard stories of the wild Braden brothers, even after they left Bitter Creek. And though she hadn't heard a thing about Matt for years, it appeared that once again Papa had been right. This time, someone had been faster than Matt.

Agitated, Laura drew the quilt tighter around her shoulders and squeezed her eyes shut to blot out the image of the man who lay near death.

"Don't die, Matthew," she whispered. "No matter what you've done, I don't want you to die."

* * *

Matt lay very still, absorbing the alien feeling of comfort. After a dizzying lifetime of living on the edge, he had always known heaven would be like this. A soft weightless feeling, like floating on a cloud. Warmth. The blessed warmth of a cocoon.

He sighed contentedly and shifted. Instantly pain crashed through him, shattering the mood. He wasn't dead, after all. He was very much alive, and his body was one large mass of pain.

He touched a hand to his shoulder, expecting the sticky warmth of blood. Instead his fingers encountered clean linen bindings. His eyes flew open.

Where the hell was he? And who had dressed his wounds?

He studied the wooden beams of the ceiling and watched the flickering shadows cast by the fire in the stone fireplace across the room. A cabin. The one he had approached last night. Though he couldn't remember, he'd apparently persuaded the owner to give him aid and comfort. There'd been something familiar about the cabin, but that was probably just his mind playing tricks. He seemed to recall thinking it was his childhood home. But that was impossible. He hadn't had a home in a very long time.

It caused him considerable torment to turn his head even a fraction, but he had to see the rest of this room. His gaze fastened on the figure in the chair beside his bed. A patchwork quilt covered all but the tip of a small upturned nose and a wide forehead covered by a spill of dark curls. As the figure sighed and shifted, he felt as if had just taken a blow to the midsection.

Laura. Sweet Jesus! It couldn't be. With a look of naked hunger he squinted through a haze of pain and devoured the wonderful sight that greeted him.

She was asleep in the rocker, the quilt tucked primly about her. The edge of the quilt had slipped low on her shoulders, exposing an ivory nightdress that clearly revealed the outline of her breasts. The sight caused a rush of heat, which only added to his fever.

How many nights had he dreamed of seeing her like this? For so long now, he had told himself that she couldn't possibly be as beautiful as the girl he remembered. But there she was, all soft and sleepy, curled like a kitten in a rocking chair. And no amount of imagination was as wonderful as this living breathing woman whose chest rose and fell so peacefully.

Before the pain had overtaken him, he had known he was on the trail to Bitter Creek. But in the confusion of the gunfight, his escape and his efforts to stay alive, that thought had been lost to him. He took a shallow breath, fighting the pain that swamped him. No wonder his thoughts had been of home and childhood. Laura Conners had been a special part of his growing to manhood. And all these years, though she had rejected his love, he had carried her in a special place in his heart.

His gaze fell on the pitcher of water that rested on a bedside table. His throat was as parched as the desert. He was burning with fever. But though he yearned for relief, it was too much effort to speak.

He returned his attention to the woman who slept in the chair, afraid that if he but closed his eyes, the vision would disappear. Though he made a valiant struggle, he could no longer find the strength to stay awake. His lids flickered, then closed.

Thin winter sunlight spilled through a crack in the curtains. Laura came awake slowly, stretching first one leg, then the other. As she did, the quilt slid to the floor. With a sound of annoyance she bent to retrieve it. Her hands paused in midair as she turned in time to see that Matt was fully awake, watching her.

The quilt was forgotten.

"How... are you feeling?"

Without waiting for his reply she automatically reached a hand to his forehead. That was her first mistake. The moment her fingers came in contact with his flesh, she jerked her hand back as if burned.

Aware of her reaction, he gave a weak smile. "I've..." He swallowed and tried again. "I've felt better." Though every word caused him pain, he forced himself to continue. "But at least I'm alive. Thanks to you."

"You gave me quite a scare."

Awkwardly she reached for the quilt, but before she could drape it modestly around her shoulders he croaked, "Could I have some water?"

"Of course." She filled a dipper, then knelt by the side of the bed. Gently lifting his head, she held the dipper to his lips. That was her second mistake. She had forgotten the shock she had always experienced whenever she was too close to this man.

Her hand trembled, causing her to spill some of the water.

"I'm sorry."

At her whispered words, he lifted his hand and closed his fingers over hers, holding the dipper steady. Though it cost him a great deal of pain, he decided it was worth it just to be touching her.

She was achingly aware of the big hand holding hers. And though his touch disturbed her, she could not deny the thrill it brought.

When he'd drunk his fill she lowered his head to the pillow and moved away as quickly as she could manage.

Needing to be busy, she bustled about, straightening his blankets, drawing open the curtains. When she spoke again, she prayed her voice would not betray her nervousness. "I could fix you a coddled egg if you think you're up to eating anything."

When he made no response, she turned. The effort to speak, to move his hand, had drained him. He had already returned to his troubled dreams.

Matt lay very still and strained to sort out all the unfamiliar scents and sounds that greeted him. How long had it been since he'd slept in a big feather bed, while the air hung heavy with the mouth-watering fragrance of apples and spices?

He was in a ranch house. Laura's ranch house.

Cattle were lowing in the field. From the barn came the sound of horses blowing and snorting. Outside his window, chickens clucked. In the other room he heard Laura humming.

He needed to see her, to talk to her before her father returned from the fields.

Rolling to his side, he tossed back the blankets and swung his feet to the floor. The room spun in dizzying circles and he waited for the feeling to pass. Focusing on the doorway, he took a step, then another.

She had not yet seen him. Bent over the oven, she removed a pan and quickly set it on the table, then placed a second pan in the oven and closed the lid.

She turned and became absorbed in a task at the table.

Her dark hair was piled on top of her head. Little wisps had pried themselves loose to curl around her forehead and kiss her cheeks. She wore a faded gown of palest pink that outlined every line and curve of her slender body.

She lifted her head and saw him. The look on her face was one of surprise tinged with pleasure.

"Matthew. You shouldn't have tried to get up yet."

"I'm fine." Like hell he was. He was as weak as a kitten and afraid that at any moment he'd fall flat on his face. But it would be worth any price to his pride just to see her like this.

"Here. You'd better sit at the table." She rushed forward, then stopped, embarrassed to offer a hand. When he'd been wounded and bleeding, it had been perfectly normal to undress him and tend his wounds. Now, his state of undress caused a fluttering deep inside her.

He was barefoot and shirtless. She had forgotten how wide his shoulders were, how muscled his arms. The faded pants only emphasized his flat stomach and narrow hips.

"Thanks." If he noticed her hesitation, he quickly dismissed it. Walking slowly, he slumped into the chair she held beside the table. "Something smells wonderful."

"I'm baking apple spice cake for Christmas gifts for some of the women in town."

"Christmas." Matt tried to think when he had last thought about the day that had been so special in his youth. "I had no idea it was even close to Christmas."

"It's just a few days away," she said with a smile. "And I have plenty of baking planned. One of my students brought me a bushel of apples."

"Students." He looked up. "So you became a teacher."

She nodded, feeling oddly pleased that he remembered her dream. Then, determined to keep the conversation light, she lifted a wrinkled apple. "I want to use them up before they all wither in the fruit cellar. Papa always said waste not, want not." She stared at the loaves cooling by the window. "They aren't much. But Papa always taught me that it isn't the gift that's important—it's the giving. Papa always said that love isn't love until you give it away."

Matt cleared his throat. "How is your father?"

She seemed startled by his question. "I guess there's no way you could have known. Papa died three years ago."

She turned to the stove to fill a cup with coffee.

"Three years." He allowed his gaze to slowly roam the tidy room. "Who's the lucky man you finally settled down with?"

"I live here alone." She placed the cup before him, then began slicing the loaf still warm from the oven.

He sipped his coffee in silence and blamed the sudden warmth on the fever that burned within him.

"How do you manage both the teaching and the ranch chores?"

She glanced at him. A smile touched her lips. "I just live the way Papa taught me. Hard work from dawn to dark every day, and the chores get done." She turned toward a pot that bubbled atop the stove. "I made some soup. I'll fix you a bowl."

Matt nearly laughed. Did she have any idea how much she sounded like her father? The old man had been as tough as rawhide, never veering from his charted course. And he'd had a Biblical quote for practically everything from raising his daughter to curing the ills of the world.

"Takes a lot of muscle to run a ranch. My father couldn't do it, even with the help of four sons."

"Papa used to say that was because you were all too busy raising..." She felt her cheeks flame. Swallowing, she filled his bowl and set it down.

"We did raise a bit too much...dust to please this town, didn't we?"

She smiled at his gentle gibe and watched as he took a taste of broth.

"I see you haven't lost your touch. You still like to cook."

"Papa always complimented me on my fine meals. After Mama died, it seemed important to make up for his loss."

Matt indicated the empty chair. "Will you join me?"

She filled her cup with coffee, then sat down across from him. When she looked at him, she felt herself blushing. It was impossible not to stare at the wide expanse of shoulders, the hair-roughened chest. His body was lean and hard, his arms corded with muscles. It was not a sight she was accustomed to seeing across her table. She stared hard into her cup.

"Tell me about Bitter Creek." He studied the smudge of flour on the tip of her nose and had a sudden urge to kiss it away. His fingers curled into a fist at his side. "Who's the mayor now?"

"Ned Harrison."

"Old Ned." Matt leaned back with a smile. "Does he still run the mercantile?"

Laura smiled back. "Yes. And he still argues with old Mrs. Smithers over the price of every bolt of fabric and spool of thread."

"Those two will go to their graves scrapping with one another." He shifted, trying to find a comfortable way to ease the pain in his chest. "Does old Ned still give out penny candy to the boys who sweep his store?"

Her smile grew. "Is that why you were always helping him?"

"And you thought I did it out of the goodness of my heart."

"I knew old Ned had a fondness for you."

Matt's eyes took on a faraway look. "He was fair with me. He never held me accountable for the sins of all the Braden brothers, the way some folks did." He quickly changed the subject. "What about the Reverend Talbot? Does he still ride all the way out to the Widow Conklin's every Sunday afternoon to read the Good Book with her?"

Laura's eyes grew soft. "Even though she's almost blind, she still cooks him dinner and he reads aloud to her from the Bible." She glanced down at her hands and added softly, "I guess nothing much ever changes in Bitter Creek."

"I expect you're right."

At the sound of a horse's hooves they both looked up. But before Laura could go to the door, Matt had crossed the room and was pressing her against the wall.

She was acutely aware of the warmth of his skin. The sharp odor of disinfectant mingled with the distinctly masculine scent of him.

She hadn't known a wounded man could move that quickly. But the pain it cost him was visible on his face. Sweat beaded his brow. His eyes were narrowed in concentration.

"Who's here?"

"Probably old Judd. He works out at the Ridgely place. He often stops by on Saturday mornings to see if I need anything from town."

"Will he want to come inside?"

She shook her head. "There's no need. I'll just give him my list and he'll be on his way."

Matt felt his strength drain from him. If there had been any danger, he doubted that he could have saved Laura. But he knew one thing. He would have died trying.

He swore loudly, violently. He was suddenly drained of all strength. He despised this feeling of weakness. Leaning against the wall, he felt the room spin.

Laura looked up in time to see the color drain from his face. "What is it? What's wrong?"

"I guess I'm not as strong as I thought." He clutched the wall for support. "I don't mean to impose on you like this. But I'm afraid if I don't lie down right now, I'll be lying on your floor."

She wrapped her arm around his waist. Gripping her shoulder, he leaned weakly against her and allowed himself to be led back to bed.

When he was settled, she lifted a blanket to cover him. Strong fingers closed around her wrist. Surprised by his strength, she merely stared into his dark eyes without a word.

His voice was low, intense. "Where's my horse?"

She licked her lips, suddenly afraid. "In the barn."

"Keep him hidden from view."

"But I—"

His eyes narrowed. The fingers at her wrist tightened perceptibly. "When the old man is gone, bring the saddlebags and rifle in here. Next to the bed."

"But you can't. You're too weak—"

"Just bring them." He paused, seeing the fear leap into her eyes. His tone softened only a little. "I'm sorry, Laura. I didn't mean to bring you trouble."

Laura swallowed. Matthew had been gone from her life for a long time now. She really knew nothing about him. But she knew enough to realize that trouble always seemed to follow him. Hadn't Papa always said...?

Very deliberately she pulled free from his grasp and straightened.

He turned his head and watched as she crossed to her own room. From a peg in the hall she removed her father's old oversize sheepskin jacket and pulled it on.

Matt heard the door slam, and the sound of her boots as she walked across the porch. He strained to hear the words she exchanged with the handyman. A few minutes later he heard her return.

She strode into the room. With a thud the saddle-bags landed on the floor beside the bed. She thrust the rifle next to him on the blanket.

"I'll need my bullets," he said, indicating the saddlebags.

She rummaged through them, then handed him a sack of bullets. "Will there be anything else?"

He heard the thread of anger and wished he could think of something to say. But sweet words and kindly gestures had never come easily to him. Besides, the damage had already been done. She had saved his life. And in payment, he had placed her life in grave danger.

Chapter Three

The heavy snowfall forced Laura to go out into the surrounding hills to round up her cattle. For the rest of the winter her small herd would be forced to stay in a fenced area near the barn. She had hoped to build a shelter for them, but there hadn't been enough time before the snow came. Next spring, she promised herself, as she mucked the stalls and filled them with clean straw. Next spring she would build a shelter big enough to hold an entire herd.

She attacked her chores with a vengeance, determined to keep her mind off the man who lay inside the house in Papa's big bed.

She turned her horse into a small enclosure and kept Matt's horse concealed in the barn, then moved on to several outbuildings to feed the chickens and pigs.

While the chickens clucked and scratched at her feet, her mind was awhirl with dark thoughts. After all her years of wondering, after all those nights of regret, Papa had been right about Matthew Braden. Even now, when he ought to be old enough to shed his wild ways, he was living as he always had. He'd been in a gunfight. And the man who'd shot him was still out there, searching for him. Judging by his reaction to old Judd's arrival, he expected retaliation from the gunman at any moment.

The snowfall would have obliterated Matt's tracks. But Bitter Creek was a small place. The man would have no trouble searching the town and discovering that Matt was not there. That would leave the outlying ranches. Sooner or later, the man would be here. And when he came...

She paused in her work and lifted her head to study the surrounding hills. He could be out there right now, watching, waiting.

It was unfair of Matthew to bring his troubles to her very doorstep. Of course, he'd had no choice, she reminded herself. He hadn't deliberately chosen to collapse at her cabin. But now that he had, she could find herself in as much peril as he.

She must stop these unsettling thoughts. Calling upon all her discipline, she swept him from her mind and flung the last of the feed, then made her way to the barn. Inside, she examined the harness and wagon traces. They were wearing clean through. One of these days she wouldn't make it to the schoolhouse and back. She'd hoped to have time to repair them this weekend. But it would take all of her energy to cook and tend to Matthew's wounds.

She gave a sigh. There were only so many chores a body could do in a day. This would have to wait until next weekend.

As she milked the cow and gathered the eggs, she realized that she was drawing out her chores, putting off for as long as possible the time when she would have to return to the house. To Matthew.

In the fading light of early evening she lifted a bucket of milk and a basket of eggs and determinedly made her way to the cabin.

To her great relief, he was asleep.

For long minutes she studied the figure in the bed. The shaggy hair and heavy beard gave him the look of a fierce mountain man. The six-gun by his left hand, the barrel of a rifle peeking from beneath the blankets on his right side, only added to the look of danger. But it had always been his eyes, those dark challenging eyes that had given him an aura of mystery. What went on behind those eyes? Matthew Braden was not a man to give much away. Especially about himself.

She lingered a moment longer, staring at him with a welling of emotion that left her startled. She forced herself to turn away.

The room was cold, as were the other rooms in the house. She added a log to the hot coals and watched as flames raced along the bark. Then she made her way to her own room to build a fire. With that done, she hurried to the main room and stoked the fire until the entire cabin was snug and warm.

She ate quickly, enjoying the soup that had simmered all day on the wood stove and the apple spice cake she had baked the day before. When she had her fill, she picked up her mending and settled herself in front of the fire. Very soon her eyes grew heavy. She had, after all, slept little the previous night. She put aside her mending and made her way to her bedroom.

Pouring warm water into a basin, she bathed away the grime of the day and pulled on her warm nightgown. Taking down her hair, she brushed it until it crackled.

As she extinguished the flame of the lantern, she heard the low moan from the other room. Moving quickly she padded into her father's room and bent over the sleeping man. She touched a hand to his forehead and whispered a prayer of gratitude. His skin was cool to the touch.

Strong fingers closed over her wrist. With no warning, she found herself hauled off her feet and pulled firmly across the massive chest of the figure in the bed.

"Matthew." His name came out in a long rush of air, wrenched from between her lips.

"Laura. Sweet Jesus." His other hand closed over her shoulder, holding her still when she would have pulled away. He felt like shaking her. An oath sprang to his lips but he swallowed it. "What are you doing sneaking up on me in the dark like that?"

"I wasn't sneaking." She wriggled, trying to free herself from his grasp.

He continued to hold her. Now he no longer wanted to shake her; he just wanted to hold her.

By the flickering flames of the fire, she could see that the surprise in his eyes was gradually changing to a look she couldn't fathom. But it was a look that caused her pulse to race.

"You moaned. I thought you were in pain."

"I am." His words were a low growl against her temple.

He rolled to his side, dragging her with him so that she lay facing him. Her hair swirled in disarray, veiling her eyes. Her nightgown was tangled about her knees.

He'd often imagined her like this, dressed in something pure and white, her hair soft and loose.

He lifted a hand to smooth the hair from her cheek. His eyes narrowed as he sifted the strands through his fingers.

"You're even more beautiful than I remembered."

"Don't Matthew." Her voice was a strained whisper.

"Don't what?"

She heard the gruffness in his tone and felt a growing sense of unease. "Don't do this. It isn't right."

"To tell you that you're beautiful? Oh, Laura. The rules haven't changed that much since I've been gone. Or if they have, I'll just have to break them."

As she opened her mouth to protest, he said fiercely, "You're beautiful. The most beautiful woman I've ever known." He shot her a dangerous smile. "There. I've broken your rules. Now what are you going to do about it?"

He had always been good at breaking the rules. "You know what I mean. You mustn't hold me here like this, in Papa's bed."

"If you object to your father's bed, we can always go to yours."

"Oh, Matthew. Stop twisting everything I say. You can't—"

He lowered his mouth to hers, abruptly cutting off her words.

Ice. At the first touch of his lips, splinters of ice seemed to shatter through her veins, shocking her with their intensity.

Heat. As he lingered over her lips, she felt a sudden rush of liquid fire that raced along her spine, then seemed to radiate outward to her limbs, leaving them heavy. She thought about what she had been going to say. But the words were quickly forgotten. She brought a hand to his shoulder, intending to push him away. But the moment her fingers encountered his warm naked flesh, all thought fled. Her fingers slid over his skin, then curled into his arm, drawing him even closer to her.

Matt lifted his head a moment, touching a finger to her lips. Lips that tasted as cool as a mountain spring. As soft as the muzzle of a newborn foal. Lips that had him so enthralled he could think of nothing else.

He lowered his head again and brushed his lips over hers. It was the merest of touches, but he felt the tremors rock him. And then he was lost. His arms came around her, pinning her to the length of him. His lips closed over hers in a kiss that demanded everything, gave everything.

She was so fragile he feared he would bruise her. And yet even while that thought flitted through his mind, he drew her even closer, until he could feel the thundering of her heartbeat in his own chest.

How long he had waited. But he would wait no more. He would take. He would give. And he would take again, until he was filled with her.

He heard her little moan and felt the excitement build as his hands moved over her, touching, exploring.

His fingers encountered the swell of her breast beneath the soft fabric of her nightdress and he heard her quick little intake of breath. Instantly his touch gentled, and moved to the small of her back, stroking, arousing, until he felt her gradual response.

Laura struggled to control the wild beating of her heart. Never, never had she allowed a man to touch her like this. His touch had her spiraling up like the dust devils that danced across the desert. And then she was falling, falling so fast her heart couldn't seem to catch up with her.

Never before had she known such conflict. She wanted him to stop. And yet she wanted him to go on kissing her, touching her, forever. She knew she had to end this. But not yet. *Oh, Papa!* Not just yet.

"I want you, Laura. God, how I want you," he murmured against her throat.

Though she wanted to protest, to shout her refusal, her words came out in a guttural moan that only seemed to inflame him more.

"Say it, Laura. Say the words we've both needed to hear all these long years. Tell me that you want this, too."

He lifted his head and studied her. Her lips were moist and swollen. Her eyes were closed.

"Look at me, Laura."

Her eyes blinked open.

She saw herself reflected in his eyes. And she saw something more. She saw knowledge. The knowledge of a man who knew the ways of the world, and of men and women. But she knew nothing of such things. And her ignorance frightened her.

And along with knowledge, though she could not put a name to it, she saw naked desire.

With a finger he traced the curve of her eyebrow, the slope of her cheek. Like a kitten she moved against his touch, loving the feel of his rough finger on her skin.

"When I left Bitter Creek all those years ago, I asked you only one thing—that you tell me you loved me." He took a deep breath. "I needed those words to carry me through the long days and the longer nights. But you never did say how you felt."

"I couldn't, Matthew. Papa forbid it."

He saw the little frown that furrowed her brow. He touched his lips to the spot with the gentlest of kisses until the frown was erased.

"Your father isn't here now, Laura. It's just you and me. Say the words."

It would be so easy. Lying here in his arms, with her blood still hot from his kisses, it would be so easy to say she loved him.

Slowly, languidly, she lifted a hand to the dressings at his shoulder. They were warm and sticky where his sudden movements had caused him to begin to bleed once more.

The blood was like a dash of cold water. She pulled her hand back as if burned. What had she been thinking of?

"Let me up, Matthew." She prayed he wouldn't notice the little catch in her voice.

His eyes narrowed. "That isn't what you really want. That's your father speaking. You want what I want." He could feel it in the way she trembled at his touch. His own hands were none too steady.

"No." She pushed herself from his arms and fought to control the tremors in her limbs. "I want you to get well enough to leave, before the man who's after you finds out where you are."

At her words, his hands dropped away in a gesture of defeat. Desire fled. "I want you to know that I didn't mean to drag you into this."

She shrugged. "What's done is done."

She stood up and smoothed her nightdress. Though her legs were shaking, she forced herself to take several halting steps. She needed to put some distance between them if she was to think clearly.

"You're bleeding again. I'll get fresh dressings."

As he lay back against the blankets, his hand encountered the cold steel of the rifle. For a moment his fingers closed over it. Then he pushed it aside and clenched his hand into a fist to stop the shaking.

"This will sting a little." Laura sponged lye soap and warm water over the wound before applying a clean dressing.

She was uncomfortably aware of Matt's eyes watching her while she worked. Not once had he looked away since she'd begun. She heard his low hiss of pain and looked down. Instantly she regretted her lapse. His gaze bored into hers.

"Roll this way a little," she said, wrapping a clean strip of linen about his shoulder.

As he complied with her request, his hand brushed the underside of her breast. Her hands stilled. Then she forced herself to go on until she had tied the final strip of cloth.

By the time she finished, sweat beaded Matt's brow and Laura felt a sting of remorse. It was her touch, after all, that had caused his pain.

"I could get you some coffee or warm broth."

"No." He caught her hand, then abruptly released it. "What I need is a good stiff whiskey."

"I'm sorry. Papa never allowed spirits in the house."

If he hadn't been in such pain he would have laughed. "I guess I figured as much. He didn't approve of guns. He didn't approve of whiskey. And he made it clear that he didn't approve of me."

Before she could protest, he held up a hand. "I'm sorry, Laura. That was unfair. Your father was a good man. A damned good man. And he was right to want to protect you. Especially from a man like me."

A silence stretched between them until he said, "I have some whiskey in my saddlebags. Would you mind if I had some?"

Without a word she picked up the saddlebags from the floor and set them on the bed. With his good arm he rummaged through them until he located a bottle.

She had fully intended to leave the room. But when she saw his clumsy attempts to remove the cork, she relented and surprised him by taking the bottle from his hand.

When she'd uncorked it, she leaned over the bed and cradled his head on her arm. With her other hand she lifted the bottle to his lips.

He drank deeply and felt the warmth snake through his veins. But was it the warmth of the liquor, he wondered, or the warmth of this woman's touch?

"Do you want some more?"

He lay very still. Her touch was so gentle, the scent of her so enticing, he wanted to prolong the moment.

"If you don't mind, Laura, I'd like to wait a minute, then have a little more."

She lowered his head to the pillow and sat gingerly on the edge of the bed. It was terrible to be this close to him. Terrible and wonderful. She felt her heart miss a beat before settling down to its natural rhythm.

"Does it ease the pain?"

"A little."

"I'm glad."

They sat in silence for several minutes before he asked for another drink. Cradling his head in her lap, she lifted the bottle to his lips a second time.

When she corked the bottle, he leaned back against the pillows and closed his eyes. Laura watched him, feeling her heart contract. If only she had it in her power to heal all his wounds.

When he opened his eyes, he saw the concern etched on her brow. Sensing her compassion, he was touched by it.

"You need your sleep, Laura. Why don't you go to bed."

She drew the chair close and sat down. "If you don't mind, I'd like to stay a while."

He stared at the ceiling, feeling the whiskey begin to numb the pain.

She cleared her throat. "You've never told me, Matthew..."

"Told you what?" He waited, his gaze still fixed on the ceiling.

"Did you ever..." She licked her lips and tried again. "Are you...married?"

He turned his head and met her look. "There's no wife. I guess a life like mine, on the trail, never left room for a wife and kids."

She felt a strange sense of relief. For long minutes they sat in silence.

His low voice broke through the stillness. "Tell me how your father died."

"He was thrown from a wagon. Apparently he had whipped the team into a run, trying to beat an approaching storm. When the team returned with an empty wagon, I went out looking for him. I found him along the trail. He was still alive, but unconscious."

"How did you get him home?"

She glanced at the fire for a minute, deep in thought.

"I had to drag him into the wagon, then from the wagon into the house. He lingered for nearly three days. But I couldn't leave him. He was in too much pain."

"Were you alone the entire time?"

She nodded.

Without thinking, Matt reached out and caught her hand. "It must have been terrible for you."

"I was so afraid. I remember breaking down and crying several times, wishing fiercely that someone would come by and offer to go for the doctor. If wishes could come true—" She seemed to catch herself. Her tone sharpened. "But Papa had always said no one is ever alone. There is always One by our side, giving us help when we most need it."

He marveled that this fragile woman could have such inner strength.

"After his death, didn't anyone from the town offer to come out and lend a hand?"

"Oh, yes. They were very kind. The Ridgelys sent old Judd over to tend my cattle until I could handle the chores again. And Ned Harrison sent supplies from his store. The women in the town sent food and baked goods. But everyone is so busy with their own lives, Matthew. They can't keep helping me forever. Besides, I've been alone a long time now. I manage very well alone.''

"You certainly do." He loved listening to her voice. It washed over him, soothing him.

She felt him squeeze her hand.

She turned to watch the flickering flames of the fire, feeling oddly contented. It had been a long time since anyone had asked about her father's death. The story had been bottled up inside her for too long.

"Would you like any more whiskey, Matthew?"

She heard the smile in his voice. "Did you know that you and my mother were the only two who ever called me Matthew? Everyone else has always called me Matt."

"Do you mind?"

He shook his head. "I don't mind at all."

"Then," she said, matching his smile, "would you like any more whiskey...Matthew?"

"No. That did the job. I'm feeling no pain."

"Then I'll put it away and go to bed."

As she reached for the bottle, he closed his hand over hers to stop her. There was an immediate rush of heat between them. And though neither wanted to admit it, they were both aware of it.

"Leave it. In case I wake up in the night in pain."

"Yes. Of course."

She dropped her hand to her side and turned away. As she crossed the room she heard his voice, low and gruff.

"Sleep tight, Laura."

"Thank you. And you, Matthew."

"Laura."

She turned.

By the light of the fire, she could see the laughter in his dark eyes. "If you'd like to check me during the night for fever, be my guest. But I won't be responsible for what might happen."

With heat staining her cheeks, she fled the room.

Chapter Four

Laura lay in the feather bed and drew the blankets up to her chin. Though she had worked since sunrise, sleep eluded her. Her mind was crowded with thoughts. Memories washed over her. So many memories. Many of them were too wonderful to imagine. A few were so painful she had kept them buried all these years.

She turned and stared into the flickering flames of the fire. Once again, in her mind's eye, she was a girl of fifteen.

Every Sunday, Laura had accompanied her father and mother to town. After church, while Papa loaded supplies in the back of the wagon, Mama would visit with the ladies from town and study the latest merchandise in the mercantile. Those few precious hours away from the ranch gave Laura a sense of freedom, which she treasured. Often she studied the pages of the books in Ned Harrison's mercantile, dreaming of exotic places she would never see. Once she had ridden young Billy Harrison's bicycle, until Papa saw her and admonished her for such unladylike behavior. At her age, he scolded, it was improper to hike her skirts above her knees.

"Billy's only ten, Papa. He doesn't care."

"You heard me, Laura. You will not do it again."

"Yes, Papa." She hated growing up; hating being too old to play with the children, too young to enjoy gossiping with the ladies.

The following Sunday, Laura left the mercantile in search of something to occupy her time. The women were busy examining the new bolts of fabric that had just been delivered. Papa was off to a nearby ranch to see a bull that had been brought all the way from Missouri.

At the end of town stood Purdy's stables. As Laura ambled along the dusty road, she heard voices raised in raucous laughter. Curious, she rounded the side of the stable and paused beside a split-rail fence. Several young men sat atop the fence, laughing and shouting words of encouragement to the rider attempting to stay in the saddle of a bucking horse.

Fascinated, Laura leaned against the rail and watched. Though the rider was only a few years older than she, he handled himself like a man born to the saddle. His shirt was stretched tautly across shoulders that were muscled from years of farm chores. The front of his shirt clung damply, revealing a lean flat stomach. His hat flew into the air. Beneath it the dark hair was plastered to his head and fell across his forehead in an oddly appealing way. As the others whistled and shouted, his eyes danced with excitement. His lips were parted in a grin.

"He's going to throw you, Matt. You know you can't hold on much longer."

"There wasn't a horse born who can throw me," he taunted.

"Whoa, boy. Are you going to feel silly when you land in the dust."

"You'll eat those words, Cal. I'm going to tame this beast."

The horse, its eyes wide, nostrils flaring, leapt high in the air and executed a twisting motion that left Laura dizzy just watching. And though the idea of a man and beast pitted against each other was distasteful to her, she found she could not look away. The scene unfolding before her was too terrible. Terrible and wonderful.

She watched as the rider knotted the reins about his hand until the horse stopped fighting him. At the nudge of the rider's knees, the horse began to prance smartly around the ring.

The rider gave a laugh of pure enjoyment. As he waved to the young men atop the fence, he spied the lone girl. For several seconds their gazes met and held.

Laura found her cheeks growing hot. The young man in the saddle looked so sure of himself, so brave. She was so embarrassed by her reaction to him that she began to turn away.

Out of the corner of her eye she saw the horse begin to race toward her. For a moment she was too stunned to move. Then, as the others shouted and hooted, she backed away from the fence and watched in horrified fascination as the horse came to a sudden halt. The rider sailed through the air, over the fence, landing in the dust at her feet.

While the others jeered, he lay very still. A cry was torn from Laura's lips as she bent to him. *Please Lord,* she prayed as she touched a hand to his shoulder, *don't let him be dead*.

He lay perfectly still. Even when she shook him, he didn't move. Tears sprang to her eyes and she glanced up at the young men who still sat atop the fence.

"How can you sit there when your friend is dead?"

The onlookers' voices faded.

"He's faking it. Come on, Matt," one of them called, breaking the uncomfortable silence. "Get up."

"I tell you he's dead." Laura knelt in the dust, unmindful of the fact that Mama would scold her for soiling her gown. And Papa. If he found out she was at the stables with a group of roughnecks, he would be furious. But at this moment nothing mattered except the daring young man who lay at her feet.

As she tenderly touched a hand to his face, his eyes opened. The laughter that he had kept under such control now burst free. "Had you fooled, didn't I?"

"Oh." She jumped up and took several steps away from him. Then she bolted.

Instantly he leapt to his feet and ran after her, while behind them the others laughed and shouted.

"I'm sorry," he called, trying to catch up with her. "I didn't mean to scare you."

Struggling for breath, she stopped and faced him. "Why would you do such a foolish dangerous thing?"

"I didn't know how else to meet you."

Her mouth dropped open. "You mean you let that horse throw you just to . . ."

He nodded his head. "I saw you there, and I was afraid you'd leave before I finished with that old nag. So I just did the only thing I could think of."

"But you could have been killed."

"I've been thrown from plenty of horses." He shrugged off her protest. "A few more bruises won't matter."

For a minute she stared at him, then turned and began to walk as fast as she could toward the mercantile.

He matched his stride to hers. "My name's Matthew Braden. What's yours?"

She kept her mouth firmly closed.

"Not going to tell me, are you? I'll bet it's a pretty name. Because you're just about the prettiest girl I've ever seen."

She felt the heat return to her cheeks.

"Do you live in town?"

She gritted her teeth. He was too bold. She would not dignify his questions with an answer.

"Do you come to town often?" he asked.

She stepped over a boulder and continued walking. Up ahead Laura could see her parents seated in the wagon. Papa was looking at his pocket watch.

"Oh, dear. I'm late." Lifting her skirts she began to run.

As she ran toward the wagon, she could feel his gaze burning into her back. And though she longed to turn for a final glimpse of him, she kept running until she reached the wagon.

"Was that one of the Braden brothers you were talking to, Laura?"

"Yes, Papa." She frowned. She'd forgotten to tell him her name. She saw her father and mother exchange worried glances.

"The Bradens are new in town," her father said softly, "but there are already rumors about them.

They're a wild sort. Not much good at ranching, from what I've heard. Without some supervision, they're apt to drift into trouble. You'd be wise to stay away from them."

"Yes, Papa."

Climbing into the back of the wagon, she seated herself on the sacks of flour and watched as the town receded from view. But that night as she went to sleep, she could still see the dark laughing eyes of Matthew Braden.

The following Sunday she told herself firmly that she had no intention of looking for the fool who had thrown himself at her feet. But as soon as their wagon rolled into town, she could think of nothing else. She felt a wild sense of anticipation as she stood beside her parents in the church, singing the words from the faded hymnal. And then she knew. Without turning around, she sensed that Matthew Braden was watching her. And though she continued to stare straight ahead during the long service, she could feel his dark gaze.

When she finally walked out of the church beside her parents, she saw Matthew and his brothers standing beneath the branches of a gnarled old tree. His hair was slicked back from his face. His faded shirt was freshly washed.

When she glanced his way, he winked. She felt her cheeks grow hot and looked away quickly. But later, when Papa and Mama went off to the mercantile, Laura refused to run away when he cautiously approached.

"I found out your name," he said proudly.

"Who told you?"

"Ned Harrison at the mercantile. I give him a hand sometimes, when he needs someone to lift heavy sacks. When I told him about the girl who looked as clean and shiny as a Sunday prayer meeting, he said there was only one person I could mean." A smile lit his eyes. "He said your name is Laura Conners."

She had never thought much about her name. But Matthew whispered it as though it were a prayer.

"It suits you," he said, his voice gruff. "A pretty name for a pretty girl."

"I bet you say that to all the girls in town." Laura kept her gaze firmly on the pebble she had uncovered with the toe of her boot.

"I never said it before."

"To anyone?"

"Not to anyone."

They both looked up as Matthew's brothers approached. "You coming, Matt?" Cal asked.

"I'll be along."

"Don't keep Pa waiting. We got chores."

"I said I'll be along."

When they were once more alone, Matt said, "There's a new foal at the stables. Want to see it?"

Laura nodded her head.

"Come on then."

They walked side by side, careful not to touch. When they reached the stables, Laura paused at the doorway, but Matt walked boldly inside. As her eyes adjusted to the gloom, she could make out the forms of the mare and her newborn.

Matt approached, his hand outstretched for the mare's inspection. When she nickered softly, he caught

Laura's hand and placed it on the foal's velvet muzzle.

"Isn't that just about the prettiest little filly you've ever seen?"

Laura was too overcome to speak. She continued to stroke the soft quivering little creature until, on wobbly legs, it made its way back to its mother. In silence Laura and Matt watched as the foal nuzzled its mother, then began to suckle.

When they emerged from the stables, Laura's eyes danced with pleasure. "Oh, Matthew. She was so beautiful. More beautiful even than the calves at our ranch."

"I knew you'd like her." He studied the way Laura looked, and felt as if he'd never shared anything so special before.

At the other end of town Laura could see her father and mother already waiting in the wagon.

"I have to go."

"I'll walk with you."

"No." Laura thought about the things Papa had said about Matthew and his brothers. It was not her intention to do anything wrong. But today had been so special. She didn't want anything to spoil this happy feeling. "You stay here. I'll run back."

"Will I see you next week?"

Laura looked away. "Maybe."

"I know I will."

She glanced at him and saw the laughter in his eyes. "Even if I have to be thrown from a horse again to get your attention," he added.

In the next year, between her fifteenth and six-teenth birthdays, she had come to know the man be-hind those laughing eyes.

Matthew Braden was like no other person she had ever met. He was a tease who would go to great lengths to make her laugh. She loved his silly jokes, his mocking humor. When she fretted about her moth-er's fragile health, he could lift her spirits with a sin-gle word. And when she worried that Papa might lose the ranch because of debts, he offered to rob a bank for her. Of course, she knew he was only joking. Still, she told him that he must never say such a thing, even in jest.

"Someone might hear you and turn you in to the marshal."

"Believe me, Laura," he muttered, "if the bank gets robbed, the first person the marshal will look for is me. Haven't you heard? The Braden brothers com-mit all the crimes in the territory."

"Papa says a man's reputation is his most valuable possession."

"Then I guess you know what I'm worth."

"You're worth everything to me."

He caught a strand of her hair and watched as it sifted through his fingers. His eyes were narrowed, thoughtful. "I guess I could just about walk through fire for you, Laura."

"Don't walk through fire, Matthew." She lowered her gaze. "Just walk the straight and narrow."

When Mama died, it was Matthew who had known just what words to say to ease her grief. He had lost his own mother. He understood her pain.

Laura saw a tender side of Matthew, which he kept hidden from the world. Beneath his bravado there was a kind and sensitive man who was willing to take the time to listen to her when she needed to talk about her loss. And when she wept, he offered his quiet strength.

Papa began to depend upon her to take her mother's place. Laura had always been a good cook, but now she assumed the rest of her mother's duties, as well. She sewed and mended, and each week, when she went into town with Papa, he expected her to go to the mercantile and talk with the older women about gardening and cooking. But though Laura assumed the burdens of a woman, Papa resolutely forbade her to speak about courtship. That would come later, Papa said. And not with Matthew Braden. Matthew and his brothers had begun to wear guns and holsters slung low on their hips. There were rumors and whispers about trouble, not only in town, but in surrounding towns. Trouble caused by the Braden brothers. Matthew Braden's name was not permitted to be spoken in Papa's home.

Laura lay very still, listening to the silence of the house. A glance at the window told her it was not yet dawn. She had been dreaming again. It was the same dream she'd had for years.

It was the summer of her sixteenth year, a hot sultry day. Papa rode up to the hills to find the cattle that had broken away from the herd.

Laura's chores were finished. She sat on the porch, fanning herself. Even that would not relieve the unrelenting heat. Lifting her hair from the back of her neck, she thought about the creek that Papa had dammed up for the cattle.

She checked the pot of stew that simmered on the stove, and covered the freshly baked biscuits with a linen square. Then, latching the door, she ran toward the creek.

She had at least another hour or two of privacy before Papa came down from the hills. Peeling off her dress and chemise, she lathered them with soap, then rinsed them thoroughly and wrung them out before spreading them on some low-hanging branches to dry. Then she began to wash herself. Sitting in the shallows, she moved the cake of soap along her body in slow strokes. Lifting her foot high in the air she ran the soap along her leg, then moved to the other leg. When her body was completely lathered, she waded farther into the cool water.

Oh, how wonderful it felt against her heated skin. She submerged her body completely and came up sputtering. Then she began to lather her hair. Rubbing her scalp until it tingled, she tossed the soap onto the shore, then ducked beneath the water once more until all the suds floated free.

With a laugh she tossed her head. Her hair fanned out around her, sending up a rainbow spray.

It was then that she saw Matthew.

She ducked under the water until it lapped about her breasts. Her cheeks flamed. Her eyes darkened with fury. "Matthew Braden. How long have you been standing there?"

"Long enough." He had wanted to leave. All his common sense told him that a girl like Laura was entitled to her privacy. She would be embarrassed to have anyone watch her perform such personal tasks. And angry. She would have a right to be angry, he told himself. But despite his best intentions, he had been unable to walk away.

"You'd better get out of here. Papa will be along any minute."

"Your Pa's up in the hills. I passed him some time ago."

"Just leave, Matthew, so I can get dressed and get back to the ranch before Papa comes home."

"I thought I'd join you in the creek."

"Matthew." She saw the way his eyes danced with unconcealed humor. "What are you...?"

When she saw him drop his gun belt and begin to unbutton his shirt, she shouted, "You can't do this."

"Want to stop me, Laura?"

She recognized that look. He was such a tease. But this time, he meant what he said. She decided to try a new tactic.

"Please, Matthew." Her voice purred. "I have to get back to the ranch."

"No one's stopping you. Come on out."

"Matthew." She was no longer smiling. "I have to go. Papa will be angry."

"Then go. But I'm going swimming." As he reached for the fasteners at his waist, she turned around, refusing to look at him.

A minute later she felt a tap on her shoulder. Whirling, she found herself face-to-face with Matthew.

Her voice caught in her throat. "You shouldn't be here."

"We're only swimming, Laura."

"But we have no clothes on."

He gave her a slow dangerous smile. "Really? I hadn't noticed."

"Oh, Matthew." As she started to move past him he dropped a hand on her shoulder. She could feel the tremors clear to her toes.

"Stay a few minutes. Swim with me."

"I can't." She felt awed by the powerful width of his shoulders. She couldn't help but notice the dark mat of hair that covered his chest and disappeared beneath the water. She deliberately turned her head, refusing to look at him.

"I know I'm not as pretty as you." Laughter warmed his tone as he caught her chin and forced her to meet his gaze. "But at least you could look at me."

"I'm afraid to."

"Afraid? Why?"

She sucked in a deep breath. "You're beautiful."

They both seemed stunned by her words. She swallowed, feeling her throat constrict. "I never realized that a man could look so..."

"You're the one who's beautiful." His hand moved along her cheek. "If I had a lifetime to look at you, it still wouldn't be enough, Laura."

Why did his touch have to be so gentle? She wanted to walk away. All her senses were shouting for her to leave, now, before it was too late. But though he did not hold her, she was tied to the spot. She could not find the strength to leave.

"I want to kiss you, Laura."

"No." She was shocked by his suggestion. But even while she recoiled from it, she felt a little thrill of anticipation. What would it be like to touch her lips to his? How would it feel to be held in those powerful arms?

As if reading her mind he bent and touched his lips to hers. It was the sweetest of kisses. A mere brushing of lips on lips. Her eyes were open; so were his. Each of them stood very still, absorbing the shockwaves that collided between them.

He moved his lips to the corner of her mouth, kissing away a tiny drop of water.

"You taste so good, Laura. So clean and sweet."

She put a hand to his shoulder to steady herself. Was it the current that tugged at her, drawing her closer and closer to his arms? Or was it her need to feel, just once, the strength she knew she would find in him?

"I have to go, Matthew."

"I know. But I'm not sorry I kissed you, Laura."

"I'm not sorry, either. Don't look until I'm dressed."

He laughed. "I've already seen you."

"I don't care. I want you to turn around, Matthew."

"All right."

She turned, and felt her heart stop. Her father, astride his horse, was watching them from the bank. His eyes were dark with fury.

"Get dressed, girl." His voice was hard, tight. She knew it was taking all his willpower to keep from shouting. "And go home."

"Papa, it isn't what you—" She ran a tongue over her lips and tried again. "We didn't—"

"Not another word, girl. Do as you're told."

Mortified, Laura waded to the bank and pulled on her damp dress.

As she and her father started away she heard Matthew's low even tones. He did not sound like a man who had just been caught doing something wrong; he talked like a man who knew exactly what he wanted. "I'd like to talk to you about courting your daughter, Mr. Conners."

When she hesitated her father pointed a finger. "Be on your way. This is man-talk, Laura."

Fighting tears, she ran all the way to the ranch house. When her father returned, he told her that she was never to mention Matthew Braden's name again.

Chapter Five

Matt awoke to sunlight streaming through a gap in the bedroom curtains. A cozy fire crackled in the fireplace and from the kitchen came the wonderful aroma of coffee and freshly baked bread.

He sat up slowly, testing his strength. Though he was still weak and his arm and shoulder throbbed painfully, there was no longer a fire raging where the bullet had been removed, and the fever was down.

Spying a basin of fresh water, he moved stiffly to the dresser and peered in the mirror. He looked more like a grizzly bear than a man. With a string of oaths he reached for the straight razor and set to work. After shaving his beard, he washed, then surveyed himself again. Satisfied, he picked up a clean linen towel and began to dry himself. Turning, he paused with his hand in midair. Laura was standing in the doorway.

Watching him shave with Papa's old straight razor had caused the strangest reaction in Laura. Though it was absurd, she had been riveted to the spot, unable to turn away.

"You look..." She wanted to say handsome. But she was too shy. So she finished lamely, "...fine. You must be feeling better today."

"Today I don't feel like a whole herd of buffalo ran over me," he said with a grin. "Just half a herd."

She smiled at his humor. "I...thought you might want to wear one of Papa's old shirts." She knew she was blushing, which only made her cheeks grow hotter. "Just until I can clean and mend yours."

"Thanks." He crossed the room and took the shirt from her hand.

As he pulled it on, she stared, fascinated at the width of his shoulders.

"It fits fine," he said, tucking it into the waistband of his pants. Her eyes followed his movements.

When he noticed the direction of her gaze, she blushed again and forced herself to look up at his face. He seemed much less fierce without the beard. But every bit as dangerous.

He sat on the edge of the bed and winced as he pulled on first one boot, then the other. While he struggled with the task, Laura noted the beads of water that glistened in his dark hair. She fought a nearly overpowering urge to touch him. How would it feel to be free to run her fingers through his damp hair? To reach a hand to his smooth clean-shaven cheek?

She turned away and headed for the safety of the kitchen. Over her shoulder she called, "Breakfast is ready. If you're feeling up to it."

Matt paused in the doorway and watched while she stirred something on the wood stove. How strange to have a woman cook for him, fuss over him.

She turned from the stove and found him standing in the doorway, watching her with a strange intense look.

He took his place at the table and sipped the strong black coffee while she filled his plate. Then he dug into eggs, fried potatoes and thick slabs of beef. There was a loaf of crusty bread still warm from the oven, as well as slices of apple spice cake.

"It's been a while since I watched a hungry man eat my cooking."

"I don't believe I've ever tasted anything this good," he said, spreading a third slice of warm bread with apple preserves.

Be careful, he cautioned himself sternly. It wouldn't do for a man like him to start enjoying this kind of pampering.

He studied her across the table and she felt her cheeks grow hot.

"I guess there isn't much time to cook when you're out on the trail," she said.

"Or to eat." He finished his coffee and sat back, content. "Or even time to just sit and talk." He glanced at her. "Tell me about Bitter Creek. And the people. And about what you do there."

She stood and began gathering the dishes. While she worked she told him about Jed McMasters, the banker who owned half the town. And about Nate Burns, the hardened widower with two small children.

He studied the way her gown narrowed at her tiny waist, then flared over her hips. Just looking at her made him ache with a hunger that could never be sated.

"Sounds like the town of Bitter Creek is teeming with eligible bachelors."

Laura poured him another cup of coffee and laughed. "I'm thinking of hiring a couple of gunmen to keep them from beating down my door." With a twinkle she added, "Would you care for the job?"

"You might be sorry, Miss Conners. I might be tempted to shoot all of them and keep you for myself. You'd be in big trouble if I was the first in line to get through the door."

Though his humor was light and teasing, she heard the gruffness in his tone and tried to ignore it. But the thought of Matthew's breaking down the door and forcibly taking her had been playing through her mind, especially at night when she lay just a few steps away from the sound of his steady breathing.

She turned the conversation to more mundane topics. She told him about Beth Mills, and how helpful and sweet she was at school. In a soft voice she spoke about Beth's mother, Wanda, and about how confused her life had become since the loss of her husband.

"That woman's playing a dangerous game, working in a place like the Red Garter. She ought to give more thought to her little girl." Matt's tone was harsh. It was odd, but he sounded the way Papa used to.

"I know. The Red Garter is a bad place for a lonely woman like her. But there aren't any other places in Bitter Creek where a woman can work." Laura's voice lowered. "Her only other choice is to marry a man she doesn't love, in order to be taken care of. I respect her for trying to survive on her own, even though at times, it's almost as if Beth is the mother, and poor Wanda the lost child."

"Seems to me you care a lot about that girl and her mother."

"I do." Laura shrugged. "I just want Wanda to find a way to build her life again. And Beth." Laura wasn't aware of the sadness that came into her eyes. "Sometimes she's like my own child. The one I never had. And I share her unhappiness."

When Matt remained silent, she realized how much she had revealed of herself. Feeling a need to fill the silence, she began to tell him about the mischievous Thompson boys, five rogues who kept her on her toes all day.

"They sound a bit like the Braden brothers of old," he said with a grin.

She poured him another cup of coffee and laughed. "Oh, they try my patience. But I know that with the proper guidance, they can grow up to be fine citizens."

"You talk just like a man I once knew." He chuckled when she shot him a quick look. "Your father said the same thing to me."

She turned away. "I guess I do sound as foolish as my father."

He scraped back his chair and stood so quickly she didn't have time to react. In one quick motion he turned her to face him.

"I didn't say he was foolish." Matt looked down at her, his dark eyes serious. "I never forgot what your father said to me. He was the only one who ever cared what I did with my life."

She heard the intensity of his words every bit as much as she felt the intensity of his touch. She pulled away and took a step back, determined to break contact. When he was too close, when he was touching her, she couldn't seem to control her emotions. And during the long night she had convinced herself that she would keep her distance from this man until he was well enough to ride away.

Very soon, she thought with a pain in the vicinity of her heart, he would ride out of her life, as he had done before. And it would be the best thing for both of them.

Crossing the room, she said, "I guess I'll see to your things. Your shirt and jacket need washing and mending."

He watched her disappear into her father's room. As she emerged, she had his shirt draped over her arm. In her hand was the torn bloody jacket.

"I'll wash these first and try to get all the blood out. When they're dry I'll..." She was holding up the jacket, but it wasn't the blood that she was seeing. It was a badge. A shiny silver badge pinned to the cowhide.

She studied it for long moments, then looked up to see him watching her.

"You never told me. I thought..." She paused and started again. "You're a marshal?"

He nodded. "A territorial marshal."

"You aren't running from the law?"

His voice was low and grim. "I am the law."

"But all the stories of the Braden brothers..."

"Were true. My brothers were always in trouble. And they all died violent deaths. But somewhere along the trail I got to thinking about what your father said. And I knew he was right. Unless I took my life into my own hands, I'd never amount to anything."

She felt a sudden warm glow of pride that her father's words had not been spoken in vain. Those same words had sent away the only man she had ever cared for. But Papa had been right to stand between them. Matthew had needed time to see the error of his ways.

A marshal. A territorial marshal. She hugged the knowledge to her heart.

And then the warmth was swept away by another thought. There was still a wild streak in him, one that caused him to face down cold-blooded killers. He was still a man whose life was spent killing others.

"But Matthew. Why a marshal?"

He shrugged. "Living by the gun was the only thing I knew. And there were people willing to pay me to use my skill."

"Pay you. Is that all you thought about? Getting paid to kill?" Her eyes filled with tears and she quickly blinked them away. "Weren't you listening to Papa?" Her voice was little more than a whisper. "Whether you're on the right side of the law or the wrong side, if you live by the gun you'll eventually perish by it."

He could feel his energy draining. Hadn't he had this same argument with himself a hundred times? He was sick to death of defending his choice. Still, he owed her a reply.

"I've never doubted how I'd die, Laura," he said tiredly. "There are too many gunmen out there just waiting to see if they're better than me, quicker than me, tougher than me. But this is the job I chose." He leaned heavily against the wall, cursing the weakness that plagued him.

Noting his sudden pallor, Laura felt a twinge of regret. "I'm sorry, Matthew. I had no right to attack you for doing your job. Here." She caught his arm and helped him back to the bedroom.

She could sense buried beneath the pain his frustration at his weakness. "I need my wits about me," he said through clenched teeth. "Those men—"

"Men?" She felt her heart lurch. "More than one?"

"Four," he said softly, closing his eyes. "Part of a gang of gunmen who've been robbing and murdering their way across Arizona Territory."

Laura felt a terrible despair wash over her. It was even worse than she had imagined. There was not a single gunman to deal with; there were four. And Papa had been right all along. His words of warning rang in her mind. Woe to any woman who foolishly gives her heart to the wrong kind of man.

As she eased Matt onto the bed, she noticed that his hand automatically closed around his gun before he drifted off into a troubled sleep.

"Where are you going?"

Laura looked up from the dough she was kneading to see Matt lifting her father's old jacket from a peg.

When he pulled it on, he inhaled the soft womanly scent of her that seemed to linger in the folds of the jacket.

"Thought I'd go out to the barn and check on my horse."

"He's fine. You should save your strength. I've seen to it that he has food and water."

"Thanks. But I'd like to check on him, anyway." He frowned. "Are you sure he won't be noticed if old Judd happens by again?"

"Old Judd won't be back again until next Saturday." She laughed. "He was headed to the barn when he was here. I practically threw myself against the door to keep him from going inside."

Matt joined in the laughter. "You never were very good at lying as I recall."

"That was Papa's fault. He raised me to believe that lying was the devil's handiwork."

As he began to walk past her, Matt paused and ran a finger along her jaw. With a thoughtful expression he murmured, "For once in his life your father was wrong."

She looked up at him with a questioning arch of her brow.

"The devil's handiwork was woman."

He moved past her and pulled open the door. She shivered at the blast of frigid air as he slammed it behind him.

Wrapping her arms around herself, she stood by the window and watched as he strode across the snow-covered expanse to the barn.

By the time he returned she had the table set.

He sniffed. "Something smells wonderful."

"Since it's Sunday, I thought I'd make something special for supper."

He removed the jacket and his wide-brimmed hat, then filled a basin with water and washed his hands. When he sat at the table she ladled chicken and dumplings onto his plate. Steam rose from biscuits wrapped in a linen square.

"You sure know how to spoil a man." He bit into a tender flaky biscuit and rolled his eyes heavenward. "I don't know when I've tasted such good cooking."

Laura fussed with her apron, feeling pleased yet awkward. "Papa set great store by Sunday supper. But now that I'm alone, I sometimes forget what day it is. With the preacher off to Kansas, Sunday seems just like all the other days."

He heard the loneliness in her tone. "When will he be back?"

"Any day now." She got up to poke at a log that was smoking in the fireplace, then returned to her place at the table. "The Reverend Talbot promised us he'd be back to Bitter Creek by Christmas."

"He picked a tough time to travel through these mountains."

Laura nodded thoughtfully. "So did you."

"I had no choice." He finished his meal and sipped strong hot coffee.

"Choices." She smiled. "Papa said we spend our whole lives making choices."

For a long moment they both remained silent, thinking about the choices they had made and the consequences of those choices.

To break the uncomfortable silence she asked softly, "How long have you been a marshal, Matthew?"

"It's five years now."

"Was it your choice?"

He drained his coffee and touched a hand to the pouch of tobacco in his pocket. Thinking better of it, he dropped his hand. "You might say the job was just thrust upon me. The sheriff of a small town was shot and killed by a gunfighter, who decided to stick around and terrorize the citizens. They asked for my help to...eliminate the problem.''

"You killed him?''

He heard the accusation in her tone and fought down a wave of anger. How could he describe to a sheltered woman like Laura the fear and desperation of the people of that town?

"I gave him a choice. Leave town or face my gun.''

"What choice did he make?''

"The wrong one.'' Matt stood and lifted her father's sheepskin jacket from the peg. Walking to the door he muttered, "Think I'll take a turn in the night air.''

As the door closed behind him, Laura sat stiffly in her chair, staring at the empty space across the table. The thought of Matt calmly facing down a dangerous gunman left her stomach churning.

She stood and touched the end of her apron to her brow. She must have been mad to indulge her fantasies about Matthew Braden. Regardless of the badge, he was as dangerous as the gunmen he tracked. And as unpredictable.

When the kitchen was tidy, she peered through the window into the darkness. Where was he? And what would keep him out on a night like this?

As if in answer to her question, she heard a sound on the porch. Opening the door, she found him seated on a railing, watching the gathering storm clouds. In his hand was a thin paper. From his pouch he poured a generous amount of tobacco onto it, then rolled, licked and sealed it. A match flared in the darkness, and he held it to the tip of his cigarette. He inhaled deeply, then emitted a stream of smoke. The sharp bite of tobacco stung the air.

"More snow coming," he said as she stepped outside.

"Aren't you coming in?"

"When I finish this." He held up his cigarette. "I didn't want to violate any of your father's rules."

Laughter warmed her words. "Matthew, come inside before you freeze. And smoke your cigarette in front of the fire."

"You don't mind?"

"I think it might be kind of nice."

Before he followed her inside, he bent and retrieved something from the porch.

"What's that?"

"Your harness. When I went in the barn earlier I noticed it was frayed. Thought I'd mend it."

She flushed as he removed the jacket and eased himself into the big chair in front of the fire.

"I would have gotten around to mending it one of these days."

He shrugged. "I don't mind. Gives me something to do until I get my strength back." He glanced at her as she picked up a basket of mending and sat in the opposite chair.

He smoked the cigarette until he could no longer hold it in his fingers. Laura watched as he tossed the last of it into the fire. She inhaled the fragrance of the burning wood and the tang of tobacco, and thought how long it had been since this old cabin had been filled with something so distinctly masculine.

They worked in companionable silence. Occasionally Laura glanced toward the man who was so intent on his task. How strange to have his presence filling the room. How...comforting.

When Matt finally hung the mended harness on a peg, she looked up to see him rubbing his shoulder.

Tossing aside her mending, she stood and crossed to him, touching a hand to his arm in a gesture of concern. "You've taken on too much. You should have gone to bed right after supper."

"I wasn't tired, Laura. And I was glad for the chore." When she started to draw away, his fingers closed over hers. His voice lowered seductively. "If I'm going to share this cabin with you, I'm going to need a lot of things to keep me busy." His gaze roamed her face before coming to rest on her lips. "Or I might do something we'll both regret."

She felt a rush of heat and knew that the stain on her cheeks would give her away. There was no way she could hide her reaction to his simple touch. And yet, if she was to survive this time with him, she would have to keep fighting. Fighting him. Fighting herself. And fighting her reaction to his simplest touch.

"I'll say good-night now, Matthew."

As she pulled away his grip tightened. Surprised, her glance flew to his face.

His dark eyes narrowed. He could read her fear and indecision. But needs pulsed through him. Needs that fueled a hunger stronger than anything he had ever known.

He reached a hand to her face. With his thumb he stroked her lips.

"Soft. Sweet Jesus, you're so soft, Laura."

She knew he was going to kiss her. And she knew, too, that if she allowed it, she would be lost. Calling on every bit of willpower she possessed, she took a step back, breaking contact.

His hand dropped to his side.

"Good night, Laura."

She swallowed, but the words wouldn't come. On trembling legs she made her way to her room. And when at last she lay alone in the darkness, she fought down a wave of abject misery.

She had wanted him to kiss her. God help her, she had wanted to throw caution to the wind and kiss him back.

When she finally fell into a troubled sleep, her throat was raw from swallowing back the unshed tears.

Chapter Six

Matt prowled the sitting room, achingly aware of the woman who slept just a wall away. After pacing in circles, he finally paused in front of the fireplace. Sinking into the chair, he studied the glowing coals that offered the only light in the cabin.

He could ignore the pain that radiated from his wounds. He'd spent a lifetime living with pain. But the pain around his heart was harder to bear.

He had thought that all of this had been put to rest many years ago. He had made his peace with the fact that he could never see Laura again. He had convinced himself that in time her image would fade until he would no longer remember what she looked like. She would be like those blurred images he carried in his heart of his father and mother and brothers.

But Laura was different. She haunted him. Whether waking or sleeping, he could see her beloved face in his mind; could hear the sound of her voice, the trill of her laughter whispering over his senses. And all through these years he had carried the image of the shy sweet girl who had captivated him one summer's day and had never released him from the sweetest bonds he'd ever known.

What strange fate had brought him back here? Was this the price he had to pay for his past?

He had left her once because he had loved her. Her father had convinced Matt that a girl like Laura could never fit into his rough life-style. If he truly loved her, her father insisted, he would be man enough to walk away and leave her untouched, unspoiled by his ways.

His hand clenched at his side. The old man had wisely known the one thing that Matt Braden could never turn away from—a challenge. He'd been man enough. Oh, yes. He'd been man enough. But he had regretted his decision every day of his life.

Not that her father had been wrong. Matt knew that his life would have been a cruel fate for a sheltered woman like Laura. She deserved something better.

He glanced around. At the windows the faded curtains shivered against the chill wind that blew through the cracks in the walls. The sagging door barely held to the rusted hinges, which creaked in protest. Outside, the cattle were forced to stand in an unprotected area while the wind howled about them. And daily, Laura was forced to brave the elements in a rickety wagon, miles from her nearest neighbor. It was not the life of ease he had envisioned for her.

It was plain to see she needed a man around the place. This old ranch was coming apart at the seams. But Matt was familiar with that damnable pride of hers. She would work herself into the grave before she would ask for help.

He walked to the window and stared at the darkened shape of the barn. Oh, he'd had a firsthand taste of the Conners pride.

He rolled a cigarette and held a flame to the tip, then inhaled deeply.

As snowflakes danced past the window he thought back to that special Christmas when he'd returned to town after many weeks away. He'd driven a team from Bitter Creek to the railroad, nearly two hundred miles distant. There, he'd spent a month driving spikes with a sledgehammer while freezing in a near blizzard. With his pockets full of his pay he'd headed to the mercantile, happily made his purchase, then ridden out to meet Laura.

She was so cool, so beautiful, he felt robbed of speech. For long minutes he could merely stare at her and marvel that this perfect creature was here waiting for him.

She invited him inside, and he stood, stiff and awkward as her father studied him from across the room.

"I brought you something." He thrust the package into Laura's hands.

"I didn't want anything, Matthew. Except you back home. I prayed every night for your safe return."

He grinned, feeling so proud. "Open it. I know you'll like it."

With the enthusiasm of a little girl she tore the paper and stared at the delicate pink gown with white lace at the collar that had been admired by every woman in Bitter Creek.

She looked up at him with glowing eyes. "Oh, Matthew. How did you know?"

He puffed up his chest, feeling so pleased with himself. If hard work put that glow in Laura's eyes, he would work until he dropped.

"I saw you admiring it in the mercantile."

"But it's so expensive."

"I don't care what it cost. I want the whole town to see you in that gown, Laura."

Her father's stern voice shattered the mood. "I can afford to buy my daughter what she needs."

Laura glanced at her father, then back to Matt.

"Of course you can, Mr. Conners. But I wanted to spend my first pay on something special for Laura."

"It isn't fitting," the older man said, "for a man to buy such things for a woman who isn't his wife."

Matt couldn't prevent the smile that touched his lips. "I'd like to talk to you about that very thing, Mr. Conners."

Laura's eyes widened in sweet surprise.

Her father's words abruptly cut off anything more that Matt might have said. "We've talked about it before, Braden. My answer is still the same. Now about that dress. The whole town knows that you and my daughter are not man and wife. I will not permit her to keep your gift."

Laura turned to face her father. His lips were a thin tight line of anger. For a moment she merely studied him. Then she glanced up at Matt with a stricken look. "I couldn't possibly accept this from you, Matthew."

"Of course you can. You know you like it. You've been staring at it for months in the mercantile."

"Oh, it is beautiful." She sighed. "More beautiful than any dress I've ever seen."

"Then what's wrong, Laura? Don't you want to be the envy of every woman in town?"

She gave a soft little laugh before touching a hand to his sleeve. Even that simple touch caused him to tremble with need.

"I don't care about making the other women envious, Matthew. I just know that what Papa says is true. Everyone in town would know that I let you buy this for me. And since you aren't my husband, it wouldn't be proper."

"To hell with being proper."

She looked shocked at his rough language. When she glanced across the room, she saw that her father had come to his feet in anger.

Matt frowned. "I'm sorry, Laura. But what's wrong with wanting to see you wearing the prettiest gown in the world?"

"Nothing." She gave a last lingering glance at the dress, then folded the paper over it and handed it back to Matt. "But I can't accept this, Matthew. Papa would never approve."

In his anger, Matt had tossed the parcel on the rough wooden table. "I'm not asking for your father's approval. I bought it because I know how much Christmas means to you. I wanted this to be special for you. I know you'd look beautiful in it. You have a right to pretty things." His tone lowered to a dangerous pitch that she had never heard before. "You have a choice, Laura. You can wear the dress I bought you, or you can just let it gather dust on a shelf. Either way, it's still my Christmas gift to you."

He turned away from her, feeling bitter and frustrated. All the way there he had imagined a grateful

Laura falling into his arms and pressing kisses to his hungry lips. Instead, he had left without even touching her. And the words between them had been far from tender.

The next day, he learned that Laura had thought of a third choice. Or maybe her father had. The pink dress once again hung in the mercantile for all the women to dream over. And Ned Harrison returned the money he had spent.

Matt took a last drag of his cigarette and tossed it into the fire. For a moment it glowed, then curled into ashes.

He stuffed his hands into his pockets and headed for his bedroom. That was the last time he had celebrated Christmas. From that day on, he knew that the things he wished for were never to be.

The Conners pride. It was a fearful thing.

He pried off his boots and lay atop the blankets, his hands behind his head. A half smile touched his lips. Just thinking about Laura made him grin. What had she ever seen in him?

It had never ceased to amaze him that a sweet innocent like Laura Conners could be attracted to a rough character like him. She was an only child; adored by her parents. He was the last of a litter of pups who'd been raised without any guidance except that of the fist. Besides trying to please his father, he'd had to contend with Jase, Cal and Dan, three older brothers who never looked back to see if he was following. But he had followed. Followed them into wrangling horses, followed them into working for the railroad, and even followed them into strapping on a gun and learning to use it better than anyone else.

And through it all, Laura had believed in him.

There was a time, when he was young and foolish, that he had actually believed that her goodness would be enough for the two of them. He'd thought that somehow her integrity would rub off on him, and the gunfights, the brawls, the troubles, wouldn't touch him. Or her. But her father's words had had the desired effect. When Matt had asked permission to court Laura, her father had pointed out Laura's flawless reputation. How long, he'd reasoned, before she would be subjected to the humiliation of seeing her name tarnished beyond repair? If she were to marry a man like Matt Braden, her dreams would be forever shattered. The town would never hire as a teacher the woman whose husband was suspected of committing every crime in the territory. Worse, she and any children she might have would suffer the shame of his imprisonment if he resorted to using the gun at his hip.

"Laura might be heartbroken for a little while if you leave her," her papa said matter-of-factly, "but she'll get over it. But if you take her with you on the trail, the pain could last her a lifetime. If you really love her, Braden, you'll leave her free to chase her own dreams."

Matt frowned now in the darkness. Her father had been a smart man. He'd made Matt see the wisdom of his words. And even now, wanting her with a desperation he would have never believed, he knew he'd made the right choice all those years ago. The trail was no place for a woman like Laura.

He glanced at the snowflakes that swirled outside the window. A storm was moving in. He really ought to get back on the trail before the gunmen came after him. But the thought of leaving Laura so soon was too painful to contemplate. She had taken such good care of him. Whatever he could do in return was little enough thanks.

As he eased out of his clothes he came to a decision. He would stay for another day.

He drew back the blankets and settled himself in the big bed. His hand closed around the barrel of his rifle. His eyes narrowed in the darkness. Laura's pa had been right about one thing. In the dark of the night, a cold gun brought a man no pleasure.

But many a night it had kept him alive.

Chapter Seven

Laura was up and dressed early. When Matt appeared in the doorway looking rumpled and sleepy, she found herself unable to look away. Last night, pain and fatigue had been etched in his face. This morning there was no trace of pain. He looked strong, virile, untouched by the bullet that had brought him to her doorstep.

"Good morning. There's coffee," she said softly, pointing to the blackened pot on the stove. "And I left some biscuits." She finished wrapping a piece of cold chicken and several biscuits in a square of linen. That would be her midday meal at the schoolhouse. "Your jacket and shirt are clean and mended." She pointed to the stack of neatly folded clothes on the chair.

"I'm much obliged. I'll hitch your horse." He lifted the mended harness from the peg on the wall.

"There's no need. I can do that."

"I'll do it." Before she could protest further, he pulled on his cowhide jacket and strode to the barn.

A few minutes later she heard the creaking of the wheels as Matt brought the horse and wagon around to the porch.

She emerged from the cabin with a blanket folded over her arm and a warm shawl draped about her shoulders. It wouldn't do for the town's teacher to be seen wearing her father's old jacket. That was reserved for ranch chores.

Her mane of dark hair had been tamed into a tidy knot. The shapeless gown she wore was buttoned clear to her throat. Yet Matt was achingly aware of the slender, shapely body beneath the gown.

"Looks like it might snow all day." He glanced toward the sky. "Maybe you ought to forget about driving into town."

"I have to go. The children are expecting me."

As she walked up, he put his hand beneath her arm to help her into the wagon. But instead of lifting her, he lowered his head until his lips hovered a fraction above hers.

"That's too bad."

She shivered as his warm breath caressed her lips.

"There are so many things a man and woman can do on a snowy day like this."

"I guess you'll just have to do them alone."

"What I have in mind takes two." His eyes stared deeply into hers. His lips brushed hers as lightly as a snowflake.

"Matthew, I—"

Her words were cut off as his mouth covered hers in a searing kiss.

He'd given her no time to protest. Tremors rocked her. Stunned, she swayed against him. The blanket slipped from her arm and fell unnoticed into the snow at their feet. Her shawl fell away. Neither of them seemed to care.

He brought his arms around her until she was pressed tightly against him. The heat of his body warmed her. The fire in his blood seemed to radiate to hers, until they were both inflamed.

"I should have done this last night," he muttered against her lips.

Before she could form a reply he kissed her again, a kiss so hungry, so demanding, it left her limbs weak, her breathing ragged.

How sweet were her lips. How innocent her touch. She tasted as clean as a mountain stream. The fragrance of evergreen and pine seemed to surround her.

Clean. Untouched. Those were the words that came to mind whenever he thought of Laura.

He fed from her lips again and again, feeling the heat of desire rise within him.

He knew he had to end this or he would take her here, now, in the snow. But reason and logic were pushed aside. His wild pulsing need drove him to linger over her lips for a moment longer.

"Matthew. Matthew."

He heard her cry in the far recesses of his mind, and fought to surface.

He lifted his head.

Her lips were swollen, her eyes soft. Little wisps of her hair had become pried loose from the neat knot at the back of her head.

He placed a hand on each side of her face and stared deeply into her eyes. "It's snowing too hard to travel all that way. I shouldn't let you leave here."

"I have to go. But if it continues to snow, I'll dismiss the students early."

"Then I hope it snows all day."

She lowered her lids, ashamed of the betraying blush that stained her cheeks.

A sudden thought caused her eyes to widen. She stared up at him. She hated herself for asking, but she couldn't stop the words. "Will you be here when I return?"

The moment hung between them, and she felt her heart stop.

"I'll be here."

At his reply she released the breath she had been unconsciously holding.

He held her another moment, then, taking a deep breath, he took a step back and bent to retrieve her blanket and shawl. He caught her hand lightly in his and assisted her up onto the seat of the wagon. When she was settled she picked up the reins. The horse broke into an easy trot.

As the wagon pulled into the snow-filled trail, she stared straight ahead. If it killed her, she was determined not to turn and look at him. But despite her best intentions, she turned at the last moment to find him still standing where she had left him, staring intently after her.

As the horse and wagon dipped below a rise, Laura drew the shawl tightly about her shoulders. Now that she was no longer in Matt's arms, she felt the chill of the winter day seeping through her clothes. The hours spent at the schoolhouse would seem endless.

She was not, she told herself firmly, eager to return home tonight to Matthew. Unknowingly she touched a finger to her lips. His kiss had held the promise of something. Something terrifying. Terrifying and wonderful.

* * *

Before Laura could even see her ranch, she spied the smoke coming from the chimney. It was an oddly comforting sight. Since Papa's death, she had been forced to return each night to a cold empty cabin.

When the wagon rolled to a stop, she was surprised to see Matt standing on the porch repairing the sagging door. It no longer hung at a lopsided angle, but straight and sturdy. Matt tested it several times, opening and closing it. Satisfied, he picked up the jacket he'd flung over the porch railing and looked up with a smile.

"I got tired of hearing those hinges squeaking. Figured I might as well make myself useful."

"Thank you."

How handsome he looked without the bushy beard. How tall and muscular. As he pulled on his jacket, she watched in fascination as the muscles of his arms bunched with each movement.

"You sew a fine seam." He ran a hand along the freshly mended cowhide.

"Thank you. I'm glad I was able to mend it."

All the way home she had known she would feel awkward and uneasy in his presence. Especially after that intimate kiss. But despite her initial discomfort, she felt more alive than she had in years. He was still here. He had not left her.

"I guess this old place does need a man's touch." She prayed her voice hadn't trembled.

When he held the door, she walked past him into the cabin. Her mouth rounded in surprise. The table was set for supper. Slices of salt pork sizzled and snapped over the fire. And the cabin was as warm as toast.

"You're making supper, Matthew?"

"You might call it that." He grinned. "It won't be much, I'm afraid. I'm used to eating cold beans and jerky. But I thought, since I'd already collected the eggs and milked the cow, I'd try my hand at making some scrambled eggs."

"For supper?"

He shrugged. "It's all I know how to make."

He watched while she lifted the lid of the blackened pot and inhaled the aroma of freshly made coffee.

She turned to him with a worried little frown. "Oh, my. Mama and Papa believed in a proper time and place for everything. Papa would have never approved of having breakfast at suppertime."

He fought to keep all trace of emotion from his voice. "I know what your mother and father wanted. But what about you, Laura? What is it you want?"

She was startled by his words. It had never occurred to her to question the rules set down by her parents all those years ago. She'd never thought about her own wants.

"Have you never done anything just for the pure fun of it?" Seeing her indecision, he goaded her further. His tone was low, intense. "What does it matter, Laura, if it tastes good and satisfies our hunger?"

What indeed? She could think of no answer. And yet, judging by the way he was looking at her, she wondered whether he was speaking of a need for food or another kind of hunger.

Hesitantly she said, "It might be fun to have breakfast at suppertime."

She accepted the chair Matt held for her and watched in anticipation while he served their plates.

She tasted the eggs, then bit into a slice of bread covered with apple preserves.

In her most sugary tone she said, "Why Marshal Braden, sir, I do believe you are the best cook who has ever crossed into Arizona Territory."

"And you, Miss Conners, ought to be ashamed of yourself for lying so sweetly. I thought your father taught you to always tell the truth."

"So he did. But right now, after a day of dealing with all my little darlings, especially the Thompson boys, nothing in the world could taste as good as this."

"Were your students worse than usual?"

She nodded. "With a snowstorm headed this way, and Christmas almost here, the children are a bit of a handful."

While they ate, she regaled him with details of her day. By the time they had finished and were lingering over coffee, they had shared a great deal of laughter.

"I think, for all your complaining about the Thompson boys, you really care about them."

"I didn't think it showed." The corners of her eyes crinkled with unspoken laughter. "They have a way of disrupting things without ever being mean. They're really good boys." She laughed. "But such imps."

They cleared the table together, then drew their chairs close to the fire. While Laura picked up her basket of mending, Matt rolled a cigarette and stretched his feet toward the flames.

Drawing smoke into his lungs, he turned to study the woman beside him. In the flickering light of the fire, her eyes gleamed like precious stones. Her hair was dark and lush.

These few days together had been like a special gift. More precious than gold. Though it had been such a short time, it felt right. As if they had always been together like this.

Dangerous thoughts, he warned himself sternly. There was no room in his life for a woman like Laura.

Her words broke into his dark reverie.

"When you...encountered the gunmen did you know that you were so close to Bitter Creek?"

He stared into the flames. "I was too caught up in the chase to know or care where I was. Then, when I was wounded and unable to go on, I thought this cabin was my boyhood home. I imagined my father and brothers inside waiting for me." He watched a stream of smoke curl toward the ceiling, then said softly, "I felt soft hands and thought my mother had come for me. And when I awoke in that feather bed of your father's, I thought I'd died and gone to heaven."

He glanced at her and gave a bitter laugh. "That was the strangest part of my dream. We all know where I'm going when I die."

"Don't say that, Matthew." In her fervor, Laura pricked her finger with the needle. Tears filled her eyes.

Seeing her distress, Matt took the mending from her and dropped to his knees before her. He lifted her finger to his lips. "Now I've caused you to hurt yourself."

"It's nothing." She tried to pull her hand away, but he held it fast.

"Then why are you crying?"

She felt the tears spill over, and though she despised her weakness, she couldn't stop.

"What is it, Laura?" He was genuinely concerned now. It wasn't like her to weep. "What have I done?"

"Don't talk about your death." She wiped at her eyes but they instantly filled again. "I can't bear to hear you talk about your death."

"I was making a joke." He stood and pulled her into his arms.

"It isn't funny, Matthew." She pushed away and took several steps back, until she was pressed against the cold wall of the cabin. "I can't bear to think about you facing the barrel of someone's gun."

At her angry words he felt a sudden rush of heat. His eyes narrowed. She cared about him. Though she had never said so, she cared. Why else would she cry at such a silly thing?

He walked closer, resting his palms on the wall on either side of her. Then he moved one hand and caught a strand of her hair, twisting it around his finger. In a voice that was barely a whisper he said, "Then I'll never speak of it again."

"Stop it, Matthew."

She shook her head in an attempt to free herself, but he caught her by the shoulder and held her.

"I'm not a child to be teased. I know what a marshal does. I know that you spend your whole life confronting men who care nothing at all about your life. And I know that as soon as you're strong enough, you'll go back out on the trail of those men who shot you and left you for dead."

"All right," he said with no trace of emotion. "The truth, Laura. My wound is healed enough to ride. In the morning, I'll be leaving."

She reacted as if he'd slapped her.

For a moment she couldn't find her voice. The only sound in the room was the hiss and snap of the logs in the fireplace.

She looked up into his dark eyes, then looked away, blinking back tears. She would not cry in front of him again.

Pushing roughly away, she reached for the old sheepskin jacket.

"Where are you going?"

With her back to him she pulled it on and opened the door. A blast of frigid night air rushed against her, bringing with it a spray of fresh snow.

"I'm going to check the stock before turning in."

She crossed the porch and stepped into snow that was already to her knees. If it continued, by morning it could be as high as the porch railing.

She walked to the enclosure where the cattle huddled against the blizzard. Steam rose from their nostrils as they lifted their heads to study her. She checked their feed and saw to it that the gate was firmly closed.

She crossed to the barn and let herself in, grateful for the shelter. She ran a hand along the velvet muzzle of Matt's horse, then sat down on a bale of hay and gave vent to the tears she had been holding inside.

From the first, she had known that Matthew would have to leave when his wounds were healed. And though she had always known that his gun would be there between them, she had steadfastly not permitted herself to dwell on that fact until now.

Her tears ran in little rivers down her cheeks and she wiped them with the back of her hand.

She had foolishly begun to allow herself to believe that he would stay. How childish. What a silly old spinster she had become. Weaving fantasies about herself and Matthew Braden, one of the West's fastest guns. How he must be laughing to himself at her ignorance.

She wept for Matthew, for the life he had chosen. And for herself, the happiness she had glimpsed then lost. And she wept for Papa and Mama, who had tried so hard to mold her into an image of themselves.

At last, there were no tears left. Straightening, Laura let herself out of the barn and started toward the house.

"Forgive me, Papa," she whispered. "But even knowing who and what Matthew Braden is, I shall miss him terribly. And I would give anything if I could persuade him to stay."

Matt leaned a hip against the windowsill and watched as the figure emerged from the barn. Snow gusted and swirled about her, giving her an ethereal appearance.

When the door opened, he remained by the window. Even from this distance, he could see that her eyes were red and puffy. Snow dusted her dark hair like diamonds. She shook it from her skirts as she removed the jacket and walked to the fireplace.

When she had warmed her hands, she turned toward her room without even glancing at him. It would be too painful, she knew. She needed to salvage what little pride she had.

"I'll say good-night now, Matthew."

"Don't go, Laura."

She paused, but still refused to look at him. "We'll say our goodbyes in the morning. It will be easier then."

"No." He crossed the room and caught her arm.

When she looked up at him, she saw the same look that had caused gunmen from Kansas to Arizona Territory to tremble. His jaw was clenched, his mouth a grim tight line of anger. "It isn't over between us, Laura."

"It has to be."

"No, it doesn't."

"Papa said—"

"Dammit, Laura. I'm not interested in hearing another of your father's famous quotations. This doesn't involve him. This is between you and me."

"There is nothing between us, Matthew. We...cared about each other once. But we can have no future."

"We have tonight, Laura."

His words whispered over her senses, causing the hair at the back of her neck to rise.

"I couldn't." She turned away from him and shook her head, as if to add emphasis to her words. "I just couldn't."

He stood behind her, a hand on each of her shoulders. Drawing her back against the length of him, he brought his lips to her ear. "One night, Laura. If we can't have a lifetime together, at least we'll have this."

When she lowered her head, he turned her into his arms. The hands at her back were strong and firm. She felt them move up and down her spine, igniting fires wherever they touched.

He drew her closer and pressed his lips to her damp lids. She felt the tiny thread of pleasure curl deep inside and begin to spread.

"Is your finger still bleeding?"

"What?" She felt deliciously warm and languid in his arms, and completely incapable of thought.

"Your finger."

"Oh." She glanced down as he caught her hand and lifted it to his lips. He kissed her finger, all the while watching her eyes. Then, before she realized what he was doing, he raised her hand and brought his lips to her wrist.

A tiny pulse fluttered, then raced.

"Your skin is so soft, so fine." He drew her hands up around his neck and pressed his lips to her ear.

She felt her pulse quicken even more as his breath feathered the hair at her temple. And then, without warning, he darted a tongue to her ear and she gave a soft quiet moan of surprise.

She tried to pull away, but he held her firmly against him.

Desire curled in the pit of her stomach. "Matthew. Do you know what you're doing to me?"

He ran his mouth along her jaw, then brought his lips to the sensitive hollow of her throat. "The same thing you've been doing to me, Laura, since I first woke up in your father's bed."

She caught his face between her hands, determined to still his movements. "I can't think when you touch me like this."

"Then don't think, Laura. Feel. Savor." His eyes gleamed in the light of the fire. "I want you. And have from the time I first met you."

"That's your answer for everything, isn't it, Matthew? You see something you want, you take it. But life is never that simple."

That had once been true. His younger days had been wild and undisciplined. But for years, it seemed, he had walked a narrow straight line, expending all his energies on the safety of strangers. The years of discipline seemed to fall away. At this moment, he felt exactly the way he had in his youth, when he'd done as he pleased. His voice roughened. "Then I'll make it simpler. You want this as much as I do."

At his words she lowered her face, but he lifted her chin and forced her to meet his knowing gaze. "Admit it."

"Oh, Matthew. I'm so afraid." She wrapped her arms about his neck and drew him close. "Hold me. Please hold me." At least through the night, she thought. At least until morning comes, when she would go back to being the town's spinster schoolteacher, and he to chasing outlaws until they were dead. Or he was.

Tentatively she lifted a finger to his face, tracing the outline of his lips, the curve of his brow. She would commit everything about him to memory. And years from now, when she was alone, she would still be able to recall the way he looked this night.

Standing on tiptoe, she offered her lips to him. In a trembling voice she whispered, "Love me, Matthew. At least for tonight, please love me."

How long had he dreamed of this? How long had he yearned to hear her whisper these words?

He reached up and took the pins from her hair. Free, it tumbled in dark silken waves about her cheeks and shoulders. With a sigh he plunged his hands into the tangles, drawing her head back.

His gaze raked her, and the look in his eyes revealed the depth of his desire.

His arms came around her, pinning her to the length of him. He wanted to be gentle. His lips were avid, his kiss taking her higher than she'd ever been. His hunger fueled her own.

His lips roamed her temples, her forehead, the corners of her eyes. She thought she would go mad waiting for his lips to claim hers once more. But slowly, lazily, he kissed her nose before following the slope of her cheek to her lips.

Her mouth moved beneath his, opening for him, as their tongues met and tangled.

He tasted faintly of tobacco, and she knew that scent would forever remind her of him.

His mouth moved lower to follow the column of her throat. With a soft sigh she moved in his arms, loving the feel of his lips on her skin.

His fingers were strong and sure as he reached for the buttons of her gown and undid them, drawing the dress down over her shoulders. As it whispered to the floor, his gaze burned over her.

No man except Matthew had ever before seen her in a chemise and petticoat. But though she trembled before him, afraid and shy, she reached for the buttons of his shirt. Her fingers fumbled until he helped her.

His naked flesh was warm. So warm. She touched a finger to the dressings at his shoulder, then pressed her lips to the spot.

Stunned, he felt his breath catch in his throat at the tenderness of her touch.

With his fingers pressing into the tender flesh of her upper arms, he dragged her roughly against him and brought his lips to her throat. She moaned and arched her neck, inviting his touch. But when his mouth moved lower, to close over her breast, a low moan shuddered from between her lips.

Never, never had she known such feelings. She was hot. So hot she felt as though her flesh were on fire. She needed to be free of the last of her clothes.

As if reading her mind, he untied the ribbons at her shoulders, freeing her chemise. His look burned over her. With a groan he bent his head again to her breast.

His hands caressed her thighs as the petticoat joined the clothing at their feet. Just as quickly he shed the rest of his clothes.

Now they stood, flesh to flesh. And as his mouth covered hers in a burning kiss, his hands caressed her until passion, need, desire became an all-consuming inferno.

Dropping to their knees on the rug, Laura clung to him while his fingertips, his lips, brought her pleasure beyond anything she had ever known.

"My beautiful Laura," he murmured against her lips. "I've carried you in my heart for such a long time."

He dragged her against him, while his hands moved slowly over her, learning all the new intimate places of her body.

Her breathing was growing shallow now. Caught up in all the strange new sensations, she moved in his arms, lost in delights she had never even dreamed of.

Matt stared down at the woman in his arms. Her hair spilled across the rag rug in a cascade of dark silk. Her skin was as pale as ivory. But it was her eyes that held him. Eyes that burned like molten gold. In her eyes he saw himself reflected.

"Touch me, Laura."

For a moment she forgot to breathe. How could she touch him as intimately as he had touched her?

"I've waited a lifetime for you to touch me."

Her heart thundered as she reached a hand to his shoulder. She paused, feeling the corded muscles there. How powerful he was. Strong enough to break her in two. And yet his touch was so tender.

Her fingertips moved over his hair-roughened chest until she encountered several raised scars.

"What are these?"

"A gunfighter's wounds." His voice was low, gruff. "I did too much fighting in my youth."

"Oh, Matthew. If only we could erase the past."

"Don't." He touched a finger to her lips to silence her. "Tonight I don't want to think about the past. Or the future. Just tonight."

She moved her hand lower, across the flat plane of his stomach, and felt his quivering response. Then her hand moved lower still, until she heard his low moan of pleasure.

Instantly his mouth covered hers in a kiss so hot, so hungry, she felt herself reeling. And then his lips, his fingertips, moved over her body, arousing her until she thought she would explode.

There was no longer any fear or hesitation in her. With her head thrown back, she drew him into her.

As they began to move, he covered her mouth with his. He wanted her first time to be as gentle, as easy as possible. Her hands clutched at him, drawing him even closer. Her strength matched his. Her heartbeat raced, keeping time with his. And as they reached the first crest, Matt forgot to be gentle. He forgot everything except this exquisite woman who was no longer shy but bold. His need for her bordered on insanity. And for tonight, for what little time they had left, she was his. His woman.

A cry broke from her lips as she soared higher than the stars. A million bright lights seemed to explode behind her closed lids. And as they reached the heavens, Matthew murmured incoherent words of love.

At last they lay together, their bodies damp and tangled, still joined as one, neither of them willing to break their fragile bond.

Chapter Eight

Nestled in Matt's arms, Laura felt the last of the shudders subside.

He rolled to one side and drew her close against his chest, pressing his lips to her closed eyelids and tasting salt.

Instantly he pulled away to study her. "I've hurt you."

"No."

He lifted a work-roughened finger to the tears that spilled from her eyes. He swore, low in his throat. "What was I thinking of? All day my thoughts were about you, about how wonderful it could be between us. But I swear, Laura, I never planned to take you like a savage here on the cold floor."

"That doesn't matter. And it isn't why I'm crying." Her lower lip trembled. "It's just that...it was so wonderful...I never dreamed..."

He touched his lips to the corner of her mouth. "It was wonderful for me, too. More wonderful than anything I could have imagined."

They lay in silence for several minutes, listening to the quiet of the night.

"For years," he murmured against her temple, "I've dreamed about you. So many nights, lying beneath the stars, I've thought about you here in this cabin. And I used to imagine what it would be like to face your father's wrath and steal you away to some lonely mountain cabin."

"What a nice dream." She sighed and snuggled closer to him. "Why didn't you follow your dream?"

He shrugged and kissed the tip of her nose. "I'd convinced myself that by now you had probably turned into an old hag, your skin burned and wrinkled by the sun, your teeth missing, your hips as wide as that barn out there."

She giggled at his description. "Sounds just about right."

His voice warmed with laughter. "Yes, I can see that the years have been unkind to you." He ran a finger over her flawless complexion. "Any day now this skin will turn to leather." He traced the fullness of her lips, then dipped his finger between them. "Hmm. These teeth will probably last no more than another month or so."

Laura laughed harder now. She teasingly bit his finger. Then, with an agility that caught him by surprise, she rolled on top of him. As she straddled him, her hair swirled about, she kissed his cheeks. Then she lowered her mouth to his. "And what about these hips, Marshal Braden? Are they as broad as a barn yet?"

He placed a hand on each of her hips, then ran his hands lightly up her sides. "Any day now you'll lose this maiden's figure and rival that cow out in the barn."

She wriggled over him in a seductive manner and brought her lips to his. "I can see that I'll just have to look for a lonesome cowboy who could want a fat toothless hag."

"I believe you've already met him, ma'am." How was it possible that his passion could be aroused again so soon? He wanted her. God in heaven how he wanted her.

He thrust his hands into the tangles of her hair and pulled her close for a long hungry kiss. With a little moan she clung to him, pressing her body to the length of him.

With quick movements he rolled them over and stood, lifting her in his arms as easily as if she weighed nothing.

"This floor is too cold and too hard," he murmured against her lips.

"And I thought you were a tough lawman."

Cradling her against his chest, he crossed to her bedroom and placed her gently on the feather bed, then crawled in beside her.

"Now. What were you saying about being tough? Come here, woman," he muttered, pulling her roughly into his arms. "There were some more things I was hoping to teach you."

He groaned as she pressed her lips to his throat. "You have my complete attention, Matthew."

And then they were lost in a world of gentle sighs and soft words. A world where only lovers can go.

Some time during the night, they awoke to the howling of the wind. It whistled down the stone chimney, sending sparks flying. Icy snow and sleet lashed the windowpanes.

Matt climbed from bed and hurried out to the fireplace to add logs to the glowing embers. Instantly flames licked along the dried bark. In no time the room was bathed in the glow of the fire.

He returned to the bedroom and climbed back into bed and drew Laura into the circle of his arms. "Sounds like our snowstorm has turned into a full-blown blizzard."

She sighed and snuggled close to him. "Does that mean you won't be leaving in the morning?"

He seemed distracted by the line of freckles across her shoulder. Bending his lips to the place, he felt her stiffen in his arms.

"Matthew."

"Hmm?"

"Are you going to answer me?"

"I forgot the question." He ran his mouth along her throat, then nipped at her earlobe.

"I asked if—"

"Be quiet, woman. Can't you see I'm busy?" His tongue explored the shape of her ear.

A delicious lethargy seemed to have robbed her of the will to move. She lay, soft and pliant in his arms, while he continued to weave his magic.

"Now." He brought his lips to hers. His hand found her breast. "What was it you wanted to know?"

She opened her lips to him and felt the scrape of his teeth as his mouth teased hers. "I don't remember."

"Mustn't have been important."

He took her with a savageness that had them both shaken. Despite her languor only moments before, she was now charged with energy. She moved with him, matching his strength with a new strength of her own. And when at last they lay sated, their bodies were covered with a sheen.

Content, they slept, still locked in one another's arms.

In the stillness of predawn, Matt lay quietly, studying the woman who slept beside him. She lay on her side facing him, one arm flung upward beneath her head, the other curled against his chest. Her breasts rose and fell in a quiet steady rhythm. Her breath was warm and sweet as it drifted across his cheek.

For the rest of his life he would remember this night. She had given him a most precious gift. The gift of her innocence. Her love.

It had been wrong of him to stay. All through the previous day he'd argued with himself, knowing that he ought to be gone when she returned from the schoolhouse. He owed her that much; to leave her as he'd found her. Innocent. Untouched. But she'd looked so anxious when she'd asked if he'd be there when she returned. And so he'd given his word. And the truth was, he hadn't been strong enough to walk away without one final glimpse of her.

He'd known. He'd known that if he stayed, he'd find a way to seduce her.

She sighed and he studied her, memorizing every line and curve of her lovely face. And then he smiled. Who had actually done the seducing? Could any man resist what she had offered?

He saw her lids flicker and his heart forgot to beat. What if she regretted their night of passion? What if, in the cold light of morning, she felt ashamed of what they'd shared? What, after all, had he offered her, except a few moments of pleasure? He had nothing else to offer. She was opposed to everything he stood for.

"Matthew."

His heart seemed to freeze in his chest.

She touched a finger to the line between his eyebrows.

"Why the frown?"

"Was I frowning?"

She pulled his face down and pressed a kiss to his forehead. "Do you always wake up grumpy? Or have I made you so unhappy?"

"You could never make me unhappy, Laura." His voice was husky with sudden startling desire. "But I was afraid you might wake up with regrets."

"Regrets?" She wrapped her arms about his neck and buried her lips against his throat. "Oh, Matthew. I'll have many regrets in my life. But this night will not be one of them."

He felt the warmth of her words melt the last of the fear that had imprisoned his heart. And when she boldly began exploring his body with her lips, the heat became a fiery blaze.

"Miss Conners. What would your pupils say?"

"Be quiet, Marshal Braden. I'm practicing my newest lesson."

Their laughter stilled in their throats as they moved together. The town of Bitter Creek, the snow, the wind that howled outside the windows, were all forgotten. There was only this room, this bed. And a passion that had been too long denied.

* * *

"I wonder how much it snowed."

"We could get up and look."

Laura moved her head slowly from side to side. "If the snow hasn't drifted to at least the height of the porch railing, I'll have to dress and leave for the schoolhouse."

"Is that the yardstick you use for canceling school?"

She nodded.

"I'll check."

"No, Matthew." She drew him back down on the pillow and dropped light kisses on his temple.

He gave a sigh and twisted a strand of her hair around his finger. If only life could always be this gentle. A warm cabin. A feather bed. And Laura.

"You stay in bed, Matthew. I'll check."

As she started to rise he pulled her down and gave her a long lazy kiss. "We'll both get up."

Drawing a blanket around her for warmth, she padded to the window, with Matt beside her. She drew back the curtain, then stared at the expanse of white. The snow had drifted above the windowsill. The barn and the little cabin were nearly buried in snow.

"Looks like you won't be going to town today," Matt said softly.

She turned to him with a warm smile. "It doesn't look like you could do your job today, either, Marshal Braden."

He gave her a roguish smile that started her heart tumbling. "Looks like we'll just have to spend the whole day locked away in this cabin."

He lifted her in his arms and carried her back to bed.

"What about some breakfast?" she asked against his lips.

"Maybe later. Right now, I'm hungry for something else."

Their lovemaking took on a new sense of freedom and joyousness. They had been given a reprieve. For this one precious day, they would not think about the world beyond their door. They could concentrate only on each other.

"What was that?"

At the sound of a wild shriek, Laura looked up from the table, where she and Matt were enjoying a leisurely breakfast.

Before she could even react, Matt was across the room, rifle in hand.

"Stay here. Bolt the door behind me."

Without even taking the time to pull on his jacket, he yanked open the door and was gone.

Within minutes Laura had retrieved the rifle from her bedside. Slipping into her father's oversize jacket, she made her way through the snow toward the barn.

A gunshot rang out in the still air, and for a moment she thought her heart would never start beating again.

She broke into a run, nearly losing her footing in the deep drifts.

As she rounded the corner of the barn, she saw Matt on his knees in the enclosure where the cattle were penned.

"Oh, no. Please, God, no!"

She raced to his side, then came to an abrupt halt. Lying in the snow was a huge wildcat. Beside the cat lay a wounded cow.

He saw her ashen features and knew that she had feared the worst. Then he noticed the rifle in her hand and arched an eyebrow. "You, Laura? Actually holding a rifle?"

She gave him a wry smile. "It's of no use to me really. It hasn't worked since Papa died. But I thought it would make me look tougher."

Grinning, he took the rifle from her hands and examined it. "The firing pin is missing. With a little work it can be like new."

"There's no need," she said quickly. "I'd never be able to use it."

"Not even against one of these?" He indicated the wildcat.

She shook her head.

"In that case, these cattle need a shelter from predators."

"I had hoped to get one built before the snow." She shrugged. "Maybe by next year..."

This ranch was too much for one woman, he thought with a trace of anger. "Go back in the house," Matt said roughly. He unsheathed a razor-sharp hunting knife. "I'll put the cow out of its misery."

She nodded. Without a word she turned and fled to the cabin. With trembling hands she returned the rifle to its usual resting place on the table beside her bed.

It was several hours before Matt announced that the cow had been slaughtered, its meat carefully wrapped and stored for future use.

"What of the wildcat? Do you think it has a mate nearby?"

Matt nodded. "I'm sure of it. And when this one doesn't return soon with food, the mate will be lured out of hiding."

"Then I could lose more cattle."

He smiled. "I hope not. I've already set the bait." He pointed to a young bull, tethered just beyond the fence.

"Matthew. I need that bull for breeding more stock next spring. What if the cat gets him before you get the cat?"

His smile grew. "Trust me, Laura."

She gave him a tentative smile. "I guess I have no choice."

Humming a tune, he poured himself a cup of coffee and positioned a chair in front of the window.

Within the hour, a second cat was seen creeping through the snowdrifts toward the tasty offering.

Laura marveled at the stealthy way Matt moved as he crossed the room and let himself out the door without so much as a single sound. From her vantage point at the window she watched as the cat crouched flat, stalking its prey. Suddenly, without warning, the cat leapt high into the air, lunging for the bull. A single shot rang out, echoing in the still mountain air. A moment later the cat lay quietly as a circle of crimson stained the snow beside it.

Matt led the bull back to its enclosure with the rest of the cattle. Then he dragged the body of the cat into the barn.

While she finished her chores around the cabin, Laura thought about the number of cattle she had lost in the past year. She had known about the predators, but this was the first time the wildcats had ventured this close to her home.

"Thank heavens Matthew was here, Papa," she whispered. "No telling how many cattle I would have lost to those two cats."

By the time supper was ready, Matt had still not returned to the cabin. Puzzled, Laura pulled on her father's old jacket and plowed through the deep drifts to the barn.

By the light of a lantern, Laura could see Matt seated on an upturned milk pail, his head bent as he carefully worked over the wildcat's pelt.

"What are you doing, Matthew?"

He looked up, and she saw on his face a look of almost boyish happiness.

"I'm making you something."

"For me? What is it?" She took a step closer.

He held up the two pelts, which he had been carefully scraping. "It doesn't seem fitting for the town's teacher to wear a thin shawl and an old blanket for warmth. There's enough here to make a fine wrap when they're dry."

"Oh, Matthew." She studied the thick white pelts, tinged with shades of yellow, gray and black. "They're almost too beautiful to wear."

"Not nearly as beautiful as the one who'll wear them."

She gave a joyous laugh and caught his hand. "Come on. You've sat out in this cold so long it's addled your brain."

"Ah. Is that why you look so beautiful, Miss Conners?"

"And that's probably why you look so handsome tonight, Marshal Braden."

As they sprinted the distance from the barn to the cabin, their laughter rang on the clear night air.

The fragrance of baked apples and cinnamon permeated the air of the cabin, along with the aroma of freshly baked bread. Their simple supper took on the festive air of a sumptuous feast.

While Laura tidied up the kitchen table, Matt went back out to the barn with a lantern to work on the hides.

When he returned a few hours later Laura looked up from her mending with a shy smile.

"I wanted to give you something, Laura." He cleared his throat. "Those pelts are my Christmas present. I feel I've taken from you, and I have a need to give, as well."

"Oh, Matthew." She put her work aside and rose to stand in front of him. Wrapping her arms around his neck, she drew him close. "I don't need presents. And you've already given me something special. This whole day has been a gift."

"For me, too." He ran his hands across her shoulder. The words rushed out before he could stop them. "I wish I could stay."

She couldn't hide the excitement in her tone. "Will you?" It was the only gift she wanted.

He looked down into her shining eyes and felt his heart grow heavy. "We both know it's impossible."

She had thought for many years now that she had learned to live with disappointments. After all, she was a simple woman with simple tastes. But these past few days had brought changes that she had never dreamed of. And for just a few minutes longer she wanted to believe that every wish could come true.

"You could just put away your badge and stay here with me."

"And what about my job?"

"You've given enough to the law." When he opened his mouth to protest, she said quickly, "Matthew, I've seen the scars you carry. How many times must you risk your life?"

"And what about the killers who are out there, Laura?"

"Maybe they've moved on. Maybe you'll leave here and never find them, anyway. Think about it, Matthew. You might risk everything for nothing."

"And how will I live with myself if those men are out there killing again?"

Her voice trembled with emotion. "Are you saying that it won't end until you kill them or they kill you?"

"Don't do this, Laura." His own tone was low. "Don't spoil what little time we have left with this argument. Because neither of us can ever win."

She turned away, fighting her tears. With her back to him she felt his hands as he caught her roughly by the shoulders and drew her against him. Pressing his lips to her ear he whispered, "These are our last hours together, Laura. I want to spend them loving you, not fighting you."

With a sob catching in her throat, she turned and lifted her face for his kiss.

He swept her into his arms and carried her to the bed.

Born of desperation, their lovemaking was more passionate than anything they had yet experienced. They came together with the fury of a mountain storm. And long after their desire was spent, they lay tangled together, afraid to release for even a moment their tenuous bond.

Chapter Nine

There wasn't even a hint of a breeze to rifle the snow-laden branches of the evergreens. A dazzling sun glinted on a countryside buried under mounds of snow. The landscape was so white it burned the eyes. At least that was the reason Laura gave for the tears that threatened each time she glanced out the window.

How could this morning be so excruciatingly lovely when her heart was breaking?

Matt was in the barn, saddling his horse and hitching hers to the wagon.

They had said their goodbyes.

Through the long night, Laura had fought her battles with herself and had come to a decision. She had no choice but to let him go without a word. He had a right to his life. She had a right to her beliefs. She also had a need to salvage her pride. And so she would not beg or plead. She would pretend that these days together had been nothing more than a pleasant interlude.

She did not love him, she told herself firmly. She could not afford to love a man who lived by the gun.

She heard the creak of the wagon wheels and saw Matt astride his mount, leading her horse and wagon.

She pulled her shawl around her shoulders and, picking up the blanket and a linen-clad bundle, stepped out into the frigid air. As she walked from the porch, she carefully avoided looking at him.

He slid from the saddle and walked toward her, intent on helping her into the wagon.

"I wrapped some food for you, Matthew. You'll need it out on the trail."

"Thank you." He placed it in one of his saddlebags, then offered his hand.

"I hope you stay well, Matthew."

"And you, Laura."

As he caught her small hand in his, he felt the first tremors rip through her. "I'm sorry, Laura. You'll never know how sorry I am."

"Don't." She tried to pull away but her strength was no match for his.

He drew her into his arms and pressed his lips to her temple. "I want you to know that I'll never forget you, Laura. And I wish with all my heart that I could stay with you. But I have a job to do."

"I understand." She prayed her voice would not betray her.

Before the words were even out of her mouth, he drew her close and covered her lips with his.

"I love you, Laura. I always have. I always will."

She went very still, allowing his declaration of love to wash over her. But even as she thrilled to the words, she knew they were not enough. She needed to hear that he would give up his guns and his life on the trail.

His lips were warm and firm on hers. She felt his strength, his determination, and clung to it.

Love. He loved her. And though she knew that he wanted desperately to hear the same thing, she could not bring herself to say the words. Papa would be proud of her for her firm resolve. Woe to any woman who loved a man who...

The kiss deepened. And then, abruptly, they both pulled away. He had his pride. She had hers. They would not prolong this agony. Both of them stood, memorizing the beloved features of the other.

With stiff awkward movements he helped her into the wagon. She watched as he pulled himself into the saddle.

Matt touched a hand to his hat, then wheeled his horse and took off at a gallop.

At the top of a rise he paused and watched as Laura's wagon rumbled across the snow-covered trail toward town. When she was out of sight, he gave a last glance at the small ranch, then moved out at a fast clip.

The days before Christmas were always a time of high excitement for the children of Bitter Creek. This special day meant a break in their routine. Ranch chores still had to be tended to. But there were secrets and whispers, and the rustle of paper as gifts were lovingly wrapped and hidden beneath beds or out in the barn. Though even the Thompson boys were on their best behavior, the children twitched and fidgeted at their desks, waiting for school to end.

This year, even their teacher seemed distracted. Behind their hands the students whispered, wondering about Miss Conners as she stared out the window and watched as a hawk made slow deliberate spirals in the sky.

Where was Matthew now? Laura clutched her hands to her sides and stared at the vast expanse of snow. What if he were wounded again? Who would be there to tend to his wounds? *Please, Lord,* she prayed silently, *keep him safe.*

When she became aware of the silence in the room, she turned. The children were looking at her in puzzlement.

"You may continue, Joseph."

"I already finished, ma'am."

"Yes. Of course."

Laura crossed the room and sat down at her desk. When she looked up, the children were still watching her.

"I have a special treat for all of you for Christmas." Even she was startled by her words. Where had they come from? She never did anything spontaneously. "I am dismissing school early. I hope all of you will have a very pleasant Christmas."

Within minutes the schoolhouse was alive with the sounds of children laughing and chattering as they pulled on their heavy boots and coats and made their way outside. A chorus of voices called out to her as they began the long trek home.

The small building was strangely silent as Laura took a rag and began to wipe down the desks and slates. When that chore was finished she swept the floor and carefully banked the fire.

Her hands were cold as she hitched the horse to the wagon. Pulling herself up to the seat, she flicked the reins. As the horse and wagon plowed across the snow she realized that she had been drawing out the time when she would have to go home. Home. It would be so empty now. There would be no smoke coming from the chimney; no supper simmering on the stove; no one waiting for her.

The first tears surprised her; the second angered her. She admonished herself for her show of weakness. She had been alone for a long time now. Matthew's brief visit had changed nothing. She wiped the tears with the back of her hand and stiffened her spine. She would continue as she had before. She would live as she always had. She would survive. She would endure.

Matt sat astride the big roan and stared down at the tracks in the snow. He'd picked up the trail several hours ago, and there was no longer any doubt in his mind. The outlaws had circled several times, and crossed the river looking for signs of him, but they were definitely headed for Bitter Creek.

Laura. He bit down hard on the oath that sprang to his lips. Turning his horse, he whipped him into a gallop.

The hills were steep, the valleys frosted with snow, which slowed the horse's efforts. And while his mount picked its way through belly-high drifts, Matt's thoughts were on the scenes of carnage he had witnessed every time these killers had unleashed their violence.

He was sick of the killing. But he could see no end to it as long as men like these threatened the innocent.

* * *

Laura added kindling to the log on the grate and watched as the thin flame flickered, then caught and spread along the dry bark. She blew on her hands, then drew the shawl tighter around her shoulders and made her way to the kitchen. As she lifted the kettle to the stove she glanced out the window and saw the horse and rider.

For a moment her heart skipped a beat. Could it be...? In the distance she spotted a second rider, then a third and fourth. Despite the cold, tiny beads of perspiration dotted her forehead.

Four men. Matthew had said there were four of them.

Wiping her hands on her apron, she moved quickly, bracing the front door with a heavy timber, pulling the shutters closed and securing the latch. She gave a little groan as she glanced at the roaring fire. The smoke would alert the strangers that the cabin was occupied.

From a crack in the shutters she watched as they approached. Two of the men urged their mounts toward the front porch. The other two circled toward the back of the cabin.

She heard the sound of booted feet crossing the wooden porch. Lifting Papa's rifle to her shoulder, she faced the door and waited.

Matt crouched in the shadows and thought about the number of times he had been in this situation. He had faced death too many times to count. He did not fear it. He had always known, in some dark place in his mind, that the day would come when another man would be faster, or more accurate. It was one of the risks he was willing to take.

But Laura. She had not been part of the bargain. He hated the fact that it was his carelessness that had placed Laura's life in peril. Seeing the woman he loved shot down before his eyes would be the most terrible price he could pay for his past.

With a little luck, the four men would soon be his prisoners. Without it, he and Laura would both be dead.

For the first time in his life, Matt felt his hand tremble as he reached for his gun.

As the heavy boots crossed the porch, Laura heard a man's voice, low and chilling. The footsteps paused. Then she heard the voice again and realized that it was Matthew's.

For a moment she felt a wave of such relief, she had to lean a hand against the wall to steady herself. It was Matthew. She was safe. Then she froze as she heard a gunshot. And then another. And then a series of them in quick succession.

With no thought to her own safety, Laura dropped the rifle and threw herself at the door. "Matthew!"

Shoving aside the wooden barrier she flung open the door and rushed out onto the porch.

The silence was deafening. The gunman who Laura had seen on the porch now lay still in the snow at her feet. His gun trained on the two outlaws who remained standing, Matthew cautiously approached the fourth who lay sprawled next to the horses.

At Laura's quick intake of breath, he addressed her without taking his eyes off the man. "Go back inside,

Laura. Bolt the door and don't open it until I tell you to.''

Laura whirled around and raced into the house. Slamming the door behind her, she dropped the timber into place and sagged against the solid wood.

It seemed like hours before Laura heard footsteps on the porch and Matt called to her to open up. As she swung back the door and he entered she fell into his arms.

She was so relieved to see him unharmed, she had to fight back tears. "You're..." She licked her lips and tried again. "You're not hurt, Matthew?"

"I'm fine, Laura. They won't be bothering you or anyone else for a long time."

"I'm grateful that you came, Matthew."

"So am I." As he stroked her face he saw the pallor on her cheeks and noted the way her hands were clenched tightly at his back.

He wished there was time to hold her, to offer her a few words of comfort. But in his line of work there was no room for such luxuries. "I have to go, Laura."

"What are you going to do?"

"I'm taking these two to federal prison in St. Louis. I'll stop in town and send someone for the others. I have to get moving."

Placing a soft kiss on Laura's brow he turned to go.

Laura followed him out onto the porch and watched as he mounted. The gunmen sat astride their horses, their hands securely in front of them. Matt reached down and untied the reins of their horses from the railing.

"You're safe now, Laura."

Until the next time, she thought as she watched him turn into the road leading the other horses behind him. For the first time she realized how precious a man like Matt was to her quiet community. Greater love hath no man...

The horses' hooves raised a cloud of snowflakes as they rode away.

After the men had departed with the bodies of the two outlaws, Laura wrapped the last loaves of apple spice cake in linen squares and placed them on the windowsill. In the morning she planned to give them to her friends after Christmas services. Christmas. Despite the ache around her heart, she clung to the hope that Christmas had not lost its magic.

The cabin smelled of apples and cinnamon and the darker scent of wood smoke. Snow frosted the windowsills. Laura's hair fell in damp tendrils about her neck and cheeks. She had forced herself to work until she was exhausted. That left no time to think about what had happened earlier. Or to brood about the man who had breezed into her life for a second time only to ride away with her heart.

She heard the sound of a horse's hooves and peered into the night. There was nothing to see but darkness. With her heart pounding she ran into the bedroom and returned with her father's old rifle.

At the sound of footsteps across the porch she tensed.

"Laura. It's Matt. Open the door."

At the familiar voice she threw open the door and drank in the sight of him. His cowhide jacket was covered with snow, as was his hat. He removed the hat, sending a spray of snowflakes into the air. His eyes were dark, intense.

"I thought you'd be halfway to St. Louis by now."

A gust of wind caught her hair. He slammed the door shut and turned to study her.

"I should be." A slow smile touched his lips. "Then I thought about you alone in this cabin. With that rusted old rifle that won't fire. And I knew I couldn't leave again."

Her throat went dry. For a moment she couldn't speak. She swallowed and tried again. "Are you saying you've come back to stay, Matthew?"

"If you'll have me."

"But what about your job..."

"It's over. I decided to turn those men over to the sheriff in Bitter Creek. He'll keep them in jail until a federal judge comes through the territory and they can be tried."

She felt her heart begin to hammer in her chest. "You left me before. Why should I believe you'll stay this time?"

"Laura." He took a step closer and kept his hands at his sides. He couldn't afford to touch her just yet. "I want you to marry me."

Laura thought about how foolish she had been all those years ago, when she had believed with all her heart that Matthew would return and make her his wife. He had broken her heart instead.

"The last time, you went away without a word."

"I left you before because your father convinced me that I had nothing to offer you. He was right. Life on the trail is no life for a woman like you." He breathed in the rich spicy fragrances that would always remind him of Laura and Christmas. "I still have nothing to offer you. Except this." He held out his hand.

She looked down at the gleaming silver badge, then up into his dark eyes.

"What are you saying, Matthew?"

"My life as a lawman is over. I'd like to try my hand at ranching now. There's a lot that needs fixing around this place."

She swallowed the lump in her throat. "Aren't you afraid you'll miss the adventure?"

"I think," he said, his smile beginning to grow, "that marrying you might just be the greatest adventure of my life."

"Oh, Matthew." She blinked back the tears that threatened. "We've wasted so many years."

"They haven't been wasted. We've learned, we've grown. There's still plenty of time left. Even time to have a family if you're willing."

"A family." Her eyes grew dreamy.

"Say yes, Laura. Tell me what I've always wanted to hear. Tell me you love me."

Oh, Papa, she thought. *Please understand and be happy for me. What did you always say? Love isn't love until you give it away.*

"Yes. Oh, yes." She threw her arms around his neck and hugged him fiercely. "I do love you, Matthew. I've always loved you." Through her tears she whispered, "Welcome home, Matthew."

Home. He'd waited a lifetime for a place he could call home. And it had been here all along, just waiting for him.

"Merry Christmas, Laura," he whispered against her lips.

And for the first time in years, he found himself believing again, as she always had, in the magic of Christmas.

*　*　*　*　*

A Note from Ruth Langan

I love Christmas. I love all the baking, the shopping, the wrapping, the whispered secrets. With five children, you can imagine the excitement at our home each Christmas. Traditions, once begun, seem to take on a life of their own.

Because no one at our house, especially Santa, can stay awake until midnight on Christmas Eve, we attend a special children's evening mass, complete with the wonderful Christmas story acted out by four- and five-year-olds. I always cry. I love the feeling evoked by all the beautiful, familiar carols. Afterward, we have a huge family dinner with turkey and all the trimmings.

On Christmas morning, we go to Grandma Ryan's house for a big breakfast. Christmas afternoon is spent with Grandma Langan, along with several aunts and uncles and assorted cousins. By evening, we're all happy to get home, to sort through all the gifts we've opened and to enjoy the feelings of peace and joy that are generated each year by this glorious holiday.

This Christmas and every Christmas, I wish each one of you peace, joy and, most of all, love.

From *New York Times* Bestselling author
Penny Jordan, a compelling novel of ruthless passion
that will mesmerize readers everywhere!

Penny Jordan

Silver

Real power, true power came from
Rothwell. And Charles vowed to have it,
the earldom and all that went with it.

Silver vowed to destroy Charles, just as surely and
uncaringly as he had destroyed her father; just as he had
intended to destroy her. She needed him to want her . . .
to desire her . . . until he'd do anything to have her.

But first she needed a tutor: a man who wanted no one.
He would help her bait the trap.

**Played out on a glittering international stage,
Silver's story leads her from the luxurious comfort of
British aristocracy into the depths of adventure,
passion and danger.**

AVAILABLE NOW!

 HARLEQUIN

SIL-1A

Take 4 bestselling love stories FREE

Plus get a FREE surprise gift!

Harlequin Historicals®

COMING NEXT MONTH

#59 HEAVEN'S EMBRACE—Lynda Trent

When ex-gunfighter Jess Darnell rescued convent-raised Kate O'Connell from the Mexican bandits who murdered her companions and stole her convent's most precious possession, he didn't expect her to accompany him in pursuit of the outlaws. But the longer they spent together, the more inevitable it became that Kate make a choice—heaven's embrace or Jess Darnell's.

#60 STRANGER IN MY ARMS—
Louisa Rawlings

Impoverished aristocrat Charmiane de Viollet was swept off her feet by handsome, brooding cavalry officer Adam Bouchard. After an impulsive night of glorious passion, she married him. But her romantic dream turned into a nightmare when the hero she thought she married became inexplicably moody and violent. Would her heart be forever ensnared by the stranger in her arms?

AVAILABLE NOW:

#57 THE YANKEE   #58 AN AMERICAN BEAUTY
Kristin James   Erin Yorke